PAPERCUTS

Michael James

authorHOUSE®

AuthorHouse™
1663 Liberty Drive
Bloomington, IN 47403
www.authorhouse.com
Phone: 1 (800) 839-8640

Published by AuthorHouse 01/18/2016

ISBN: 978-1-5049-7438-7 (sc)
ISBN: 978-1-5049-7439-4 (e)

Print information available on the last page.

This book is printed on acid-free paper.

Contents

I

OUTBURSTS (LISTENING TO HATE)

"Hey Gina! Gina! When's supper going to be ready? I'm getting hungry. And don't be putting the meat and potatoes in the same pot! Then all the potatoes turn brown and taste like shit! You hear me? Randy? Randy! Go help your mother so we can all eat before midnight!"

I'll never understand why my dad couldn't get his lazy butt off the couch and help mom. Most families treat dinner time as family time. He could have put the dishes and glasses out on the table. He knows how to use the potato peeler. All afternoon the TV is on, but instead of watching whatever program is on, my dad keeps falling asleep.

The 1970 action-drama film Living Free and Riding Free is on channel eleven. He has seen the movie several times already. I do like the film though. The leads are former football player Rob Nesbeth and Ann Marin. She is best known for her role as Rebecca Martin in the dance-drama film Viva America. Joe is TC, a loner-rebel biker who joins a gang but lives by his own rules. Ann Marin is the damsel in distress who is rescued by TC. She then falls for his charming ways. The two of them start going out together, then he saves her from a kidnapping, and after TC's bloody brawl with a rival biker, decide to go away together leaving their boring lives behind. Clearly, we are not talking Oscar material.

Every Sunday mom works up a tiring sweat carrying two baskets of dirty laundry down the basement steps, ironing my dad's work shirts and pants, peeling the damn potatoes, vacuuming our living carpet, sweeping the kitchen floor, and dusting the rooms in our home. Then without any rest, she cooks the strips of meat over a hot stove and heats up a can of peas.

I'm glad our home is small. Makes all the cleaning that my mom and I do take only a few hours. My dad, mom and I live on one side of a duplex. My grandma, dad's mom, lives on the other side. Grandma also owns the duplex. She doesn't ask for any rent or help with the personal property tax bill. Her reason is why charge rent to your own son? I dust my own room floor and dressers. I help mom fold clothes and dry dishes so she can rest some. My dad never helps mom with cleaning up after dinner. He just scarfs his food down, burps, then goes back into the living room to watch television and eventually fall asleep.

Grandpa Clyde and two of his friends, I can't remember their names, built a makeshift bedroom and bathroom for me. About a fourth of the basement was used. I have everything I need to survive -bed, dresser, TV, baseboard heater, clock radio, portable cassette player, stacks of music trivia books, professional wrestling magazines, comic books, and plenty of records and tapes. My favorite records or tapes to listen to are either my disco albums or my hard rock cassettes. Next to our washer and dryer is a black pipe that hangs down from the basement ceiling. There are two round faucet knobs you turn to the left or right to get hot or cold water to pour down.

No one really talks to one another while eating at the dinner table. Mom's afternoons are kind of dull. She reads, cooks, cleans, and naps during the day. She will pick up extra money babysitting for Joan. Joan lives five houses to the left of us on our block. She and her husband, I think his name is Ray, have four kids. All of their kids are under the age of thirteen. None of their kids go to the same school that I do. I don't even know the kids names.

Dad's sullen mood tonight suggests he had a crappy day at work. I want to tell both of them that my grades in school are A's, B's and C's. My homeroom teachers are rewarding me and my classmates with an upcoming field trip. I have a crush on Kelly. She's the prettiest girl in the eighth grade. What are we going to do for fun this summer?

I'm tired of eating overcooked breakfast steak. It's not mom's fault the meat is cooked so long that it tastes like a rubber hockey puck. Dad orders her to cook the steak well done. Sometimes, we'll have fried chicken. Of course, my dad will grab the biggest breast on the plate. Mom and I get stuck with drumsticks and puny thighs. And we always have mashed potatoes. No rice or any other starch. My dad hates rice. He's mentioned that fact hundreds of times to my mom.

He despises cheese more. Not sure what the history is between him and his loathe of cheese. I guess his taste buds or his ass had a bad reaction the first time he put a piece of Gouda or Swiss in his mouth. When the fast food place messes up his burger order by putting a half melted piece of cheese on top of his burger, my dad gets so angry. He will stomp out of the house and drive back to the fast food place demanding a fresh new burger. I hope the manager on duty there is prepared for my dad's rage. When he comes back home, he's pissed all night because his food was either cold or he had to eat after six pm.

I have learned NOT to backtalk dad or make any comments about his eating habits. I'm not sure what possessed me one time at the dinner table to turn my head towards dad while he was stuffing his mouth with meat and carrots and say

"Why don't you chew with your mouth closed?"

My dad darts his head in my direction and snorts back with

"Why don't you shut up?!"

Then he grounds me for a week. I can't watch any TV programs.

I'm about ready to finally talk about everything happening in my life when dad interrupts me.

"So the company decided to let two people go. These guys were two of the hardest working WHITE people there was. And get this, they got replaced with two blacks. Two of the dumbest, laziest niggers I ever been around. The one bootlip doesn't work at all. All he does is go outside to smoke. Then he complains all day the work load is too much, my back hurts, aww boohoohoo. He expects people to just hand him stuff. The other one is about as retarded as an ape. He can't even read! I hand him a list of the items we need to put in the truck and this guy points to the words yelling no English or what Rich what Rich! He's probably an illegal immigrant. I'm tired of working with stupid, uneducated niggers! I'm sick and tired of all this shit! I come home tired and the house is filthy! My dinner is cold and the floors are dirty, aw, I'm sick of this! I oughta just quit my job and move out! I'll find myself a studio apartment and live by myself. You all can stay here and live like slobs."

"Oh Rich, I wish you wouldn't use that kind of language in front of Randy."

"I'll say whatever fucking words I feel like. He needs to learn what the real world is like. Grow up and start taking some responsibility around here. If you let people push you around you'll end up being a big pussy the rest of your life. The two of you will be begging me to come back once I'm gone."

So get out. Mom and I are used to your rants. She ignores you or goes into her bedroom. I hear you only because your voice carries. But most of your yelling, arguing, whining, venting, pouting, pissing, moaning, growling, and having a temper tantrum goes in mine and mom's one ear and out the other.

My dad used to be an office product salesman. SD Adams was the name of the company he worked for. He was schooled in the fine art of using bullshit as a tactic to sell copiers and office chairs. I still snicker every time I see an old Polaroid of him. His bright tan leisure suit glows in the dark. That kind of suit was the style back in the mid and late nineteen seventies. He never told me why he stopped working there. I say he got fired for treating customers and employees terrible.

Now dad looks like an aging biker. The short hair has grown to shoulder length. His sideburns and mustache almost connect. The suits have been replaced with torn jeans, plain old navy colored pants that he wears to work, and white T-shirts. It's only when dad gets a moonlighting gig as a security guard does he cut the hair and puts on a pressed pair of navy blue slacks and matching color collared shirt with an arm patch that says ALERT SECURITY. His main job, the day job, is working inside a warehouse. From what he has mentioned to me, his job duties include loading and unloading trucks, and providing maintenance.

My dad is not physically violent. A few times I've seen him roughhouse or even smack my mom on her arm. He says he's just playing around. Mom needs to smack him back. Give him a hard, swift, left backhand across his puss. He has never spanked me or even hit me with a belt. And something else worth mentioning, my dad will not drink alcohol or smoke. He thinks people are stupid for lighting up or getting drunk.

No, when my dad gets angry, he becomes impatient. His vice is rage. He yells, screams, throws items across a room, and cusses. Those growls coming from his mouth are demonic sounding. I never disobey or argue with him when he's in one of his anger phases. It's frightening to wonder what kind of violence dad could spew out. His cussing goes beyond excessive. I'm proud to say that my dad would easily win any cuss word contest. Fuck. That word is my dad's favorite and the most used. Many times he will add in you, me, this, or that after the word fuck. Then it's shit. The two together-shitfuck!. Or he will reverse the two words. Ass and asshole. Goddammit. Sonofabitch. Bastard. My personal favorite is when he combines a few of the words together. A great example of this would be awufuckinsonofabitch.

Then comes the slurs. He calls the dark skinned people niggers. Or spooks. Did he come up with the word bootlip himself? In addition to black people, he hates Mexicans, Indians, gays, even Chinese. I'm not sure how he feels about Samoans. To him, women are the inferior gender. The man works and makes all the money. The woman cooks and cleans. I've only heard him call a woman a cunt once. That was the time he was driving on the road and a lady cut him off.

Some of my dad's outbursts are embarrassing, some are serious, many comical. If I'm nearby, I have to bite my lip otherwise I'll bust out laughing. Sometimes, my dad will catch me trying to laugh. All that does is makes him angrier. Then I have to hear him yell out *and you think it's so Goddamn funny!* A few of the incidents could be the result of my carelessness. Others are his fault alone.

Here are some of the more memorable dad tirades:

THE CEILING LIGHT

I'm excited because I received five dollars from grandma. When I add the five to the amount I already saved up, the total becomes a whopping six dollars and eighty two cents. Hey, for a thirteen year old living in the year 1979, that's good money. My grandma and I are taking a trip to Arkansas. We are going to be with several other people riding on a tour bus. I put the additional money in a small yellow envelope. I'm running through the house and run down the basement steps. Not paying any attention to who or what is around me. My dad is in my room. There's no lock on my door. Or any of the doors in the house for that matter. Hell, you could be jerking off or taking a messy shit in the bathroom and if someone isn't aware or doesn't year you moan or scream, they could be walking into an awkward situation.

One of the ceiling lights has to be replaced. There are two sets of two long white florescent lights. A plastic cover fits over the space where the lights are. The covers serve as protection and safety. I wasn't paying any attention to where the covers were at. One cover was sitting up against the edge of my bed. When I accidently bumped into the cover, the cover slides down on the floor. *"Watch it!"* dad says to me in a harsh whisper. He was attempting the replace the other cover. Dad then walks over to the knocked down cover. *"Aw."* His voice had been quiet, my grandpa and his wife were visiting. Grandpa was taking a nap in my parent's bedroom. Mom and dad's bedroom was right above my room. Suddenly, dad's voice became louder. *"Aw! You broke it"!* His vocals went from soft to ear splitting in seconds. *"AW YOU BROKE THE SONOFABITCH!"* Then my dad takes the small cracked cover and throws it across the room. Now the cover cracked in several places. Dad continues to bark at me. *"Pick it up and throw it away!"*

I'm carrying the damaged cover outside to the back dumpster. My grandma is outside. She must have heard my dad's yelling. She asks me if everything is okay. I nod my head and tell her yes. At this point, I should have gone next door to visit with grandma. Or, stayed upstairs in my own home. For some reason, and I still have no reasonable explanation to this day, I walk back downstairs to my room.

My dad is having major difficulty putting the other cover back into its grooves. He would gently or sometimes not so gently hit the cover. My facial expressions range from curious to surprise. Inside, my gut is howling hysterically. I'm doing everything I can NOT to laugh. I'm sure by now grandpa has been awaken from the noise and loud cussing.

"Get IN there!" "Fuck!" "Shit!" "COME ON MMMMMMMM!" What can I do to help or calm him down? I'm smart enough not to open my mouth and offer any suggestions. He could end up punishing me by not letting me go on my trip. Dad keeps making frustrating sounds out of his mouth but no coherent words would form. Suddenly, dad takes the

cover and throws that one across the room. Lucky for me, I was standing in a corner. Otherwise, the damn thing would have hit me. Then I see dad squatting down, like he's about to poop. He balls his two hands into fists. He screams out *BAAASSTARD!!!!*

I walk over to the cracked cover and proceed to the outside dumpster again. This time, I wisely visit grandma.

Another one of dad's tirades:

THE DIAPER

Uncle Ted and Aunt Gloria have left their infant son with us to babysit. My mom got all gushy emotional as soon as she saw the baby. Spending time with and caring for the baby made her feel important and needed. Dad seemed to be okay with watching the kid. He and Ted spent some time outdoors admiring my dad's Pontiac. Dad also showed Ted his two guns. The smaller gun is a pistol that my dad brings with him to his security gigs. His other gun is a larger and heavier one called a Colt Diamondback. Neither gun is ever loaded. Having the two guns make my dad feel important, above the law, and unstoppable.

Mom is in the kitchen or bathroom changing the baby's diaper. She asks me to put the wet, shit filled diaper in the sink. Later in the evening, I'm tired and ready for bed. As I start to fall asleep, I can hear mom and dad yelling back and forth to each other. I hear mom say something like is it in the bathroom sink. Then I clearly hear dad yell back THEREIN THE KITCHEN SINK! Oops. Soon, I hear thump-thump-thump. Dad is pounding his feet as stomps down the steps. He blurts out a loud sounding GO IN THE LIVING ROOM! Then he swings my bedroom door open so hard it slams up against the wall. He is walking over towards me. His facial expression is all knotted up. His face is inches over mine. He points a finger right in my face and spits out

"Randy Goddammit! Those dishes smell like piss!"

The above two incidents were the result of my carelessness. Other rants from dad were caused by his own lack of being careful. One of the more serious ones was the time he touched a hot pot handle. Mom did warn him to be careful. My dad just couldn't wait for the handle to cool down. He's too much of a man to use a potholder. I felt dad's pain as he jerked his hand away from the hot handle. He then clutched his sore, red hand and began flapping the flesh up and down on his leg.

Another round of his poisonous venom was when he forgot a bag of groceries at the store. He didn't realize the bag was missing until he got home. He took his anger out on an innocent and unsuspecting two liter bottle of soda. I'm in the basement ready to go upstairs. All of the sudden here comes a bottle of soda tumbling down the steps! I quickly grabbed the bruised but still breathing bottle and rush to the downstairs bathroom sink. This bottle was going to make it! I place the top part of the bottle in the sink and slowly twist the lid off. I hear a fizzing noise. I wait until the fizzing stops then tightly screw the lid back on. The tough little bottle of cola survived!

Dad can get riled up and frustrated so easy. Uncut grass, when his good work or dress pants get in his words *you're wrinkling the fuck out of them!*, trouble filling out a fax form *I don't understand ANY OF THIS SHIT!*, when a guy named Walter E Wesser sideswiped the right side of dad's car. This happened in the parking lot of Arno's Barbeque. Walter was backing up and not paying attention to how close he was to my dad's vehicle. I hear my dad yell *hold it! Hold it!* I go inside Arno's to order food. Sometimes, I get confused. My brain stops thinking logically. My dad and I went to Arno's because he was hungry. I go back outside and interrupt my dad who is surveying the damage to his car. I ask him

"Dad, do you want an Arno's?"

His fender bender was not funny. Someone could have gotten hurt. Not to mention the cost of repairing any damage. What was funny, and I held my laughter in until after I got home and went into my room, was my dad's response. His face got all scrunched up as he formed a scowl and replied

"y-y-y-y-y-y-y-y-y-y-essss!!"

Even if I bust open a can of Lee's oil or knock over grandma's portable TV by accident and not on purpose, it's fuck this, shit that, and your ass is mud. The your ass is mud situation was the only time that his anger towards me caused me to cry. My dad and I were next door visiting my grandma. He brought back burgers from a fast food joint for the three of us to eat. My mom already ate some fish that a neighbor made for her. I'm in the kitchen waiting for my dad to give my burger. He kept unwrapping everyone's order to see if all the hamburgers were plain. I never got the chance to ask for mayonnaise on my burger. I had to settle for two pickles from a jar in grandma's kitchen.

My grandma's kitchen is tiny. She had a portable television sitting awkwardly on a stand. The stand was really too small to even hold the television. All I was trying to do was move out of everyone's way. I kept walking backwards and bumped into the television with enough force the television falls off the stand. I'm sure I said sorry several times. My grandma was forgiving. As I'm starting to eat my dinner, my dad leans in to me and whispers *your ass is mud.* I already felt bad busting grandma's television. A few bites in, I lose control and start weeping. My grandma does her best consoling me.

I made a promise to myself that night from now on I refuse to shed any tears. Be a man. I'm sure when dad was my age he broke a few of his mom's belongings. My mom rarely gets mad at me. Her idea of anger is banging on the basement wall when I'm playing my Standing Hampton record too loud. That's her subtle way of telling me to turn down the music.

My eighth grade class is going on a school field trip. All of the kids, our two homeroom teachers, and some of the kid's parents are riding our bikes to the zoo. Our parents have to sign a release. I guess for safety purposes. We also have to pay twenty five dollars. The cost will provide for entrance to the petting farm, food, and a train ride. I've had the paper with me for about a week. I need to turn the release in to my teacher soon. I wait until dad is in a good mood. Yesterday, I spent an hour outside in the sweltering heat trimming the edges of our lawn. Right before he's ready to watch TV, I hand him the paper.

"Our science class is learning about animals. Our teachers are taking us on a field trip to the zoo."

I make the trip out to be more important than what it really is. My dad's response went something like this:

"What! Twenty five dollars! No way! I'm not giving that school another fucking nickel. I keep giving and giving them all kinds of money and I get in return is nothing up the ass! They don't need any more money. And for what? A trip? Where? To the zoo? They can provide the money themselves. You don't even ride your bike that much at all. Hell, I gave you a bike last year and it just sits in the shed. No,

I'm tired of getting reamed in the ass. This time Rich isn't going to let the school put one over me. Maybe next year, if you're good and your grades are good then we'll see."

What next year? I'll be in high school. Does this mean if the high school has any field trips planned I'm shit out of luck? I grab the paper and stuff it back in my pocket. I tell mom and dad I'll be riding my bike around the block. I want to cry but will show him that not going doesn't faze me in the slightest. I'm in the backyard about to take off when my grandma approaches me. She puts a finger over her lip.

"Shhhh, don't say a word to anyone."

She hands me some money. Twenty dollars. I already have the five dollars.

"Thank you." I say to her while giving her a hug.

My mom and grandma sign the release. My dad left for work early that day. He always believed I stayed at school that day.

Where, when, and how did my dad become so selfish, greedy, stubborn, loud, impatient, and mean? I know dad is an only child. So that's part of it. All of his toys, books, clothes, and games were his and his alone. My grandma can be a bit impatient when waiting in line or mad at someone who she believes is pulling a fast one on her but that's about the worse she gets. Mom has four sisters and two brothers. Mom learned to share whether or not she wanted to.

To be honest, I didn't care if I went to the zoo or not. My only friend in school, Joe, was in the seventh grade. So therefore, I would be spending most of the time at the zoo by myself. I was not a cool kid. The cool kids were friends with other cool kids. I'm shy and awkward. I never had the guts or nerve to hang around with any of the girls in my class. The girls would want to be with the cool boys anyway. I didn't care. I liked older women anyway.

The cool kids wore hiking boots, had knapsacks, combed their hair in the current fashion, and bragged to one another about watching R-rated movies. I got stuck with ugly black goulashes, a tan satchel that looked like a gigantic purse, an uneven part down the middle of my hair, and a no to watching any film that showed a boob.

Rob was the leader of the cool kids. He was athletic, smart, and popular with the girls. And he probably wore girl's underwear. His second in command was Matty. Matty is best remembered for his big pair of ears and a no doy expression. Danny was the tough but dumb enfor.. wait, that word is too good to use for him. Danny was just a big oaf. Danny could win any after school fight but couldn't remember how to spell the word school. Davey and Dougey were the cool troublemakers. Those two would be the one responsible for tee-peeing a tree. As a group, the cool kids would pay soccer during school recess. All of them thought it was, well cool, to take their school shirts off while playing. None of them ever asked me if I wanted to play with them. Instead, I sat with and talked to Joe, dorks, and the straight A students.

One day as I'm walking home from school I can hear a loud, angry voice resonate throughout the neighborhood.

"Yeah that's right, keep blasting your music! I'll call the cops! Yeah, I know who the cops are in this neighborhood. I even know who the sergeant is too! You'll will be spending the night in jail!"

Mom and grandma made feeble attempts to get my dad to come inside.

"Oh Rich, come inside. You're making a scene."

A few minutes later he steps inside then slams the door shut. Dad continues to spew out his contempt for the people he was arguing with. Our new neighbors. Technically, they live three houses down from us.

"Bunch of ignorant niggers. It's no wonder the property values in this area are going down the drain. We have people living here who trash the area. And that lady is the dumbest person I know! Holy Jesus! A white woman living with a black man. She must be desperate. And they even got kids! Pee yuke. The older ones smoke and leave the butts all over the sidewalk. I know for a fact those kids steal, vandalize, and sell drugs. I tell the police all the time about what they are doing but the cops are more concerned about keeping little old ladies safe or hanging out at the donut shop. I'm sick and tired of hearing all of them play their awful music! I'm going to have to buy a security system for the garage and the house. That'll be at least a hundred dollars!"

My dad makes an exaggerated point. Yes, the kids smoke and play horrible rap music. Yes, the woman looks like she was born in a park trailer. And the older guy who stays in the same house could be her pimp. But, the kids keep to themselves. I've haven't heard about or seen any of them get arrested. Dad's just pissed because she's white and he's black. I've said hello to all of them. They are all polite when saying hello back to me.

When the cops do arrive at our front door, dad is always telling them he knows a guy named Danny O'Shea. Dad also brings up the time he spent in the military. The Marines. Semper-Fi. Of course, Dad and Danny are not friends. They barely know each other. Danny O'Shea used to be Dad's boss at Alert Security. Dad was never in the armed services. He was a working man, the draft was over, and he became a family man.

I recognized the two officers who came one night. One of the cops reminds dad to stop calling them for no good reason. Dad has no proof of drugs being bought and sold, damaged property, or any other illegal activity dad dreams up. I'm surprised the neighbors haven't sued dad for slander. Soon the neighbors will move out. Once new ones move in, dad sticks his nose in their business, and begins the façade of accusations all over again.

My final grade school report card had great grades. I received A's in English and Religion. My B's were in social studies, math, and history. My lowest grades were one high C in science and a low C in physical ed. Dad frowned upon the low c.

"How could you get a C in gym class? All you do is run around and play games. That should be an easy A."

My dad took me to the arena to see a monster truck pull. This was his way of bonding with his son. He was also rewarding me for not flunking out of school. I had no interest in this event. I wanted to stay at home and watch a rerun of the TV crime drama MacDarby and Wives. I pretended to be excited so that my dad would think I was having a great time. I will admit though, the motorcycle stuntman's jump over thirty monster trucks was awesome to see. The truck pull itself never happened. From what I understood at the time, the dirt wasn't set enough on the field. The trucks couldn't accelerate properly. So the event was cancelled.

A whoosh of booing began. I could hear rowdy chants of *this is bullshit! This is Bullshit!* The crowd of spectators were upset because they didn't like or understand the refund policy. As my dad and I were leaving the building, two guys got into an argument. The argument escalated into a fistfight. The two guys were getting close to me. My dad yanks me by my shirt and pulls me away. I wasn't scared but it's cool that he was looking out for me.

The next night at home, my dad tells me where I'm going to high school.

"In case you didn't already know, you'll be going to Bishop Pettit High School."

"Oh wow, okay. For a minute I thought I would be attending Roosevelt."

Many of my classmates will also be attending Bishop Pettit. Bishop Pettit is a well-known, crowded, co-ed, and expensive catholic high school. Roosevelt is the public high school my dad went to.

"No way. Your mother and I talked about this. There's no way in hell you're going to be one of those kids who gets bussed every day. You can ride on the public transportation or even walk. I don't want you in a school that's all black people."

"Fine with me. I'm going to my room."

"Wait a minute. Here, this is for you."

My dad hands me a small silver box that was sitting on the small table next to the couch. I open the box to see a face staring up at me.

"All right! I could use a watch. I'll wear it when I go on my trip. Thank you!"

The watch wasn't anything fancy. A small wristwatch with a leather band. My dad and I know better than to say the words I love you or hug each other. Saying thanks and not ruining the watch is all each of wants from the other. Mom's gift for me is a hug and cooking a fancy dinner. So we will be having fried chicken and mashed potatoes. I also received congratulations graduate cards from my aunts, uncles, and cousins. My grandma is the most generous. She gives me a card along with fifty dollars inside the card. I also find out the two of us will be taking a bus trip to Indianapolis.

I was hoping my dad would grow out of his infantile behavior. Sadly, he has not.

Dad and Trent are laughing so hard and loud that I'm beginning to laugh too. And what they are laughing about isn't even funny. Trent and dad used to work together at SD Adams. The two of them have remained friends. Trent must be my dad's only friend. I never see any other male or female who is not a relative with my dad.

"Hahahahahaha I never seen anybody who was so stupid! I'm driving along and minding my own business when the two black kids were playing ball in the street. One of them kept looking at me. So I roll up my window then yell out BOO! I honk my horn thinking he and the other kid will get out of my way. They never do! I'm honking! Beep Beep! Beep Beep!"

Mom and Trent's girlfriend would keep waving their arms up and down and asking him to calm down. My dad even walked around the house pretending to have a limp. He's letting everyone know how the new guy walks and talks. I have never seen my dad act like a complete donkey. If anyone is not all there, it is my dad. My mom is embarrassed.

"I'm tired. I'm going to bed."

"Good night Regina." Trent's girlfriend says back to her, also embarrassed by my dad's infantile behavior.

Even Trent is embarrassed. He steps outside on our front porch. I am ashamed.

My dad doesn't keep is berates to the outside world only. Mom is studying to retake her driver's exam. She already told dad about going back to beautician school and work. My dad complains about not making enough money but balks at my mom getting a job. Dad couldn't stop her from perusing employment. My grandma supports her and even gave her some dollars to help buy a car. Dad refuses to pay for one cent for any school costs. He's already paying for mine which is all he can afford. I'm not positive, but I think mom received financial help from the government. Good for her. Dad has no confidence in mom's future plans. He thinks mom will fail her driver's exam the first time. And the second. Mom will get fired from her job a few weeks after she starts. My dad thought he was being funny making fun of mom's driving.

"And remember in America we drive on the RIGHT side of the road. And the big red sign you see on street corners is called a STOP sign. Hahaha! And don't forget we YIELD to traffic already on the highway! That is called giving them the right of way. Oh my God look out! Here comes Regina Stevens! BETTER STAY OFF THE ROAD! I hope the driving instructor has a bible in the glove compartment. Hahahaha!"

Now you can add hypocrite to dad's faults. My dad is an abysmal driver. While he is driving, he makes jerky stops, speeds past the yellow stoplights, and can't parallel park worth a shit. The back end of his car always sticks out like a plump human butt. He will not help mom study or practice driving with her.

Mom has developed thick skin all these years. But she is tired of all dad's rants, tirades, and bullshit. So one Saturday or Sunday, I'm in my room reading a Batman comic book. My dad walks down the basement steps and comes inside my room.

His facial expression shows sadness and disappointment. He may have been crying. His eyes look sore and red. My first thought is that one of my relatives died.

"Put the magazine down and sit up. I want to talk to you. This is so difficult I don't know where to begin. Your mom and I, we are getting a divorce."

"Why?"

Dad assures me the reasons have nothing to do with me.

"We just are calling it quits. I want Gina to stay at home and be provider for us. But she wants to go to work. Her priorities have changed. You and I don't come first anymore. She wants to spend all her time going to beauty school. I think some of friends around here twisted her arm into going back to school. I don't know why. She's not going to make a lot of money cutting hair. I'm tired of arguing and fighting with her. But she is not going to stay here. She can find a place of her own. But you did nothing wrong. We both still love you."

Good to know. I can't think of one good reason I would be the cause of their split. Mom and dad weren't getting along for a couple of years. They rarely see each other anymore. The last time I can remember those two going out was back in 1980. They saw the western drama Texas Cowboy. I nod my head as my dad continues to talk even though I don't believe a word he's saying to me. Dad never cried or displayed any anger. He seems shocked by what is happening to him.

Come on. How stupid do you think I am? You treated mom like she was useless. When was the last time you said thanks to her for cooking and cleaning? Now you're lonely. Did you actually think mom was going to be your house slave forever? Mom would have stayed if you showed more support for her decisions to be more independent. The two of you could have combined your earnings to become a successful team. You have nothing to complain about. Now you and Trent can go to the nude girl bars and not feel guilty. That is, if you even do feel guilty.

My mom showed even less emotion about the divorce. At least towards me. Hell, she didn't even say goodbye. Packed up all her shit fast and silent. She picked a day that I was at school. I could have handled watching her walk out the door. She was the one who couldn't handle the situation. My mom went from being a shy housewife to a cold sniper. My dad made it crystal clear where I was going to live.

"You are still going to live here and stay at Bishop Pettit. Gina is moving out to find a place of her own. I will have sole custody over you."

"I don't want to live anywhere else. Bishop Pettit is close to the house. But I am going to visit mom."

"Fine. Just let me know when you do."

"Why?"

"Because I said so, that's why."

I didn't go to the courthouse with mom or dad. Dad already had it planned out for me to say a bunch of rotten lies about mom to the judge. He even gave me a piece of paper that had all of these lies about my mom written on it. 1- She doesn't care about my education. 2-She stopped cooking home meals. 3-the dirty clothes kept piling up. 4-The bathrooms are filthy. 5-she put added stress on my family.

I wasn't about to miss out on making money mowing lawns or skipping a class just to lie for him. My final grade school exams were more important than his quest for divorce victory. I gave Mrs. Dailey my word that after school I would mow her lawn. She told me I would receive ten dollars.

My dad did everything he could to make mom look bad so he would look good. My Dad would take any shortcut or do something unethical to get the judge to award him a large amount of child support money. All of those items written-my dad would tell those to the judge himself.

I'm outside finishing trimming our own lawn. My grandma is sweeping up grass on the sidewalk. I look up to see dad driving by. He's returning from the courthouse. His driver side window is rolled down. He sees me and his mom and sticks his arm out the window then gives a thumbs up. Did he win a court prize? I find out that he has won child custody. Mom will have to pay him child support. I'll visit mom later to hear her side in all this. The truthful side. Right now though, I have other, more important stuff going on in my life. Bishop Pettit offers a cooking class. I want to read and study recipes so I'll already have a good idea how to prepare them when I do take the class.

2

ORIGINS (THE ADDICTIONS BEGIN)

My favorite show as a preteen was Super Woman. I still watch reruns on television. Lisa Caldwell is the actress who portrayed Desiree Prince. Desiree is really an Alien in disguise. She saves a pilot named Steve from danger, then travels with him. The first season takes place in Germany circa the Hitler era. The next season fast forwards to a contemporary location, Hollywood, I believe. Any time Desiree sensed danger, she would transform into the voluptuous, bullet dodging, heroine Super Woman. I wished Lisa Caldwell was my girlfriend.

Besides her, there were several older ladies who I wished were my girlfriend: The Bleach Blonde's lead singer Christine Miller, the actress Donna Patton, she's one of leading ladies in the 1977 cop film Barracadeland, country western singer Barbara Thompson, and my buxom sixth grade homeroom teacher. If I remember, her name was Louise and the color of her short, stylish hair was auburn.

During my grade school years, the only other woman I spoke to who wasn't related to me was a local librarian. I don't count saying hi to my female classmates or my teachers. There I'm just being polite. One day the local librarian visits my homeroom class. I don't remember her name. I will call her Susan. Susan would help me with checking out various cookbooks or reference materials for an assignment. I loved reading the detailed recipes for cakes and pies. Susan and I never talked about anything on a personal level. I didn't know if she was married, had a boyfriend, a girlfriend, was part of a swingers group, a convent, or happy to be a single woman.

I'm not aware Susan is in the classroom. Blowing her completely off, I walk in then proceed to the back of the class. Once I sit at my desk, I see Susan standing next to my teacher. Susan is a full figured woman. She could be in her late twenties or early thirties. She wears big rimmed glasses and favors long, frumpy dresses. Susan begins talking to the class. She spots me, then waves to me. I do not wave back. Susan continues to talk, sees me, and then smiles and waves to me. Again, I do not respond. My eyes glaze over towards the window. By now, the other nosy, close to mentally retarded classmates of mine begin to whisper among themselves. They want to know if I know Susan. Yes, I know who she is, but I'm too much of a pussy to respond back to her.

I never wave back, smile, wink, or say one fucking hello to her. I regret being rude to Susan. I'm positive if Susan and I got to know one another we would have become a couple. Our age difference of at least ten years would be the hot smoke topic for all the gossipy broads to languish over.

Susan is not the only female I blew an early sexual opportunity with.

Ever since my cousin Mary laid next to me in my bed, I've been hoping to have sex with a woman. Mary, her mom, and Mary's two older brothers Kevin and Jacob were visiting my family for a weekend. Everyone except me was going to Six Flags. I had promised two of our neighbors that I would mow their lawns. My dad sternly reminded me that I made a commitment and to stick with it. Mary feigned a minor stomach ache. She blamed the hot dogs my dad had burnt. She stayed at home with me.

So everybody is gone, I'm lying on my bed reading a music entertainment magazine, and Mary decides to lay against me. My heart begins to beat fast. C'mon Randy, you know girls have boobies and once you grab a hold of them, you can tickle, scratch, fondle, squeeze, and suck them. I never summon the balls to make any sexual move towards her. As Mary got older, I saw less of her. All of her. Mary moved to Maine after she graduated from high school. My mom had mentioned to me that Mary now has four kids from four different men. Two of her kids have dark skin. Mary doesn't care what nation you come from as long as you have a working penis. To this day, I still miss her. And I regret not fucking her before any other guy had the chance.

Thank God I didn't have to hear any talk about sex from mom or dad. What preteen guy wants to hear sex talk and how babies are born from their parents? I would rather have any of the Jamboree Good Time girls tell me then show me. This show which ran from the 60s and 70's was a country western themed variety show. You tuned in the see the regulars Marlene Sutton, Gunella Heaton, Lisa Tidd, Kathy Bennett, Ronnie Lee Davis, and Lucille Rowan. Jamboree Good Time was one of my dad's favorite television shows. The comedy sketches were goofball on purpose, but the country music performed by A-list singers like Loretta Quinn and MJ Haggard were first class.

My grandma preferred The Lawrence Timmons show. The Lawrence Timmons show was also a variety and music show. But where Jamboree Good Time focused on idiotic comedy skits mixed in with country and gospel music, Lawrence Timmons emphasized a gentler, easy listening approach. There were no sketches, only a relaxing atmosphere. Grandma's favorite show featured a lot of beautiful female singers too. The two I can remember are Latin Sensation Louisa and down home girl Sandy Jacobs.

Neither of my parents showed the slightest interest in me learning about sex anyway. I learned about dicks, vaginas, and how to fuck a woman from movies, books, and magazines. Another great educational tool to learn about women and sex from is the film His Eyes Said Yes. The film was already four years old by the time I first saw it. The movie's plot is about a female doctor who has an addiction for having meaningless sexual relationships with different men. She couldn't stop her addictions and ultimately paid a price.

We need to go back even earlier. My obsession with women and sex began with Playpen magazines. Damn you Frank Cecero for a brilliant idea! My dad collects Playpen magazines. He doesn't hide them well. When mom and dad are gone, that's when I take full advantage of sneaking a peek. All I have to do is walk into his unlocked bedroom. Then I open the closet door, grab a stepstool from inside the closet, and reach up for a magazine. My favorite issue of Playpen is the one from December 1979. The centerfold features a lady named Camella Coltier. She's only wearing a paper thin, unbuttoned white night shirt. Camella has the most beautiful breasts and cunt I have ever seen.

Playpen wasn't the only adult magazine my dad collected. He also had issues of Kitten, Teaser, and Amore. I thumbed through the pages of them to. I didn't care as much for those magazines. The ladies were not too attractive and the pictures of them were not as classy or tasteful as the pictures in Playpen. I would read articles in the magazines written by men or women who would describe the time they had a sex with someone. So that's how you fuck! So that's what a 69 is!

One time during high school homeroom period, I overhead a classmate tell a joke to another classmate. The joke was about a person learning about sex. The punchline had the classmate who was telling the joke move his arm in an up and down motion. Now I know how to masterbate. And once I started, every day before I went to sleep and after I prayed, I jerked off.

After school, I went downstairs to my room. My dad was at work and my grandma was next door. I laid on my bed then pulled my pants and underpants down half way. I began stroking my cock. I kept stroking until cum shot out on my chest. Then I hear my front door open. Oh shit! I wipe cum off my chest using my shirt. I was able to put up my pants right before my grandma began walking down the steps.

My mom hid her adult novels better. These novels would include several pages describing explicit sex between a male and female. So that's how you fuck a woman! Who knew my mom had an erotic side to her? I always made sure to put dad's magazines back the exact same way I found them. I had to be careful when putting mom's books away. She hid the books under her panties in one of the drawers. It was always risky anytime my hand slid under one of her panties. I'm proud of how careful I was. I was never caught red handed or questioned or accused by mom or dad.

Friends and strangers were another fast way to learn about sex and the type of sex to avoid. My friend Joe invited me over to his place for a sleepover. The only reason I said yes was because my dad's bragging about winning his divorce case was getting on my nerves. I didn't want to be around him. Since Joe's house was only a half mile away, I walked there. Joe opened the door wearing a pair of blue and white boxer shorts. No shirt, socks, or shoes.

"My mom and dad won't be home until Sunday night. We can stay up all night. I have the new PureVision space invaders, monte carlo, and red baron games."

"Oh okay, I can only stay over tonight. My dad is bugging me to help him with cleaning the blinds."

Joe's bedroom was too small for both us to be on the floor. We both spread out our sleeping bags on his living room floor. Joe has laid his sleeping bag right up against mine. I had to borrow an old one from my grandma. Each time I would move my sleeping bag over some, Joe would slide his bag over in the same direction. I'm beginning to regret my decision about staying the night. Joe is an intense video game player. His eyes are gazed upon the television screen. Without even looking at the game remote, he uses his hands and fingers to move the stick around.

"Hey when you're done, can I try?"

I could have said *hey your house is on fire* and Joe wouldn't budge. Another young lady opens the front door and walks in. She walks right past the television causing Joe to stop playing.

"Thanks for messing my game up dorkface. I was going to beat my high score."

"Your sister?" I ask already knowing who the babe was.

Joe lets out a big sigh.

"Yeah. I call her dorkface or buttface."

Joe goes back to playing his spaceship video game. I excuse myself and walk into his kitchen.

"Hey I'm Randy."

"Hi."

She must be Joe's younger sister. A preteen who should race past puberty before Joe even starts his. Her body is developing nicely. She's wearing a red and white dress that stops right below her kneecaps. Ooh, I so want to date your sister.

"Do you want to play a game or not?" Joe yells out from the living room.

Let's see, choice one is to go back in the living room and shoot down enemy spaceships. Choice two is to follow your sister upstairs into her bedroom. She turns around to see me and leaves her bedroom door open. I watch your sister take off her candy cane dress, white bra, and powder blue panties. Then I walk into her bedroom, grab her by the shoulders, and toss her naked body on the bed. Then as you come upstairs, I say to you *get the fuck out of here, can't you see I'm busy* then slam the door shut and lock it. The only dork or buttface I see around here is you.

"Guess Joe wants to play teams or against me. Maybe I'll see you around."

"Maybe, see you." Joe's sister says as she gives me a wink.

Man, I am uncomfortable laying so close to Joe. I'm nervous that he's going to reach over and start touching me. Man, why can't you be somewhere else? It's hard to have sex fantasies involving me and your sister with you all up next to me.

"Listen, my back is starting to hurt really bad. It's not you it's me. And this piece of junk for a sleeping bag. My dad's too cheap to buy a new one. I'm just going to sleep in your recliner."

I didn't think what I said would offend Joe. Hell, we're only talking about my health.

"Why? You're supposed to stay on the floor. That's why it's called a sleepover."

Aw man, I hope Joe doesn't start crying. I could tell he was getting mad at me. His lips were puffy and his face morphed into a pout.

"Yeah I know but I don't know how much more my back can take. I'm sorry."

"God, you're such a wimp."

Yeah, I'm a wimp, but a wimp who doesn't nestle up against guys.

After the weird night at Joe's, I would make up an excuse for not spending the night at his place or if he asked to spend the night at mine. After several months of pushing him away, he finally stopped calling. The sad part was I also never saw Joe's sister again.

I didn't see Joe again for about a year. He and his dad were shopping at the same store that my dad and I were in.

"Hey Joe, how's it going. Long time no see."

Joe gave me a quick wave then walked away. I think he's still sore that he didn't get to touch my dick. I was going to talk more, but then

I see him hanging out with another boy. From that moment on, I only wanted female friends.

My trip to Arkansas with my grandma was forgettable. I don't remember a damn thing about the trip except that we stayed in the city of Mountain Home. Any activities from the trip are a total blank.

My next trip with her to Indianapolis was a much better experience. Both trips were taken during the summers in 1981 and 1982. The bus ride began in front of the Downtown Westin Hotel. Several couples, mostly old folks but a few young ones were getting on the bus. I felt like a baby compared to everyone else. Our tour guide is a short, red haired man named Jasper. He looked like a cross between a leprechaun and an Alaskan bear trapper.

Anyway, as we rode along the highways, Jasper would speak into his microphone and tell everyone a little history about the local landmarks we passed by. The bus stopped for lunch at Bennigan's. Bennigan's was located in the middle of nowhere. Springfield, Illinois to be exact. The eating place served up hearty helpings of burgers and fries, fish and chips, and ribs and slaw.

Our first night in Indiana was a relaxing, spend time on your own affair. The hotel didn't have cable TV, only local channels. I just walked outside while grandma read a local newspaper. I didn't see anyone from our tour outside. The humid evening stopped any of them from stepping out. I was too young to drink. The only places nearby was a grocery store and a barber shop. Indiana isn't impressing me.

My grandma and I had a tiresome second day. We saw the Indy 400 racetrack and museum. A shuttle bus drove around the track as we listened to the local guide talk about the track itself. You could see the tire marks left by speeding cars still on the track. At the museum, I walked around the entire area. Plaques of the past race winners hung on the walls. The plaques had a picture of an Indy 400 winner along with his name and the year he won the race. Okay, the track and museum were impressive.

Grandma and I went inside the museum gift shop. She purchased a T-shirt for dad. The light red shirt had INDY scrawled across the front in black ink. The back of the shirt listed every Indy 400 winner. I was going to buy some shot glasses but changed my mind after I saw the seven dollar price tag. The hot sun made both of us too tired to go out again after we got to our room.

Back at the hotel, we decide to eat dinner at the restaurant next door.

"I had a lot of fun at the racetrack. Are you still staying in tonight? I overheard Jasper mention something about a bus ride to the theatre. Some play is showing."

"If you want to go, go. Have some fun. I'm going to stay in and watch TV. I had enough excitement for today."

"Nah, the play doesn't interest me. All I know is that play is about a group of people building a new church. I'll stay in with you."

"We'll see what's on TV."

Once we get back to our hotel room, my grandma turns the television on.

"Do you want to watch the baseball game?"

"I need to take a shower first. I'm sweating and I stink."

Once I'm finished, I step out and grab a towel. Next, I squint my eyes and peer through the crack between the bathroom door and wall. I can barely make out grandma standing in front of a large sink with an attached mirror. She is combing her hair. Is her pajama shirt unbuttoned? I hurry drying off, then put my shorts on. Slowly, I open the bathroom door. My instincts were correct. I camouflage myself so grandma could only see my head. She's blind to the fact that I'm staring at her. She stretches her arms out causing her shirt to expand. I catch a fleeting glimpse of her brown nipples. I'm too nervous, scared really, to act upon my feelings. I slam the bathroom door shut.

My dad keeps secrets from mom, grandma, and myself. He never told mom about the strip clubs he was at, the money he pockets for himself after receiving a refund check from the IRS, and getting more money on his paycheck but expecting mom to pay him now for my child support. Dad will find the easy way out and not stop until he is satisfied with getting what he wants. Well dad, I have secrets too. I look at your Playpen's. I saw grandma's breasts. I want to see and suck my mom's.

Sex isn't the only type of insatiable desire forming.

"I'm going to be working nights from now on. Sometimes I'll have to cover the graveyard shift. When you work the night shift, you get paid more. It's called shift differential. I'll be working with more white people too. None of these lazy niggers, foreigners, and other idiots anymore. Some of these old guys who work late nights are old enough they should be retired. I hope none of them collapse on me while I'm working with them! Jesus. My boss needed someone younger, smarter, and stronger. Someone who knows all about the shipping and receiving. What's that? Yeah my guns. Not those guns. These guns, at least fifteen inches. Yeah, Hahaha! Hell. If anybody fucks me with me they will come face to face with both of loaded guns. What! No! These guns! Yeah, a chest full of led. Oh, and something else I learned, my boss tells me that once the old timers do leave, he's already lined up some younger and experienced people for me to work with. Thank you Jesus!"

Dad must be talking to Trent. Trent is the only person on this planet who tolerates my dad's arrogance and ignorance. From what I heard, dad is transferring to the night shift. He and his supervisor were butting heads over stocking and inventory.

The main reason for the change is so my dad can earn more money. He's already milking mom dry. I make no allowance. How much more of a tightwad can he be? He was bitching all the time to me and his mom about how lousy of a review he got at work. No shit? In his words, he works hard only to get royally screwed up the ass.

Up the ass. Take it up the ass. Reamed in the ass. Fucked in the ass. My dad uses those words and other similar phrases like screwed over and bent over so much I wonder if he really did have an uncomfortable object rammed, jammed, or alakazamed up his ass when he was a child.

The great news about dad's change in work hours is that I will see him less. I'll be in school for at least eight hours, five days a week. When I do get home, sometimes late if I need to go somewhere for school research, he will be leaving or already be gone. But with mom gone, I could become his personal verbal punching bag. Shit. Oh well, I'll just tell him I have homework and stay in my room all evening.

In his spare time, Dad has been frying up hash browns and small sausages. This is his idea of cooking gourmet food for the two of us. I have to admit, this combination of meat and starch tastes good. Neither the hash browns or links is burned to brazen hell, but I'll still be eating plenty of microwave Hot Pockets and Pizza Rolls. Since my dad works a lot when I'm at home, I even can hear Donna Summer sing Love to Love you Baby to me without using the headphones.

Bad news is dad still off on the weekends. If he's tired, he'll just watch TV all day. During auto racing season, he will be glued to the set cheering on his favorite racer, Richard Gold to win. If Richard Gold crashes then dad will cuss at the TV screen. If nothing on TV interests him, he may get the urge to diligently clean the house. I'll have no choice to help him sweep and mop floors, wash a car, wipe piss off the side of a toilet, do his and my laundry, I keep my clothes separate, and help wash the blinds. It's too bad if I'm the one who is tired.

Most of the time, he will re-do what I already cleaned. What did you have me do all this cleaning for if you're going to just clean the same thing yourself! All of his mumbling about the poor job I did cleaning gets old. I've learned to tune him out.

I hate the winter months. The howling cold winds mixed in with frigid temperatures cause my hands to become numb and my butt cheeks to freeze. On one blistering afternoon, the high school let all of the classes out early. A winter storm was coming. I made it home about two hours before my dad would arrive. The snow was falling fast and hard. I kept shoveling the snow off the sidewalk next to my dad's driveway. I already opened the garage door for him.

I see a pair of bright headlights but the light was facing in another direction. That's because the Pontiac was sliding sideways down the alley. My dad's lips are moving as he struggles to turn the car straight. What's he yelling at me? He stops a few inches past the garage. As he backs in, the tires spin viciously in the snow and gravel. I get in front of the car and with all my strength push the car towards the garage. The car's back wheels spin viciously on top of the snow covered alley.

"AW JUST GO IN THE HOUSE!"

Well excuse me for trying to help. I knew my attempts at moving the car were fruitless. I was wanting to prove my manhood to him. Instead, I show off my feminine side. My dad finally comes in the house fifteen minutes later all huffy and puffy from the ordeal.

"How come you didn't shovel the Goddamn sidewalk?!"

"I have been shoveling the Goddamn sidewalk. The snow keeps falling. If it stops before I go to bed, then I'll go back out."

I've made decent money over the years shoveling snow, mowing lawns, and carrying the neighbors' groceries up their stairs. Having pocket change has allowed me to buy sno-cones in the summer and cans of vegetable soup in the winter. I'm not old enough yet to apply for a paycheck earning job. I do however go to our local bowling alley. A flyer pinned to the library's community bulletin board advertised the need for additional help at the alley.

My interview, if you want to even call it that, was with an old, gaunt looking man who may have also been a graveyard caretaker. He was skinny like me with wrinkled skin. He took me behind the lanes to have me watch the boys who were working.

"Think you can handle it?"

"Yeah."

"Come back Friday at six PM."

The machines were still hand pulled by pinboys. The other kids and I ranged from ages twelve to fifteen. We were paid twenty in cash after working our machine or machines. I never worked with these machines before. Steve was the one who showed me how to operate them. I learned fast and soon I was manning one or two of the machines myself.

Leagues were held on Mondays, Wednesdays, and Fridays. On Mondays, the parish ladies would bowl. The ladies were around my mom's age. Some of them were nice looking but also too religious for my taste. Only one or two of them drank beer. Most of them would talk about an upcoming church event. Wednesdays were when the teams made up of rowdy teens, rowdy male adults, and their rowdy friends bowled. Most of them were terrible bowlers. They were more talented drinking beer and burping. Several of them rode cool looking motorcycles. I knew a few of the kids from going to Bishop Pettit. On Fridays the alley was packed. This is when the male church parishioners, including two priests, came to the bowling alley. These guys knew how to bowl and most of them did well.

During school, I worked Fridays and some Wednesdays. Depends on how much school homework I have. During the summer between my freshman and sophomore years, I would try to work all three days each week. Most of the other kids don't even bother to show up when they are scheduled to work. I don't feel bad at all when Jack calls me to ask I can fill in. The money fits better in pants pocket. In one month I could make up to two hundred and forty dollars. Plus, any tip I would get from a generous bowler.

If you were fast enough, you could work two machines, next to one another. Jack, my boss, didn't hesitate to have me operating two of them. I didn't want to be like Jimmy and Stevie. The slow boys. Once the pins were knocked down, I had to hurry my ass up and scoop up the pins, slide the bowling ball down the rack, and make double damn sure the pins were placed in the correct slots. There was no fucking around. You either hustled or you were gone. Working behind the alley was a dirty, smelly job. Some of the other kids would take off their shirts. If their pale, hairless, white skinned chests didn't blind me, their excessive body odor gagged me.

Some of the kids who worked there didn't take their job serious. I still remember one Wednesday night when Eddie got his butt chewed out by Jack and some of the bowlers because he was goofing off all night. The highlight of that particular night was when an angry bowler swung the back area door open and blurts out *WHO THE FUCK'S ON FIVE?!* I couldn't hear any talking after that because I'm now in my pit working. When I got up, I noticed Eddie's face was all red. He may have been crying. Eddie is such a baby. Brian and I had to finish Eddie's night. Didn't get out of there until ten thirty at night.

Another dope, that would be Greg, got fired when he threw a pin down the alley towards the bowlers. Greg was all upset and boo- hooing because he claimed a bowler tried to nick him with a pin on purpose. As nasty as the job was, it was working at the bowling alley I learned working fast is what gets you ahead. You will yourself to work faster, but also smarter than everyone else.

The best advice, well its more words of wisdom, I got an ear of came from a high school senior named Bruce. Bruce was a tough looking senior at Bishop Pettit who was also the star football running back. He and I were in the school's weight room with about ten other guys. Bruce was talking to another guy about football and scoring. Bruce began lifting barbells when he said *some coaches and other people don't mind winning by a point. I don't want to win by a point. I want to blow them away. Let them know they're fucking with Bishop Pettit.* Sounds like the same advice my dad would dish out. The words stick with me. I use them to motivate myself at the alley. Anytime you finish off a night under two hours, the guys will give you tips. I don't mind the handful of quarters, but I relish the ice cold cans of soda the bowlers will buy for me.

I'm getting too old to continue working at the bowling alley. I was the only kid working there not in grade school. Besides, I'm looking to work at a place that will allow me to get a foot in the door relating to my career as a chef.

Jack Bennett is my idol. Not the only, as I have others. Ted Dane, Paul Ellison. But Jack Bennett was my first. Jack is a fictional character on the TV comedy show Turn of Events. Jack is a single, successful chef who discovers that his two roommates are dating one another. The show created a lot of controversy due to the adult subject matter. Jack can be a bit clumsy (an act I'm sure), has a different girlfriend in each episode, and has a good heart. He treats his female roommates with respect. I have a crush on the actress Joyce Vitt. She plays Mandy, one of Jack's roommates. Joyce is down to earth, successful, and perky. I'm turned on by her short, jet black hair.

Jack went from cooking school, to working as a chef at various restaurants, to owning his own French bistro. He gave up the playboy lifestyle to settle down with one woman. I want to achieve everything he did. From his success as a chef to the causal meeting and dating several women.

It's time for me to study for my driver's license.

"Hey dad, I applied to work for some restaurants, hotels, and retirement homes. A lot of them are local grease spoons but a few of them are located downtown. When you have some time, can we go practice driving?"

My dad seems supportive. His philosophy has always been get a job. He never went to college. Don't be sitting on the couch all day was is mantra. My dad does care that I'm passing my classes, but he has yet to be a part of my school activities. And by activities I mean going to the parent-teacher-student conferences.

"Yeah, I guess so. Why don't you get the book from the department of revenue first? Kind of go over it and read it. We can go out Sunday morning and practice on an empty parking lot."

At first, dad and I went out in his Pontiac. Most of the time I would drive the car around in an empty parking lot. Only one time did he allow me to drive in the street. How am I supposed to learn driving if all I do is drive around in circles on an empty lot? MY dad is the WORST passenger and a back seat driver. He made me so fucking, and I mean fucking, nervous. Every time we go out to practice, I have to hear him yell out *Stop sign Randy! Slow down dammit! EEEEEEEEZZEE!,* and *Turn the wheel Randy!* And this is while I'm driving in a parking lot!! His lack of patience made me have a deeper appreciation for public transportation.

When I mentioned to him that Bishop Pettit offered a free drivers education program, dad stopping giving me his lessons (lessons is a word I use very loosely). I end up learning how to drive through an independent company called A+ drivers. My two instructors Isaac and Abe were smart, patient, and complimented me when I made smooth left turn. Once I passed the written and driving tests on my first try, I had to, otherwise my dad would give me constant shit for failing something any male should easily pass, then he and I went car shopping.

He could have gone to all the car dealers all by himself. Even before we went to one, I had to hear him say a thousand times to me *don't you start talking to them, I'll do the talking. I used to work in sales so I know how these people operate. They'll sweet talk you into a fancy looking car and you'll end up with a lemon. You have to know to bullshit with these people. I know how to bullshit. I'll make sure you don't pay a lot of money for any car.* After he said those words to me on the way to our fourth dealer, I had the words memorized.

My dad never let me get a word in. I was ready to say fuck it and take my chances riding on the city bus. After his useless negotiations, I finally own a white 1983 Ford Escort. The car only had about two thousand miles on it. The sticker price was seventeen five. My dad was a real ace when it came to wheeling and dealing as I paid around fifteen grand. My grandma lent me ten grand. I already had the five thousand. I promised her that I would pay her back. She kept a journal and would write down the date and the amount that I gave to her on that day.

A few weeks after driving around places to hand in my resume, I receive a phone call from the Clarion Hotel. The hotel is located in the heart of downtown St. Louis.

"Hi is this Randy Stevens?"

"Yes ma'am."

"My name is Jane. I work in the personnel department at the Clarion Hotel. We received your resume and we have a current opening for a steward and purchasing clerk. I would like to meet you and set up an interview."

"Wow! That's great. Thank you."

"Let me tell you a little bit about the position. This is a dual position. The steward will assist the chefs and utility workers in a variety of functions. One time you could be helping with washing dishes and then be asked to help the banquet chefs prepare dishes to go out. The purchasing part of the job will be a lot of stocking deliveries and filling kitchen orders. You'll be working with a number of kitchen staff but you report to our executive chef."

"What about my school? Will that be a problem with the hiring?"

"Not at all. I've already coordinated all of your school days and hours to Chef John. From the information given to me, you will be working evenings and weekends. In fact, the only time you would work in the day is during the summer when you are not in school of course. John, he's our executive chef was impressed by your grades and is aware that you are currently taking a cooking class. He also is aware of your previous employment."

"That's great. Will I have an interview with him?"

"Not right away. Once I'm done screening and doing the preliminary interviews then John and I go over them. He will be the one who decides which candidate he wants to hire. He was impressed by your resume though. You would meet him on your orientation day."

"That sounds good to me."

"Can you come in Tuesday at ten?"

"Yes."

"Great. When does school start for you?"

"About two more weeks."

"Okay then, I'll see you Tuesday."

"Absolutely. Thank you."

Jane is aware of my school days and hours. She's coordinated that information to the executive chef. The chef was impressed by my good grades in the Chef Cookery class that I'm in, and my past employment at the bowling alley. Having reliable transportation was a plus to getting hired. I let Jane know that during the summer, I am able to work days as well. Having flexibility put my resume ahead of the others. After meeting her in person for an introduction interview, I wait for a phone call. One week later, the home phone rings.

"Hello?"

"Hi, may I speak to Randy Stevens please?"

"This is him."

"It's Jane from the Clarion. I would like to have you come in for a drug test and background check. How does Thursday at ten sound?"

"Great. I'll be there. Thank you!"

"So dad, I got a phone call from the Clarion Hotel. I was told to come in so they could give me paperwork to take a drug test."

"Hey alright, you got the job!" My dad beams. I've never seen him this proud of anything I've done.

"Well, I'm not hired yet."

"When someone calls and tells you to take a piss test, you got the job." Dad explains to me. Now he's an expert on the hiring process. This time though, he's right.

I wasn't looking forward to telling Jack that I found another job. But the reality was I am going to work for a place that will provide me with a great future.

"Um, Jack. This is my notice in writing. I got another job working at the Clarion. I'll be working in the kitchen which relates to my school work. Thank you for everything."

He didn't seem to care if I stayed or not. To him, I just another kid who moves on.

"I don't need that. I got two guys who asked me if I had any openings anyway. You can make tonight your last night if you want. You're a hard worker. Good luck to you."

On my final night. I tear through a Friday night and set the alley on its ass. My killer instinct propels me to lifting six to ten pins a frame and firing back shiny black balls down the rack at thirty miles an hour. I was finished in under two hours. My last night there resulted in a ten dollar bonus given to me by all the people who bowled on the two lanes I was in charge of.

Now that I have a real job, I wanted to celebrate my asking a girl out on a date. There were plenty of high school girls to choose from. I have no idea if any of them had boyfriends so I would be taking some chances. My first pick is Cheryl. She's a perky brunette who is in several of my classes. I also have a crush on Darlene. Darlene is a spunky little blond whose lack of boob development is made up by her outlandish personality.

Another girl I want to go out with is Annette. Annette is a quiet homey girl who keeps to herself. We worked on an American history project together in our sophomore year. If any of these ladies would say no to me I could always ask Miss Day out. She was my high school guidance counselor. Her plain jane appearance reminds me of a skinnier Susan.

Before I had a chance to ask Cheryl or Darlene out, I saw each of them outside the school with a boy. Cheryl and her jock boyfriend were kissing each other by the school's track. Darlene and her leather jacket wearing boyfriend were taking turns smoking a cigarette. Annette transferred to another school. I was getting desperate. I began nervously asking girls out who I hardly knew. The rejection was humiliating. There were plenty of women, older women, who worked at the Clarion. My odds of hitting one of them up for meaningless sex seemed promising.

3
SEPERATION (LIVING ALONE)

My dad, grandma and I live in a middle class neighborhood. The homes can be divided into singles, duplexes, or four family flats. The flats always appear crowded. I would see several men and women enter and exit from the doors. Their cars or trucks lined up single file up against the curb. The walls were built so thin, you could hear your neighbor's conversation. With the exception of a newlywed couple living down the block, several of the men and women around here were mom and dad's age. Their kids were typical teens and almost teens. The boys would ride their bikes for fun and the girls would relax next to their blown up swimming pools.

Crimes never occur in my neighborhood. No burglaries, murders, or grand theft auto happens around here. Between the nosy old ladies and constant car doors opening, and house doors slamming shut at night, someone would always be up and alert. My dad pretends to be the head of our pretend neighborhood security watch. He keeps a keen eye out on the block by snoring loudly on the couch. How would he knows what is going on? The blinds and his eyes are closed.

I get the feeling these older ladies do not want any minorities in the area. They are not racist, rather suspicious, maybe overly concerned that a minority will create trouble. Or bring in trouble. None of the homes are large or lavish. No one around here wants to pay city officials to have a technician install a security camera or gate. Besides, the block has six tall bright street lights.

Compared to my mom's new area where she's living, I am in Beverly Hills. When mom gave me her address, 55 Dade Street, I got an uneasy feeling in my stomach. She went from middle class to lowest class. I'm driving north, towards the airport, past the large water tanks, rusted railroad cars, and boarded up business that have been closed for years. I see too many busted out windows. I have be on the lookout for any nails or other sharp objects laying in the road. The last thing I need to have is a flat tire. For starters, I'm not an expert at fixing or replacing a tire. Second, I'm stranded in a dim area where hoodlums walk back and forth.

A lot of poor, black people live in this area. Yes, a few whites too, so don't start with the remarks about hating blacks. Every person I see standing aloof on their sidewalk or in the street are dressed as if they were robbed. Their faces form a droopy pout, which makes sense, they were robbed. Their shirts have holes in them. I even saw a guy who was wearing socks that didn't match. One argyle sock on the left leg and one white sock on his right leg. The chubby looking kids would be in the street throwing a football or dribbling a basketball.

None of the kids pay attention to the cars driving by. If they don't move out of the way at the last second, they remain in the street. The person driving has to slam on the brakes. And the adults are just as dumb, not paying any attention to how close one of these kids could get hit by a speeding car.

I make sure my windows are rolled up. I smell smoke coming from either a house or a sewer. Either someone's house is on fire or a group of homeless people are building a fire. Where in the hell are the cops? Is there even a police station nearby? The cops always arrive to ticket you for doing twenty five in a twenty mile an hour speed zone. But if you need one to chase down an armed robber, forget it, the cops are slurping coffee and eating blueberry muffins inside a bakery.

What was mom thinking by moving into an eyesore of an area like this one?

Mom lives in a duplex too. Her block is off the main road. The flats and duplexes are camouflaged by large trees full of leaves. I had to drive backwards up to her place as the street was one way. Mom is standing outside talking to a woman who may live next door. I open my car door, quickly lock the door, and wave to mom.

"Rannnnndy!" My mom is gushing with excitement upon seeing me.

"Hi mom." I smile and give her a loose hug.

"Nice area. So if you don't mind my asking, how did you find out about this place?"

"Oh, Betty told me about a vacancy here. And I already knew Kate from work."

"Hi Kate, I'm Randy."

"Hi."

Kate is a busty redhead who reeks of cigarette smoke. Her grey tanktop barely fits over her chest. I can see a quick peek of a flower tattoo above her right breast. A guy who is either Kate's boyfriend or husband is working on something underneath the hood of a car. He has to be at least six feet six. I have a funny thought. If she stands face front of him, she is right up to his dick. The big man has multiple tattoos on both his arms. I jumped when he spits out *shit!* This guy's rough and surly demeanor reminded me too much of my dad. Even so, I'm glad and I feel better that those two are mom's neighbors.

"Kate and I were talking about going to the bar that she hangs out at."

"I finally twisted your mom's arm. She needs a girl's night out."

My mom, at a bar!? I can't imagine my mom drinking a beer much less even walking into a bar. Don't get me wrong. I want my mom to live a little. Have fun with her new friends. I want to her to play in the adult sandbox with Kathy. But Kate could be too bad of an influence. Offering her a cigarette, a bottle of JD, that's Jack Daniel's, and getting into a fight with some slut who causes trouble at a biker bar.

Dad would have a massive kanipshin fit if he ever finds out where mom is living. He might get along with Kate's boyfriend only because they both enjoy fast cars, fixing cars, and saying the shit word a lot. Dad would despise Kate for being a trashy smoker. I'm sure dad would voice his strong opinions about the condition of mom's home. Her brick home is sturdy on the outside. I didn't see any visible cracks in the foundation or sidewalk. There was no broken windows or busted fences. She has a working AC/heat unit.

"I hope you're hungry. I made dinner for both of us."

"My stomach is growling already. I'm going in. Nice to meet you Kate."

"I'll talk to you later."

I say goodbye to Kate and walk inside mom's home. I instantly recognize the large black hard plastic chair. Her TV is about as small as mine. She also took some of the living room pictures with her. One picture is of me and her. Another one is with me, her, dad and grandma. The green kitchen table and matching green chairs belonged to grandma. Mom's bed and dressers, one in the bedroom another in hallway near the bathroom, looked used and worn. Those may have been given to her by a co-worker.

"So what's your dad doing tonight?"

"He and Trent went to the stock car races in Pevely."

"Why didn't you go? Sounds like fun."

"Yeah, for him. Not my scene. I told him that I would go with him to another one later."

He knew that I having dinner with mom. I promised my dad that I would go with him to a future stock car event. I prodded mom to cook dinner early so that I could leave while it was still light outside. I haven't had the chance to buy a club for my car. Or a high tech alarm to scare off potential thieves.

Mom bakes fish patties served with macaroni and cheese. The tender fish patties were cooked to a perfect golden brown color. Sure beats the rubbery breakfast steak I was getting. I brought over a loaf of wheat bread and a yellow cake. The cake was made by me and two other students. I already cut two slices for my dad to have.

"How are doing in school? Are you enjoying your classes? Making friends? Do you have a girlfriend?" Mom chimes in, asking a new question before I can even answer the first one.

"I'm doing fine. I'm passing my classes, in fact, I'm getting an A in the cooking class and English class. I've started a new job at the Clarion Hotel so I don't even have time to be hanging around other schoolkids."

"Are you working in the kitchen?"

"Most of the time. They have me doing all kinds of work. Some days, I wash dishes all day and other days I'm prepping and bring up cases of food."

"Oh, that sounds good. Hopefully, with you working now maybe your dad will stop pestering me for more child support. He's already taking a big enough amount out of my paycheck."

I feel bad for mom. I'm already giving dad fifty bucks a month, he lives rent free, and now he's taking pleasure in raping mom for more money.

"I doubt dad will be able to collect any more than what he's already getting. Here, I wrote the name of the person down who handles the child support stuff."

I hand mom a piece of paper with the name Hubert Pill written on it. Underneath the name is the number 456-2020.

"You can call him to see if you can find out more information. Yeah, dad can be a greedy tyrant. Let this Hubert guy know I'm working a steady job. Unfortunately, since I'm under twenty one and living at home, I think dad still gets money. Maybe if this guy has proof of my earnings, the money will be less."

"I don't want to get your father all upset. I know he will he yell at me."

"So play dumb and don't tell him. It's not like the support will end. I think it goes on until I'm of age."

"Well, I'll manage."

I'm ready to talk about something else. Certainly not the divorce itself.

"Randy, you know the reason I left your father had nothing to do with you. I just don't love him anymore. I will always love.."

"I know I know. I love you too."

Mom was getting teary eyed and too emotional. I changed the subject.

"Let's talk about your new job at the salon."

"I love working again. And I can choose by my own hours and days as long as the salon is open."

"Sounds great. I now know where to go if I need a trim."

I keep looking out her front window. I'm nervous somebody is going to steal my car. Two fat black kids in their teens keep bouncing their basketballs near my car.

"I need to leave so I can pick up food for dad."

"Oh okay, well come here, I want a hug."

"I'll walk out with you."

"I'll keep in touch and let you know how school and work is going."

"Okay, remember I love you."

"Love you too."

I manage to leave mom's area while the sun is still out. I gave mom one last hug and wave goodbye from my car. As I'm driving way, some burly black guy yells out some words at me. I couldn't understand what he was saying. I didn't steal your clothes. I breathe a sigh of relief once I'm on the highway. When I make a ton of money, my first priority will be moving mom out of her poor, run down, filthy neighborhood.

A tale of two dads:

"FUCKINSONOFABITCH!!"

Another terrific Stevens family moment ruined when dad and I happen to be off work together on a Saturday. Well, not quite. I have to be at work at five pm. I'm unsure if dad woke up in a rotten mood or if the bad mood started off small in the morning and became infected in his ass by the afternoon.

He's repainting the living room and hallway walls. After hours of going over samples at the hardware store yesterday, he made up his mind on a light green color for both walls. He stayed up for several hours the night before putting masking tape over the crease where the wall and baseboards connect. So he was probably cranky from the lack of sleep, like a baby, than angry.

"I'm totally dissatisfied. Totally dissatisfied."

Paint kept getting splattered on the dropcloths or on part of the baseboard that wasn't taped over. I'm waiting for him to either kick or throw a can halfway across the kitchen. You have to think that even my dad would be smart enough not to. My dad is not a professional painter. He's too cheap to call and pay for a real one. His anger over the paint job triggers a chain reaction of him tearing into me for uncompleted chores.

He storms outside to the garage and then drives out the Pontiac. He parks the car up against the garage. No sooner he walks back in the house and barks out an order to me.

"Go outside and wash the car! It's filthy! And the sonofabitch better be clean. AND WASH YOUR CAR TOO GODDAMMIT!"

As I'm walking outside, there are two scenarios running around in my head.

The first: I will commit suicide. No, not by running out in front of a car, but by walking back inside the house, face my dad, and give him two middle fingers all the while saying wash the damn car yourself.

The second: Be a wimp by enduring the hot sun while I wash two cars. It's the second one that actually happened. Earlier, I helped dad trim the edges of our lawn, and washed the dirty dishes in our kitchen sink.

My dad forgets I have to be at my new job in a few hours. I'm exhausted from all his demands. I take a long shower and jerk off while washing myself. Both the shower and the masturbating helped me get replenished. My dad needs to get out of the house more often with Trent. Hell, meet some women. A woman who can put up with his erratic behavior. A woman who will fire all of weapons back at him.

My prayers were answered. My dad begins to date various women. He's going through a newspaper's dating service section. He wrote a short paragraph pointing out what he is looking for in a woman, his likes and dislikes, and a brief description of himself:

Single white male early 40s about six feet tall and weighing in close to one hundred and eighty pounds looking for attractive single white female. I enjoy getting cozy on the couch, backyard barbeques, and TLC. Wants to travel and explore the world. Must have a sense of humor and enjoy the same activities. Let's have some fun and let the good times roll! Rich

His ad is sweet and honest. But he left out all kinds of prevalent shit. If I was writing the ad for him, the ad would read something like this:

Single white male looking for white women only. I enjoy slouching on the couch after you cook the meal. I want to travel all over the United States in my 1979 Pontiac. I drive! It's my car! You just sit next to me. And don't fiddle with my car radio! The stations are pre-set. Must have a sense of humor and not get all bent out shape when I cuss and use racial slurs. No kids at all! I'm not a babysitter. Let's set this dump of a town on its ear and show everyone why WE are the main attraction! Yours forever, Rich

Tonight, dad is all dressed up. He's looking dapper in his pressed tan slacks and light blue long sleeved collared shirt. His mom ironed the shirt for him yesterday. His shoes are a darker brown with a soft sole. Personally, I think he sprayed on WAY too much cologne. Damn, I was in the living room while he's in his bedroom and a whiff of his man perfume burned my nosehairs. Dad and his date are going to the same steakhouse place, the sizzler, where he and my mom went to.

I'm meeting one of the ladies who responded to his ad.

"So how many replies did you get from your ad?"

"Fourteen".

"Wow, do you like any of them?"

"I've talked most of them already. A few of them seem real nice. I would rather see someone who doesn't have any kids. I'm meeting one lucky lady tonight."

The lucky lady is Peggy. After the doorbell rings, I jump up from the couch to let her in.

"Hi. I'm Peggy."

"Hi. I'm Randy. Come on in."

She's cute. Probably five seven at best, one hundred fifty, top heavy with elbow length, semi curly brown hair.

"My dad's in the bedroom getting ready. Can I offer you a drink?"

"Oh no thank you. We are going out to eat."

"Cool. Anyway, I hear him coming. I have to study for exams. So I'll leave the two of you alone."

About twenty minutes later, I can hear my dad and Peggy move towards the back door.

"You hittin' on my woman!"

"No just being friendly."

"I know, I'm just teasing you. Okay we're leaving now. Make sure you keep the doors locked but not the screen doors."

"I will. Have a good time. Nice to meet you Peggy!"

Dad has a gift for shutting off his rage when he's with a female. He morphs into this goofy, joke telling, charming phony. Dad will put me on the highest pedestal. He brags to the ladies how smart I am in school or how successful I am at the hotel. He makes the Clarion sound like it's the Sistine Chapel. You can tell your dates that my job consists of washing crap off dishes and put tags on tenderloins. It's kind of him to show that he is aware of, and even care about my grades and work.

I should pretend that I ruined one of my records. I'll starting using a barrage of foul language. Maybe fling the record across the living room. I'll go in the kitchen and throw a dinner plate out of spite. I want dad and whoever he brings over to see and hear how ridiculous he can act. Dad and Peggy leave for the evening. Time for me to embrace the peace and quiet.

High school has flown by. My overall grades were no lower than a C. And once again that was in freshman and sophomore gym class. I studied my butt off, especially in the Chef Cookery class. I did have a slight advantage over the other students as I was already doing some prep work at the Clarion. Ms. Telu, my home ec teacher, offered me a teacher's aide class in my senior year. Hell yes I said yes! Not only would I be in a class in several hot girls but I could substitute the aide class for a less interesting elective, like shop.

I ended up working at the hotel on senior prom night. I didn't care. I struck out with the two girls I finally did ask out. Sherry and Sharon. The two of them shot me down faster than a high powered machine gun. It was the Americans versus the Russians in heavy combat times ten. Hell, the pain was comparable to having some fat guy jam his finger up your ass and leave it in there for five minutes. Who gives a fuck anyway?

There are plenty of women working at the Clarion. These women are taking over the hotel. The front desk, housekeeping, transportation, and even security departments are all managed by women. The entire banquet set up and marketing departments are all women and gay men, so all women. I would rather date these ladies over any phony high school girl. The Clarion ladies are sexier, naughtier, and made enough money to afford high dollar tans that only intensified the pure sex oozing off their sun kissed bodies.

The Clarion is a busy place. Profits have to pouring in. During orientation, I took a tour throughout the place. You could walk barefoot on the plush velvet carpet spread out in the front lobby all the way to the back door leading to the parking lot. The large glass chandeliers hanging above must cost a fortune. Their restaurant has a coat and tie policy for dinner. Our transportation department provides a shuttle and limo service. There are two large rooms to host banquet events. I grabbed a menu to peek at. You can whet your appetite on various chicken, steak, and seafood dishes. A weekly Sunday brunch is served. Prices range anywhere from ten up to twenty five dollars a person. All of the dinner items have the name of a wine listed underneath.

I meet my new boss in his office right after the hotel tour.

"I'm Chef John, welcome aboard."

"Thank you. Glad to be here. This is one busy place."

"We are always moving. You got to hustle around here. We have food orders going out and dirty dishes coming in. Constantly. You'll be working with different people depending on what you'll be doing. I'm a little short in the utility area so that's where I'll have you start. Hopefully, I can get you in the kitchen soon."

"That's great."

"For now I'll have you work Friday and Saturday nights. On Friday start at six and Saturday come in at four. Those of course are our busiest nights. What about during the week?"

"I can come in after five. Takes me about twenty minutes to get here."

"Okay, let's do Tuesday and Wednesdays from six to close. You should be done by eleven. We can play Thursdays by ear. This way you'll have Sunday and Monday off. Sometimes on a holiday like Easter, you'll need to be here. We host all day banquets on Easter and Thanksgiving. I try to work the schedules out so that you have time to be at home."

"All of this sounds great to me Chef. I'll be here."

"See you Friday at six."

My poor hands are wrinkled and sore from the many hours washing dishes. I've never seen so many dirty plates, silverware and glasses at one time. The hotel usually hosts large banquets Fridays or Saturdays. In the dish area, I work with three other guys. One of the guys, a black guy named Albert, becomes my sort of supervisor and fast friend. Albert is the lead night time dishwasher. I had helped Fred prep some fruit salad earlier, now I'm needed in the fast paced world called utiltyland. When I first met Albert, his greeting set the tone for the evening:

"Greetings my main man." Albert then forms two imaginary guns with both of his hands then pretends to shoot me. "These cats are crazy for throwing you in the fire on your first night."

Albert is the hippiest, loosiest, jive talker I ever met. Okay, the only one. But he moves like a panther. About every twenty to thirty minutes or so, he or someone else will bring over a full queen. A queen is a giant cart filled with trays of the dirty dishes, silverware, and glasses. I spend most of the time helping him stack up the dishes so they can be run through the dish machine. I also help Marty out by putting away the pots and pans.

Five hours in and Albert stops me from working.

"Say man let's go outside and take a short break."

My first impression of Albert is that he partakes in getting high. A man who smokes weed whenever he feels the need to. A man who sells on the side along with some watches and rings. Here at the hotel, he had to be contempt with smoking a cigarette. My intuition about him toking reefer was proven right when I saw his T-shirt through his thin baby blue smoke. A picture of a young black guitarist showed through.

"Sometimes it gets crazy in the kitchen holmes when we get superbusy. Think you can keep up my man?"

"At my last job I had to work fast and bust my ass off each night I worked. I'll be ready."

"What kind of work did you do?"

"I was a pinboy at a local bowling alley. You learned there how to move fast or you ended up getting fired."

"That's what I want to hear my man. You and me will be working together as brothers."

Right before Albert and I went back inside, he gave me another handshake that involved six different hand movements before completed.

Working slow in the dishroom is not an option either. And you have to be careful not to break anything either. This is not easy when you're working at rocket speed. In my first week alone, I busted three plates and one wine glass. Fred warned me to be careful dozens of times. Fred is the head banquet chef. Another laid back black guy who stresses the importance of getting the work done. I can hear him bellowing out commands at the other chefs.

"Hurry up with that tray of chicken breasts. Dave! Get ready to start busting open the tubs of ice cream! Shit! Where's my big knife! Hey Stevens! Take this requisition with you and go down to the purchasing department to fill it. Thanks man!"

Once we get a break in the dish action, I walk to the purchasing department. I had to have one of the security guys open the cages. In the day time, Mike works inside the cage. He's the head purchasing clerk. He and my official boss John, the executive chef, orders the food items. Mike showed me how to properly fill an order and stock deliveries.

"Okay Steven. A few but very fucking important things to know. You need to remember to make sure you give them the correct tagged meat. Put the older meat out front and the older date supplies out front. And man most important never, unless it's the lobby happy hour, never give the kitchen an opened bottle of liquor."

Mike and Fred are in their mid to late thirties. I know nothing about Fred other than he can cook excellent meat and chicken dishes blindfolded. Mike loves listening to hard rock music. He's dating Joann, one of the banquet servers. They have yet to be caught screwing around in one of the refrigerators. Fred and Mike have become my mentors. John is too busy working in his office or the kitchen. Fred and Mike have a lot in common-young, aggressive, cuss, call me by my last name, and are money hungry pirates. Their work ethic motivates me to kick ass in everything I set out to do.

I love all the work I'm doing. The food prepping, stocking and delivering, serving food, even washing pots and pans. I have to smile at the pretty female banquet servers when they approach me. I feel beneath them because the servers wear pressed black pants or skirts with pressed white buttoned down shirts. They talk among themselves about the latest lipstick color or a fancy necklace one of them received from a boyfriend.

My high school graduation was blur. The stupid math teacher preceding over the ceremonies mispronounced my name as Randy Stephans. The entire gymnasium filled with students, teachers, and parents heard the wrong last name.

When I came home, there were gifts and cards on the kitchen table. My dad gave me a new CD player, the CD Born in the USA by Bruce Springsteen, and money. My grandma and grandpa also gave me cash. Grandpa's check was for one hundred dollars. He wrote *and go get 'em* in the memo part. Before college starts up, I work as many hours as I can. I want to pay off my car debt. Plus, I can get more prep and stock work in the daytime.

A fancy culinary school was too expensive. I was disappointed that no university said hello to me. Then again, I never applied to one. I wind up going to Forest Hills Community College. I use a chunk of the money I received from my relatives to purchase a new set of kitchen knives. Unbeknownst to me, my dad swiped the knives and had my full name engraved on each knife. So unless I plan on selling my knives to another Randy Stevens, the knives are mine forever.

The chef program at Forest Hills lasts only eighteen months. In addition to the core kitchen related courses like purchasing, intro to kitchen equipment, and food prep I, II, and III, I'm also required to take three electives. I chose introduction to broadcasting, English literature, and beginner computer use. I can't wait to use a chainsaw in the ice carving class! The menu planning course is cool, I can show off my creative side. Ironic, the difficult class is purchasing. I learn quickly that purchasing is more than tagging loins, storing booze, and delivering cases of breasts. John has a copy of my school schedule. I do what I'm told and where to go. John is flexible working with my crazy school schedule. I even find time to help dad with laundry and keeping the inside and outside of our home looking presentable.

My long hair is becoming a hassle to take care of. Most of the time, I wear a hat or pull the back of my hair in a ponytail. But long hair is going out of style. The classy ladies, those at the Clarion, prefer short hair. I call mom and ask if I can make an appointment with her.

"Raanndy, it's so good to hear your voice. I'm sorry I missed your high school graduation."

I hate when mom gets choked up. Then I feel responsible in some way.

"Don't worry. You didn't miss anything. Anyway, I need a haircut. Can I make an appointment with you for this Thursday?"

"Sure. Now I may not the one who cuts your hair. Is that okay? I'll have to check my book to see if I have anyone else. If you want you can wait."

"Doesn't matter. I can only go Thursday. I'll see you either way."

"Okay by me. I'll see you Thursday. I love you."

"Love you too. Bye."

Mom's work is close to her home. I'm not crazy driving north again. The cost at her school come salon is a lot cheaper than any other place. I walk in an immediately get a nostril burn from all the chemicals. Old ladies are everywhere getting their hair washed, dried, and cut. I spot and make eye contact with mom.

"Hi Raannnndy!" Mom squeals my name so loud that everyone inside the shop looks up to see who she's yelling at.

My mom is taking curlers out of an old lady's head. She stops to tell me what is going to happen.

"Listen Randy, Mary is going to cut your hair okay!" Mom shouts out to me.

Mary appears to be a few years older than me. I'm guessing she is in her late twenties. She's a plump blonde with long razor thin blonde hair. A part of the package for me is to have my hair washed first, then cut. Mary is standing over me while my head is under the faucets. Every time Mary bends down I get a fantastic view of her big, round, breasts. I wonder if Mary is single. Shit. I see a fancy looking ring on her finger. My hopes are further dashed away when Mary starts talking to her co-workers about an upcoming camping trip with her husband and kids.

Mom has been working all the time I'm there. She is more happy and alive than she has been in a long time. She is no longer tired or exhausted. She's excited having new clients ask for her to cut their hair. Maybe she will start dating again. My mind keeps wandering as I sit in the chair now waiting for mom to finish her shift. I told her I would give her a ride home.

I look over to see a young lady sitting in the chair next to mine.

"Hi, how are you?" I quietly say to her.

"Hello."

"I'm Randy. My mom works here." My damn hands are shaking from having a conversation with her.

"My mom, aunt, and I come here to get our hair done."

I'm already attracted to her. Her skin color is darker than mine. I'm guessing she's Hispanic.

"Couldn't help but notice the textbook. Are you studying to be an animal doctor?"

"Yes, I go to Brookdale House."

No shit. Brookdale House is an invite only, expensive ass private college located way out of the country. The school is known for teaching people how to become vets.

"That's awesome, I'm in a culinary program myself."

"What's your specialty?"

"Hmmm. I like desserts and pastries."

"My mom and I make cookies together all the time."

"That's cool. So do you have any pets at home?"

"No. I want to take care of farm animals. What about you?"

"Pets? Oh no, my dad couldn't handle a dog or a cat. He would get mad if the dog or cat pooped in the house and if the dog keeps barking, that would drive him up the wall. I should ask him if I can get a big puppy just to see what kind of reaction he has."

"That's funny. My dad knows people who have horses. We go there in the summer to see them. One day I hope to own one."

"Can you ride a horse?"

"Sure, it's easy to learn."

It's great we share each other's interests. I mean I like animals too. I need to make a move fast or I may never see her again.

"So…maybe we can get together sometime and help each other study. Then go for some food afterwords. You're an interesting and attractive woman."

She laughs at me but doesn't say no. She pulls a paper and pen out from her purse.

"Here, put this in your pocket but don't open it here."

Soon, two ladies approach us. Once of them, a short and not as full figured as Mary woman motions for the lady to come here. Must be her mom. The other woman is a Playpen centerfold. If not, she needs to send tasteful nude pictures to Frank pronto. Her built body has sleek curves all over. Her long, light brown hair shines in the light. Her smooth skin is a golden tan. The hot body centerfold smiles at me then turns around. A cool breeze suddenly give me goosebumps. I have met my new future wife. All three ladies are whispering to one another. Sometimes one, two, or all three of them will look at me, then giggle. I have no idea if they are making fun of me or thinking *hey he's a cute guy, ask him out.*

I drop my mom off and wait until she goes inside her house before I drive off. I unwrinkled the piece of paper that was stuffed in my pants pocket. A long smile forms on my face as I'm driving home. Well I'll be damn, written in blue or black pen on the piece of paper are the letters and numbers *Rosa 546-5511.*

4
ROLE MODELS

Christmas time around my household was not a festive event. Dad was always harping about driving to work in the bad weather or having to spend money buying new holiday lights because the old ones never work. When I was little, I usually got two presents total from my mom and dad. Both gifts would be a generic toy such as a remote controlled racecar or a plastic snowman that had a small slit on top of its head. The purpose of the hole was for me to put coins inside. I never received an allowance from my dad nor was I working. Therefore, the few coins I had in the snowman came from me picking up loose change I found on the sidewalk.

I never got from my mom or dad any of the items I asked for. My mom would ask me to write out a list. Some of the items I can remember writing down were the new Tyler Brothers album Spirits All Around, a new pair of tennis shoes, and a subscription to The Justice League comic books. Instead of getting any of those, I get plastic cars that have a faulty remote. I have doubts neither mom or dad even read my list. I tossed the car in my closet. I may have broken the remote before even trying the car out. The snowman stayed on top my dresser for several years. By the time I went to the bank the following year to exchange the coins for cash, I had collected twenty nine dollars and fourteen cents.

My grandma never asked me what I wanted for Christmas. Or my birthday. Her gifts to me were always clothes. I was fine with receiving new clothes. Having a variety of shirts and pants to choose from made me feel like a wealthy, stylish man about town. I wasn't crazy about the short sleeve pull overs though. I prefer shirts that you button. At least she my blue jeans size right. I hate wearing pants that are too short in the leg. If bell bottoms were still in style, I would wear those.

I had to be creative when coming up with a gift for my dad, mom, and grandma. My dad was easy to shop for. For him, I would pick up the most recent issue of any car magazine. My mom liked to wear jewelry. The diamond studs I saw in the case ranged from one hundred dollars on the low end all the way up to three thousand for the most expensive. I had around forty dollars to spend. The earrings I did buy for my mom were made of cheap metal. The same company who designed my piece of shit remote control car was probably the same company who designed mom's nine dollar piece of shit earrings.

My grandma would remind me not to buy her any clothes, jewelry, of any item that would need to be dusted. She forced me to be more creative. Come up with a gift that comes from my heart. So for her, I froze my balls off washing her car in the blistering cold weather and then I paid for her meatball sandwich with fries order from Luigi's.

Every year, maybe up to high school, my presents to mom, dad, and grandma were the same. A car themed magazine, plastic jewelry, and free labor. Give or take a food order and how cold it was outside. The element of surprise vanished.

As I got older, the gifts my parents gave me got worse. One year I asked my dad for the new Night Thrillers greatest hits CD. The Night Thrillers are a trio of ladies who are not afraid to rock with the boys. I even wrote down in big, legible letters OWN THE NIGHT- THE VERY BEST OF THE NIGHT THRILLERS. On Christmas day when I unwrap the gift I get THE NIGHTLIFE'S GREATEST HITS. The Nightlife are a mellow country-rock band. Well Fuck! I put on my bravest happy face for my dad when I opened the gift. My mom give me a Christmas card with five dollars inside. She's struggling with her own cash flow so I tell her not to give me anything. We'll have dinner together I say.

I had to improvise with all of them later on. One year I gave my dad a car cleaning set. I thought he would have used the set once spring arrived. He didn't open the package I gave him until two years later. My mom received jewelry that cost more than forty dollars. At least my grandma told me what she wanted, then would buy the box of assorted candies and hand the box to me. She kills the whole concept of being surprised.

My grandma thinks that my pants and shirt size are the same as it was three years ago. I could barely put my new short sleeve pull over without choking myself to death. My new, stiff pair of jeans were certified floodwear. Not to mention that when I tried to button the pants, my waist cried out in excruciating pain caused by the tightness of the pants.

From that point on, I never asked for any specific gift from anyone except to say all I want is cash. I'll buy my own gifts.

With my dad's child support nearing the end, I'll be twenty one next month, my dad has been desperate to keep the monies coming. I threw my dad a bone by mentioning to him that since I was in college, he could argue that money was needed to complete my education. The truth was though, my mom had no extra money to give to him. A set dollar amount for a set period of time was agreed upon both of them. Mom still has the legal paperwork. Didn't matter if I was in school or not. Besides, my dad wouldn't use the money to help me out. He would buy a brand new carpet for his living room.

One night I turn in early. My dad thinks I'm fast asleep. I was resting but had to get up and go to the bathroom. As I walk to the bathroom, I could hear my dad talking to someone on the phone. I tiptoe to the bottom of the steps so I can hear better what he's saying.

"Good evening. I'm from the child support division."

"Regina Stevens."

"Not paying her support in full."

"I haven't received anything since last April."

Then I hear my dad hang the phone up. Is he done? No.

"Hello, I'm calling about Regina Stevens."

"Regina Stevens. What word do you not understand? Do you speak English? English."

"Okay goodbye."

A few minutes later, my dad dials yet another number.

"Yes ma'am I would like to place an order."

"Okay. I need one leather PTS jacket. Large. Yes, insulated. Does that cost more? That's not bad. Okay. The name is Richard Stevens. S-t-e-v-e-n-s. Yes. Can I pay over the phone? Okay. Wait though I want to order more stuff. I also want the six piece screwdriver set. Silver. Can those be engraved? Oh, no that's okay. No. My name is Ken Archer. The mailing address is 3150 Watson Road. Yes ma'am. But I have a different billing address. That is, wait a minute."

I knew what my dad was doing. He was going to give whoever he was talking to over the phone my mom's home address. If not hers, then he's probably picking one out of the white pages. I stomp up the stairs on purpose so he knows I'm coming up. I can faintly hear a click.

"Who were you talking to this late?

"Oh that was Trent."

I stay in our living room pretending to be interested in whatever program was on television. My dad stopped calling people. After a while, my dad left the kitchen and went into his bedroom. He knows I'm on to his underhanded tactics.

The next day I went into my dad's bedroom while he was still at work. I rummage through his top drawer searching for any piece of paper with my mom's address. I was unsuccessful, dammit. Why did he say a different billing address? I made a mental note to remind myself that if any items were delivered to find out where from and then call them to give them the proper billing address. I also give my mom a warning.

"Hi mom, it's Randy."

"Hi, is something wrong?"

"I'm not sure yet. My dad's been calling people late at night. He's ordering stuff but telling these people a different billing address. He doesn't want to pay for the items. He was also talking to someone about child support. The conversation wasn't making any sense though. He's trying to act like you aren't paying."

"That's dumb. But that's your father."

"Yeah, you need to watch your mail. If you receive ANY mail from child services, let me know. I'll call them myself and make sure they know you are doing your part. And if you get any bills from a place you don't recognize, call me. I'll know if it's a company my dad called. Also, the name on the invoice may be Ken Archer."

"Who's that?"

"Either some name my dad got out of the white pages or a name he made up."

"Why is he doing this?"

"Who knows? Maybe he's bored at night or in the daytime when he's not sleeping. Or he's still got a hair up his butt from not getting more money. He sees all this stuff on television and in magazines that he can't afford so he buys the stuff but then refuses to pay for any of it."

"I think he needs help."

"If I could provide ample proof, I would have him committed."

"Haaa!"

"Anyway, keep your guard up. By the way, you never told him your new address? It's not in the phone book either right?"

"I haven't told him anything. My number's unlisted. Does he know where I work?"

"Probably not. Even he wouldn't be stupid enough to go to your work for anything but a haircut. If he did, you could get him for harassment."

"Let's hope that doesn't happen. I'll watch my P's and Q's."

"Good. Keep it that way. I'll call you soon and talk more."

"Okay, you be careful too."

"Trust me. He don't know shit about my job or my finances."

If my dad made any more secret calls, they would have been while I was not in the house. Mom hasn't called me since the last time I spoke to her. However, packages have been delivered to our front door. I didn't want any item from him if the item was never paid for. I only saw one of the items. It was a plaque made from either copper or fake gold. The inscription read *HAMMOND MOTORSPORTS CUSTOM OF THE YEAR*

"Hey Randy, I'd like to get you a new chef's coat. What size is the one you wear?"

"Oh thanks but not necessary. The college actually supplies us with the coats. I have another one in my locker, I really don't need another one."

My dad must have changed his mind about the PTS jacket and screwdriver set. I never saw him wear that jacket or mention to me that he got a new screwdriver set.

One of the Clarion's annual holiday fundraisers was the holiday can food drive. The hotel management team makes the announcement about three weeks before Christmas. To motivate us, hotel management treats the event as a contest. The department that brings in the most supplies wins a prize. This year's prize is two hundred dollars for the entire winning department to share. Last year, when the front desk crew won, they gave their one hundred dollar prize to the food bank.

Last year, I only contributed five cans of vegetables. This year I want to bring in more. I went to Savmore Foods. The store is located near my mom's place. I didn't mind going only because Savmore is right off the highway. There's no need to drive through any of the neighborhoods. Buying cans if vegetables is cheap. One small can of corn is fifty cents.

For a low grade grocery store, Savmore keeps their shelves stocked. I begin putting several cans of fruits and vegetables in my cart. When I add all the items together, the cost only comes to twenty dollars. I still have enough money to buy more. I go back to the aisle and put more cans in my cart. The stocker gave me an odd look.

"I have an addiction to peas and corn that come from a can." I say with authority.

Well that was better than saying I have an addiction to pussies, tits, cocaine, and whiskey. The checker paid no attention to my snide remark. Her facial expression and lack of excitement told me that she was working there because her skills were no better than a checker.

The next day, I carry in two large paper bags filled with items I purchased. Our restaurant cashier, Christine, was in charge of keeping track of the items collected. The items were being stored in a small break room next to the cashier's kiosk.

"I'm going to set these down in there, okay?"

"Wow thank you!"

"It's nothing. I'm glad to help out."

"You're very generous."

"I know what it's like not to have and then to have luxury items. Everyone deserves to have something, even if it's a nice dinner around the holidays."

"The food bank will be very grateful. Oh by the way. I was talking to John earlier. We have an employee who wasn't working out too well in the restaurant. I asked John if he had any open spots in the kitchen. He's supposed to get with you about training him."

"As a chef?"

"No, I would assume that he will be working in the utility department."

"Well that's Albert's area, not mine."

"John says you're the best person to train him."

Of course, John was on vacation and none of the other chef's knew anything about a new utility worker. Well except Fred who enlightened me on my new job duties.

"Hey man, the boss wants you to train our newest worker. You're still working in the kitchen for a few hours but once the new hire gets here then you're out of here."

I've only been at the Clarion for a couple of years. My name is still on one of the lower tiers of our seniority privilege pole. Hearing that John wants me to do any training does make me feel confident in my abilities. Yet, I wasn't excited having to train a new hire. The action was in the banquet kitchen, not in the utility area.

"Aw man, why can't Albert do this?"

"Don't know, ask him."

When Albert arrived, I did.

"Hey Albert, Got a minute?"

"How's my brother tonight?"

"Thrilled to be here. Did John ask you to train a new guy who's supposed to be working in the utility area."

"Ohhh, sweet Lord." Albert sings back to me, off-key that is.

"Shit. What's wrong?"

"Man, when I showed you how we do things, you learned fast. I need to keep an eye out on Marty and Marco. Those two without proper supervision? Shit, I'll have dishes piled to the ceiling. Man, I can't be keeping a pair of eyes on them and having to watch over a new boy. I need help my brother, John also has me helping out on the line. Man, I can't be over there and over he-ya at the same time! My man, my brother, you got to help me please."

"So you asked John if someone else would train him."

"He and I know you are the right person for the job."

"I touched. I'm not confident having him pull off the dishes, much less pull a queen. God knows how many broken plates we would have. Does he at least know how to fill the sinks properly?"

"That's what I was showing him. I also thought he could put the clean dishes away."

"Fine. Fred already has me off for the time spent in here. No reason why you need to be ball slapped."

"Oh Lord thank you. You are the man around here."

"I have a feeling you and I will be smoking plenty of weed after this."

About an hour later, I meet the new worker. A scruffy man probably in his early thirties. He walks with a limp but moves along at a brisk pace. Derrick introduces me to our new co-worker.

"Randy, this is Jerry."

"Hi Jerry, Good to meet you."

I extend my hand out but Jerry only smiles back. He doesn't take my hand.

"Are you clocked in yet?"

"Yes."

"All right then, come with me. I'm going to show you the ropes. I'll work with you for the rest of the night you're here. I'll work with you for a few days as well and then I'll turn you loose. But don't worry, I'll be in the kitchen and Albert, he's the head utility guy, will help you out too. Sound good?"

Jerry responds by nodding his head.

"We like to train the new guys on pots and pans first. Get a feel of putting your hands in hot and cold water."

I fill the first sink with hot water, the second with cold water, and the third with warm water.

"The third sink is used for sanitizing. As the water runs, take some of this liquid and pour a little in the water, like this."

"Sometimes, the chefs will bring over the dirty pots and pans. Most of the time, we go in either that kitchen to grab any or.... Follow me, we grab the big pan underneath the chef's main station. If you ever hear one of these chef's yell PAN RUN that means the tub is overflowing. Just make sure you say excuse me and grab the tub quickly. And, try not to get in their way, get in and get out."

"We'll rotate. I'll wash a few first, while you dry and sanitize. Once we get a lot stacked, then I'll show you where the pots and pans go to."

About two hours into the job, Jerry is learning fast. I mean how difficult is it to scrape shit off a pot and scrub it down. Marty and Marco aren't the speediest workers. A much needed kick in their backside might motivate them. I can see Albert sweating his ass off hustling to get the piles of plates off the queens and into the dish machine. Sometimes while Jerry is washing, I rush over to help Albert clear off his queen.

"Wandy! Hey Wandy!"

"What's up?"

"Are de pans queen?"

"Say what?"

"Are.. de. Pans and pots queen?"

"Oh yeah. You're doing a great job. Here's some lotion to put on your hands. You may not like the smell of this goopy shit but your hands will be glad you used it."

Jerry worked hard for his first night. His physical impairments didn't affect his job performance.

"Say Jerry, you get a fifteen minute break. If you're hungry there's some extra plates of chicken and green beans in those containers. Help yourself."

"Twanks."

Jerry had no problem going into the kitchen to grab a plate of food. Marty and Marco left to go to the hotel break room. This was a good time to let Albert know how great Jerry was doing.

"Say man, Jerry's going to work out fine. He knows what to do, then does it. I don't think he can pull a full queen due to his limping but let's see how fast he can unload. Shit. Have him help you instead."

"I need someone as fast as you."

"I'll bet Jerry works faster than the other two guys."

After Jerry's break was over, I motion for him to come over by the dishwasher.

"I was talking to Albert. He's the guy I mentioned earlier to you. I'll have him work with you on the queen while I stack up. Whenever Marty and Marco come back, they can do the nasty stuff."

Jerry's transition from potscrubber to dishloader was seamless. Albert and I looked at each other. We weren't gazing in each other's eyes. But we both were thinking the same. Jerry can kick some dishwasher ass.

"Here you go. Dere do these go?" Jerry asks holding a large tray."

"Right over there holmes." Albert chimes in.

"Damn, he moves faster than you."

I give Albert the middle finger but then switch gestures to give him a thumbs up.

After the shift is over, I let Jerry know how the training went.

"Hey, listen. For your first night, you did really well. I mean you hustled. Albert and I will make sure John knows how well you did. Most of the time, you'll be in the pots and pans area, but man, make it your own. Not one time did one of the chefs have to bring back a pot or a pan. I'll let you on a secret. When Marty and Marco are doing that, shit comes back. On out slow days, I'll get Albert to have you do work of the dish work. You keep this up and hell, I'll even talk to Fred or John about having you help out in kitchen."

"Tanks for training me."

"You're a part of OUR team now."

I extend my hand out once again. This time, albeit a limp one, Jerry shakes my hand.

I wave goodbye to Jerry as he gets into a car. The driver may have been his mom. I had to wave my hand back and forth to get rid of the black smoke spitting from the muffler.

On Wednesday, I show up to work a half hour earlier. I want Jane to be aware of Jeff's first night. I'm also hoping to obtain more information about his family.

"Hi Jane, thanks for seeing me. The reason I'm here is to let you know how well Jeff did on his first day."

"I'm happy to hear it. I'll make sure John knows too."

"This isn't his first job, is it?"

"Hmmm, no, his resume had two other places listed."

"I'll bet he was let go from both places due to his walking and speech problems."

"I wouldn't know the reasons why."

"This guy moves faster than other guys who aren't physically challenged. He understands what he's told. He doesn't complain, or whine, and makes sure the work gets done right the first time. What happened in the dining room?"

"What do you mean?"

"I was told he didn't work out. It wouldn't be for a lack of effort and hard work. I think some of the servers or guests didn't want him around."

"Now now. Let's not make any accusations. Sharon worked with Jerry the entire time Jerry was in the dining room. I don't know all the specifics. Let's focus on Jerry being a valuable kitchen employee."

"He'll have no problem fitting in with me, Albert, or any of the kitchen crew. He shows up, works hard, and listens."

"That's the type of employee we want. Did you mention any of this to John?"

"Hasn't been around. He and Albert joined forces to put me in charge of showing Jeff the biz."

"I'll make sure your comments are noted in Jerry's file."

"Great. I have idea about the prize money relating to the food drive."

"By the way, your department is way ahead of the others."

"No sh.. I mean no kidding? That's great. Must be Paul. He knows someone who actually works for one of our suppliers."

"I hear you've contributed plenty as well."

"Some. About the money, I have a feeling that Jerry's family is struggling financially. The car his mom drives is on life support. Is there a way we can provide Jerry with the money?"

"Wow. That's generous of you. Unfortunately we have an agreement with the food shelter."

"I understand."

"Besides, we can't single out one hotel employee."

"I shouldn't have brought it up."

"You're fine. It's wonderful you're being thoughtful and selfless. Maybe you should talk to your co-workers. Some departments are having their own gift exchanges."

"Yeah good idea. Thanks again for meeting with me."

"See you around."

Derrick was getting ready to leave for the day. He was not in a good mood. A three hundred banquet party was in full force during the hotel dinner hours. Marty showed up two and a half hours late for his shift. He says it's because of car trouble. Marco took his sweet ass time unloading a queen. The reason Albert wasn't in the dish area was that John had him help out in the restaurant. Only Jerry was working hard in the dish area. I had to know why Derrick was peeved.

"Rough night huh?"

"I'm fed up with those two jackoffs. I ended up finishing washing the dishes myself."

"I heard that you and Marty got into it. What for?"

It was nothing. I asked Jerry if he and Marty could pull a full queen. Jerry was some trouble with it. But he made the effort. Anyway, Marty got a hold of Marco and told Jerry to get lost."

"Get lost!?"

"That was the gist of it. Anyway, I made sure that little prick knew that you don't disrespect the people you work with. Not in this kitchen."

"We need to let John and Fred know that these two aren't pulling their weight."

"All John's going to do is slap them on the wrist. And Fred doesn't want to get involved. That's okay though, I have some ideas."

"Yeah, me too. I'm going to talk to Albert. The three of us need to be on this together."

I caught up with Albert the next day.

"Hey Albert, gotta sec?"

"Always for you my man."

"Listen, Derrick had it out with Marty last night. He and Marco aren't doing their jobs. They also treat Jerry like shit. You know and I know that those two are bringing the utility department down. It's time for us to let them know that they need to start working or personnel can find out."

"Man, I know. What can we do?"

"Put them on pot and pan duty. Have them mop the kitchen floors. You, me, and Jeff take care of the queens. Come on man, this Saturday we have a four hundred party sit down. Not only are salads being served along with the main course and dessert, but Fred told me that appetizers are being served prior to the dinner. That's a ton of dishes. No one wants to be here all fucking night. The chefs are going to expect us to be on our toes all night."

"John put me in charge and I'm going to let him down."

That Saturday Albert ordered Marty and Marco to stay away from the dishes. When those two complained to John, all John said was Albert's running the area to do what he says. Marty and Marco whined all night. I loved it. I didn't give a shit how much Marty and Marco were complaining. Derrick didn't give a shit and Albert only gave a whiff after the shit. Our shift began at four pm and thanks to Albert's quarterbacking, our shift ended at twelve thirty.

Marty didn't show up to work on Monday. He didn't call John, Fred, or anyone else at the hotel so he was fired. Without his butt buddy, Marco floundered like a dying fish. He too would have quit however personnel fired him for getting caught with a bottle of booze in his gym bag.

I need to find out a way to help Jerry without raising suspicion. Over the next few days, I prodded Jerry for a little more information. I told him about my common last name. He told me his last name was Duncan. I asked him if he lived close to the hotel. He too lived in South St. Louis. But where I was closer to the downtown area, he was further south. I was able to get a handle on his location by asking him how he gets to work. He inadvertently told me his street name. Now I have Sedens Street.

Jeff has no clue as to why I'm asking him in a roundabout way for this information. I hope he doesn't think I'm going to give him a ride to and from work. I don't have the time to make extra time playing chauffeur. Maybe when the weather is sunnier and dryer, I might do that one time.

At home, I'm flipped through the white pages until I reach the Duncan listings. Damn, there's about sixty names. Slowly I finger down the names and address until I reach Duncan, T. 2110 Sedens St. 63119. I didn't see any other address with that street name. I already brought Christmas cards to send to my relatives. I pull a card out, then put in five twenty dollar bills.

My pay check was larger than I expected. Raked in a cool four hundred ten dollars! With my school hours slowing down, I was able to pick up some additional hours. I write the address from the pages on the envelope. I do not use any return address. I'm hoping the address is not for a relative of Jerry's. It's a risk I'll have to take.

The kitchen and banquet chefs won the prize for most can goods brought in. I was thrilled to see several boxes, I think there was nine, of canned and small box items. One of the boxes had a large package of toilet paper rolls and a three boxes of tissue.

I'm in a giving mood. On this Christmas day, I give my parents gifts they could use but not expect. First my dad-

"Oh wow! This is the good stuff. It's expensive as all hell but it's the best. I'll be going through this in no time when the new season starts."

"I know how much you like to use Maguire's. So I got a hold of their catalog through one of your magazines."

"You sneaky little shit."

"This is for you grandma."

"I didn't want anything"

"Are you really going to pass on the popcorn?"

"I'm not going to turn it away. There's so much here."

"Just hide the box from him."

"Fuck you!"

"Hey, hey, let's watch the language. No, I'll share with both of you. I know you like the butter and he like the caramel."

The snowy streets prevented me from seeing my mom on Christmas day. Instead, I waited until Saturday morning to drive over her place.

"Here, this is for you."

"Oh you didn't have to."

"Just open it."

"Oh Randy, I love it."

"There another one underneath. I had to sneak a peek in your drawers to make sure I got the right size."

"Oh great, you went through my drawers."

"Not all of them. I didn't thumb through your bra and underwear drawer.

"That wouldn't have helped you."

"The receipt is there in case you need to return or exchange."

"I hope you didn't spend a lot."

"Not at all. Got them when they were on sale. Now you have something brand new to wear when you go to work or go out."

"I don't go out that much, I'll wear them to work."

I'm too old to be writing a Christmas present list. I mentioned to my dad that I wouldn't mind receiving a new car stereo system. The one in the car now is a radio player only. I saw one at the store that had a built in cassette player. I didn't receive any new stereo, but I did receive a five dollar bill from my mom, a new long sleeve blue button down collared shirt from grandma, and a new pair of white chef pants from my dad.

Back at work after the holidays, I've returned to the kitchen prep area. I see Albert and Jeff working in the dish area.

"Hey Albert! How was your holidays?"

"Just fine brother."

"Did you get the girlfriend the ring she wanted?"

"Yeah, I gave her a ring. We're engaged to be engaged."

"Congratulations, my friend."

I then turn towards Jerry.

"How was your Christmas?"

"Fine."

Jerry never said anything to me about money. He may have too much pride to say something. If he or his family didn't get my money, then someone got one hundred dollars from me. A stranger will never know where the money came from. I enjoyed playing Santa, but I'm done buying expensive presents.

5
STICKY SITUATIONS

My dad has been going out on dates with several different women. There is one lady, I don't remember her name, who may have been with dad more than once. His playing the field doesn't bother me at all. Better to find the right woman by hunting for the right one rather than pick one out of desperation. His newfound dating life is making me happy. For one thing, he's not at home as much.

He's also backed off berating me when it comes to cleaning the house. I still do two loads of laundry, shop for groceries, sweep floors, and wipe down the toilets. When I was a little kid, my dad would scold me for pissing on the side of the commode. Now it's my dad who can't control where his stream goes.

I must be doing a satisfactory job scrubbing, trimming, and washing because he doesn't re-do my work. He's also in a pleasant mood more times than a shitty mood. At least when a woman is in our house. One moment he's cheerful and laughing at the program he's watching and in the next moment he's having a temper tantrum because the kitchen window will not open and close properly. I give dad and the woman he's with plenty of privacy. Even when dad asks me if I want to watch a movie with him and his date, I politely say no. Besides, I have too much homework or in some cases I have to work.

My dad is buying a new car. He wants to display his Pontiac in car shows and car cruises. Trent printed off some flyers of different car shows and cruises coming up. My dad went to a place called Steinman Unlimited to get information and samples relating to painting and putting custom designs on his car. I had some rare free time on my hands, so I tagged along with him. This was a horrible idea.

"Don't touch anything around here. All of this stuff is expensive. On second thought you just need to stay in the lobby. Hey Lou!"

"Hi Rich. I have some samples for you to look at for your car."

"Here's the one I like. It's a dark maroon. This will go well with the red pearl. Feel how soft that is."

"How much we talking?"

"I can have the entire upholstery installed for three hundred."

"Hmmm..."

"Trust me. You won't find a better price from anyone."

"Will I have the car back by the middle of April?"

"You should. I only have one other job. I know how eager you are to get the car out."

"Let's do it then."

After two hours of sitting in the lobby, bored out of my mind, my dad finally made up his mind what new color the car would be. He chose a ruby red pearl.

Because my dad hogs the one phone in our house, I have brief, and I mean ten minutes tops, conversations with Rosa.

"Hi Rosa, its Randy. I can't talk long. Just calling to say hi."

As I'm listening to Rosa tell me what her and her mom are cooking, I see some papers on the kitchen table. One is from Southtown Motors.

"I can't wait to meet everyone and have dinner with you. My dad's wanting me to get off the phone. I'll see you soon."

"Can you come over?" Rosa shyly asks me.

"Damn, I'd love to but I have to be at work at five am. One of the morning chefs is on vacation. John asked if I could fill in for the week."

"Oh, okay. I can wait until we have dinner."

"I'll be thinking of you all night. Sweet dreams."

After I hang up the phone, I ask my dad about the additional vehicle he now has.

"Awwww. Are you done playing kissy face?"

"For now. I see you purchased a pick- up truck. Is it new?"

"No, but I had the vehicle go through a diagnostic test. I only need another vehicle to get me from home to work."

"How's the Pontiac coming along?"

"Should be ready in a few weeks."

My dad now owns a dark blue Chevy pick- up. He will not admit it, but with his child support coming to an end, he doesn't have the cash flow to afford a brand new car. He's ticked because grandma couldn't help him out financially. She told me that she wasn't going to shell out money so he can make fancy, unnecessary changes to his car.

My dad is determined to succeed and have bigger rear tires, custom pin striping done, even a brand new engine. It's his car and money to burn, so I stay out of his car business. I have six hundred dollars left on my own car debt. Then I will be giving both dad and grandma one hundred dollars a month. I know my dad will use the money I give to him for useless car accessories like fuzzy dice to hang from the Pontiac's rearview mirror, and decals of Indian heads to put on the sides of the car.

Without much of an advanced warning, I have to ask my work for a Friday, Saturday, and Sunday off. I just got done letting John know that I'm now available full time and can work weekends. Now I'm going to come across like an unreliable liar. I was planning on calling and hopefully seeing Rosa after work on one of those days.

The reason dad wants me off is so we can go Bagnell Dam together. The trip is dad's college graduation gift for me. Rosa still has several months to go before she is finished with her school. My dad was unable to attend my college graduation because he was working extra shifts. I didn't care if he was there or not. No one in my family, not even one relative, showed up. Mom was not feeling well, grandma didn't want to go out at night, my aunts and uncles had other plans. One excuse right after the other.

Most of my classmates, and most of them black, went to celebrate finishing college at the Clarion's bar. Our graduating class voted on the Kool and the Gang song Celebration as our theme to be played during the graduation ceremony. After saying goodbye to my teachers and some parents I knew, I met up with my classmates. We all sit together at a table inside the bar.

"Does anyone already have a job lined up? Lloyd asks us.

"I'm still at the Red Barn." Quppied Anton.

"Not yet, got an interview next week." Said Aaron.

"You looking for work?" Lloyd wants to know.

"I'm working at the Clarion." I tell him.

"What you do there? Do they have any openings?"

"I help out in the kitchen. I do everything from stock cases of food to grill fish to wash dishes. I'm not sure about openings, might be for line cooks or banquet and restaurant servers. I've only been there a short time and have already seen different servers.

"You put in a good word for me."

"Yeah of course, we went through this together and still do. Come down to the hotel. I think applications are taken Monday through Fridays"

"Thanks man."

What my dad never gets is that I don't look at people on the outside. I could care less how much darker your skin is than mine. You could come from the island of Bora Bora or the planet Uranus. I look at people from the inside. How you act towards me and my friends. You can be the whitest person in the world but if you are disrespectful, I'm not going to like you.

I'm not much of a drinker. I had one vodka mixed with orange juice. The drink is called a screwdriver. A lot of my classmates drank several mixed drinks, beer, and downed shots of hard liquor. So I'm the class pussyweight. I order a plate of Crab Rangoon to dilute the alcohol. My grandma gave me fifty dollars. I probably spend thirty of that on the screw and crabs.

I mentioned to my grandma that I'm seeing a young lady.

"Her name is Rosa. I met at my mom's work. Here's a picture of her."

"She's an attractive young lady."

"Thanks. I'm hoping to get you and my mom together and be on my side in case dad throws a shitfit when I tell him."

Anyway, back to my escapade at Bagnell Dam. I had to kiss John's, Fred's, and Mike's ass to get the time off. I gave John a valid doctor's note regarding an appointment dad had. I'm also going to work a heavy, flexible schedule when I return. The note turned out to be a fake.

To whom it may concern:

Please excuse Randy Stevens from work for the dates of July 7th, 8th, and 9th. His father Richard Stevens will be recovering from foot surgery. Richard will be unable to stay on his feet and will require assistance.

Regards,

Peter A Feller DPM.

My dad is going to the foot doctor but he's having his toenails trimmed and dead foot skin shaved off. My dad did a good job of creating a horseshit note. I keep getting off the subject of our trip-

At Bagnall Dam you can rent and ride boats out on the river. Or bring your boat if you own one. The daredevils will rent waverunners. There's also a bunch of theatres hosting country or rock and roll music shows. The main boulevard, named the strip, has plenty of antique shops, an olde time photo shop, bumper car and boats, and a large arcade filled with pinball and skeetball machines. The entire area is Las Vegas only without the casinos, grand scale hotels, hookers, pimps, drugs, and seeing a couple fuck one another on the hood of their car.

"Rise and shine big boy! Up and atom!"

My dad wakes me up at five AM Friday morning. I pack some clothes and toiletries quickly so we can get a move on the road. No rest for the wicked. My dad puts in a cassette of Ricky Olson music. Ricky's breezy bluegrass songs cause me to doze off. Before arriving at Osage Beach, we stop at Hartman's Truck Stop to eat breakfast. The check came to fifteen dollars. Dad walks out without leaving a tip. He just gorged himself on plates of hash browns, ham steaks, sausage links, and biscuits. I reach in my front pocket to pull out two singles. I toss the dollar bills on the table as I walk out.

We stay at the Elk Motel. The motel is a few miles away from the Dam. This place only accepts cash for payment. Our room is dim, small, and has stained curtains. While at Osage Beach, my dad and I go on two boar rides. The smaller boat is a paddleboat named Tom Sawyer. I'm glad to have a magazine with to read. The ride was kind of boring. A slow, lazy ride along the river. Later in the evening, he and I see a show called Rock and Roll Legacy. The show was a flashy musical with the spotlight on 1950's rockers.

The second boat ride was on a larger boat named The Commander. The ride around the lake was at least two hours. The boat had no live music or a café to order a soda. I spent half the time sitting in the lower tier because being in the shade felt cool. When I went up to the top tier, my skin started to bake. I didn't want my dad to be by himself for the entire trip, so I became company. Dad made small talk bringing up college and the Clarion. When I start talking about Rosa, he becomes disinterested and his mind drifts off. At least he's not giving me any third degree. Not yet, but it came and came hard.

"So what's the name of the place Gina's working at? I want to call her work and get my haircut and get a shave. Do you know the name of her boss? Is she working part time or full time? I have some information for her boss to read. Have you seen what kind of car she has? Do she even have one or is relying on the bus? I'm sure her car is a lemon. Where's she even living? It's probably up north where all the blacks live. Give the name of her work and phone number."

Are you done yet with all the inane questioning? He seems to already have the answers to his questions. The only reason he wants any information is so he can pillage mom for more money. Dad received a letter stating his child support will be coming to an end. My dad makes phone calls to the DFS trying to extend the support for as long as he can. I believe he's losing his case. I give out enough information to pacify him.

"I don't have mom's number with me. I don't know her work number off the top of my head. The name of the company, and I believe it's a school also, is called St. Louis Beauty Salon. You've passed up the place before. It's the small building near the auto parts store on Mackland. I haven't met mom's boss. I met one co- worker who ended up being the one who cut my own hair. I doubt mom is working full time, she didn't say. I didn't talk to mom a lot, I do remember her saying something about the place relocating to a bigger building."

My dad is not the only one who can spin a white lie.

When dad's working, I can call Rosa. I'm not pushy at all. If she's not there or too busy to pick up, I leave a message for her to call at her convenience. I call today and her mom picks up.

"This is her mom Amelia."

"Hi Mrs. Carvella. I'm Randy."

"Yes, Rosa has told me a lot about you. She really likes you."

"She's great. And I'm guessing she's either studying or asleep."

"She went to bed about an hour ago."

"Did she mention me coming over for dinner?"

"Yes. Next Wednesday. My husband and I can't wait to meet you."

"I'm looking forward to meeting everyone. I have to get up early so I guess I'll be hanging up. It was great talking to you."

"You have a wonderful night."

"You too, Bye."

The sugar was making my teeth rot. I didn't want to have a long conversation with Rosa's mom as I knew her parents would drill me when I came over. Dad was going out on a date the same night I'm going out. God pointed his finger on my side for once.

Wow! Someone in Rosa's family is wealthy. She gives in West County, near Chesterfield, Missouri. Her neighborhood is a grated community where I had to get the secret code from her so I could even drive through. The large houses are spread apart with driveways on both sides. Everyone's front lawn is professionally taken care of. Rosa's place is a two story ranch home. The two huge windows in front have thick black curtains hanging inside. One of the cars parked in the driveway is a bright red Camaro. The second car in the driveway is a gray Honda Accord. I wonder what kind of sports car is in the garage.

I walk up to the front door and ring the bell. My hands feel sweaty as I tightly grip the flowers in my left hand.

"Hi! You must be Randy. Come on in."

A tall man with an overly pleasant voice says to me while extending his lanky hand. He's dressed all dapper like with pressed blue jeans and a golf course green colored short sleeved polo shirt.

"Do you go by Randall or Randy?"

"Doesn't matter, I'll answer to both."

"I'm Daniel Carvella. Nice to meet you."

"You too. I spoke to your wife earlier when I had called to talk to Rosa."

"Oh boy, I hope Amelia was gentle with you." Daniel chuckles as he walks away from me and heads into another room.

I sit down on their beige couch. Man, this feels likes a waterbed. The thing is deep and makes my rear sink down. There is a mid -size TV in their living room and a huge wooden bookcase next to the TV. I can't make out any of the books. They appear to be textbooks or self -help books. The coffee table already has flowers in a vase on top of it. A group of white and pink carnations that make my bouquet look like a piece of shit. A huge picture is hanging on the wall closest to the front door. Rosa, her mom and dad, and older guy who is probably Rosa's brother.

Rosa, her mom, and dad are all in the kitchen. Rosa pokes her head out from the kitchen to give me a big smile and wave.

"Hi! Dinner's almost ready. I hope you're hungry!"

"Starving."

The food smells great. Could be fish, chicken, or pasta. In addition to the flowers, I also bring a bag of rolls and a small white cake with white icing. I get up from their couch and have to walk through their dining room to get to the kitchen.

"Hi Mrs. Carvella. These are for you."

"Awww you're sweet. And call me Amelia."

"Okay, I'm Randy. We spoke on the phone."

"Hey Randy, I want to show you my arts and crafts before we eat."

Rosa has a talent for making homemade bracelets. She hands me a red and pink coral-like one to wear.

"Wow! This is really nice. Damn, I'm sorry. I didn't bring you anything. The rolls and cake are for everyone."

"That's okay. You've been the one treating me and paying for the food when we go out."

All of us eat baked enchiladas smothered in a spicy red sauce. Damn, these are too spicy for me. I had to drink three glasses of cold milk in order for my tongue to cool off. Amelia also made a tossed salad and yellow rice to accompany the enchiladas. Rosa and Daniel were in the kitchen a lot so I'm sure the two of them helped.

During the tabletalk, I find out a ton of information about Rosa and her family.

Daniel works as a computer repairman for the US government. It's no wonder the family rakes in the money. He didn't mention the name of the company. His work assignments are classified. Amelia works as a secretary at a dentist's office. She alone is pulling in some good money. And neither of them had to shell out tuition for Rosa's school. They didn't have to. Brookdale offered, well actually gave, Rosa a full college scholarship. The other guy in the family picture is Rosa's older brother Gino. He is serving in the US air force.

Every week, sometimes on Monday or Tuesday, a woman from a house cleaning company comes over to wash their floors, clothes, and appliances. I'm surprised our food wasn't served to us by a butler.

"Rosa enjoys listening to music too. I wish she would take dancing lessons."

"Oh mom!"

"Don't worry. I'm not the ballroom dancing type of guy. I do know how to disco dance though."

"Just like the guy in that disco movie huh?"

"Yes, and watching reruns of Dance Fever with Denny Terrio."

"There's plenty of food left over. Take some home with you." Amelia insists.

"Thanks. I'll take some with me for my lunch tomorrow."

I grab a spoon to scoop up an enchilada. I also scoop up a few spoons of the rice. My dad will have to settle for rolls and cake. Rosa's parents kiss each other before they walk into the living room together. I overhear Daniel say thank you, dinner was wonderful and I love you several times. The two lovers don't stay in the living room for long. Daniel whispers in Rosa's ear then kisses her on the forehead before heading upstairs with Amelia.

"Thanks for the wonderful meal. The food was delicious." I say as Rosa's parents go up the steps. Daniel stops and turns his head around towards me.

"Thank you. I think we'll being seeing more of you. Good night Randy."

"I can only stay up for another hour." Rosa informs me.

I look at my watch. It's ten at night. My time with Rosa went by too fast.

"I need to make a quick call to my dad. Let him know I'm still here."

I had to leave a message. As long as my dad knows where I'm at and I'm not in any trouble, he doesn't care how long I stay out.

"Want to look at some photo albums?"

"Sure."

I have to use a lot of willpower here. Don't be aggressive. My heart is beating fast. I want to give Rosa a kiss on her lips. She may push me back. Then I risk fucking up the only realistic chance I have of having sex with her. The sweet smell of her perfume only feeds my sexual craving more. The hour went by too fast.

"I had fun tonight. The food was great, your mom can cook. Can I keep seeing you? I want to."

"I had fun too. Um. Yes I want to see you too. I still have to study for exams but you can quiz me. Will you come to my graduation?"

"Definitely."

I will also come tonight as I close my eyes and experience pure sexual fantasies between you and me. As I'm driving home, the feeling inside of me is pure euphoria. Her parents are too lovey-dovey for me to digest. But it is sweet. I can't wait to see the look on my dad's face when I tell him then show him a picture of Rosa.

Rosa and I do continue to see one another. Most of the time at a library near her place. When we do get back to her house, I will make a move. A kiss on the cheek, a brush up against her chest. Rosa kisses me back but there is no intensity. It's the brother kissing sister feeling.

Even though my dad has been dating his own set of women, he's lonely. Only one lady that I know of could be a potential girlfriend. My dad is always pestering me to go with him to a car show, car cruise, movie, or to a nightspot. He's been on a cruise, and even back to Bagnell Dam with a lady he's dating, but I'm still his go to buddy. Trent still comes over to visit though. My life is too hectic to be my dad's pal. I'm already making time to see my mom, grandma, and continue to help with household chores. I was surprised to see Trent come over on a Saturday night. My dad tells me that all three of us are going out. Now my dad wants to celebrate my graduating from college.

"Does Randy know where you are taking him?"

"No."

"Nothing quite like a little father and son bonding."

The flashy bright lights blink continuously on the billboard. DIAMOND SHOWCASE CLUB. Large industrial tanks and rusty railway cars hide the building away from the main highway. My dad drives onto the well- lit parking lot.

"Hey Rich, remember the time we came here and saw all those ladies wrestling in mud?"

"Oh yeah. I remember a few of them losing their tops in the mud too. Hahaha!"

After showing my ID and getting patted down by a hulking security guard, I walk inside the place. The ten dollar cover charge is ridiculous.

I haven't figured out what Rosa and her family do for fun. Daniel is a nerd. A smart and wealthy nerd but still a nerd. I doubt he ever went to a strip club. Their leisure time is all spent going to churches and flea markets. My going to the Diamond is not something I will ever tell Rosa. Who knows how upset she and her parents could be if any of them found out.

I can't help but look at all the women inside. I call myself a wolf but act like a puppy. Four women are dancing provocatively on four different stages. A tall blonde dances on one stage while her large banana shaped breasts wiggle up and down. A petite brunette wearing a plaid mini skirt dances on another stage. Her pure white short sleeved shirt is unbuttoned. Another lady, this one a tall, buxom black woman, climbs up a pole then slides her naked body down the pole. She has the most men sitting at the edge of the stage that she's performing on. The fourth lady could be an Asian. She doesn't do much dancing. She appears nervous around the few men gawking at her.

"Hey Randy! Bet you never been in a place like this before!" Trent points out.

"It's the pages coming to life."

My dad, Trent, and I sit down in front of the stage where the brunette is dancing. After several minutes, the brunette faces me. She kneels down then removes her top. Her strong watery smelling perfume makes my nose itch. Her lips are moving but I can't hear a word she is saying. The awful hip-hop music is too loud.

Trent and my dad laugh at me as the brunette puts her rear end in my face. Close up, her butt is huge. I'm staring at the center of her ass crack. She swings around then grabs both sides of my head. She gently pushes my head towards her breasts. As soon as my head is pushed back to me, the brunette stripper stretches out her red panties. I know what this means. She wants my money.

She's thinking: Hey you drooling puppy dog, I let you see and feel my tits and ass. Now give me all your money you pathetic, horny, young male.

I'm thinking: Whore, slut, cockteaster, baby doll, greedy wench, what a fine choice you made and lifestyle for yourself, and damn I'm hungry. I could go for a ham sandwich on rye.

I reach into my left pants pocket and pull out some one dollar bills. I tuck two or three between your thong and thigh. My dad warns me to be careful about women approaching me for a private dance. These women seduce dumb men and steal their money. Having a private dance could cost anywhere up to one hundred dollars. I only had sixty dollars in my pocket.

Later on, as I'm exiting the club's bathroom, I see my dad's face buried in the blonde's chest. When he removes his head, he and Trent laugh and put their arms around each other. I shake my head back and forth in disbelief as I watch my dad shake his butt back and forth to the synthy-dance music. Naturally, my dad has no rhythm in his moves.

"It doesn't get any better than this right buddy?"

"Only if she comes home with me. Hahaha."

"Hey, next time we're here we need to get her and five of her friends to join us in the back room for a private dance."

"Oh you better fucking believe it! They can all take turns sitting on my face! Hahahahaha!"

If he's looking to have a serious relationship with a woman, he may need to cease going to strip clubs. We stayed at the club for about three hours. I'm tired and ready for bed.

"Hey Trent, It's like one in the morning. Can you help me get my dad to leave? He forgets I have to work the next night."

"Yeah, we'll be leaving soon. We're running out of money to throw at them anyway."

Trent helped me get my dad to leave the place when one am occurred. My dad was in a great mood even after we got home.

"Well Randy my boy, you popped your cherry! Hahahahaha! We'll go back again, just you and me."

I have no intention of going back ever. I play along with my dad's game though because now is a good time for me to tell him about Rosa.

"Okay, that will be fun. Oh by the way, here is a picture of Rosa. She's the girl who I've been seeing. We've gone out a few times already. I even met her parents."

"Randyrandyrandy." My dad is shaking his head back and forth.

"Where did the two of you meet?"

"I met her at a library close to the college."

"She's pretty. I'm happy for you. Don't tell her about going to a strip club though."

"Was taking that to my grave. She's studying to be an animal doctor."

Dad laughs at my remark about the grave. Had my dad not been surrounded by bouncing boobs his reaction to my dating a non- white person would have been him spitting out racial remarks towards her. My dad doesn't have to say the words. I know he wants to date a white woman.

Whose truck is this parked in front of my house? The shiny paint job done on the truck is either hell black or midnight blue. The word DODGE is spelled across the back trunk. My first thought is dad already sold or traded in the other pick up. Then I see fuzzy pink dice hanging in the rearview mirror. The small lipstick bottles laying in the passenger front seat assured me this vehicle belongs to the lady who is in my home. I walk in the front door to see my dad sitting on the couch with the lucky lady.

"Hi there. I'm Nancy. Your dad and I met at the grocery store. I never been approached by a man in the produce section. He couldn't stop asking me out. He would call me all the time. I finally said yes."

"Hi I'm Randy. So have the two of you gone out before."

"Oh yeah lots of times. He can be a real pistol sometimes. I'm sure you already know. I can deal with him, most of the time anyway."

"She means, I put up with her not the other way around."

"He's full of it. But you already know that too don't you?"

Sounds to me like my dad was stalking Nancy. Then again, maybe Nancy was stalking him. Whatever the case may be, Nancy is loud and direct. My dad gets off being in charge and in control. Everything is his way or no way. My first impression of Nancy is that she wants to tug on the relationship rope in her direction. Out of all the so called relationships and dates my dad has been on or with, this one could be a fiery mix of oil, water, and matches.

"So how was work?"

"Busy as usual."

"What kind of work do you do?" Nancy bellows out.

"I'm a chef at the Clarion hotel."

"Yeah, he's like the top chef there. Has people working under him." My dad brags.

"Not even. I work with the banquet chefs. I still wash dishes."

Nancy is full figured but not fat. Her busty large frame makes her chest seem small. She's wearing torn faded blue jeans and a t-shirt with Dolly Parton's face on it. When Nancy stretches, the shirt rides up just enough so that her bellybutton is exposed. She doesn't do much with her long straight silver hair. Many of my dad's dates took a cautious approach being with him. Not Nancy, she's a bull who gorges men with her horns.

I'm in the kitchen drinking a glass of chocolate milk. I almost spit out the milk when I hear overhear Nancy say something like we can go in your room to look at your dirty magazines or watch a porn movie. Her brashness and standard of living is the anti-mom. The two of them are laughing as if they are high school sweethearts having their first sexual fling.

"I'm turning in! Nice to meet you Nancy!'

"Goodnight!"

"See you in the morning slim!"

As I'm getting ready for bed I realize the trimmer was leaning up against the side of our house. It's a strange but satisfying feeling not having to help dad with cutting the grass. I'm already beginning to like Nancy.

What I don't like is Nancy spending the night at our place. Okay, I need to be more specific. I don't like that my dad's bedroom is directly above mine. Nancy has a loud, booming voice I can see my ceiling tiles vibrate when starts talking. I clearly hear her talk about being married to an asshole for ten miserable years. She had a kid who died when he was only sixteen. Something about him being the victim of a robbery gone wrong. Nancy has developed some tough skin to deal with those situations.

I also have the unsatisfying pleasure of hearing Nancy and my dad have sex. I know the two are fucking each other. Neither one of them takes in to consideration that I'm right below them. Nancy keeps shrieking or grunting UHHHH! or AHHH! My dad must be pounding away hard because his bed backboard kept going BAM BAM BAM BAM BAM from what seemed like the two of them fucking all night long.

Nancy is the one woman who is not going to put up with dad's ranting and complaining. My mom and grandma would walk away. Those two were too exhausted to fight or even argue with him. Not Nancy, she would be in his face. He yells at her and she yells back even louder. Nancy would have no problem throwing a dish at my dad. She is the type of woman my dad needs to have, the type of woman I want him to have, to put him in his place any time his behavior spirals out of control.

6

WINNER AND LOSERS

My dad has never taken any interest in my hobbies. All throughout my time in grade school and high school he would dismiss any activity I would take a part in as either a passing fad, something I wouldn't like, or something I wouldn't be good at.

Some of my grade school classmates collected baseball cards. I began buying packages of cards myself. I always hoped to get a player card that showed a lot of statistics. Any time, I would show the cards to my dad he would say something like *what are going to with those? You don't watch baseball.* I end up throwing all my cards away. At the time, I probably collected five hundred different baseball cards. I remember having Rickey Thunderson's rookie card and an old Oscar Smith card. It was after I pitched them that I find out how valuable the cards were. Who knows how much money was flushed down the drain?

One of the electives I chose to take during my sophomore year in high school was weight training. If you thought the class was an easy A, you found out quickly that this class was hard work. Three times a week I would lift dead weights or ones on the machine. The teacher, who also was the varsity football coach, taught us the importance of safety and proper conditioning. We had to use each one of the six sets. You worked out using your legs, arms, or a combination of both.

The other two days during the week, we ran. Most of the time, we would run outdoors on the school track or had to run a set number of miles from the school and back. We were graded on our production, how much lifting or running we did in class that day, and on how much improvement we showed as the classes went on.

When I tell my dad about taking the class and buying some small weights, his reply is *oh that's just a gym class. Why are you taking that class? You never did well in any gym class before. You're not going to be able to lift more than any of the other kids. You're not a fast runner. The weights are going to just sit in your room just like the bike sits in the garage. All you're doing is wasting your time.*

Since I love music, I thought about going to college to study radio broadcasting. I figure that my radio DJ career would be a great alternative to my chef career. My dad loves listening to music. This one should have been an easy for him to be supportive. He's always listening to rock and roll or country music on the radio. When I mention to him about taking classes, his retort is *all they are going to do is train you on how to use your voice. You don't have a right kind of voice.* I never follow up on the broadcasting classes.

I don't care anymore if my dad loves or hates any kind of hobby I want to pursue. I didn't criticize him when he was working part time as the concert cop or as the animal shelter Santa Claus. My dad was getting spoiled rotten. As a security officer at the arena, he saw country singer Kenny Nelson and the shock comedian Manson for free. He also had to bear watching and hearing music from the new wave band The Cenns and a showing of the movie Go Behind the Curtain. The animal shelter paid my dad one hundred dollars each night as Santa. He also received an invitation to the shelter's annual Christmas party. The only reason he went was because all of the employees, including him, got a fifty dollar cash bonus.

I have no desire to going to any of the free concerts or Christmas parties with my dad. I don't care for any of the musicians performing nor do I want to stand around while my dad brags about his false glamourous lifestyle. He's got Nancy to be his lapdog.

I'm also saving up money so I can buy a DJ mixer with microphone. I may not be on the airwaves, but at least I can create my own radio show. The air waves aren't playing any decent music anyway. It's all bland classic rock or syrupy today's hits. The songs are always in edit format, either for language or length. I'll call my show *Injection.* The program would feature a mix of female fronted rock band music with a dosage of floor shaking disco and dance music.

I decide to take a small interest in my dad's hobby of showing off his Pontiac. He and Trent have gone to a few shows together already. I had a rare weekend off from the hotel, so I ride along with my dad to a car show. Trent also went to the event. He drove over to my dad's place and followed us to the show. Trent owns a white 1956 Chevy. Before we left, Trent popped his hood to show my dad whatever new upgrades were made to his car. The engine inside Trent's car was smaller than my dad's. The interior was mostly white which gave the back seat a plain feel than my dad's red carpeted interior.

The event was held in the parking lot at Parkmore West high school. If you wanted your car to be judged, you had to pay twenty dollars. You could also have the option of putting your car on display only. Then your cost would be five dollars. The money raised from the show went towards the school's booster program. I think this program aides the parents with supplying the students with school sport uniforms.

After my dad gives a twenty to the man standing in front of the lot gate, he drives around the parking lot several times searching for a place to park. I saw about a dozen empty spots but kept my mouth shut.

"Shit. All the good spots are taken. And look at these assholes putting a lawn chair out on an empty spot."

"What are you trying to do?"

"I want to find a place in the sun so the paint job shines."

My dad finally finds a parking spot. Before I can even close the door, he's giving me orders.

"Get my cleaning supplies out. Take a damp rag and wipe off the car doors, hood, trunk, and fender. When you get done wipe off the wheels with a different rag. Use this bottle for the tires only. Then find out where we register. I don't want to turn in my paper until I know how many cars are in my class. We need to find out what class I'm in. I may be able to choose from more than one car class. Hey Trent! Trent!"

My dad walks away from the car and heads towards Trent. Hey thanks for leaving me here. What am I, your car cleaning slave? After wiping off the car, I sit down in the lawn chair and observe the people around me. They too spend several minutes either brushing off their car or lining up their trophies and plaques they had received. The car parked next to my dad's was a 1962 light green and white Chevy Bel-Air. The guy who I'm guessing owns the car was placing photo albums out for people to look at.

"Hi'ya doing. That's a nice car you have. Don't see too many of those."

"Thank you. Is that a 78?"

"No 1979. Grand Prix."

"My son owned a white 78."

The guy stopped talking to me as soon as another guy approached him. They must have known each other by the way they hugged one another.

This was not my scene and I'm not a car kind of guy. Every car on the lot, including my dad's, had their hood propped open. If your car was going to be judged, you must have your hood raised, passenger door opened, and card displayed somewhere on your dashboard. The event was a competition. Someone would leave this event as the winner of the best engine, best interior, best paint job, best under the hood job, or best overall car on the entire lot. Each class had a first, second, and third place trophy for the winner. When my dad returns to his car, he's not happy.

"I told you to wipe off the car. I can still see dust on the trunk. Sigh. Give me a damp rag. You need to go over the front and back fender like I'm doing. Any idiot can do what I'm doing. People are already starting to register. Go over to where the table is so we can register."

"Here's a flyer with the classes."

There were thirty classes listed on the flyer. The two main headings were stock and modified. Stock means original parts to the car. Modified means you have at least three or more changes made to the car. The engine in the Pontiac is a 350 Chevy small block. A sunroof was installed about three years ago. Those changes alone would put our car in the modified category.

Then the classes were broken down into year, make, and models. A few examples were Class A Stock 1900-1920. Class F Stock 1970-1980. Class J Modified 1950-1960. Class N Camaros 1950-1965. The Pontiac was in Class S which is Street Machines 1970-1989. My dad could have also gone in the K class for Modified 1961-1989.

"So what class do you want to go in?"

"Shit. I don't know. I guess S. I hate when they have a wide gap instead of a decade by decade class. The people putting on the show don't know how to properly set up the classes. Find out who else is in our class and let me know."

I didn't feel like walking around but at least I wouldn't be bored shitless. These old guys take pride in their cars. The lot was filled with rows of classic cars and modern sports cars. The most popular makes were Chevy and Ford. I saw several old Chevys from 1955 to 1960. Someone is the owner of a 1948 Ford Street Rod. The color of the car was a light shade of red.

Some of the owners had cars that were identical to famous cars in television shows or movies. I passed by a 1975 red and blue El Camino. This was the car that a rebellious 70's teen drove. Someone else has a 1977 black Pontiac Trans-Am. This was the same type of car featured in the film Deadly Race. This car was in the S class too. The two cars that stood out to me were a 1937 Ford Humpback and a 1990 Dodge Viper. A large trailer was parked near the viper. I couldn't tell how many cars were in the same class as my dad's car. I'm guessing around eight. I wait my turn at the registration table, then finally register the Pontiac.

"Here's your card. Make sure it's displayed on the dashboard."

"So how many are in my class?"

"Maybe eight. Not everyone had their card showing."

"Shit. I'll bet half of them are trailer queens. They shouldn't even be allowed to enter. We may have to change classes. What was the other class? Go around and see how many are in that class. I'm getting hungry. What do they have to eat?"

"Hot dogs and hamburgers."

"Hey Trent, you hungry?"

"Yeah. Give me a sec."

Once again, my dad just walks away with Trent. I'm not walking around the lot again. My dad brought a milk crate filled with cans and bottles of car cleaning supplies. I should have brought my own basket for dad as well. My basket would include a diaper, a bib, a pacifier, and a box of tissues. He is acting and behaving the same way a pouty baby does.

The flyer also mentioned that each class would have three trophy winners. The presentation could not have come any sooner. I toughed out a hot day of walking around the lot several times, getting weiners for my hungry father, eating a bland cheeseburger for lunch and listening to my dad bitch all day about how the new cars don't belong at a car show.

When the announcement was made as to who won in my dad's class, I didn't hear the guy say 1979 Pontiac Grand Prix. I was surprised. There were several Pontiacs, but my dad had the only Grand Prix. The first place trophy went to a guy who owns a 1988 Chevy Stringray. The bandit car received second place. I think a GTO received third. Trent on the other hand, received a second place trophy.

"Let's blow this dump. Start putting all the stuff away. Make sure you don't scrape the car with the lawn chairs."

My dad is disappointed and even a little angry. He doesn't help me put any of his shit back in the trunk or back seat. Instead, he is walking towards the judge's table. I quickly finish putting the last of the items away the run towards the judges myself.

"You have a ten year gap in all of these classes but when you get to this one it goes all the way from 1970 to the present or you have at least twenty years! That's not fair! You need to have ten years in all the categories. And stop letting all the fucking trailer queens pull in. They don't drive their cars so it's no wonder the cars look great. I know nobody here knows how to put on a car show so maybe next year you'll ask for help. I would be available but I wouldn't be seen here even if I had a pinto.

The lady my dad was yelling at wasn't even one of the judges. She was one of the cooks. One of the show judges comes up to my dad. This guy has no problem getting in my dad's face.

"Sir, there's no need to use that kind of language. Our judging was fair and honest."

When you take a stick and keep poking the stick at a bear, the bear will eventually roar.

"Fair and Honest?! Oh Bullshit. You play favorites with the locals and shut out those who actually drive a great distance. You can be sure that I will never come to this show again. And I'm going to tell everyone how bad this show sucks."

"I'm sorry you feel that way."

My dad had to get the last word in.

"Yeah, this show SUCKS!"

Trent finally came over to calm my dad down.

"Hey buddy, let's cruise on out of here. Later on we can stop off at the tittie bar. How about you Randy? Does that sound good?"

Honestly, I didn't want to be anywhere near my dad.

As we drove home, I tried to soothe my dad's sore by siding with him on the car judging.

"I don't understand. You had the only Grand Prix on the lot. You have brand new paint job. Why would the trophy go to some brand new car or a car that wasn't even cleaned? Man, you got robbed."

"Fuck the trophies. This is why you go to a cruise instead. At a cruise you pull in, park your car, and walk around looking at the other cars. You don't have to even bother cleaning up the car. There's no trophies given out."

"So let's go to a few of them."

"We will. What I'd like to do is go on a Hammond Motorsports Power trip.

"What's that?"

"You meet at one location then cruise through four or five states before circling back. This year the trip starts in California."

"Any stops in St. Louis?"

"I haven't seen any yet. I think there was one in Kansas. I'll have to look at the magazine to see where the stops are."

"Maybe I can ask off work if and when you do go. I could follow you in my car. That way we would have an extra car to load stuff in."

"Yeah. We'll see."

"Are you going with Trent to the nudie bar?"

"No, of course not. He was just kidding."

The talk I have with him temporarily soothed his sore spot. Every weekend if it wasn't raining, my dad would drive the Pontiac to a car show. I would make up a work or even school related excuse just so I wouldn't be obligated to go with him. I didn't want to hurt his feelings so I did go with him to a few. I could tell if my dad came home empty handed because he would start going off on a tangent about the show being rigged and why we go to cruises instead.

It wasn't long though before my dad started winning trophies and plaques. The bigger the trophy he won, the better mood he was in the rest of the day. At one show, after he won a first place trophy, my dad grabbed a microphone off of a table.

"I want to thank the academy. How does my hair look? I'm styling! I want to thank everyone for showing up and voting for my car. I'm the original owner! Bought it new in 1979."

I lean in towards Trent, who was also at the show.

"Does he always act this way? A sore loser when he doesn't get a trophy and a jackass when he does win one?"

"Hahaha. No, he's just being Rich."

I observe the other people around including the ones who put the show on. Most of them walk away and ignore my dad. My dad didn't win all of his trophies or plaques in an honest manner. He made it a habit to either pester or butter up the judges. He would change classes right before the judging began. Sometimes, the judges would catch him going into an incorrect class. At one show, my dad came across a box with some trophies inside. My dad was able to swipe a trophy that said voter's choice.

Many of the judges or people putting on the show grew tired of my dad's bad behavior. The time for my dad to stop going to shows came to a head. We were on our way to a car show in Columbia, Missouri. When we pull up into the entrance of where the show was, a young man walks up to my dad's car window.

"I'm sorry sir but I have orders for you not to come in."

"What are you talking about? Move out of my way!"

"No sir. If you continue to drive or step out of the car, you will be arrested."

"Oh Bullshit! Let me through!"

The guy did flash a badge but who knew if it was real or fake. He was probably a friend of someone at the show who owned a badge.

"Hey! Hey! You step out of that car and I will kick your ass! The police have already been notified!"

"Aw fuck you! Fuck you!"

"Turn around now sir! You are not welcome to be here!"

"Here comes a police car dad."

"I'm going! Yeah fuck you too! Fuck this show."

At least now I can go home and finish reading the cookbooks I had started. My dad can go to these shows without me. I waited until Monday night when my dad was at work to let Rosa know how thankful she was that she didn't have to endure my car show escapades.

"Oh my God, are you kidding? The police came?"

"Yeah, but nothing happened. My dad turned around and we left."

"Why was acting like that?"

"He just wants to show everyone how macho he thinks he is. He's all talk and no action. I'm glad the car season is over. Next year his girlfriend can go with him."

"Does he always act like that in public?"

"No, only around other car show enthusiasts."

"That's good. I have exams to study for. After my exams are over, do you want to come over more?"

"Sure. We'll celebrate together with wine and…whatever goes with wine."

"Oh okay. My mom and dad are home. I will see you later."

"Okay, bye."

During football season several employees participate in the pro football pool. Andy, who works as a front desk clerk is in charge of gathering the papers turned in to him. He and Kim, who works with him, have been coordinating this unofficial and very under the table activity before I even started. The cost to take part in the pool is ten dollars per week. The payoff though could be as high as two hundred dollars. I've never seen anyone win less than one hundred dollars.

Andy is strict with the rules. He always attaches a page of guidelines to every sheet.

1-HAVE FUN

2-DON'T COMPLAIN IF YOU LOSE

3-DON'T BERATE, TEASE, OR PICK ON THE WINNER

4-BE COURTEOUS OF EVERYONE PLAYING

5-BE DISCREET-WE WANT TO KEEP PLAYING

6-DON'T CHEAT

IF YOU DO NOT ABIDE BY THESE RULES AND GUIDELINES YOU WILL BE BARRED FROM PLAYING-FOREVER

THIS IS NOT, I REPEAT NOT, TO BE TAKEN SO SERIOUSLY. ENJOY AND WIN SOME CASH!

I didn't watch or even keep up with enough football to know who the good teams were and who stunk on a regular basis. There were a few guys who would win regularly. They were the ones who kept track of every player who was injured, inactive, and insubordinate. It never ceased to amaze me any time a female employee would win. All of the ladies were the only ones who picked teams based on prettiest color, sexiest ass on a player, and coolest team name. I lost around one fifty total and finally said fuck it.

I used to be an uncompetitive person. Several co-workers have told me about various baking contests they have read about or even seen. I attended a food and drink convention at another hotel a year ago. One of the activities was a fried chicken contest. One of the female chefs won a large ribbon for her winning recipe. Personally, I thought the chicken she made was too dry.

I share my homemade cookies, cakes, and pastries with the hotel employees and guests. I pass some around to the front desk clerks. The idea is for them to put a few samples out for the guests to have. The response from the guests sampling desserts have been positive. I always tell my co-workers thanks but I'm not interested in any contests.

I never was. I didn't need to be the fastest kid in grade school. I didn't need to be kid who scored the most goals playing soccer. My grades were good enough, but not high enough to win any academic awards. So what. I still managed to get into college, graduate, and make a decent salary at work.

New hotels, restaurants, and banquet centers are being built. The downtown area is a mecca of the new and trendy eating places. One place called Sapphire got rave reviews for their eclectic décor and innovative sushi menu. I read somewhere that the managers of Sapphire are planning to add a one hundred fifty seating banquet center to their restaurant. This could hurt the Clarion's business. I bring up some ideas at kitchen staff meeting.

"Is there a way we can expand our advertising to more than flyers? What about a commercial or even a radio spot."

"A radio spot might not be so bad. Television commercials are too expensive. I'll reach out to Marian. She has a lot more knowledge about advertising."

"The open bar we do on Wednesday generates some word of mouth among the guests. What about adding some appetizers? If we try something new and the product goes over well, maybe can we add it to our menu?"

"Okay, I'll keep that in mind. You want something more upscale rather than meatballs or cocktail franks?"

"I was thinking more exotic. Maybe we can have paper surveys for the guests to fill out. We could present a few of our ideas along with a space for them to add their own. I hear sushi is becoming a popular dish."

"Mmm. We tried the sushi bit once. We actually lost some money on that one. Seafood isn't too popular with our regular guests. They are more steak and chicken people."

"Even with the women? Lately our large parties have been female dominated. I can't see all or most of them craving something that was killed before grilled."

"Right. I hear what you're saying. With the women, and the men too, we should focus on creative but healthy foods. I think we succeed with our salads, sandwiches, and pasta dishes. So I want that to remain."

"Our field is rapidly growing. Everyone wants to be the place that serves the hot new items or pamper the guests with the latest new spas. We need to spend the money we are making to stay one step ahead of the others."

"I agree. Piss on being number two."

"Our guests keep returning because they are familiar with all that we offer to them. Any sudden jolts, we could risk losing them and they stay elsewhere."

"Our profits have been great and I believe we already have returning guests coming. So let's keep on doing with our menu, we will talk more about adding healthy alternative and I will follow up with Pat and Marian about getting mentioned on the radio. On a different note, our awards banquet is next month. Several of our kitchen staff will be present. I'm going to start making up the work schedule soon so we are not short staffed. Okay then, Thanks everyone."

One of our recent banquet events was Channel seven and its sister stations celebrating fifty years in the television business. Our general manager and one of the station general managers must have met prior to the event. A deal was made where Channel seven would televise a segment showcasing the Clarion and the Clarion returning the favor by giving all the television employees a discount on their stay at the hotel.

A small television crew walked around the Clarion. The only people who were given any interview or real screen time were Pat, our general manager, Sharon, our food and beverage director, and Tessie, a long time housekeeper. I came into work late that day as my shift didn't begin until five pm. By then the crew was finishing up their shoot.

At the hotel awards ceremony, John and Fred each received a plaque for their continued success in the kitchen. Derrick received a silver pin for his ten years of service. Another employee Doris, who works in the laundry area, received a gold pin for her twenty five years of employment. After her name was announced, everyone in attendance stood up to give her a standing ovation. Doris was so shocked that she fought back tears and lost.

John had smaller plaques made for each of the kitchen staff. Mine read *Randy Stevens*

culinary award recipient

for excellence in the kitchen

I felt proud of myself. All of my studying paid off. This is my first award. I'll repay John and Fred back by continuing to show up, work hard, and help out. If all the Clarion hotel employees follow this mantra, then any new trendy sushi loving places will eventually fall off the map.

When I arrive home from the hotel, I'm excited to share my great news and show my plaque to dad. Damn, I had to wait until morning since he was in his bed asleep. I didn't see Nancy's truck outside.

The next morning I hurry taking my shower. For breakfast I eat a couple of waffles, waiting for the right time to tell and show my dad my plaque. After he got done shaving and washing his hair, I showed him my award.

"Hey dad, look what the hotel gave me. My boss has these made up."

"That's nice. You should see the trophies I'm winning. Sheesh, I have two of them that are at least six feet tall! Another show gave me best interior and another show gave me best engine. Best engine! Pretty soon I'll need to hook up a trailer to the car so that when I bring all of them with me, I'll have more room! I'm just kidding of course. I'll never trailer my car!"

My dad walked away and never bothered to even look at my plaque. What an asshole. He's become blinded by his own greed. I made a decision that day to never show or even tell him about any of my accomplishments. The next day I went to Rosa's. I showed her my plaque.

"Wow, this is really great. You must be doing well at work."

"It's a team effort. From Albert to the chefs, to marketing, I'm just glad to be a part of all of it."

"I'm happy for you."

"You're doing great too. I can tell all my friends and relatives that I'm with a doctor."

"Oh, not yet. But thank you."

Not only did channel 7 show a half hour piece on the Clarion but several pictures were taken for the local newspaper and Taste of America magazine. The entire kitchen staff had a group picture on page twenty four. I purchased five copies and gave one to my mom and one to my grandma. I videotaped the fifteen minute segment and gave a copy of the video to my mom. One of my neighbors who must have seen the segment came up to me when she saw me standing on the front porch.

"Hey! I saw you on television! How does it feel to be a celebrity?"

"Oh, I'm not any celebrity. But thanks."

7
HELLO AND GOODBYE.

My relationship with Rosa is becoming more serious. I'm working a lot of hours at the Clarion in order to save up enough money for an engagement ring then a wedding ring. Then I need to buy mine right? The thought of me getting married gives me goosebumps. I don't want to spend a lot of money only to end up hearing her say to me no, not now, let's wait, or I have a confession, I'm really a lesbian or even worse, I'm a guy.

"Yeah. So I'm looking forward to spending the night with you."

"So am I. My parents are going to Kansas for the weekend. My aunt Karen is going to be here though. I think my mom and dad told her to be here since you are coming over. I wish it was just us."

"They just want to make sure you're safe."

"I am. Will you be here soon?"

"In a few hours. I have to finish baking a cake for a class project. I also make some peanut butter cookies. I'll bring some over."

"Okay. See you soon. Bye."

The timing couldn't be better. Nancy is spending the night at my dad's on the same night I'll be at Rosa's. Daniel and Amelia will be in Wichita. What the heck is in Wichita? I quickly open up my wallet to make sure I still have the two unused large size lubricated condoms inside. I hate wearing condoms. My fear is that some woman will yank on the damn thing so vicious and maliciously that half of my pubic hair will be pulled out of my skin.

Rosa did mention during our phone conversation that her aunt Karen would be staying. I didn't mind. I think Karen is the lady who I saw with Rosa's mom at the salon. The thought of Karen spending the night at the same house I'll be at gives me an erection. On the other hand, Rosa is not happy. Rosa sounded pouty when she spoke about her. Rosa believes her parents stuck Karen on her as a babysitter. Rosa should be more sensitive. Karen is having her living room and kitchen fumigated so therefore she needs to stay away from her place for at least twenty four hours.

"Hi there, come on in!" Rosa is all excited to see me.

"Thanks. Your parents are great for letting me stay the night."

"I wanted you to. Oh by the way, my aunt Karen is here. We ordered a pizza, half sausage and half cheese and some toasted raviolis."

"Sounds great. I'm hungry. I have peanut butter cookies for dessert."

I follow Rosa into her kitchen. Karen is getting paper plates out from the package.

"Hi Randy."

"Hi Karen. I actually met you at my mom's work. We saw each other but didn't speak to one another."

I reach into my pants pocket to pull out some money for the food.

"Thanks for the food. Here, I want to pitch in." I say as I hand Karen a ten dollar bill.

"Oh quit. Or give it to Rosa."

Karen refuses to take my money. She brushes her body up against mine as she goes into the dining room. I live the smell of wet grass and ripe strawberries. The three of us sit at the dinner table stuffing our faces with slices of thin crust sausage with diced green pepper pizza.

"I'm glad to see you. My work's been busy. That's why I haven't called as much. It's finally died down for now. How have you been?"

"Fine. A baby calf was brought in. The calf injured her leg. I helped give her medicine and bandaged her leg up."

"That's great. I hope the calf gets better." At the end of my sentence, I turn my head towards Karen.

"So are you a doctor too?"

Karen hurries to finish her slice of pizza.

"What. Who me? I do administrative work."

After the chit-chat and eating, Rosa heads for the small closet in between the living and dining room.

"Do you know how to play Sorry, Life, or what about Yahtzee?"

"Sure I'm familiar with all of them."

So the three of us play board games for most of the night. Rosa won Sorry, Life, and kicked both my ass and Karen's in Yahtzee. I also saw the games Battleship, Uno, Candyland, and Monopoly crammed in the closet. Well I now know one of the activities Rosa's family does together. Her family may not have a pulse, but at least they take pleasure in being together.

"Do you want to watch to watch some home movies?" Rosa exclaims as she grabs the tapes. I'll be watching them whether I want to or not.

"Sure. This will be fun."

I notice Karen rolling her eyes. She seems less than thrilled. I put my arm around Rosa's shoulder while we sit on the couch watching the time Rosa received a giant dollhouse for her birthday. I also saw one of her early thanksgiving dinners with her family, and a time when she was outside in her front lawn hugging her brother. I look over at Rosa who is teary eyed.

"I take it that's when your brother left to go wherever he was stationed at? These are very cool."

"Thanks. Yes. He's in Hawaii now. I'm hoping he will come home soon."

I did an impressive job masking my boredom. I glance at their wall clock.

"It's later than I thought. I'm getting tired, long day at work."

I didn't notice Karen had left. She went into the guest bedroom. Rosa's bedroom is upstairs. Rosa grew up a spoiled girl. What a shock, Rosa sleeps in a king size waterbed. The dollhouse I saw from the movies is sitting on top of her dresser. I trip over the twin size mattress next to the waterbed.

"Oof."

"Oh sorry. That's where you'll sleep. I have an extra pillow and blanket for you."

You can't be fucking serious. I want to sleep next to you dammit. I didn't bring any pajamas because one, I don't own any and two, I'm hoping they wouldn't be needed. I sleep in my white shorts and grey T-shirt. Rosa takes off her mini skirt. Her bright red panties are sexy. I reach out to touch them but Rosa moves out of the way too fast. She then removes her top. Her bra is white with lace around the edges.

"Um Randy, I really like you but I don't want to have sex until after I'm married. But we can kiss and hug and kiss and hold each other."

Rosa's words didn't exactly fuck up the evening. I did see a luscious strip show. Besides, with Karen in the same house, I didn't think Rosa and I would be fucking each other brains out. So all I could do and did do is kiss Rosa on her lips and neck. My hand slid over her left breast and Rosa moans when I pulled down the ride side of her bra so I could suck on her right nipple. I feel her hand slide down my shorts. She is stroking my cock up and down. The sucking, massaging, and kissing go on for a while. All of our physical action ends there. At first, I was elated to have a killer erection. After an hour, and convinced that Rosa meant what she said about not fucking before getting hitched, my stiff dick was feeling uncomfortable.

Rosa is a heavy sleeper. It's already eight thirty in the morning. I'm ready to start my day. As I get up to leave, I stumble over the mattress I had to sleep on. Rosa mumbles something I couldn't understand then rolls over on her right side. I finish buttoning my pants as I walk out the door. When I get downstairs, I can hear running water coming from the bathroom.

I tiptoe to the bathroom door. The door is opened about an inch. I turn my head around to make sure Rosa isn't walking down the steps. I turn my head back then squint my left eye between the door crack and wall. Suddenly, the water stops running. I move my head over a bit to the right. Rosa could walk downstairs at any time. I look in again to see Karen's naked, wet body step out from the shower. Her large tanned nipples are a bright velvet color. Her brown pubic hair has the feathered look. I'll bet she spends a lot of lonely evenings in her bathroom or bedroom styling her hair. While she's drying off, she stares at herself in the bathroom mirror. She then tosses the towel on the floor.

My heart is beating very fast. Does Karen even suspect someone is standing outside the door? If I don't move away fast enough, Karen may get a jolt from my watching her, then scream. Karen is pushing her breasts together, then up and down. She also takes her left hand and slides it underneath her pussy. Sometimes her eyes will close, then open. I move away, then move toward the door. I have to leave now. Seconds after I leave, Rosa walks down the steps.

I spend many more nights at Rosa's. When her parents are home, they do give us our privacy. I have not seen Karen since. One morning while eating a corn muffin at Rosa's dinner table, Daniel mentions he want to meet my parents.

"Oh absolutely. My mom and dad want to meet all of you too. I'll have to set up a date and time when we can all get together. I want my grandma to come too. Also, my dad is seeing someone. Her name is Nancy. Is it okay if she comes?"

"Yes of course, the more the merrier."

"My dad is a picky eater. We'll have to find a place that serves a steak."

"No problem. Are your parents still together?"

"Daaaad!"

"No no that's okay. They've been divorced for about eight years, maybe more. But my mom and his mom still go out and do stuff. My dad does appreciate her stopping by. He's dating other people, I think she isn't seeing anyone but no we still all get along."

"That's what's most important. Even though your parents are apart they can still remain friends."

Yeah, my mom and dad haven't been together since their divorce. Any topic about money, homes, and skin color could trigger some nasty words. That's why I want my grandma and Nancy to be present anywhere my mom and dad are.

Forever Cosmetics Company is having their annual convention at the Clarion. Some of the company executives already visited the restaurant. I think a small business banquet was also held for them. Their district vice president was impressed by the kitchen and room service. She must have told her partners about the hotel. At least six hundred people representing the company's various locations around the world will be arriving. Many of them will be staying at the hotel overnight.

John called me into his office the day before. He was in a bad mood.

"I lost two bartenders. Garth was fired this morning for stealing money out of the register. Then Alan doesn't show up for any of this shifts. We have an important function coming up. I need your help in the banquet area. You will be working with Josh. He's going to need your help getting ice, liquor, even serving the soda. You move faster than all the other banquet workers so I know I can rely on you."

"No problem. Never did any barbacking but I can do those jobs."

"I never had any doubt. And look at it this way, instead of sweating with men in the kitchen, you'll be in the presence of a lot of attractive ladies on the floor."

Robert, the lead breakfast line cook, was leaving for the day. He told me how busy the kitchen staff was in the morning and afternoon. I'm guessing that several people from the convention arrived early and had time to eat. I thanked him for the heads up. Albert was already in the utility area hand washing some dishes. The other two night time utility boys Nate and Jerry would be starting their shifts soon. I didn't recognize the fourth guy. Must be a new hire. Come to think of it, Nate was a new hire too. David, our sous chef was present, working with him were Nate, Todd, and Tony. John would be working with Fred and another banquet chef, Paul. Mike even came in to help with setting up the tubs and cases of beer bottles.

Josh is a hefty guy with tons of personality. We have worked the night shift together before. He also digs listening to some rock and dance music. My main duties are making sure the tubs are filled with ice, he doesn't run out of booze, and when the line gets long, help pour soda, water, and beer. The only task I couldn't do was pour any mixed drinks as I didn't know the right amounts to booze to pour in.

Josh and I are surrounded by long legged blondes, brunettes, redheads, and a few ladies who dyed their hair pink. The men attending were all wearing expensive three piece suits. Most of these guys had to be gay. Their voices and laughs were high pitched and they spoke fondly of other guys they had been with. One by one and order of Jack and coke, rum and coke, a vodka drink, beer here, wine there were flying from the bar. I had to have one of the security guys go with me so I could get more booze from the cage.

Josh and I worked great together. He poured the hard stuff while I filled the tubs and popped the tops of bottles. We would flirt with all the ladies and laugh at the dirty jokes the men told. The men fantasized about getting laid by any one of the ladies. One straight male lush gets in my face and asks me *Whoa did you see the pair of kuchalakalakas on her?!* Which I did, a plastic blonde bimbette who was a dandy D-cup.

All night long I would hear Josh say *what can pour for you lovely ladies* or *this one's for you baby.* He's the suave prince with a belly so portly, you could poke your finger in his bellybutton and his reaction would be to laugh. I'll say hello, flash a quick smile, wave to the ladies and say thank you and you're welcome to all the women there. Simple shit I should have done when Susan was in the classroom. Josh's tip jar was overflowing with coins and bills. Damn, I have to run into the kitchen to get more ice. Fred and Paul were frantic tearing apart tubs of ice cream. For a second, I wished I was back in the kitchen.

"How's it going in the VIP section?" A smart-ass Paul blurts out.

"Busy. I've never seen so many people drink booze at one time."

"Are the women good looking?"

"You have got to see for yourself." These ladies are a hot! And they are loaded."

"What do you mean? Loaded from all the drinking or loaded as in money? Daaaaammmn!" Hey Fred! Can you handle it back here?"

"You ain't going nowhere. Get your ass back here and help me finish."

The Clarion had to make money that night. The dinner course consisted of chateaubriand, new potatoes, Caesar salad, and cherries jubilee. The booze was NOT free, champagne was passed around, the limo service was rolling, Hell, even our dry cleaning service was busy, at night! Seemed a few guests had too much to drink, spilled wine and puke was the winning combination. And who knows what the room charge was? We charge thirty a night to the peasants, what do we charge to the kings and queens?

I'm curious to know how much of a profit was made. I walk into our accounting department. My department has a portable radio on one of the shelves. Classic rock is the choice of music. Even the colored guys dig the loud music. My department is employed by people who brag about money, food, and who they laid last night. Our accounting department relaxes to piped in classical music. Our accounting department is made of people who would fit in as funeral directors.

"So do you know how much money was made last Saturday?"

Phil looks up at me, flashes me quick smile, then looks down at his papers. Phil has been with the hotel a long time. He might have been one of the hotel's first employees. That is, if the hotel was built in the eighteen hundreds.

"I do not have an exact amount. I am aware though of the amounts of liquor the hotel went through. That amount alone is staggering. When you add in the food, limo, room, and other costs, I would say the event was very successful."

Phil wasn't going to give me any amount anyway. He's too uptight. Our general manager is supposed to have a meeting with the other management. Maybe John will have the total dollar amount made from the banquet. John held an informal meeting in the kitchen. Albert, Paul, Dave, Tony, Derrick, Todd, and I were in the banquet kitchen. I also saw Tina and Sally, two of our lead banquet servers. They too joined in the meeting.

"Listen up everyone, and spread the word to those who aren't in here. This past Saturday we kicked some major ass!" John is pumping his right arm back and forth. "We made a ton of mun-ney! The food looked and tasted great. The people were served fast, I know we almost ran out of liquor. Josh told me the booze was flowing! We easily pulled in ten grand. Pat is ecstatic! She is working with all the managers and supervisors and they are all hoping to reward everyone for their hard work. I'll keep all of you informed as to what they finally decide. I'm sure Debbie will do the same for the banquet servers. So once again, THANK YOU to everyone one of you!"

This was awesome news. I'm never leaving the Clarion.

I'm with my grandma having dinner with her. We picked up food from a local burger joint. Dad had to eat his burger and fries in a hurry so he wouldn't be late for work.

"So I'm asking Rosa to marry me. I have the ring picked out. You will like Rosa's family. They are giving people."

"You will make Rosa very happy. You're a decent person."

My grandma walks into her bedroom. I can hear her going through one of her dresser drawers. She comes back into the kitchen and hands me some jewelry.

"It's an old necklace my mom gave to me. I think Rosa will love this."

The necklace is a light blue color and made of ivory.

"Wow, thank you. Rosa will love this."

"I want you and Nancy to be present when my dad meets up with Rosa's parents. My mom will be there too. I will probably ask Rosa to marry me afterwards. I need you and Nancy there to keep my dad in check. Rosa is not all white."

My grandma nods her head and laughs at my comment.

"I'm sure he will know better than to do anything he's not supposed to."

Her voice sounds assuring but did nothing to change my mind about have enough firepower.

I ask dad where he wants to go for the dinner. I also bring up the reception. I'm thinking of having the reception at the same place. Gino would not be able to come. He sent Rosa a letter saying how sorry he was. Karen couldn't be at the get together either. Made other plans. Shit. I could have used both of them as extra ammunition.

"I know a place where we can all go to. The Sizzler." My dad barks out.

The sizzler is a moderate priced steak house. The restaurant also serves chicken and seafood dishes. It's also the same restaurant, the only restaurant, my dad goes to.

"Sounds great. I'll let Rosa's parents know."

Daniel and Amelia agreed to meet my parents at The Sizzler. The found the whole idea of going to the same place all the time amusing. Since we would be leaving at four in the afternoon, I picked up my mom first. I didn't want her to drive home by herself at night. My dad, grandma, and Nancy all rode together. I gave Rosa directions to The Sizzler. My family and I waited about twenty minutes in the parking lot for Rosa and her parents to arrive. Everyone said their hellos and introduced themselves.

"You brought both of your daughters with you!"

My dad uses this line often. It's his humorous way of telling a guy that his wife looks as young as his daughter. Daniel and Amelia laughed at the remark, I shook my head in disbelief.

Daniel and my dad talked more than I thought.

"I'm working on customizing my Grand Prix. I'm going to have all chrome underneath the hood. I'm even having the engine and carburetor on redone in chrome."

"Sweet. I used to own a 1981 Mustang. I kick myself for not keeping the car."

"Uh-oh, did a certain someone have anything to do with it?"

"No, I needed a more economical car."

"Sure. Got to watch out for those ladies. They run the household and soon enough they will running the work force."

"Rosa is heading down that path. She's in school studying to be a vet."
"My son is a chef at the world famous Claron."

"THAT'S THE CLAR-E-AUN HOTEL!" I respond with.

The only time I got uncomfortable was when my dad starting talking about his guns.

"We live in a safe area. If anyone starts trouble, I can reach for my guns."

"Oh my. What do you have?"

"I have a pistol I use when I'm on security patrol. I work at different concerts. Most of the time, I'm busting kid for smoking pot. When it gets real bad, I reach for my Colt."

"I don't believe in the use of guns. Don't get me wrong. You have to protect yourself. I just installed a new security system for our home."

"Me, I'm the security system."

"Uh-Oh!"

Nancy steps in to change the subject.

"Yeah, but I keep him in line."

"Hahaha. The woman always do, don't they Rich?"

"I'm in trouble."

Nancy, mom, Amelia, and my grandma were all talking about future wedding plans. I haven't proposed yet and already they're gushing at the mouth that Rosa and I are getting married. Rosa could say no, no way, nyet, nada, let's just be friends, are you out of your fucking mind, or I don't want to marry you I just want to have porn style sex with you every weekend. Another topic of the ladies were my bad habits. Forgetting to pick up a gallon of milk is not a bad habit. Picking your nose in public or peeing on the front lawn is a bad habit.

I pulled out a twenty dollar bill and placed in on the table. The twenty ended up being the tip. My dad and Daniel split the entire cost of the bill. My dad's share was about forty dollars. Nancy had to work early the next day. She's a freelance caregiver for wealthy families. I asked Rosa if she would want to ride with me to take my mom home first, then I would go over to Rosa's. My plan was to propose to her then.

My mom slept in the car the entire time. Rosa and I listen to my Heart CD on the way back to mom's place. After dropping mom off and waving goodbye, I drive Rosa back to her place. I walk with Rosa up the steps and fall to one knee right behind her. Rosa is surprised by my kneeling down. She knows what I'm about to do. Here come the tears.

"Rosa I Love you and want to spend the rest of my life with you. Will you marry me?"

I take the ring out from my pants pocket then place it on her finger. My hands are shaking a little.

"Yes. Yes Randy. I will. I love you too."

Now she's crying more. Her parents were listening in through the door. Amelia opens the door and hugs both of us. She too is wailing away.

With a choked up voice, Amelia whispers in my ear.

"Welcome to our family."

I drive home and see that a light is still on in the living room. My dad will want to know if I'm getting married. He and Daniel shook hands as they said goodbye. My dad behaved himself. So I'll give him the good news. After I tell him, my dad laughs some then lets me know what he really thinks.

"Randy. Randy. Randy. She's a nice girl. But her family is stuck up!" My dad sticks his nose in the air. "Did you see the big ring he had on his finger? Shit, who's he trying to impress? And the mom was wearing all that flashy jewelry. They all show in around because they're millionaires. Sheeit. Oh he's a nice guy, not sure why he married a Mexican. But for someone who doesn't believe in the right to carry, the right to carry dammit, he's okay. He would end up falling on his ass anyway after firing a gun. Hahahaha. Hey, I'm just messing with you. Rose. Rosa. She is a lucky woman to have you. I'm happy for you son."

I allow dad to have his Jeckyll and Hyde outbursts. I'll be out of here soon. I'm working a ton of hours at the Clarion. Have to, her wedding ring cost five hundred motherfucking dollars! My poor credit card is taking a beating.

Rosa's parents, aunts, female cousins, and female friends plan most if not all the wedding. I was hoping to have the reception at the Clarion. I could have saved on the costs. Daniel called a buddy of his who manages a place called The Orzo Spot. It's a family owned Mexican and American restaurant. As a favor, I asked Daniel to make sure the chefs cook up some kind of meat or steak for my dad.

Daniel and I split the cost of the reception. I owe another ass thumping two hundred dollars. Then a DJ has to be paid one hundred forty. At least that is cheaper than a live band. I will paying a part of the home Rosa and I buy. Rosa already said she wants us to purchase a home together. Well lick my nads. I was afraid I may have to work a second forty hour job to get out of my hellacious debt.

Rosa wants, and needs, a huge church wedding. The ratio of her family versus mine is going to cause the church to tilt. Daniel's family is flying in from Utah. Daniel's parents are travelling from Tennessee. That's eight people already. Then Amelia's three sisters, not counting Karen are arriving. All three of her sisters are married with at least three kids and four or five grandkids. Rosa invited all of her co-workers and maybe a dozen of her classmates, college and high school, and friends she's known since she was a little girl.

I have mom, dad, grandma, Nancy, Trent if she shows, Kate and Kate's boyfriend, if he decides to come. I did invite Albert, Fred, Mike, John, Josh, Jeff, Dave, Derrick, Paul, Tony, and Charles. Charles is only one who gave me a yes to the wedding. He is the Clarion's print worker. I met him at the hotel bar one night after work. He rides the bus to work every weekday. He only lives five minutes away from me. When I told him that my grandma rode the same bus to her work, he nodded his head and tells me that she and Charles talked to one another.

My dad is a control freak. The house, car, work, grandma, and everyone else's life have to meet his approval. So it's tough for him not to have a say in where I'm going to live and what kind of house Rosa and I are buying.

"Have you given any thought about where you are going to live? I hope not up north where your mother is. What about staying here or with her parents? Have you looked at any houses yet? You should look at what they call a starter home. Those are nice homes and cheaper."

Are you done with the questions? I sure in the shit wasn't living at home.

"We've already looked at various houses. Rosa wants to move closer to her work. I'm okay with that. I can always spend the night at the hotel during any bad weather. Rosa has the realtor info with her. He's helping us find an affordable place. Rosa and I may stay at her parents until everything is finalized. Here's some pictures of the homes we have looked at."

As my dad is thumbing through the photos, he nods his head up and down.

"I like these. My favorite is the one that's all brick."

"Yeah, I emphasized a brick home to the realtor."

"Just make sure you get a licensed building and home inspector. Make sure he checks the roof, the foundation, plumbing, walls, gas, outlets, basement for any cracks, and NO WOOD! Otherwise you'll have a termite problem. If you have outside lights, be sure they are working. You better make sure all of this is checked and done before you sign any paper. You hear me? If you don't you'll be the one paying for all this shit to get done."

"I have a checklist that outlines all of what you said. Don't worry. I'll make sure the home is trouble free."

My co-workers celebrated my upcoming wedding by throwing whip cream at me. The whip cream was squirted in a coffee filter. This is how the kitchen will celebrate your birthday as well. After I clock out, I meet Charles at his print station. We decide to get a drink at Mario's Tavern. Once we get inside the tavern, Charles bellies up the bar and orders two shots of Glenlivet. After we toast, I ask him how he and his female friend Danielle are doing.

"I'm through with her. She says one thing then does something different the next. I'm telling you randy, Danielle is nothing but a fucking cunt. She keeps pissing me off and I'm tired of her. I'm happy for you my friend. I wish you and Rosa all the happiness in the world. But listen to me, you be sure to be happy for you. Don't let her push you around. Okay? I need another drink. Bartender!"

For a minute, I thought my dad was sitting next to me.

My dad wants to celebrate my upcoming party by having a bachelor party.

"Please no strippers or anything too wild."

"Don't worry. I know the perfect place."

"Daaaad. Look…"

"Stop. Trust me. You'll like this place. It's a small out of the way place to go and relax."

The Key Club. You wouldn't know the place existed if you never been there. The strip mall shops on either side are empty. The only other business nearby is a gas station. I walk inside and nearly throw up. The patrons are Hell's Angels, ex-cons, or fat horny white collar men. Four burly men are sitting at the bar. A lady who could be mom's age is tending bar. She's flirts with the burly bears. It's too easy-all she needs to do is lean over and expose three fourths of her tits. I sneaked in a look myself. Her boobs look good. Two softball size mounds with a dark red nipple on each. What in the fuck is my dad doing in a place like this?

You can't miss the big silver earring in the female bartender's nose. If her black tank top was cut down any lower, her bouncing boobs would pop out. When the bartender comes over to my dad, she plops on his lap.

"Well hell-o there!"

"Hi Cutie. What are you up to tonight?"

"My son's getting married. I'm letting him see what he's going to miss out on."

My dad only drinks a soda. And gives the boob lady a couple of one dollar bills. I am bored to death.

"Hey dad, I had fun tonight but I do have to go in work early."

"Allright. Yo! We got to go!"

We leave about an hour after I tell him for the third time. I wasn't in the mood to talk while driving home.

"Thanks again dad for the good time."

The drinking. The magazines. The films. My grandma, cousins, Karen, and Rosa. Desire is poison. Rosa is the antidote I don't have. I'm the only one home on my side. I go through the yellow pages and stop at the E section. Here's one. One Intimate Night. I call 866-200-2000 and I'm greeted with

"Hello, may I help you?"

"Hi. Do you do outcalls?"

"Yes."

"Okay, I want to have an escort."

"It's one hundred and twenty up front. Any more is between you and the other person. You'll receive another phone call. The two of you will set up where you want to meet. You must have a current pay stub with you. What's your name and number sweetie?"

"Randy. My number is 745-8400."

"Someone will call you back soon."

You have to be careful when choosing an escort service. Any one of them could be a front for an undercover police sting. You must build trust with the company and their clients. Feel them out. If they sound like the fuzz, they are the fuzz. If you are satisfied with your escort then keep using them. You won't get any discounts, but you will be priority so long as you have the money. Twenty minutes later, my home phone rings.

"Hello?"

"Hi is this Randy?"

"Yes."

"Hi, I'm Annette."

"Hi. I asked if you do outcalls. Is that okay?"

"Yes, that's fine. Where are you coming from?"

"South city."

"Do you know where the Sennett Motel is?"

"Up north. I know it."

"I'll be in room 210. Did the service tell you how much and what to bring?"

"Yes."

"Okay then. You have my number. Call me when you pull in the parking lot. I'll watch for you."

"Okay I will."

"See you soon darling."

Up north. Great. I put three hundred dollars in my pocket then drive off. I hope to have some of the money still in my pocket when I leave. I pull in the lot, park by the room, and call Annette.

After knocking, the door opens partway.

"Hi I'm Randy."

The door closes, unlocks, and opens again. Annette is a short but endowed brunette with curly hair. She's wearing black gym shorts and a plain red T-shirt. I show her my pay stub.

"He's here." She says talking to someone on the phone.

"Okay its one twenty up front."

I give her two hundred dollars. She then recites the rules:

"You can stroke, massage and suck my breasts. Be gentle when you suck my tits. If you start to finger my pussy and I can't take it, I will tell you to stop. You cannot suck my pussy or cum in my hair or on my face."

Annette removes her shorts and pulls off her T-shirt. I quickly take off all my clothes. I lay on the bed and Annette gets on top of me. I begin to kiss her neck then move my tongue down her chest. I slide my tongue over her nipples. As I'm doing this, she is stroking my cock. I start of insert my index finger in her pussy. Her pussy feels wet. Did she already cum? While I'm fingering her I realize I forgot all about Rosa's bachelorette party. When was it? Why wasn't I invited? Hey, how come Annette and I aren't fucking? Annette grabs a hold of my right shoulder. She continues to stroke harder and faster. Oh no! Hold it! Not yet!

Annette pushes my body back down on the bed. I'm gritting my teeth in anger. I can feel cum on my stomach. Mine. That's when I knew there would be no sex between the two of us.

"Oh my God! That was incredible. You are so beautiful". I tell Annette, lying through my teeth.

We both get dressed and don't say a word to each other. I hand Annette another forty dollars. I whisper in her ear.

"I had a fantastic time." I lie to her once again.

As I'm driving away, several thoughts run through my mind. I spent two hundred forty dollars on a whore who refused to have sex. I could have been with Rosa who might have been in a sexual mood after her dildo swinging party. I feel rotten. I miss Rosa more than ever.

The sun shined all day. Hot, but not scorching the skin. Rosa's white lacy wedding dress was the kind you only see in magazines but now Rosa was wearing it. Amelia went through a box of tissues. Gino made a surprise visit that got her whole family weepy. Gino reminds me of a stout powerlifter. He showed off his many medals worn on his Air Force Uniform. I didn't mind that his presence became the front burner. Rosa was in such a good mood that I figured to have all night sex with anyway.

"With this ring I thee wed..."

I gave Rosa a promise. My Promise. To love and care for her. No more going to strip clubs and no more calling the escort services. I am going to flourish as a chef. I will serve Rosa breakfast in bed once a month on a breezy Sunday morning. I will make sure our home is warm and welcoming for everyone who visits us. I will not have violent outbursts of rage and anger. I will listen.

Rosa gave me her vow to love and care for me. Rosa admires how much I care for my family, including my dad. She loves that I am not a judgmental person. I do not want to grow up the same way my father had, a racist or a bigot.

A few more people sat on my side of the church than I originally figured. Trent did show up, and he invited a bunch of guys who were in his and dad's car clubs. I asked my dad first to be my best man. He blew me off by letting me know the groom's dad is never the best man. Albert was a no show, so I asked Charles. As Rosa and I run down the aisle, avoiding thrown rice, I see my dad out of the corner of my eye. He is sitting in the last pew with his mom and Nancy. Dad doesn't speak. He smiles at me and give me usual thumbs up.

At the reception, dad was a lot more talkative. I wasn't paying any attention, Nancy was at his side, so my dad was being good. He did have the nerve to ask my mom for the name and phone number to her work. I made sure that mom did not give him the information. Other than that, Nancy and my grandma did a great job of keeping him on a tight leash. Nancy and Gino kept going outside to smoke. Dad and Gino never really met. I didn't mind. Dad would have started spewing lies to Gino about the time my dad served in the marines.

My dad, Nancy, and Grandma are among the first to leave the reception.

"It's getting late. Mom's getting tired. Rosa! You keep my son in line and let me know if he gets out of line!"

"Bye Mr. Stevens! Thanks for everything!"

"I meant what I said! Keep him on a tight leash!"

Yeah okay, let's not make an ass out of yourself dad. Just say goodbye. I get up from the table and give my grandma a tight hug.

"Thank you for coming. I'll never forget all of what you did for me. I love you."

8

CRIMES OF HATE

Rosa and I got married on August 10th 1995. We moved into our new home three months later. I got spoiled living with Daniel and Amelia. At least five nights a week, I had the pleasure of eating homemade tacos, burritos stuffed with shredded chicken and white rice, sloppy joes, spaghetti with meatballs, tuna with eggplant casserole, made from scratch pancakes and waffles, not the frozen kind in a box that always turn out hard as a brick from being over toasted, and made to order scrambled eggs. I would bring home from the hotel's kitchen any loaves of wheat or white breads that would have otherwise been tossed.

Charles and his buddy Scott helped me and Rosa move to our new place. I felt like the weakling since I couldn't lift any dressers, recliners, or bedroom furniture.

"Thanks man for helping bringing in the heavy shit. My back just can't take it. Here's a ten for you, and Scott, here's a ten for you."

"Thanks dude."

"Yeah thanks. If anyone else you know needs help, just call. Of course we may have to set up a fixed price."

I'm a married man. I have all this nervous energy in me. The unpacking can wait. My stuff anyway. I walk around the house staring at the kitchen and bathroom walls. I'm standing in front of the large mirror that is attached to the bathroom door. Rosa is in the living room unpacking some of her stuff. Charles and Scott are smoking cigarettes outside. I smile and point to myself.

You did it! You married the girl of your dreams. Throughout grade school and high school no one ever thought you would get married. Much less even talk to a girl. Yeah, well I did, so fuck all my classmates who said or thought I was a big pussy. This pussy will get pussy all the time. Me. Not you. I'm married and successful. Big house, big bed to share, a great career where I'm rolling in the money. And not one of you pissants will ever be invited to come over and share in my success. My life is awesome!

I walk into the living room to let Rosa know I need to get out of the house. It's time to unleash my nervous energy.

"If it's okay, I want to buy Charles and Scott a round for helping us move. I won't be gone long I promise. We are just going down the street. Why don't you take a break and join us?"

"No. I want to keep unpacking. But go and have fun. Be careful."

Once Charles, Scott, and I are in the bar, the two of them waste no time squashing my balls.

"Dude, you had better say goodbye to your man jewels."

"Yeah. She's going to put a dog collar around your neck. HERE BOY COME HERE BOY!"

"What do you mean his neck? She's going to have an electronic dog collar strapped around his little testicles."

"Yeah BUZZZZZZZZZZZZZZZZZ Hahahaha!"

After about forty minutes of bearing their juvenile teasing, I've reached my limit.

"Yeah okay funny ha ha fuck both of you. Rosa knows I like going to the bars. As long as I'm not drunk when I get home, she's fine with me going. Besides, I would much rather spend time with her than you two pubic hair loving assholes."

"Duuude. We know. We're just kidding around with you. She is the luckiest woman in the word. RAISE YOUR GLASS LADS! To Randy and Rosa!"

I couldn't believe all the wedding gifts Rosa and I received. I was shocked that my dad purchased a new lawnmower for us. I doubt Rosa knows how to operate one. Thank God the size of our lawn is no greater than what my dad's was. My grandma gave us one hundred dollars. Rosa and I decided to keep our separate bank accounts and open one new joint account. Any money we got as a wedding gift would go into the joint account. My aunts and uncles gave me the typical wedding cards with money. I added the fifty dollars to the joint account.

Rosa must have registered for wedding gifts. Her family and friends gave us new bed sheets, new bath towels, new curtains to hang in the living room, a new large bookshelf, new drinking glasses and plates, and a new outdoor table and chair set. Daniel and Amelia bought us a new bedroom set. I had taken apart my old bed and kept the parts in the basement of my old house. If my dad ever needed cash to burn, he can sell the bed. It's not like anyone is going to get a lot of money for the bed. The box spring is worn and the mattress is stained.

Rosa's dollhouse was placed on top of the new dresser. My stereo system now included Rosa's portable radio, which was set on top of one of the system's shelves, her music cassettes and CDs, and some of her mom's old records. The combination of AZETC's Gold and Billy Garnder's rocking Hell No made for an odd pairing. The remaining living room and kitchen furniture was a mix of hand me downs from my grandma and her family. The entire set up reminds me of a county bumpkin cabin hidden in the woods. That's not a complaint-the peace and quiet is a welcome relief.

I AM PISSED

Not because my disco and hard rock albums are now in the same spot with Rosa's feathery goop.

It's been several months since I've visited my mom. The last time I saw her was at my wedding. I've been so busy working at the Clarion, I haven't had a chance to visit anyone in my family. I did get a chance to see where Rosa worked. At first, I thought I wrote the address down wrong. I'm at a place that could be someone's home. The building looks like a cottage. There's a shed out in back sitting on about 3 acres of farmland. There's an eerie similarity between our house and Rosa's work. Both places are located in desolate areas where no one can hear your screams for miles.

No, the reason I'm mad is because my dad, in the past year or two, has taken trips to the Ozarks, Las Vegas, and Florida. For no other reason other than a vacation. He has shelled out a lot of money to have the parts underneath the hood of Pontiac all redone in chrome. His program guide has expanded to include a premium movie channel. During the winter, he moonlights as Santa Claus at an orphanage. But he still pesters my mom for more money!

I was dropping off some old cookbooks for my mom. While mom is talking to Kate, I tell her that I need to go inside and take a piss. After I'm done going, I sniff around her kitchen. When I open her refrigerator all I see is a half of a gallon of milk, four eggs, a few slices of cheese, and an opened package of generic lunch meat. I close the door, then open her pantry. In her pantry is a half loaf of white bread, an almost empty box of cereal, an opened package of graham crackers, and a roll of paper towels.

I see that her small table near the fridge has two bottles on top. I read the prescriptions. Both are some kind of painkillers. Underneath the bottles are papers. I glance at the letters. They are bills from providers. One of the bills have a total of one hundred dollars. The other bill has a cost of one hundred and twenty. Shit, doesn't mom's insurance help cover the costs?

I decide to open her freezer. All she has in there is a near empty box of frozen toasted raviolis. She also owes sixty dollars to the electric company. She is drowning in debt.

My dad spoils himself buying four tubs of ice cream, three packages of Oreo cookies, and gets pudding and pound cake from his mom. Shit. My recent job review resulted in a big pay raise. The Clarion food and beverage director told me about five large banquets the hotel will be hosting. So I know the hotel will be rolling in the money.

"I'm taking off mom. Listen, I coming back tomorrow night. I'll call when I'm close by."

"Okay. What for?"

"You'll see. Don't worry, it's all good. I'll see you then."

As promised, when I arrived at my mom's the next night, I was not empty handed. In one grocery bag was four cans of vegetables, three cans of chicken noodle soup, a jar of creamy style peanut butter, a box of graham crackers, and a giant bag of butter popcorn. In the other bag was a quart of milk, a quart of orange juice, and a box of those small cereals that come in a variety pack. In my shirt pocket was a white envelope.

I know my mom pays rent. The rent is what swallows up her income. I put four one hundred dollar bills inside the envelope.

My mom is surprised to see me and shocked by what I have done.

"Oh no Randy. Stop all of this now. Here take your money back."

"I'm not taking jackshit back with me. You're not aware of all the luxuries that my dad has. All the places he's been to. He still bugs you for more money which is bullshit. I'm doing great at the hotel. The money is tumbling in. So you take this. Take it! Give yourself a breather for once. Just do me a favor and don't say a word to anyone."

"I won't. But why?"

"I just explained. I want to help you out."

"Well thank you very much. I love you."

"You deserve to have fun too."

Rosa and Amelia went to my mom's work to get their hair cut and get pedicures. My dad called me the day before. He wants to see me as he has something extremely important to talk to me and his mom about. My only guess is that he's going to ask Nancy to marry him. When I get to my dad's, Nancy's truck is not parked out front. I knock on the front door and immediately hear a loud COME ON IN! My dad and grandma are sitting on the couch. I sit in the recliner, anxious to hear what my dad is going to say.

"What I'm about to tell the both of you goes no further than here. I'm telling you first because WE are a family. You, You, and me. Nobody else needs to know. About a week ago, no two weeks ago I guess, I was let go from my work. From Pittman. I didn't receive any advance notice or any decent reasons why. Since then, I have never been so bitter and angry."

I was waiting for my dad to raise his voice. Never happens, he remains calm.

"I am so bitter against the company and Pete Lawton for what he did to me. Motherfucker. I took a can of red spray paint and sprayed a big fuck you Pete Lawton on the side of the building. I also dumped bags of trash all over their parking lot. Hoohoohoo. I love it. Anyway, I got caught and the company is going to prosecute."

I look over at my Grandma. She opens and closes her eyes while shaking her head back and forth.

"I've already spoken to an attorney. Whatever the company decides to do I'll know if and when I'm in the courtroom. I want you two to hear this and know what the truth is from me."

"Does Nancy know anything about what you did?"

"I spoke to Nancy yesterday. She's mad at me but understands why and how I feel. Her dad was also let go from his job. She tells me he did much worse than I did so I don't know."

"You don't know yet what kind of punishment you'll get?"

My dad raises his right arm in the air then swings the arm down.

"I'm sure the company will want to sue. So let them. They won't get a dime. That ungrateful bastard won't get a fucking nickel. Jackoff. You had better not say anything to anyone, your mother or wife. YOU HEAR ME!"

"I'm not saying a word to anyone."

The last thing I need is for my friends and co-workers to know or find out that my dad got caught spraying graffiti on a building. I'm sure all of what he did will blow over in a few weeks. I go home and do my best to forget about his revenge tactic. Little did I know that my dad wasn't telling me and grandma everything he did after getting the boot.

Rosa keeps poking me in my right side.

"Randy, please pick up the phone."

Aw shit. Why can't you answer the phone? Oh right, you moved the phone over by my side of the bed. I glance over at the clock. Eight am and it's my one day off. I never got a chance to say goodbye to Gino. Maybe he's calling to let me know this. I reach over to the phone. I grumble "Hello?"

"Randy you need to get to the police station as soon as you can."

Nancy's voice sounds frantic.

"I'm here now. It's your father. When you get here I'll fill you in more."

"Allright."

Click.

"Nancy called. Something is going on with my dad. He and Nancy are at the police station. The one near his place. Nancy is all bent out of whack."

"Is he okay?"

"Yeah, he probably was yelling outside at someone. He may need to pay a fine. I'll know more when I get there. I shouldn't be gone long."

"Okay, I hope he's okay."

I kiss Rosa on her cheek before I leave.

I arrive at the police station about forty minutes later. Once inside, I look for Nancy. She is coming out of the restroom.

"So what's going on?"

"He's been arrested. Police and a detective came by the house around six thirty. I'm waiting to talk more to the detective."

"Do you know if it's worse than his vandalizing?"

"With the cops involved, I hope not. I know he was upset at being laid off."

A cop comes over to escort Nancy and me into a small room. He took out a notepad and started writing. A few minutes later another guy enters the room. His tan suit was wrinkled. His breath reeked of cigar smoke.

"Hi there, I'm detective Hawk."

Hawk is tall and built rock solid. He comes across like one of those tough guys who take pleasure in beating up criminals to teach any of them a lesson not to do the crime again.

"Hi, so can you tell me what's going on with my dad?" I ask, regretting what I could hear.

"You're his son, Randy right? And you are..?"

"Nancy, his father's girlfriend."

"Your father is being charged with trespassing, vandalism, arson, assault and battery."

"WHAT! He told me that he sprayed bad words on the company building and then dumped trash on the lot."

"He did a lot more and a lot worse. There's enough evidence and witnesses to support the criminal activities. The information I have is that he drove to Pittman Industries Tuesday night. He may have tossed trash on the sidewalk but he also took a lit match and tossed that in a windowsill. Another fire began in the dumpster. Somehow, and I don't have the full report from the fire department, the building suffered significant damage. There was a witness to this. Another report was made later that same night. A man fitting your dad's description and car drove to a Pete Lawton's home."

"Pete. He's his boss now his ex -boss."

"Okay then. Anyway, the report says that multiple gunshots were fired at the location of Pete Lawton. Witnesses claim to hear shattered glass and gunshot noises. Three people were seen leaving the home. Pete's wife told the police a man was attempting to run them over. Your dad struck the man."

"He hit someone!"

"Oh my God! Now Nancy's face finally shows shock and stunned.

"Does anyone know how bad he got hurt?!"

"The last update I have is that he's in stable condition."

"I take it you have spoken to my dad about all of this?"

"I talked to him earlier."

"I want to know what he's said to you."

"He's a character all right. The prints on the gun will match his own. He was in denial then changed his mind. Also claimed self- defense and not of sane mind."

I'm exhausted hearing all of this.

"So any idea of what happens now."

"He's going to remain in a holding cell until his court date."

"For how long?"

"Maybe a few weeks."

"What about bail."

"I'm not sure. That will be up to the judge. You can talk to the public defender."

"He's not exactly admitting guilt. If you don't mind my asking, is he showing any kind of regret or being sorry."

"He didn't show any remorse. Sometimes he laughed by what he did. Seems proud of every crime he committed."

"Oh, something else. As he was being arrested, he told me about letters he wrote to his boss and to the company. He wanted to make sure I got a copy. He gave permission for the letters to be retrieved. I asked one of the officers who was still there to find the letters."

"Can I see the letters?"

"He told me the same letters were mailed to you with a note."

"Christ. I get the feeling these letters will not help him out. Do you want my copies?"

"Um. Pete's wife gave a copy of the letters to a police officer, then I got those. So no I guess not."

"Okay, so when can I talk to my dad?"

"Wait here some. You'll be able to talk for a few minutes."

"Okay, thank you for letting us know what happened."

"Sure. Take care."

Nancy and I walk out and head towards the lobby.

"I'm going to get with the defender real quick. Do you want to talk to my dad?"

"Later. I have errands to run. I'll come back later."

"Okay, thanks for calling me."

"Your welcome. Let's keep in touch."

I meet up with the public defender before I visit my dad. This guy could be past the retirement age on his way to the rest home.

"Hi I'm Randy Stevens. Rich Stevens is my dad. I just spoke to the detective about what my dad has done. Can you tell anything more about what kind of punishment he's getting?"

"Well, I'm Frank Chils by the way, I'm sorry but I don't have any specifics for you. He isn't admitting guilt which I advised him to do. He plays the sanity card. What any witnesses or what he says in court could affect any jail time."

"He doesn't have a past record."

"That will help some. I'm hoping he will admit guilt and show remorse. Could lessen his time greatly."

"Can I say or do anything to help?"

"Well, you just told me he has no past record right?"

"Right. Nothing. He was never violent towards me or my mom or anyone that I know of. I guess he just snapped."

"That's what I'll sell to the judge."

"Will there be a jury?"

"Doesn't look like it."

"Okay thanks for your time."

"Sure, please keep in touch and I'll do the same."

I call Rosa to let her know that I'm going down to my dad's place. She didn't answer so I left her a brief message.

"Hi it's Randy. I'm going to my dad's. I may visit my grandma. I'll be home later and talk to you more. Bye."

I go inside dad's place and begin looking for these letters. I walk into his bedroom. In a drawer, underneath his tube socks, is a legal size yellow envelope. The name Randy Stevens is written on the outside. The letters are copies of the originals.

LETTER ONE:

To Pete Lawton

You uncaring selfish no good backstabbing rotten motherfucker. You made the worse mistake of your life. NOBODY screws with me or my family. I work my butt off there day in and day out. I was never late and never called in sick. All you do is spend the companys money on vacations. You and all the other bigshots with your money. You have no idea what was happening at the company. You are not even aware of incidents going on under your nose. Let me point out a few of them to you.

April 5 1995

Rufus shows up to work a half hour late. He is supposed to be here at eight thirty. He's been late three times in the past month. When she finally does show up the first thing he does is either go in the cafeteria for another half hour or go on the deck to smoke. He is a lazy incompetent person who takes no pride in his work. I'm always having to do his work all over because he can't do his job right the first time. Is this the kind of idiots you want to keep hiring? When the truck arrives I have to unload the truck by myself because Rufus and Jan don't help. Jan can't lift boxes because he says he's injured. That is a joke. He's just stealing money and faking injury. I've cut myself repeatedly on sharp objects. I strain my lower back every day lifting heavy objects by myself. I report all of this to bill and to personnel. NO ONE including you! you dummies have never even got back with me or followed up. But Rufus and Jan get better reviews and more money than me. WHAT!!! I know why. The cat is out of the bag. You are queer. I have it on good authority that you and Rufus suck each others dicks in the mens bathroom.

May 1995

I report than jan is not meeting his quota. He can't help it if he never learned to speak proper English. The company must be under pressure to hire stupid people minorities so the BBB or the equal employee bureau doesn't come in and close the place. Someone in your company needs to make sure the foreigners you hire take a class in proper English BEFORE they are hired! Closing the place would be an improvement. Put a for sale sign in front of your doors. When you needed someone to stay late I was the ONLY ONE who volunteered and didn't complain. How and why did you give Rufus, and jan, and denny, and temon more money! You are nothing but a liar and a backstabbing asshole who kisses everybodys ass to get to the top.

I will get my payback and revenge. You better not leave work or your home by yourself. I know where you and your family lives. 6532 Shalor ave. My mom needs medical help. She needs food clothing and medicine she struggles to make ends meet. What kind of human being does this to another person? You heartless piece of shit. I hope you die. I'm coming after you. Remember when you needed a favor from me. Drop dead.

Bugs Bunny

LETTER TWO:

Dear Cindy Lawton:

My name is sargent Rosco Sesame. I am a private eye who was secretly hired by a man who believes your husband is committing bad crimes. He is bringing in ILLEGAL immigrants to work Pittman. I have reported this to the bureau. He refuses to give these people any money for their time. He is stealing money from Pittman. The company bank account kept getting lower and lower. He wasn't smart enough to hide the money without getting caught. I sent pictures of him being caught red handed to Danny O shea. His excuse of that he need to the money to pay off gambling debts. Danny and I go way back. When he gets these pictures and facts, Danny and his group of elite police officers will arrest Jeff and throw his ass in jail. I'm requesting that I ride along with Danny so I see the look on his face when the cops arrest him. Maybe one of them will shoot him for resisiting arrest. Jail or dead is where that backstabbing prick belongs. He committed a felony. That's twenty years without parole. Oh I forgot to tell you, he also drove around during his work hours and picked up women. He takes them back to the hotel. They fuck and take drugs. I have pictures of all of this too. I will mal you some copies. Fuck him and fuck you! Fuck your entire rotten family.

Sargent Rosco Sesame badge number 1234

LETTER THREE

To Janet Giles

Personnel Director.

I am writing this letter to report a grave injustice. On August 10th I witnessed Jeff Lawton selling drugs at Pittman. He was selling drugs to Rufus and Jan. Rufus is a con out on parole. I have forwarded this information to the FBI. I know how the law works. If you violate your parole then you go back in jail. If you help someone violate their parole then you also go to jail. So I guess you are going to jail. It won't be long before the FBI storms in and shuts down the company for good. Goodbye ha ha!

Sincerely
Jack Meoff

The bad news never ends. Detective Hawk informs me that my dad made several threating phones to Pete's home. Pete must have recorded the messages and gave the tape to his attorney. Multiple lawsuits have been filed by Pittman against my dad. Let's see, he destroys property, threatens and almost kills someone, and shows no compassion for what he did. The judge is going to have a field day determining on how severe he or she wants to punish my dad.

I can only speak to my dad for fifteen minutes. He comes out from the cell area wearing an orange jumpsuit. A guard undoes his handcuffs. The guard stays the area so make sure he doesn't escape. My dad and I can see each other through the window. Once he and I pick up our phones, my dad begins talking.

"Randyrandyrandy! Now just listen and hear me out okay. I'm going tell you exactly what the public defender told me."

Any time I begin to say one word, my dad would interrupt me.

"Listen! Listen to me! I'm going to explain and tell you everything. I'm what they call a first time offender. Since I don't have a past criminal record and I'm not a psychopath I won't be doing a lot of time. All they have me here for is destroying property. Okay?!"

After a long silence, I finally speak.

"I also spoke to the public defender and to the detective. I'm aware of what you did to Pete Lawton and his family."

My dad is getting agitated. He hasn't seen anything yet.

"Aww Goddammit! They're just scaring you. They blow everything out of portion. Don't listen to them. I didn't do anything to Pete."

I nod my head up and down, playing along with all of my dad's lies.

"Okay. Okay. If you want me to be in the courtroom I'll check with my work. Otherwise I'll get with this Frank guy. I have to be going. I'll keep in touch."

"Fine Goodbyegoodbyegoodbye."

I actually feel sorry for my dad. He is so diluted. I am going to the courtroom. I want to hear for myself what the judge decides. My dad thinks he's mister tough guy. My dad is going to be in for a rude awaking. I do understand and can sympathize when someone gets laid off. Finding another job isn't easy in today's job market. I'm curious to know what story my dad told Nancy.

Nancy and I were the only ones who either knew or were related to my dad in the courtroom. I glanced over at a young lady sitting on the opposite side of the room. Her eyes are red and sore. She keeps clutching two younger girls. Shit, they must be Pete's wife and kids.

"All Rise! Court is in session. The honorable Judge Leonard McCallister."

A tall man in his fifties wearing a black robe walks in then proceeds to the bench.

"Please be seated."

The bailiff hands the judge a thick vanilla colored folder. I turn my head to the left and right wondering who many of these people are. They may from my dad's work. I barely hear the judge ask the public defender how my dad pleas. Did I hear right? Not guilty by insanity? There was too much evidence against my dad. The letters and calls were minor. The arson charge was major. At least five years. His fingerprints on the guns. Another year. Running over the poor guy. Fucking brutal. When the judge asked if my dad had any words to say to Pete's family, who was present, my dad never said a word or even turned to face them. Now the judge was pissed by my dad's arrogance.

"I hearby sentence you to a maximum security facility for a term of fifteen years. During your time you will be required to do public service. During that time, your stay will be at a correctional facility. Once completed, you will be transported to the city prison. You are also required to fulfill court appointed appointments with the prison psychologist. You need to learn that there are consequences for your actions. I am going to see that you deal and learn from your horrible crimes. All of your activities will be documented and turned in to me. Any appeals can be made at a date and time to be determined. This court is adjourned."

SLAM!

9
TROPICAL PARADISE

I'm the one who has to tell my grandma and Rosa what crimes my dad committed, and worse, what punishment the judge gave him. I invited Nancy and my mom over to my grandma's so all four us would be together.

"Nancy was in the courtroom so she knows what is going to happen with my dad. He ended up in serious trouble. He was charged with vandalizing, threatening, arson, assault, and battery. He attempted to run over his boss for Christ sakes. He never said I'm sorry or showed any emotion. Anyway, the judge was not lenient. He got fifteen years."

My mom covers her mouth with her right hand. My grandma closes his eyes while lowering her head. I continue to give mom and my grandma more information regarding my dad.

"He's supposed to do community service and see a psych doctor. From what I understand, I'll have to talk to his lawyer more, is that he spends the first year or so at a different place while doing his service work. I believe his lawyer said with good behavior he probably won't serve the entire time."

"I'm going to come down here from time to time on my days off. I've asked Nancy and my mom if they will also come down here every now and then too."

"I can come down too. I'll check with my doctor visits."

"You better come down."

"I told Randy I would come down and we can both take care of the lawn. If you need anything urgent call me."

"I'm also putting a security sticker on the front window. Just to be safe."

"Thank you both for helping me out."

"We'll get through this."

My grandma summed up my dad's actions.

"Boy oh boy. He's always cuts his own nose off. I guess this time he learned his lesson."

Rosa told her parents that something terrible happened to my dad. I got goaded into having dinner with Rosa and her parents. I wasn't in the mood to give any of them specific details. I'm going over in my mind just how much information I want to spill. Who knows what kind of reaction from them I'll get? I knock hard and loud on her parent's front door.

"Come on in. Oh my, is your dad alright?"

"No, I mean physically he's fine. But he's in some deep shit."

I didn't care if Rosa or her parents were offended by my foul language. It takes something unexplained from my gut not to blow my cool. I said the word shit loud enough that Rosa's parents stopped doing whatever it was in the kitchen to hear and be concerned.

"Excuse my language. I'm not happy with what he did. My dad got arrested a few days ago for destroying property. He also made threats against his ex- boss."

"Oh no!"

Rosa wasn't satisfied with what I told her and her parents. She keeps pushing for more information.

"What happened?"

"He was laid off, let go actually, at the warehouse. He got upset. This all happened suddenly. My dad wasn't expecting to be let go. He did his work and was always there. If something occurred between him and another co-worker that got him fired I don't anything about that. So he did some damage to the outside of the company. I was told by his lawyer that he also wrote some nasty letters to his boss."

"He seemed like a really nice guy. He was a real cut-up at the restaurant. We were taking and joking. Wow. I'm so sorry."

"Yeah well, don't be. My dad is not a violent person. He just made some stupid decisions. I guess he lost his temper."

"What's going to happen to him?"

"He's going to jail. The judge gave him a year's worth of community service. He'll be at what I call the adult detention center. Then he goes to prison."

"For how long?"

"He got fifteen years."

I raise my hand in the air so that no one interrupts me.

"His lawyer told me that it's doubtful my dad will serve all of the sentence. If anything, he'll have to make restitution for the damages. Once the lawsuits are settled, then my dad will need to behave and hopefully when his parole comes up he can be released soon afterwords."

"When's that going to be."

"I don't really know. At least five years. So maybe five to ten. The worse part about all of this is that he acts like he doesn't care what he did or who he hurt. He's never said that he's sorry."

"How is his mom and girlfriend handling all of this?"

"They're shocked and disappointed to say the least. Which reminds me, I need to go over to my grandmas. I'm going to help with taking care of her and watching out for her."

"Can we help?"

"You're always welcome to visit. I need to get his finances in order. Make sure the bills on his side are being paid. I want to also go to Midwest Security. My mom and Nancy said they would stop by. I'm not too worried. There's enough people in the neighborhood who look out for one another anyway. It's at night when my grandma gets uneasy being alone. I was thinking I could stop by in the evenings after work since I'll be close."

"Did he hurt anyone?"

That question from Daniel, who's been the nosiest of all three, is the understatement of the decade. What do I say? Yes he hurt someone. Jeff, his family, a business, Nancy, Mom, me, and his own mother. He torched the building, shot and ran over an innocent guy, and then gave a rat's ass as to how this will affect everyone.

"Luckily, I believe no one was in the building. Someone probably heard noises and call the police."

"So the police caught him?"

"Soon after. My dad didn't exactly hide what he was doing. I'm mean the can he used to spray paint was still in his car. I'm sure his fingerprints were still on the can."

"Fifteen years is a long time to go away for property damage and threats."

"I agree. I'll be in touch with his lawyer. I want to know myself if something else happened to either the building or to Jeff, that's his ex- boss."

Amelia wipes a tear from her eye. She and Rosa comfort me by hugging me. My facial expression went from content to volcanic.

"Listen I appreciate your concern but I'll be fine. Long as my grandma is safe and taken care of that's all that matters. My dad is a big boy. He made mistakes and is paying for them. That's all. I'll visit him later on. I can't let all of this get to me. I have Rosa and all of you now."

I regret not talking to Pete's family at the courthouse. It's probably all for the better anyway, His wife may think I'm a psycho too. I should find out somehow if this Pete guy is in better condition. If he's getting worse, my dad prison time could be much worse. Before my dad left I was ready to tear him a new one:

Hey dad, nice going. You fucked up royally. You had a decent job being a salesman. At first I didn't understand why you were not at SG adams anymore. Now I know-you had to have everything there go your way. When nothing was going your way, you quit. Then you made money at the warehouse and moonlighted as a security guard. After you got arrested, your two guns including your precious Colt were confiscated. Bye-Bye. If I was allowed to keep the guns, I would have sold both of them. You lived all your life rent free. Your mom and my mom cooked for you, scrubbed shit stains out from your underwear and put up with your excessive ranting. But there times when the two of you had fun. Then you had fun playing the field. Then you met Nancy and played with her. Now, unless you.. never mind. I need to that thought out of my mind quick. At least you had a job, a house, a car, a show car that will sit in the garage and collect dust, I sure in the heck ain't driving the Pontiac, money to burn, and now because of your temper, you THREW all of it away. Gone. You are being sued. No more luxuries. Instead of sleeping in a comfortable bed it's a hard mattress (I can relate though) and the everyday noise of a guard banging on a trash can yelling GET YOUR ASSES UP NOW! MOVE IT! Enjoy eating two day old meat loaf and runny pasta noodles. Have a good time picking up trash on the highway. I'll be kicking ass at work and sucking ass at home. Don't get me wrong. I know you are angry. I would be mad too if I got laid off for no good reason. But you would have found another job. Even one that's better than the one you had. Now you have no job and no money. Maybe being locked up will knock some sense in that thick skull of yours.

Rosa and I have not had a proper honeymoon. We have gone out to eat at fancy high dollar eateries Quintera or The Seven Seas. But those places are local. Business at the Clarion has slowed down. I get approved for a two week vacation. Rosa wants to get way too. She's been under stress studying for exams. Her boss told her to get out for a while.

"Here are some brochures I got. They are for cruises to the Bahamas or to Hawaii. Ohhh, what do you think? I would LOVE to relax on the beach or sit out in the sun. It's so romantic!"

My first choice is the bright lights of LAS VEGAS BABY! I've read enough decadent information about Vegas from magazines and I'm itching to go there. I'm already fantasizing what the trip will be like. Arrive at the hotel, stay in one of the penthouse suites at the Flamingo, toss our luggage on the floor, have hours of sex on the bed and with curtains wide open, doggy style, then 69, then in the shower, then right back to the dog, I escort you around on the casino floor, let everyone there know this hot woman wearing a tight red mini that keeps her ass locked in tight is all mine, get you to learn the rules of craps and blackjack, neither of us wins shit but we keep on betting, dance our way back up to our suite, fall asleep in our bed at 3am, wake up, then eat a late lunch, go back to the hotel to fuck each other's brains out in the broad daylight, get a surprise from the female housekeeper who forgets to knock, have her join us for a three way, she pulls out a bottle of vodka that was hidden underneath her cart, we take turns drinking an pouring the liquor over each other's naked bodies, the three of us kiss each other's naked, wet bodies, later on, you and I dance the night way at the disco club, take a cab to the seedier, grimier part of Vegas, pick up a hooker, take her back to the hotel with us, roll around naked on the bed, you two secretly suck each other's pussies while my back is turned because I'm taking a leak out the window, put her back in the cab, go back to the casino, finger you underneath your dress while you jerk the arm of a slot machine, and then I jump back and scream OH FUCK YEAH when you win ten thousand dollars!!!

"Daniel and Amelia have been wonderful. They were very generous with the gifts and didn't kill me or disown me when I told them I was now related to a convict. What if we invited them to go with us on this cruise to the Bahamas? Even if they go, I'm sure we will have plenty of alone time."

"That's sweet of you but my dad has business conventions. My mom will be going with him. Gino will still be overseas. My mom and dad are helping us out with the cost. They want me, and you, to take a break from all the studying and working a lot of hours."

"Wow, that's generous of them. Makes me want them to come along even more."

Rosa bends down to kiss me on my lips.

"I know you are being nice and I love you for that. Besides, I want to be alone with you."

"Yeah, your right. I'm ready to get the fu, to take a vacation for ourselves."

Walking into the Ecstasy lobby was a trip into a whole new world. My neck hurts from starring at the glass ceiling that never seemed to end. Rosa and I pass up, then walk back to a huge aquarium nestled into a wall. The fish swim around looking nervous because they think someone is going to eat them for dinner. Our cruise director handed me a flyer of events. The ship has several bars and nightclubs. The upscale nightclub located near the restaurant is called Garden of Eden. Rosa may enjoy the sounds of a Junkapoo band playing at the more causal nightspot Ocean Bliss. I would rather laugh at the adult comedy of Tim Ellison.

Our room is a tight fit. The murphy bed attached to the wall needs to be repaired. What if I'm lying down and all of the sudden the damn thing springs back into the wall? Rosa and I couldn't fit in the bathroom together. I shouldn't be complaining. Hell, the bedsheets smell fresh, our travel agent sent us a free bottle of champagne, and a portable massager was hanging from a chain attached to the shower head. This is my vacation!

Rosa starts to unpack while I keep looking at all of the ship's amenities. A casino, jewelry store, candy store, spa, salon, two swimming pools both with slides, formal steakhouse, open air breakfasts, volleyball court, techno music hotspot, and several small cocktail lounges.

The reggae band Jamaicanation performs on the main outdoor deck. On the day we stay at sea, the country western band Straight Shootin' takes over the mainstage at night. Rosa and I hold off eating until later since a barbeque style buffet of ribs, chicken, and pork steaks will be available then.

I wasn't crazy about the buffet as barbequed food always makes my hands sticky with the sauce used. Rosa seemed to enjoy her plate consisting of a barbeque rib, corn, and hot roll. Soon after we begin eating at our table Rosa makes it clear what her future will be and what she hopes mine will be.

"So your mom asked me a while ago about having kids. She told me that she wants to be a grandmother. My mom does too."

"Moms are like that. I can go either way. I mean I would love and provide but if kids don't happen then I'm just as happy being with you."

"I want to keep going to school. Besides Gino's girlfriend might be pregnant."

"Might be?"

"Gino told my mom that she needs to start finding old clothes for his girlfriend. He gave enough hints but we all know she's pregnant. I'm happy for them but I want to stay focused on my career. I want to be the best animal doctor in the world.

"You're on your way."

"You can stay at home and cook for me and all my friends at the hospital. You could be your own boss."

"Oh I don't know about that. I may go nuts staying at home. The hotel is doing great business and I love being a part of it."

"Let's make a toast. Here's to our successes. And to each other"

If Rosa thinks I'm going to be one of those stay at home husbands who cater to their spoiled rich wives then she must be tripping on LSD behind my back. The men are the ones who go to work, make a killing at what they do, and expect their women to spread their legs once a week. I don't care if Rosa keeps learning about animals and working, but in this marriage, I will not be the female.

Our first port stop is in the city of Freeport. The area looks as run down as my mom's neighborhood. The homes in this area are so crammed tight you might as well just have one large communal living space. This worked for the San Francisco hippies of the sixties.

You could stay on the ship the entire time it's docked or take a shuttle to the beach. We have to return in three hours otherwise you're stranded. Well, you call the ship's aid line. Tell them you lost track of time and after you get laughed at, a helicopter picks you up from wherever you and mate are, flies you to where you are hovering above the cruise ship, and via a long rope ladder, you climb down until you are back on the ship.

Rosa and I hook up with another couple named Gary and Sonja. They are our cabin next door neighbors. I think it was those two I heard fucking each other through the thin walls dividing our cabins. We first meet during lifeboat drill.

"Hi I'm Randy and she is my lovely wife Rosa."

"I'm Gary and my wife Sonja. A wonderful cruise yes?"

"Yeah, I'm excited. I need the vacation."

Sonja moves in towards the three of us.

"Hmmm I love your dress. And you have beautiful skin tone."

"Oh, thank you very much."

Gary and Sonja are older than Rosa and I. I'll say they are early fifties but still in love with each other. The two of them hold hands and kiss each other a lot. Gary is desperately holding on to his youth. His grey streaks of hair blend in with the brown. He got his tan from a machine instead of the sun. Sonja has a unique, exotic look.

"Where are you two from?"

"I was born in Portugal. I met my husband there during an expedition."

"Wow, you still live there?"

"No. We live in Tucson."

"I used to live in Mexico. Rosa, are you from Mexico?"

"My mom was born there. She moved to the states after I was born. One day I hope to go there and see where she grew up."

"Lovely. Let me guess, you are Midwest. Chicago?"

"Close. St Louis."

"Oh yes. We've been there. Went up the giant Arch."

"Can't leave St. Louis without riding to the top once."

I was glad to be roaming the island with other people. You never know if and when a pickpocket could be lurking. The four of us walk into a bar located at the tip of the beach. An island man approaches Gary and me with a sign that reads parasailing.

"Are you up for a sky high view of the island?" Gary asks, nudging me in the chest. A teenage girl walks up to the man holding the sign. She too wants to parasail. That gives me a sinister idea. I lean into Gary and speak in a hushed tone.

"I'm up for it. I can't go alone though because of my weight. I'll end up flopping around in the air like a human kite. How about you, me, and the young girl over there go up together."

Gary moves his eyes only towards the young lady.

"I like it. Let's ask her."

"Excuse us please, I'm Gary and this is my friend Randy. We are about to go parasailing. We would love for you to join us. What do you say? I'm sorry I do not know your name."

"Rebecca. I've never done this before. I'm a little nervous."

I decide to inject some of my own sweet talk.

"It's much safer when more people can go up at once. You can have at least ten people under one large balloon. Besides, if I can go, anyone can."

"Sure, you only live once."

"Sonja honey! Randy, myself, and this young lady are going to do some parasailing. Please join us!"

"Oh no. I would rather stay here and talk to Rosa. Have fun!"

Once all of us are strapped in, the boat takes off. And soon after Gary, Rebecca and I all run in unison, all three of us are dangling high above the Freeport Island. Rebecca's bathing suit was made of flimsy silky-feeling material. I made sure she was placed in between Gary and I. Rebecca's perfume smelled of pure clean ocean water.

After all of us return to the ship and say our goodbyes and nice to meet yous, Rosa and I head back to our room. We want to clean up and relax before heading out on the ship at night. It would have been great to have showered together. While Rosa is in the shower, I take off all my clothes. I then lay in our bed and pull the covers halfway over my body. Rosa steps out of the shower, still a little wet and her towel is only held up by her right hand.

"Oh you are sooooo sexy!" I tell her as I slide the covers off of me.

She tosses the towel on the bathroom floor. Her naked body is a mere inches from mine. I pull back the cover enough so that Rosa can get into bed with me.

"It's getting dark in here, want me to turn on the lamp."

"No, I'm fine."

Rosa leans lover towards the small dresser next to the bed. I can hear her unwrap something.

"I love you but I don't want to get pregnant. I do want to have sex but protected sex okay."

"Okay, hand me the condom."

I couldn't tell Rosa that I wanted to have sex without a condom. Could fuck up the whole trip. Fuck. I hate wearing a condom. They hurt like hell when a woman rips it off my dick without feeling. Hurts even when I gently slide the damn thing off my cock. Rosa and I embrace each other and begin kissing. I start kissing her neck, shoulder, right breast, and left breast. I then stop kissing so I can slide my tongue down her chest and over her pubic hair. Rosa begins to moan.

"Mmmmm that feels so good. Please don't stop."

I spread our Rosa legs and push my head in between them. My tongue continues to move across her pussy lips. I don't stop sucking until Rosa comes in my mouth.

"Ahhoo God!"

I roll over so that Rosa can be on top of me. Rosa sides her arms back and forth across my chest. She then grabs my cock and moves in inside her pussy. She starts thrusting up and down. Her still wet breasts bounce up and down. While she's a thrusting, my hands cradle her breasts and nipples. She's thrusting harder and faster! I push my cock up and down, up and down, I can feel my cum burst inside the condom that is inside of her! We both exhale.

"Ahhhhh!"

Rosa leans forward so that her face is on top of mine. After more kissing, we fall asleep in each other's arms.

Day two of our cruise was a stop in Nassau. Nassau is more populated with plenty of locals. Reminds me of the landing back home. One of the most popular attractions in Nassau is the Glass Bottom Boat Tour. The boat coasted off from the ship about six miles to another island. I've never seen water so crystal clear blue before. The tour guide offered us an island dish called Kong. The food looked like a cross between low mein noodles and slimy eels. I warned Rosa earlier about not eating any food served off the ship. Who knows how long the food has been sitting out? The last thing I wanted was for her or me to get food poisoning.

The only fish I saw in the ocean that I knew of were small guppies. The cool ocean breeze gave me goosebumps. The fish made me hungry. Once we got back on the ship, Rosa and I treated ourselves to a shared banana spilt. Dinner at the restaurant tonight would be coat and tie. Rosa wore a long, sleek, purple dress that hugged all her curves. And where in the hell did she get that shiny rock of a necklace?

"Rosa my love, you look sensational. You're the most beautiful woman on the ship."

"Ohh. Thank you. You look handsome yourself."

"It's kind of nice to have a private table instead of sharing with like eight other people. We can be more intimate."

"Of course. So.. how are you doing?"

"Great. I'm not letting what's happened to my family get to me. I'm still going to watch over my mom and grandma, keep working, and spend time with you."

"I'm glad. I want to travel to Mexico. And Spain. See some of my ancestry."

"Let's make that happen. In the meantime you have your wine, I have my seven up, and the grilled fillets look dynamite."

"After we eat, let's go up to the upper deck. The sky will be dark and we can look at all the stars."

"The prettiest one right in front of me."

Rosa ate up all my romantic comments.

Our last day was a full day of fun and sun on the ship. We meet up with our new friends Gary and Sonja. Rosa and Sonja laugh as they walk up to the top deck.

"We can take off our tops?" I overhear Rosa mention to Sonja.

"And our bottoms." I hear Sonja whisper back to Rosa.

"Randy, I think I'll be in the casino. I'll come out here a little later."

"Okay Gary. Maybe I'll join you in bit. I want to hang out here in the open air."

The volleyball court was also on the top deck. I join a makeshift team and play a game of volleyball. I have no idea how to really play. When I'm told to hit the ball or move to a different spot, I do. I'm up here on the top deck because I want to get a glimpse of Rosa and Sonja's naked bodies.

I'm slapping, pounding, and hitting the ball but keep darting my eyes in Rosa's direction. I should pay attention to what I'm doing otherwise I'll end up falling off the ship. I can't swim. Rosa only took her top off. She was laying on the back therefore most of her breasts were hidden. Sonja through took off her entire one piece. Man, Sonja's body was created from a molten slab of hot lava and poured evenly. Her breasts have got to be a C plus size. Not much pubic hair though, Rosa has more.

There has always been debate as to what's better. Sex with a woman who is shaved in that area or if her pubic region is a forest. A shaved woman is one who takes gentle care of her clit region. I've read in sex instruction books that women believe the sex is better for them when they are bald. Me, I prefer some hair down there. On a cold night I can nestle my chin up against some warm fur.

I couldn't help but get distracted from the game. Sonja's two perfect bundles of joy were too much for me to take. Both Rosa and Sonja wore sunglasses. Both of them could be staring at me. I didn't care. I excused myself to go back to my cabin. Once I went inside, I locked the cabin door, pulled down my pants and jerked off in front of the bathroom mirror while imaging that I was fucking Rosa and Sonja at the time.

Later that night, the main deck was transformed into a tropical island. The highlight of the evening was a midnight luau. Two men wearing grassy skirts were beating on drums in unison. In the background, you heard faint techno beats. The limbo pole was set in place. Rosa, Gary, Sonja, and myself all got in line and waited to go under the pole.

Gary and I put our arms around each other.

For the first time, I didn't mind another guy's arm around mine. I knew Gary wasn't gay. Plus, I was getting tipsy from all the potent drinks I was consuming.

"Are you ready to get down and dirty Randall?!"

"I can hold my own."

It wasn't long before all the men and women were singing as they slid and hopped underneath the limbo bar. Everyone gathered around the poles were singing *Lo! Lo! Everybody do the lo lo with me!* Sonja was the most flexible out of all three of us. She could really get her body down low. Not once did her big boobs cause the stick to fall.

One of the ship's employees tells everyone to back away from the limbo pole. WHOA! Another ship employee who was wearing a bunch of leis around his neck took a lit match to the pole. Then another man, and he was the only one who could, shimmed his body underneath the flaming pole. The flames were micro inches from making contact with his exposed chest hair.

The ship lands back at port. There was an hour delay before anyone could get off because some people has gotten sick from eating on one of the islands. Who knows how many people are throwing up in sick bay. The ship's doctors and security wanted to make sure no one else was ill.

Right before Rosa and I leave the ship, Gary runs up to us.

"Let's keep in touch. Here."

Gary hands me a piece of paper that has his and Sonja's phone number written on it. I quickly grab a piece of paper out of my wallet and pull a pen out from my shirt pocket.

"That would be great." I hand Gary a small piece of paper too.

"Here's mine. Who knows? Maybe we'll meet up again?"

"If you ever want to visit New Mexico, call us. You can even stay in our home as our guests and friends."

Rosa gives Gary a hug and sees Sonja nearby.

"It was lovely to meet you Sonja!"

"You too!"

Flying home from the islands, I look over at Rosa who is asleep. I'm thinking my life is great. Yeah, my dad is going to spend years in a prison cell for committing crimes, but my success as a chef is skyrocketing. And I have fantastic sex with Rosa. The sex and excess will not end, I'll make sure of it. Rosa and I will live the life of millionaires. There comes a point in your life when the woman you dated throughout school, then married, is the one you will be with for the rest of your life.

10

GOSSIP, TRUTH, LIES, DARES, AND FRIENDSHIPS.

Rosa and I take plenty of precautions when having sex with each other. Most of those fall into something that I have to do. Rosa is adamant about not getting pregnant. I haven't seen any bottle of birth control pills in the medicine cabinet. I'm not overjoyed having to wear a condom every time we fuck each other. The penetration feels like a slippery lunch baggie sliding on bare skin. But the thought of her getting pregnant and me being a daddy makes wearing the damn thing more necessary.

"You know, I could go to the doctor and get a vasectomy."

"Is that the procedure when they snip off part of your penis?"

"Yes it is, and they do it with a razor sharp pair of pruning shears."

"They do not!"

"Thank God. No, I've reading up on the procedure. There's nothing to it. The doctor or nurse does the shlopping right in the office. I'm in and out. In and out. In and out. Get it? In all seriousness, doing that would the easiest thing."

"No, I don't want you to that for me. You don't like wearing condoms?"

"As long as they fit snug and you're gentle when pulling it off I'm good."

"Are you thinking about wanting to have kids?"

"No, not at all. I know how important finishing vet school is for you. And my schedule is too flexible. Having a child would change everything. Are we really ready for getting up at all hours of the night? And if we never have kids, fine, then our family stays with just us."

"I appreciate your understanding."

"Do you parents ever bring the notion of you having kids?"

"Gino and his girlfriend talk about having several kids. I'm sure she will make then grandparents right after they're married."

"I've never been the homebound father type. Hope that doesn't bother you."

"No, you're like me, a career first person."

"I have a confession to make though, I'm a sex with you first person. My career is a vast second."

"Oh hush and come here!"

Rosa pulls me close to her. We roll around together on her bed. I stretch my arm out to open her top dresser drawer. I fiddle around in there until I can feel an unopened condom.

One day Rosa mentioned to her that she needed a new key for her diary. Rosa and I have to spill our deepest and most personal thoughts to each other. Sure I've been blunt to her and her family regarding my dad's situation but those emotions have nothing to do with our human connections.

I am not a mind reader. Tell me what you are thinking. I want to know your most intimate thoughts. When I found out that Rosa's diary was unlocked, I made it my mission to read those thoughts. I waited an hour after she left for work. I found her diary tucked away in a corner in her bottom dresser drawer. Wearing white plastic gloves prevented any of my fingerprints being exposed.

I skipped through the first twenty or so pages. She wrote about meeting me for the first time, her new friends at Brookdale, and the first time she helped take care of a cat. I wanted to know if she wrote about our sexual experiences. I stopped at a page that mentioned my name.

October 3 1996

Dear Diary,

Wow, last night was incredible! Randy and I had the most wonderful sex again. He's a horny little guy! He's so adorable! When we first met he wanted to get inside my panties I wouldn't let him. Randy was like a little puppy whimpering and pleading for me to have sex with him. I finally caved in. Since our trip to the Bahamas our sex life has increased a lot. Randy is so gentle with me. I love the way he kisses my neck and behind my ears. He's always careful when he's touching my boobs. I let him suck on my nipples. He likes that. He closes his eyes and sticks out his tongue to start sucking. I always get a funny but good feeling in my stomach when he starts to kiss my chest and stomach. He wants to put his cock inside of me so bad. I'm scared that I will get pregnant. I always hand him a condom to wear. He complains at first, but still wears it. Randy's whining is sometimes annoying but I can live with that.

He is so gentle with me every time he pushes his gigantic cock inside. Last night he did a lot more to me. I was not ready for everything he did. He was kissing me between my legs. I could feel one of his fingers inside of me. Then I could feel his tongue go back and forth across my clit. I was getting all wet from what he was doing. I shrieked a little when he put his own tongue inside of my clit. Oh my God! My body froze. He didn't keep it there long. He wouldn't stop fucking me. Even after he came, he wanted to fuck. He asked if I could get on top of him. We fucked some more until I couldn't take it anymore.

Oct 4 2006

I called my friend Jill and told her all about the sex I had with Randy. She just met her new boyfriend Raymond a month ago. She told me that Raymond likes to have sex with her in the shower. I may try that one time with Randy. I will surprise him one day while he's in the shower. I'll sneak up behind him and ask him the silly question do you want me to join you. Of course he will say yes! I will take a warm, soapy washcloth and wash his back, his butt, and his balls.

When I'm done, I'll let him have the washcloth so he can turn around and wash my breasts, butt, and clit area. Jill wants to me to meet Raymond in person. He's cute. He's from south Florida. His body is tanner than Randy's. I don't trust Raymond. He's the kind of guy who wants to have several girlfriends at one time. I don't want to be shared by anyone. I only want Randy. That's why I married him.

I stop reading then carefully put her diary back exactly the same way I found it. Rosa doesn't need to worry if I'm going to have secret flings with other females. I detest being compared to or even mentioned in the same breath as Raymond. Raymond sounds like some chain wearing, multiple tattooed, beach poser. Rosa has found her alpha male.

I need to know if Karen keeps a diary or a journal. The one she has must be filled with naughty sexual fantasies. She's the exhausted data entry clerk who gets plenty of wolf whistles from her drooling co-workers. She's not attracted to any of them. Too immature. She noticed a shy mail room clerk picking up envelopes placed at the ends of the workers desks.

She wants to ask him out. She knows to be discreet about this. Gossip spreads too quickly around the building. She overhears the mailroom clerk say he's having a drink at Weston's saloon. She's not crazy about going to a rough biker bar, but if it's to get what she's after, then maybe for a few minutes.

She steps inside the unfamiliar drinking hole. She shakes her head back and forth as those familiar wolf whistles pierce her ears. She approaches the shy mail room clerk. They exchange pleasantries. He may be drunk because he had no problem asking if he could take her to a cheap motel.

A motel? Never would have thought of that. No one at work would ever know. A cheap motel off the main road. A dim parking lot, no flashing signs, cash up front, and one bed in the room. The cars would be parked in the hotel's back parking lot.

The mail clerk doesn't want to engage in a small talk. His life is dull. Work, watch the news, then watch a professional wrestling show, write poems that never get published, plays with himself, then cries himself to sleep. He hasn't had sex with a woman in three years. His thirst for relentless sex is frightening. He doesn't want to know a damn thing about you. He don't care where you work, who your friends are, and if you still live with your parents. All you are to him is a sex object.

You both remove your clothes at the same time. He demands that you get on top of him. Foreplay is kept at a minimum. A kiss on the lips here and a suck on the nipple there. He presses his dick inside of you and thrusts his body up and down. You keep moaning and grunting, thrusting your body up and down. He grabs a hold of your breasts to keep them from bouncing up and down. Even after he comes inside of you, he doesn't stop thrusting up and down. You are unable to move your own body. Finally, he lets out a harrowing AAAHHH and stops.

I would love it of Rosa and Karen would compete in fuck-offs using me as their prime target. That's my own private fantasy.

From fantasy to reality.

I'm at the auto parts store picking up some anti-freeze for the Pontiac. Even though the car will not be driven, I want to winterize the car so that if by some miracle I do need to drive the car, I won't have any stalling or other problems. I see Trent in one of the other aisles looking at car floor mats.

"Hey Trent, how are you?"

"Hi Randy."

"Are you still doing some shows?"

"Not now. The seasons about over. I was talking to a buddy of mine. He told me about a big show in San Diego. There may be over five hundred cars show up at that one. I'm still unsure if I want to drive all the way there."

"I'll bet that show will be packed. So have you seen or talked to my dad? I'm not sure how much you know as to what he did."

"No and I'm going to see him anytime soon. I'm mad at your father."

"Oh believe me, I'm super pissed."

"I know, and don't take what I said the wrong way. You and I are still good. And who knows what will happen when he gets out, but right now, I can't see him."

"So you're aware of what he did?"

"A friend of mine works in that same building. I'm just thankful he wasn't inside, or anyone for that matter, when the building caught fire."

"Damn, so he lost his job."

"He was out of work for about a week. I actually know a lot of the guys who worked with your father. My friends and I helped the people who lost their jobs. Many of them already had beefs with your dad."

"Did any of them transfer or relocate?"

"I think one did."

"I hope everyone found work. I wish I would have been able to help out."

"We all pulled together."

"That's good to hear. I'm a little leery about facing any of those guys."

"They all know you didn't have anything to do with what he did."

"Cool. I'm getting the Pontiac ready for the winter. If want to earn some extra cash...."

"Doing what?"

"I need to get an oil, lube, and filter change. The tires could use some more air too."

"Thanks but no thanks. I don't have the time. Call my buddy Dale. Here, here's his card."

"Thanks. Well, I guess I'll see you around."

"Be good."

Dale pocketed an easy eighty dollars for changing the oil, pouring in the anti-freeze and replacing the filer along with a worn spark plug. He wasn't the only one who was going to receive money from either Rosa or myself.

Rosa hired a cleaning lady to well, clean our house. Rosa didn't bother telling me in advance about our new houshold helper. Rosa was just as bad if not worse than my dad when it came to telling me how bad of a job I did when cleaning our home.

"So is she going to have a key?"

"Of course. She'll be cleaning during the day during the week when we are both working."

"All right. I can get a key made for her."

"Are you mad at me for hiring a woman?"

"No of course not. I guess I was stunned to hear. We're going to be like those affluent socialites who hire caretakers."

"You know we need someone. We're never home."

"One of your friends too right?"

"Someone my boss knows."

"Cool. Thank you for doing the searching. I'll help out with paying her.

I wasn't thrilled at shelling out extra money to give out to a stranger but Rosa was right. Between her work and school and my work, our home never gets cleaned.

As I was passing through the hotel lobby, I noticed Charles sitting at the bar.

"Hey Charles, what's up?"

"Just having a drink my friend."

"Rosa is working late, so I have time to relax."

"You should be at home waiting for her."

"Don't know how long she's working."

"Yeah, but when she does get home boinkcheekiboinkcheekiboink!"

"Oh yeah."

"You ARE doing it to her right?!"

"Yes. Dr. Charles. We boinkcheekiboink a lot."

"Hahahaha, dude, are you ready for a drink?"

"I got this round. Vodka cranberry for me and what, a beer for you?"

"Two drafts."

"So what about you? Who are having sex with, not counting with yourself."

"Fuck you asshole."

"No, I'm being straight. Anyone?"

"Dude, women are weird. One minute they're crying in your arms about feeling useless and worthless and not feeling loved then when you start to make them feel good they think all you want is to get up their skirt and leave them the next day. If that's how all women think then I don't want to have anything to do with them."

"Not many females out there are willing to be locked, stocked, and rocked with the cock. Well, except for hookers."

"Hahahahahaha! And Danielle! She would be the perfect female to work as a hooker. She has no compassion, no heart, and a used thatch that if you are lucky enough to get into, then you better call your doctor the next day. Chances are you'll need to get checked for any diseases."

"Have you been to the doctor yet?"

"I haven't had the pleasure or unpleasure of navigating through the cesspool that's between her legs."

"Well then how do you know? She could be fresh, clean, and waiting for the perfect prick to fit in."

"Dude. Trust me. She goes out with plenty of guys. And all she wants is to fuck them. Then after fucking about three or four of them, she calls me crying and shit because she feels used. That's why I'm jealous of you and Rosa. She's way too pure to ever have sex with anyone else. And you're too honest to ever cheat on her."

"You're even worse than my dad. The two of you need to go out sometime. You can take turns telling stories about how the women you were with screwed you over."

"We've been around the block and back. Him more than me. I'm not saying Rosa and all women are like that. You just need to watch your back."

Charles had four more glasses of draft beer. His eyes may have looked normal but his slurring words was a sign he needed a lift home.

"Say man, let me call Rosa. I'll tell her that one of the cooks didn't bother to show up, so I had to work late. I'm giving you a ride home."

"Dude, thank you. I envy you. You can go home every night to a beautiful woman."

Then Charles gives me a hard elbow in my right side.

"And anytime you want to!"

"It's not all triple X rated sex. Rosa refuses anal, or a 69, and she got a little offended when I brought up bringing in another woman. She can forget about another guy. Wait, I can see if any of her friends or co-workers are single. Maybe then the four of us can hook up. Together, we can convince Rosa to switch off. But you will have to wrap your weasel. Rosa refuses to have unprotected sex."

"Dude, she's a smart woman. You two kids are still young and can wait."

"What about the hook up?"

"Thanks but I'll pass. I scrape up enough money to go to the strip bars."

Charles stumbled a bit as he walked with me to my car. I ask Walter to help me get Charles into my car. If Charles would fall over, he would be too heavy for me to lift up.

"Thanks man for the assist."

"I'm fine dammit." Charles slurs to us.

"No problem. Drowning in your sorrows heh?"

"Yeah, Charles was. That's what the ladies will do to you."

"That's why I'm a happily single man. Freedom!"

Walter's mention of the word freedom spurred Charles to sing an American Classic (not that great of singing either) as we took off.

"From the valleys, to the highways, you're a good man Walt, to the mountains, leeeeeeeet freedom rinnnnnnng!"

When I finally arrived home, the clock read 10:22PM. Rosa had already eaten so I didn't feel too guilty about staying out late. All the sex talk with Charles was making feel itchy. How would Rosa feel if I slapped on a condom and fucked her uncontrollably while she slept? Damn, Charles is right. Women are weird. I take my shirt and pants off then lie next to her and fall asleep.

The next morning I give Rosa the skinny on my night with Charles.

"Yeah, so Charles needed someone to take him home. That's why I was so late."

"Where's his car?"

"He doesn't own one. I didn't want him riding a bus either. He was rather toasted."

"I hope he's feeling better."

"I was thinking about inviting him and a few of the guys from the hotel over one night. A poker night. He's been having girlfriend issues so the guys night in may be what he needs."

"Well okay. I was planning on inviting some of my friends from work over too. You do yours first."

The only people who showed up besides Charles, who I picked up anyway, were Albert and Derrick.

"Rosa, you already know Charles. This is Albert and Derrick."

"Hello."

"Hi Ma'am. A pleasure to meet a woman of your beauty."

"Howdy Ma'am, I'm Derrick. Nice to meet you."

Charles had bought two six packs of beer. Once he sat at the dining room table, he popped the top off one.

"These are all mine. You all can have milk or water."

Derrick snatched a beer before Charles could stop him.

"What in the heck is that music?" Derrick asks with a funny face.

"It's called dub. It's mellow dance music to cleanse your soul."

"Aw hell, strike up the tucker boys!"

"You'll have to keep your confederate flag in your pants. We want easy listening."

"Hey Derrick," Charles had to chime in.

"When we're all gone Randy will get out his Barry Manilow albums."

"Eeeewwwww!"

"Up yours to everyone except Albert. So you guys ready to lose all your money!"

"Hey I thought you would have invited Jerry?"

"He passed on the invite."

"He's a good kid. We're going to teach him to grow some hair on his balls."

"So you heard what happened to Marco and Marty?"

"The brothers are no longer employed."

"Fuck them. Neither of them were worth a shit to begin with."

"Hey keep it down. Please. Rosa is still here."

"Sorry."

"Is it true that one of them had alcohol on them?"

"Sure is. You better watch yourself too. You big lush."

"Fuck off."

"Again. The language."

"Dude, we're men. We cuss."

"And fart."

"Man, I swear if you do.."

"Hahaha. I'll try to hold it in. I can't promise though."

"Say my man. I heard a rumor that someone planted that bottle on Marco. Man, that's rough."

"Yeah but Marco had or has no proof."

"Who cares anyway? He was stinking up the place. No offense Albert but I'm a man of class. I had to work with Jeff to get the job done. The hotel is better off without him."

"So it was you who put the bottle…"

"Hey Charles, I cannot emphasize what I'm about to say. Go. Fuck. Yourself."

Rosa is calling out my name from the bedroom. Oh shit.

Rosa didn't seem too impressed by any of my friends. She rarely came into the dining room. She never offered them any food or drink. I excused myself from the dining room and went upstairs to our bedroom. Rosa was sitting up reading a book.

"Rosa, honey are you okay. You are more than welcome to join us. We're not really playing for much, just nickel and dimes."

"I'm not feeling well. I'm sorry. Could you wrap up your game?"

"Sure. I need to give Charles a lift home."

I say goodbye to Albert and Derrick then drive Charles back to his place. Once again, Charles is hammered.

"Roll down your window. Maybe the cool wind will awaken your senses."

"Dude, I'm allright. Let's go to the tit bar."

"Can't. Rosa is under the weather."

"You don't know what you're missing anymore."

"Sorry. I want to be with Rosa. And I'm not missing any tit action."

After getting home, I check on Rosa to see how she's feeling.

"Are you feeling better?"

"Much. Your friend Derrick is not a pleasant person. I can hear what he was saying. Did he really sabotage another employee?"

"Of course not. The other guy's gym bag was in his own locker. No one would have the combination. Derrick can be a bit direct and talks out of his rear end but he's a good chef. He had a run in with another employee. I don't know all the details."

"You shouldn't be hanging out with them."

"It's not going to be all the time. We see each other enough at work anyway."

Rosa tricked me. Of course I have no proof and wasn't going to accuse her of faking an illness. Rosa wanted Derrick, Albert, and Charles out of the house. Fine by me. I can always play poker over at Charles' place. At least he doesn't have a wife to henpeck him.

Because Rosa allowed me to have a guy's night at our home, I got roped into going with her to horse and buggy event. Brookdale College was putting on the event. The activities included horse and pony rides, a hayride, and watching someone put a new horseshoe on one of the horses.

The ranch we went to was beautiful. The house in front of the barn was two stories high. The white paint looked as if someone just painted a new coat over the shingles. Several acres of farmland that were home to about a dozen horses or ponies. A yellow school bus pulled up to the front gate. I was sitting on a hard bench twiddling my thumbs. Rosa was helping feed the chickens and roosters. I wanted to help her but any time I would get close, AHHH CHOOO!!

When Rosa saw the bus pull up, she stopped feeding the poultry. She runs up to the door of the bus. She's talking to another lady but I can't hear what they are saying. Adults and kids were stepping off the bus. Oh wow. These kids did look different. But they acted as excited as any kid who got to see horses and pigs. Their parents held on to their kids hands tightly. I was amused to see how wide eyed these kids got. None of them have ever been on a farm before.

I get up and walk towards Rosa. Everyone had already introduced themselves. I had to make sure snot wasn't coming out of my nose before I made my appearance.

"Hi everyone, I'm Randy. I'm here to help out in any way I can."

"Wonderful Randy. I'm Marsha."

"You own all of this? I mean you have a beautiful place."

"Thank you kindly. My husband and I have lived here for twenty years. Before us, the property belong to my parents and before that, the property belong to my grandparents. He's out back getting ready to bring out the horses."

"Can we ride them?"

"Oh sure, that's the main reason why the kids are here."

All of the kids and adults were taken back to an area behind the house. A large closed in area was set up. The horses were either in the barn next to the barn walking around. I was wearing a pair of black tennis shoes. I had to be very careful and pay attention to where I was walking.

"Okay, one by one we'll have the kids get on up. You can either ride with them or if you don't want to get on yourself, you can walk beside the horse."

Rosa handled herself well getting on a horse. She and another lady helped pull up a young girl. I want to ride a horse too.

"Are there any horses left?"

"One more. He's the jewel out of the whole bunch."

And a large one at that.

"What his name?

"Sparticus."

"He's mauis-quam-vita!"

"He's very gentle and can handle a lot of weight."

"Well if a kid wants to ride with me that would be great."

Marsha points to a young boy sitting on a log.

"Matthias, come here please."

The young boy runs towards the horse and stops inches from him. Matthias is so short that he fits nicely under Sparticus' chin.

"This is Matthias."

"Hi partner!"

"You and Randy are going to ride together okay."

"And you're going to be right beside us I hope."

"Of course."

"We can take turns riding. I don't know how much my behind will be able to take. Hey Matthias, you ever ride a horse before?"

"No.Giddy up."

"Hope he's got padding in his pants."

"Oh hush you."

After an hour or so of riding around and even trotting down a trail, I was ready to call it a day. After the horse ride, Matthias and I went with the others on a hayride.

"Having fun Matthias?"

"Yes!"

"I'm getting hungry. Bet they'll have a big ol' steer on the grill!"

"Hey Marsha, do you know what Rosa's doing?"

"She's back at the barn. She's showing some of the kids how she feeds the baby animals."

The school bus arrived back at the ranch around three pm. All of the kids had sad looks on their eyes.

"Hey Matthias, I had a lot of fun hanging out with you. Give me five!"

For a little guy, Matthias had some strength. Slapped my hand so hard that the sting went all the way up my arm.

"Owwwwww!"

"Hahahaha".

I find Rosa and hope she's ready to leave.

"Well there you are. This was an eye opening experience. Thanks for inviting me."

"Did you make a new friend?"

"Sure did. Matthias. By the way, I need to see a doctor."

"What for?"

"Well my ass is killing me from riding, my nose is all stopped up from sneezing all day because I must be allergic to farm grass, and Matthias may have broken my left hand from the hard high five he gave me. But I had fun!"

11
ISOLATION

Nancy is a patient and understanding person. She could have easily been so angry at my dad for what he did that she winds up dumping him. Instead, she has remained loyal to him and stayed true to her words about keeping an eye on my grandma. I keep forgetting that Nancy's father also got into trouble when he took it upon himself to exact revenge on the company he was released from. What kind of revenge I still don't know exactly. Nancy doesn't talk about the incident all that much. She may have been younger than me when her dad went to jail. Nancy rarely talks about her parents. I'm guessing her mom and dad live somewhere out of state. Even during the past holiday, Nancy didn't visit or even talk about her parents.

My mom has been visiting my grandma too, but only in the daytime. I don't want my mom driving to and from her place at night. My mom will schedule appointments for her and grandma to get their hair washed and cut at my mom's work. If I'm off work during the day when grandma has a hair appointment, I will be the one who drives grandma around.

Today is my one day off during the week. I'm at my grandma's having breakfast with her. I whipped up some scrambled eggs and baked biscuits in her oven.

"I'm going to see dad this afternoon. I'll call you after I visit to let you know how he's doing. I keep asking him to give a number but the only phone the prison has is a community phone. Dad says the other inmates hog and fight over the phone."

"That's okay. He can write me a letter. I don't want to go inside the prison."

"I'll make sure he does that."

"I'll bet Nancy is mad at him."

"Not really. Did you know her dad also went to jail over doing something bad after being let go or fired from a job."

"Those two are made for each other then."

Hawk gave the name of the warden at the City lockup. Clint McDowell. I want to speak to him first so he can give me the truth about my dad's behavior. Oh and before getting with him, I want to talk to Frank. I need to know if any restitution needs to be made now. I'm sure by now the lawsuits against my dad are pouring in.

I drive into the prison's lot. This place is known for locking up the bad guys. Forget finding the embezzlers or auto thieves. In here are the serial killers, revenge murderers, violent wife beaters, drug kingpins, and suicidal thrillseekers. A cesspool of rookies and lifers crammed in isolated blocks of concrete.

Black metal bars surround each of the small windows. The silver metal fence outside rises so high you hurt your neck from looking up for too long. You also cut and slice your hands while attempting to climb over the barbed wire attached to the fence. Three security guards walk around the area. They are all clutching a rifle. Another guard walks outside with his German shepherd.

Before going in, I call Frank at his office.

"Hello?"

"Hi Mr. Chils. This is Randy Stevens. Rich Steven's son. The reason I'm calling is to touch base with you regarding my dad. I just wanted an update if any changes were made with his punishment."

"No, he did complete all two hundred forty hours of community service. I believe he has visited with a psychologist. He is still going to serve most of not all of the sentence."

"I guess it's too early to bring up parole. How does he seem? I mean is he acting okay or acting up?

"No, he doesn't talk much. Sounds like he's doing everything he's asked to do. His first parole hearing will not be for several years."

"What about any lawsuits? I haven't seen any letters in the mail."

"Oh yes. That reminds me. He will have to pay for damages done to his former employer and boss."

"Well how much?"

"His employer is suing for three thousand. And…hold on, Pete Lawton's family is suing for fifty."

"My dad doesn't have that kind of money. What's going to happen? I don't want my grandma to get hurt."

"I'm working with his lawyer to try and come up with a compromise. I doubt he will pay this much money to anyone. I wouldn't worry at all about anyone going after you or your family."

"How can you be sure?"

"The lawsuits only name Rich Stevens. No one will go after any of his relatives."

"Okay, well thanks for the update."

"Keep in touch and call me if you have any questions of concerns. Good luck and take care."

Where's a surgeon mask when you need one. The stench inside the prison is nauseating. Does anyone wash the windows, mop the floor or even take a bath? Once you're in here, the thought of escaping is the first thing on your mind. It's hard to tell, but I think a working electrical plant is located behind the prison. The plant is also engulfed by large, tall fences with barbed wire on top. Situated in the prison's back yard is a tower. I see another armed guard inside. The prisoners would have a hard time busting out of here.

I meet with Clint in his office which is located in a small, connected building next to the actual jailhouse.

"Thanks for meeting me. I just want to hear from you how my dad is holding up. I mean is he behaving?"

"Yes, he's been assigned work in the kitchen and the library. There's been no reports of any incidents involving your father."

"That's good. Do you get any information about any hearings?"

"Oh yes, but your father, if I'm right, will be here for several years. Any hearing will not be for at least five to ten years."

"I hope he can handle himself for that time. My dad does not have much patience."

"Well he's going to learn to have them while in here."

"Okay. Well thank you for meeting me and the updates."

"Your welcome. Take care of yourself."

After being frisked by the guard with the dog, I'm escorted to a large room. So much for any privacy in here. The convicts and their visitors sit down on wooden benches in the open air. The female visitors whine about not having any money for diapers or food to feed the crying kid who popped out of them by having whore sex with the men sitting next to them. The convicts retort with remarks like *bitch what am I supposed to do while I'm locked up* or *call your mama and have her watch the kid.*

I didn't even recognize my dad when he came in. It was weird seeing him wear an orange jumpsuit. His long hair has been cut off. He's sporting a GI Joe marine hairstyle. He also shaved off his thick mustache. He didn't have any handcuffs or shackles on him. I give him a wave as he sits across from me.

"Randy! So."

My dad didn't show any emotion towards me. We didn't hug each other and barely smiled to one another. He sure in the shit wasn't going to get weepy eyed in here. Not with all these multiple tattooed, scarred, society rejects around here.

"Hey. So how are you doing?"

"I'm doing okay. Let me tell one thing. There's no bullshit around here. When these guys tell you to move your ass, you say how fast and where to." When it's time for you to work you had better not be late either. There's no lip either. Otherwise, you end up in the stockcade. That's where the real bad ass guys go to. A tiny dark cell with no bathroom."

"Well, let's hope you never go there. So what kind of work are you doing while in here?"

"Most days I work in the kitchen helping the other guys out. I usually clean up after we eat. I also work in the library pushing the cart around and asking people if want a book or magazine."

"That's good. Do you go outside a lot?"

"Not really." Maybe twice a day. Most of the time I'm in my cell reading or resting. What to know something else? My dad lowers his voice. I'm one of the baddest ones around here. I'm mean there are some bad, bad, guys in here. They stabbed someone and showed no emotion. You don't mess with them. But they know not to mess with me either."

Yeah right. You're the original son of a bitch. The trailblazer hellraiser.

My dad continues to spew out a mouthful of horseshit with a hushed voice.

"There's also a large group of people locked up for losing it. These are the guys who are either so strung up on drugs or just plain cuckoo. They get locked up in an area separate from us. Thank God. Me, I just eat my food, read, mind my business and say yes sir or no sir."

"That's good. Has Nancy stopped by to visit?"

"Yeah. She's come down a few times. She waited like you until after I finished with my community service. Jees. All you do for hours is pick up trash on the side of the highway. They had an armed guard watch over us all the time. Nancy and I had some good talks. I know she's spent time with mom. I don't plan on being in here long anyway. With good behavior I'll released in a couple of years."

My dad is starting to get cocky. He needs a dose of reality.

"Look, I talked to your attorney about any release. He told me that you may not even get your first parole hearing until five years from now. He also said..."

"Oh, he's just going by what the judge said. That all can change."

"Okay, I just don't want you to get a false sense.."

"Okay okay. Look, I know what I did. I don't need to be reminded. You make sure that Regina doesn't come down here. Or mom. You hear me?"

"They're not. I'll keep you informed with what's going on. I'm putting your utility bills in my name just so the mail comes to my address. Nancy and I will keep up with the house."

"Good. So.. how's married life Mr. Moneyman?"

"I'm not that wealthy. Rosa and I keep busy at work. We go out sometimes on the weekend, nothing fancy, just out to eat."

A guard yells out five more minutes. My dad still has no clue as to how heinous his crimes are. He still doesn't care. I'm not going to argue with him anymore. He will have to face the cold hard fact. You are going to be in here for many more years.

"Okay then, I guess it's time for me to go. I'll keep in touch and keep you in the loop."

"Sounds good. Take care."

With Rosa studying for her masters degree to be a licensed vet, and to perform surgeries on animals, our personal time together has dwindled. I look forward to our nights together. The two of us lying in bed together, our naked bodies wrapped around each other. During the day though, she's locked in her own world. Fine with me. I'm a rising knight of my own.

If I thought my work schedule was flexible, working a few days then a few nights a week plus the mandatory family holiday such as Easter, Rosa's work schedule was all over the place. In one week Rosa worked a few hours in the early morning, several hours in the late afternoon, and an on call emergency on Sunday. There are several times when Rosa will tell me she's coming home around five, but not arrive home until eight thirty. I'll make enough tacos or sloppy joe's for the two of us only to wind up eating all of them because Rosa already ate or she's too tired to eat.

Aw, quit your bitching Randy. At least you and your wife are still fucking at least once a month. You can sneak over to Maury's Tavern with Charles to down a vodka cranberry without Rosa knowing. The orange flavored tic-tacs in the glove department come in handy. John offers me a sous chef position. John will be splitting his time working with Pat and Antonio on a new building project. The rumor going around is Pat, Antonio, and Sharon are developing a plan to build a high end bed and breakfast in the West County area. The hotel is in its busy period and John doesn't want David to get overwhelmed. I'm flattered John asked me. You can pull in twice as much money.

My car and school debts are all paid off. I'm ready to purchase a new vehicle. Stylish cars such as the Lexus are sporty and fun to drive but a brand new 1998 Porsche Boxter lets the schmucks know that you have arrived. It stinks that I was unable to find an automatic. Besides, even if I did accept and spot a drivable Porsche, I still couldn't afford the car.

I politely turned down the sous chef position. The hours were too flexible for me to want. Fred, myself, Derrick, and Les formed an unstoppable four man machine Together we can hammer down a six hundred banquet party in a matter of six hours. We prep fast, serve with precision and exquisite taste, and get the parties to return to the Clarion for their next event. The four of even got our picture taken for the cover of *Food and Drink* magazine. The other chefs either individually or collectively received plenty of media coverage as well.

John holds an emergency meeting with all the line and banquet chefs.

"Listen up, I'm sure you heard that I will be here some of the time and with Pat. We are in the process of owning and managing a b and b. Nothing's been finalized yet, we are in the baby stages. When I'm gone, David is charge. Follow his lead."

David then begins letting us know how the chain of command will be.

"Everything is going to remain status quo. Our focus remains serving quality and delicious food to our guests. All of you will be *required* to turn up the voltage whether John is absent or not. I have no doubts that *together* we will get the job done."

I wasn't aware there were Clarion Hotels located in San Francisco, West Hollywood, Minnesota, and Miami Beach. I would love to intern at the Miami Beach one. I'm hosting an outdoor banquet, staring out at the beach, and blinded by a bevy of gorgeous ladies. Who knows? Maybe one day that dream will come true. In the meantime, I barhop some nights at the Clarion while Rosa is immersed in her job or school. I don't go the bars anymore to try and pick up a chick. I can look and only get so close to one. My impulses are under control-so long as Rosa and I lose control.

Rosa's Party

"Your attention please! I want to propose a toast. To my lovely wife. Rosa, you worked your tail off and studied your tail off. All the hard work has paid off. NOW you are officially a doctor! I'm so proud of you! I love you!"

"Cheeeerrrrrsss!!"

"There's something else. The other day Rosa mentions to be that she is pursuing degrees in agriculture and earth sciences. So another toast to my wife. She is going to be a super genius. Keep on keeping on!"

"Cheeeerrrsss!!"

If Rosa keeps this up, she will in school until she's sixty. I don't understand how the study of dirt and grass evolves into a two hundred thousand dollar a year salary. Nor do I understand how those two fields relate to grabbing a pair of hedge clippers and telling Fido that he's about to lose his wayvos.

What Rosa doesn't know is Daniel, Amelia, and yours truly have planned a surprise party to celebrate her success. I'm happy Karen is here. I also invited my mom to the party. My grandma passed on the invite but did get a money holder and put a twenty dollar bill in it. I gave gift to Rosa earlier. Rosa was moved and called my grandma to thank her. I helped Amelia make empanadas for the occasion.

Daniel invited several of his co- workers over to join the fiesta. I thought that I was doing great financially, but these classified, top secret government computer dorks were raking in some heavy, I mean serious, money. All of them wore custom made or designer polo shirts. A few of them also fancied silk or expensive cotton made short coat along with their shirt. They were the one who drove Hummers or Mercedes. Daniel and one of his work buddies begins to bring out gifts for Rosa. Rosa covers her mouth in astonishment.

"This is for you my love."

Daniel kisses Rosa on the cheek and gives her a large brown box.

"Oh my God, I love it!" She whispers with a choked-up voice.

Daniel and Amelia gave Rosa a brand new computer. Karen played it safe by giving her cash. Her co-workers all pooled some money and gave Rosa a brand new leather coat.

"Thank you so much everyone!"

"Here's my gift."

"Oh thank you!"

Rosa quickly opens the small package. She jumps up and down all excited over my present.

"Oh my. I can buy matching shoes or a new dress."

"What is it?" Amelia asks.

"It's a one hundred dollar gift card to Ultra NuWear. I can never afford anything there. Until now."

Rosa, Daniel, and Amelia huddle together. I look over to see that Karen is gone. As I'm leaving the living room, Daniel yanks me by my shirt and pulls me towards them.

"Amelia and I are so proud of both of you. We love you so much."

All of this sappiness is going to make me throw up my eaten food.

More tears were about to flow.

RRRRIINNG!!!

"Rosa honey, will you please answer the phone?"

"All right."

"OH MY GOD IT'S GINO!"

So Daniel was able to get in touch with Gino to let him in on the good news.

I have no idea what Daniel and his top secret agents are talking about. What the fuck is a DOMINO XRS? All I could offer is the fact that our hotel is getting a new computer system. Actually it's more like an upgrade. I have nothing in common with these robots. They enjoy listening to classical or Flamenco. I give an ear to Ted Nugent's penetrating macho rock or to any hypnotic trance musician. They drink cappuccinos and iced tea. I'm a vodka drinker. Of course I don't tell any these yuppies that I pussify the vodka with cranberry or orange juice. Daniel's friends and colleagues don't have the time to play with women because work is always first priority. I cut out of work five minutes early once a week so I can spend more time with my woman.

Where the hell is Karen? I mom left early and I'm b-o-r-e-d. I'm walking outside as Rosa stops me.

"Hi! Listen, we need to talk later. Between my work and school, and your work, we should think about hiring someone to help with cleaning our house. We can discuss later okay?"

"Sure. I agree."

"Rosa! Come in here!"

I walk outside and see Karen leaning up against the end of the garage. She sees me then quickly puts out a cigarette.

"Don't worry. Your secret is safe with me."

"Oh, they all know. Even Gino smokes."

"You doing okay?"

Karen offers me a smoke.

"No thanks. You smoke, I drink. So are you doing allright?"

"I'm doing well. I guess. I had to get out of there. Daniel's friends were looking at me like I was a piece of meat. Between them and the guy I was with, sometimes it's too much to deal with."

"Bad relationship huh?"

"Not really a relationship. We only dated for a few weeks. He was fitness freak who kept saying I was the only one and he ends up screwing around with his clients. He was also a cheap ass. I kept paying for all the dinners we had."

"Man that sucks. For what it's worth, any guy would be jackpot lucky to have you as a girlfriend. So it's his loss. Fuck him."

Karen laughs at my remark.

"Yeah. Anyway, I think I'm done with men for now. I'm okay being a single woman."

"Well, if you ever want to talk or even hang out, call me."

I didn't realize how soon Karen and I would get together again.

Randy's Party

I received an invitation to my ten year high school reunion. The people putting this together were almost five years late. I already blew off my grade school reunions so there was no good reasons why I needed to attend another one. I had one friend in grade school. Joe. Joe had no friends. I did find it entertaining though to read the updates on my past classmates.

Most of my grade school and high school classmates are married with a wife and at least one kid. Ron and Dale have receding hairlines. I still have a full head of wavy brown hair. Doug and Dale have paunchy bellies. Matty's ears have become so big that he was offered a role as a stunt double in the new holiday elf movie. I've worked out to carve a solid body for my thin frame. The guys used to get in trouble for cutting class or picking a fight. Now they preach righteous to their nerdy kids. The guys have labor jobs like a plumber, janitor, or weed whacker. Want to know who the weed whacker is? Rob. The cool kid from grade school. Sadly, a few of my female classmates passed away. Lynn Gold, Betty Taylor, and Denise Franklin. I wasn't friends with any of the girls but it was still sad to read that so many people died young.

Even though I am not going to my high school reunion, I filled out the card that was mailed to me by one of the ladies putting together the reunion. The card asks for me to write down my current marital and job status. I grab a pen and begin writing on the paper.

I'm married to a smoooookin' hot Hispanic American named Rosa. She's five nine and built solid in all the right places. Her nipples are the color of red velvet. Her pussy juice tastes sweeter than freshly squeezed lemons. We live in a deluxe ranch home complete with a stereo system that comes with a pair of speakers whose deafening sound is guaranteed to cause permanent damage to your ear drums. It's a listening pleasure that I wouldn't give any of you the well, pleasure of. And speaking of pleasure, the hot piece of ass I married (did I mention that I AM married to Rosa) craves sex with the almighty Randall EP Stevens. The EP stands for enormous penis. We have sex in the morning! In the Evening! Hey ain't we got fun! All together naked in sunny or rainy weather! HEY! Ain't we got fun! Futhermore, just to rub it in your noses, I am setting the culinary world on its ass. Look me up at the Clarion Hotel. I'll be the one in the chefs' outfit serving helpings of oxtail and cauliflower to filthy rich ladies. Hey guess what? I've been in magazines and on television. Bet none of you beanbrains can say that. The same ladies who want to pillage me later in the night. I've been a cruise ship and saw so many boobies my eyes are still adjusting. So to the kids who ignored me, picked on me (especially in gym class), and treated me like shit, I say to all of you, fuck off!

Damn, I tossed the card in the mailbox and can't remember if I signed my name. I am a fucking dork.

The main reason I'm not going to my high school reunion is because the date falls on the same day as the Clarion's annual Christmas party. Usually, the party is held at the Clarion. But this time due to construction going on at the hotel, new tiles are being placed in the main hallway, the party is being held at the Westport Renaissance.

Any competition between the two hotels is friendly. We both serve a particular niche location. Ours is central and south while they take care of the north and west. John knows Ken Hall, who is the Renaissance's executive chef. Hell, between the two we can create a monopoly in the hotel business. I'm excited to go this year as I will be finally going with a date.

"This year our Christmas party is at the Renaissance. The one out west. It's on Saturday the 16th."

"Oh no. I'm sorry. I'm filling in for Amber. She's on maternity leave. I will working until eleven. Didn't I tell you? I'm sorry."

I quickly shrug my shoulders. The information wasn't important at that time.

"Maybe you and your friend Charles can go together."

Yeah right, I'm going to ask a guy to the party.

"He's already going with his new girlfriend. It's cool though, I've gone stag before."

"Why don't you call Karen? She's been feeling down lately. She went through a bad breakup. I know she would have fun."

"Good idea. You're always thinking. It would be more fun though if you were there with me."

"I know. But there will be other parties."

I wasn't even sure Karen would go, but I call anyway.

"Hi Karen, its Randy."

"Hi there."

"Reason I'm calling is to ask if you want to go with me to my company Christmas party. It's on Saturday, from five to around ten. Rosa can't go because she's working late."

"Wow. Okay."

"There's food and a drinks. Plus live music. That's after the talking by our president and other bigshots."

"Right. No, that's fine. Is it dress up?"

"No, not really. Most people dress business causal. Some will even wear jeans." I can pick you up."

"Oh, that's nice of you. Okay. Well then I guess I'll see you Saturday."

"Great! I'll see you then."

Karen looks great. She fixed her hair to make it long and straight. She's wearing a pair of tan slacks and a dark blue buttoned down blouse.

"So, this this is your new ride? I like it."

"Thanks. I could afford the Porsche Boxter. So I settled for a CRV. Besides, I like sitting up high. You look great."

The Renaissance has only been around for about five years. Their lobby is dull and uninviting. The dark brown wall to wall carpet needs replacing. You couldn't walk barefoot on the carpet because the snags would cause a toenail to rip off. I didn't see any bar. Here the clientele is more of the fitness-weed juice crowd. They do have a large swimming pool. I think the juice bar is actually located outside in the same area as the pool. Their restaurant is called the Knight's Table. It's more family style than ours. Once a month, the restaurant staff will put on a show complete with kings, queens, jacks, whores, and jesters. I'm kidding about the whores.

Our party at the Renaissance was set up no different than any banquet we set up. Several tables and chairs filled a large squared space. There were two portable open bars at each end of the room. Several Clarion employees were already waiting in line for a drink. All of the booze, served in a paper cup, cost a dollar. Even the bottled water cost a dollar! At least the fountain soda was free.

I'm glad Charles sat at a table away from where Karen and I sat. His table was already filled with his co-workers from the purchasing and shipping departments. Charles would have been too nosy wondering why I came with someone else other than my wife. I sit with Jim Daniels and his wife. Jim is one of the Clarion's computer geeks. Jim is good friends with Dale. Dale is a Clarion security watchman. Dale invited two of his male friends. I didn't know any of them too well so I figured they would not pry into my life. Karen and I kept to ourselves.

"Did you have a good time at Rosa's?"

"Oh sure, I'm so happy Gino called."

"Me too. Gino seems like a good guy. So, Rosa and I went on a cruise. It was great to get away and relax for a few days."

"I'll bet. Rosa told me about the trip. I haven't had a chance to look at all the pictures she took."

"Maybe one day all of us, I mean Rosa's parents, Gino, and you. We can all go somewhere."

"That does sound nice. Who knows? Could happen."

After eating, our general manager Patricia Sutton began talking about how successful the year was. She singled out the marketing department for bringing in new clients. Then one of the personnel ladies, Jane I think, made an announcement for everyone to get on the dance floor. The band begins playing the song Celebration.

Karen and I didn't start to boogie until the band began playing the electric slide. Karen must have moved her body to this music before as she stayed with the beats and moves. Me, I would turn my body a half second before or after everyone else. Karen and I danced to two slow songs. At least then I wouldn't feel like a dipshit on the floor. I also could put my body up close against Karen's. I couldn't get my ass off the dance floor. When the song Obsession began playing, I danced with Karen and one of the female daytime desk clerks. After the song plays, Karen yawns and grabs my arm.

"It's getting late, we should be leaving."

"Okay, I'll call Rosa and let her know I'm taking you home."

As I'm driving back to Karen's, the rain was coming down heavier. The cold wind didn't make driving easy. I could make it home but I'm tired and buzzed.

"Man, the roads are getting slick. I need to find a motel nearby."

"You can crash on my couch here, if you want."

"That would be great. Mind if I use your phone to let Rosa know?"

"Not at all."

Tonight would be the first night Rosa would be home by herself.

"Hi again. The roads are getting slippery. I'm nervous driving at night with the roads getting slick. Karen says I can stay the night here. This is weird for me. Rain is supposed to be done by morning."

"It's okay. I want you to be safe."

"Me too. Make sure the house alarm is on."

"I will. I'm also leaving the living room lamp on."

"Okay. I'll see you in the morning. I love you."

"I love you too."

Karen is already in her bedroom. I yell out thanks again but didn't get a response.

I'm unable to sleep. Shit. The clock next to the TV shows 2:15. My dress slacks are twisted to the right. I tug them to the left then slide off the couch. Her kitchen nightlight is barely flickering. I am on my hands and knees. My shoes, which I took off earlier, are pushed up against the couch. I start crawling on the floor. I pass through the kitchen and stop at her hallway. She only had one bedroom, hers.

My senses tell me that I'm right in front of her bedroom door. I can hear a faint squeaking noise. There's no light coming from her bedroom. Slowly, I push her bedroom door open. Enough so I can fit inside while still on my hands and knees. The squeaking noise gets louder, then soft again. I continue to crawl near her bed. I'm trying hard to get an image of Karen. I know she's in bed. She's the one causing the squeaking noise. My heart is beating so fast. I have to get out of her bedroom now!

The next morning I get dressed, kicking myself for not acting upon my uncontrollable erotic desires. Karen is in her living room drinking a cup of coffee. I wasn't in the mood for any small talk.

"Thanks again for letting me stay. I owe you one."

"Anytime. Tell Rosa I said hi."

I pull into our driveway. I'm hoping Rosa hasn't left for work. Nope. She's in the kitchen drinking hot tea.

"Hi There. The roads are much better. I'm sorry I didn't come home. Were you okay?"

"I'm fine. I'm just happy that you made it home safe. How was the party?"

"I had a good time. Karen and I didn't stay long. To be honest, I could have passed on the party. The food was mediocre at best, the music was all of that party dance music, and my friends didn't show up. I'm off today so I'm going to go to the store. What sounds good for dinner?"

"A hot bowl of chili."

"I'll get the ingredients. I need a shower before I go. Want to join me?"

"Mmmm. That sounds wonderful."

There is nothing better to start my day than with a little sex in the shower activity. I always look forward to the days and nights I spend with Rosa. We continue to make love, even have a little hardcore sex now and then. Sometimes though, when I'm starring into Rosa's hazel eyes, I see Karen's blue eyes.

12

WORLDS APART

I hardly see any of my mom's relatives. I used to get birthday cards, Christmas cards, even graduation cards from all my aunts and uncles. The cards stopped coming sometime after I graduated from college. I was returning the favor but my excuse for stopping was that I was too busy studying or working to even buy a card or call any of them to say hello.

Keeping up with what all of them do is a daunting task. My uncle Brian lives in Seattle with his second wife and their three kids. Two of the kids are his, one son and one daughter, and she has a teenage daughter named Sherry. Sherry received a scholarship to Ohio State University.

My other uncle Ted is still married to my aunt Gloria. Their son is now close to my age. What's the kid's name? I'm drawing a blank. Mom's mentioned that he's been in and out of trouble with the law. My guess is the kid is either selling drugs or stealing cars.

My aunt Stephanie lives in San Diego. She's done well for herself. She works as an airline agent for Omega Airways. The last time she came to visit my mom was three years ago. I still remember the gift she gave my mom. A small ceramic statue of a naked man with a huge dick. I have not seen the statue anywhere in mom's place. My mom needs to find the statue and keep it on top of her living room table. Then when Kate comes over to visit, her mouth can expand wide open in shock.

My aunt Jody and her husband Tom live in Minnesota. They are the blue collar type and can relate to my dad better than anyone. Their kids are all either going to community college or working menial jobs. The last time I saw them was two years ago at Ted and Gloria's place for a Thanksgiving get together. Jody definitely wore the pants in her family. Every ten minutes, Jody would loudly scold her kids for running in Ted and Gloria's house. Then she would chastise Tom for not doing anything about it. Tom just played it all cool like. He pretended to fall asleep in the living room while a football game was on.

My mom told me that Jody and Gloria would be coming over to my mom's place. I was able to twist Rosa's arm in getting her to come with me. My mom opens her door to let us in.

"Hi everyone! Hi Jody. Hi Gloria."

"Hi Randy!"

"Hi, look at you all grown up."

"Everyone, this is my wife Rosa."

"Hi, I'm Jody."

"Hello. It's great to meet you in person. I'm his aunt Gloria."

"Hi, nice to meet you."

"So did you bring any wedding pictures?"

"Oh no, sorry. I'll go through what I have and make some copies. You'll love Rosa's dress. I hear Tim is getting married so congratulations. I can't believe it. Last time I saw him he was this high."

"He's gotten big. He's six feet five and weighs over two hundred pounds and his fiancé is about five feet seven. She's a tiny thing."

"Well, he should have no problem carrying her over any threshold. Heck, he could carry her in one arm and have the case of beer in the other."

Aunt Gloria laughed quietly under her breath. My joke turned out to be more flat than leftover cans of beer. Jody's booming voice cut through the silence.

"So how did you and Randy meet?"

"He saw me at the salon where his mom works."

"Do you work there too?"

"Oh no. I work at a veterinarian clinic. I'm one of the doctors there."

"Oh! Good for you. I have a dear friend who is a plastic surgeon. I should have married him! Ha!"

"So how is Uncle Ted? It's too bad he couldn't come."

After I said those words, Gloria began to tear up. It's at this moment that I wished I kept track of what was going on with my relatives.

"I'm sorry."

"No I'm sorry. Did something happen."

"He had a bout with colon cancer about a year ago. Since then he's been in and out of hospitals."

"Oh man, I'm sorry. I hope he's getting better."

"He is. There's just a lot of stress. He's having a hard time dealing with not being able to work. He was at the engineering plant for a long time. He isn't able to travel as much. He's also on a lot of medications. The meds make him have headaches or diarrhea. Anyway, I'm just grateful he's recovering but it's been a slow process."

"I will definitely say a prayer." I point to my mom who is hugging Gloria.

"You and I need to go to church more often. Have breakfast afterwords. Invite the relatives."

"Okay Randy. When was the last time you went to church?"

"Hmm. Does high school graduation count?"

It's time to change the subject. Then Gloria brings up my dad.

"How's your grandma doing? I heard that your dad got into some trouble involving his work. How is she coping with everything?"

"What happened to your dad?" Jody butts in to ask.

"She's doing fine. Mom, me and Nancy who is a friend of my dad's drive down to check in on her. My dad did go to jail. He got caught stealing from his company and apparently the judge didn't go easy on him. From what I understand, my dad should be out of there soon. He will pay back what he took of course but that's about all."

"He's as bad as Tommy."

"Tom just needs a good straightening out. Let me have him for a week, I'll put him on the right track. And if I can't do it, I know Julie will."

Jody may have been born with big boobs but her manly attitude suggests she prefers pants and a dildo. I had a suspicion as to who Julie was but I wanted to know more.

"I'm sure you could. Who's Julie?"

"My girlfriend. She was in the Army for ten years. She ran a company of fifty men all by herself."

"No kidding. Are you and Tom are no longer together?"

Rosa pokes me in my side. I think she is figuring out what my intention is. Rosa doesn't want me to pry in Jody's personal life.

"Randy!"

"No it's okay. Tom and I mutually agreed to separate. Our kids were old enough to understand. He's met someone else who I actually knew. This all sounds crazy but no one is angry towards one another."

"So how long have you and Julie been together?"

"About three years. She's still in the reserves so I don't see her as much as I like to. When she is on leave we're going to take a vacation in Alaska."

"Sounds fantastic, hook me up."

So Jody is a lesbian. My mom came from a family that has raised with Christian values. I guess Jody slept through religion class. Mom's friend Kate also has lesbian characteristics, you know, the short hair, pants instead of dresses, little makeup on the face, and a beer in hand and cigarette in the mouth. My dad would have a colon burst of his own if he found out or was told that mom began dating again. But with women instead of men.

The sunlight was fading away so I took that as a sign to leave.

"I didn't realize how late it is. I have to go in early tomorrow. Listen, if it's okay with you, I want to talk to some people at the Clarion about fund raising events. Any money raised would go towards helping you and your family out. I know therapy can be expensive."

"Oh, that's sweet of you but we will be fine."

"Okay. It was great seeing everyone. I'll keep in touch."

"Bye everyone. I enjoyed meeting all of you."

Rosa and I exchange hugs with my mom, Gloria, and Jody. Driving home I was eager to get with our marketing department and discuss banquet and hotel events to raise money and help Gloria out. Having fantastic sex with Rosa later that night caused me to forget about asking anyone the next day.

The months went on and the communicating between me and my relatives became less and less. From a card during the major holidays to aw I forgot, I'll send one next time. I never do. No phone calls are made either.

My mind is focused on getting my dad's affairs in order. I'm inside my dad's place sorting out a large pile of mail. I toss out all the car show flyers or advertisements. The smile on my face becomes a frown when I see several letters from lawyers and collection agencies. I begin to make separate piles.

Pile A are the current utility bills.

His electric and gas bills average thirty a month. I still hand write a check and snail mail those out. I need to remind myself to call the cable company and cancel his television service. It's not really a utility, but his damn car insurance is due. Well now it's overdue. His insurance company is yet another place I need to call so I can cancel that service. I also call his other insurance company that he has for his Pontiac. Might as well cancel them out too.

Pile B are his bills for lawyer fees, lawsuits, and other legal shit I need to sort out. He purchased a lot of car related items and paid for them using his credit cards. One of the credit card bills is for three hundred and fifty dollars. I was paying the minimum. I'm done doing that. The interest of two to four dollars a month is starting to add up. One final check to pay the bill off. His other credit card bill is for two thousand dollars. Every month I write a check to Central Bank in the amount of one hundred dollars.

I had to create a new pile C. He had a stack of invoices from companies I never even heard of. Who in the heck is SpeedDemons? Or Your Treasures? All of the invoices had either a due now amount or past due amount. Most of the items were Pontiac car related items. What I can try to do is find the item or items listed on the invoice and return them to the company. Otherwise, I'll have no choice but to pay the amounts using my dad's checking account money. Wait a minute, my dad's name is only on one of these. An invoice from ReadyMade Trophies. The other papers have the name Henry Baker.

The name Henry Baker sounds familiar. Oh yeah, he's the guy who kicked my dad out of a car show. My dad thinks that all these companies and collection agencies are going to go after Henry Baker.

Hey dad, you used YOUR address. I throw out all the invoices except for the trophy one.

Now comes the restitution. The warehouse is suing for damages done to their property. Thirty thousand mother fucking dollars. Where the hell is my dad going to get that kind of money? The house is not in his name. I'm afraid the company or a collection agency will go after the house anyway. What if the company lawyers find out my grandma is the person who owns the house? They may start to send threatening letters to her.

Talking to the public defender about getting any monies lowered has not accomplished much. He being in jail and not having the funds doesn't really matter. Pete's lawyers also sent out a few letters addressed to my dad. They too want money, money for the medical bills Pete has received. Plus, money for the ever popular pain and suffering caused by my dad's actions. So far, the total amount Pete and the warehouse are demanding is one hundred twenty four thousand. That amount will only increase because as one letter duly pointed out *ongoing physical and mental therapy.*

I'm curious. Does Pete's family and their merry band of gypsies think that my dad has an offshore account where he is holding thousands of dollars? My dad was a laborer not a CEO. Maybe Pete thinks my dad can somehow reach inside the bowels of his ass and magically pull out dollar bill after dollar bill.

I'm not about to see my grandma get nervous about receiving a letter from some lowlife collection agency threatening her with a lien warning. How did these devil worshipers even find out where my grandma lived? I'm paying off all my dad's debt. His credit card bill and the money the warehouse is demanding. Drastic times calls for drastic measures.

To say my dad was upset when we spoke on the phone would be the understatement of the decade.

"YOU DID WHAT!! AW YOU DUMB SONOFABITCH! That car was worth at least fifty thousand! Oh my God! Why?!"

"I told you already about the letters. I..."

"Oh, those are just threats! No one is taking over the house. Quit being so naive."

"Don't be so sure. I'm giving my grandma piece of mind. I did what I felt was the right thing to do. I did my research on the Pontiac. I even talked..."

"Aw you don't know shit about cars! I invested a lot of money in that car! And who the fuck do you know?"

"I called a guy named Ken Summers. He's in charge of the Midwest chapter of Pontiac collectors. He gave the names of several people who would be interested in my car. This Ken guy knew what he was talking about. I trusted him."

"Well then you're stupid. And you got fucked. Royally fucked! You're going to end up cleaning me out."

"No, I'm not. I transferred your money into my either my name or another account. You will still have plenty when you get out."

"What are you going to do next? Sell all my mom's stuff! Her car? Why don't you sell the duplex? Make mom sleep out in the streets!"

"You know damn good and well I'm not. I had..."

"Aw I'm getting off the phone!"

CLICK.

I didn't care how mad my dad was at me. The Pontiac was going to remain in the garage for several more years. My dad was responsible for the medical bills accrued by Pete Lawton. My dad also had to pay for extensive damages to a building he ruined. No money was coming in, and maybe I was getting desperate or nervous. I wasn't about to have my grandma's home be placed under any lien.

About a month later, I drive down to see my grandma. She wasn't home when I arrived. Either my mom or Nancy took her to the grocery store. I walk inside my grandma's bedroom. My dad refuses to see my mom or his mom. Instead, all of them communicate by letters. Sometimes, the letters sent to my dad are put inside a birthday or Christmas card. I see a piece of paper folded up on the top of my grandma's dresser drawer. I open the letter and start reading.

Hi Mom!

Greetings from cell block five AKA the big house!

Let me tell you it's been an adventure in here. I was supposed to be going home soon but my attorney and the judge got their signals all mixed up. The communication between those two is poor. My file is all the way at the bottom, Go figure! I've been on my best behavior so that is a big plus. I mind my manners and stay out of trouble. The guards run the prison, not the warden. I haven't even seen the warden. He's probably plying golf with the other prison wardens. When the guards tell you to jump you say how high and when they tell you to piss you say how much. You always respond back with yes sir or no sir!

Most of the time, I stay in the kitchen. I help wash the dishes, pots, and pans. And I mop the floors. We eat a lot of beef stew and chicken noodle soup. There's no Oreo cookies or brownies! I miss your brownies. I'll talk to a guard and see if I can sneak a few in. I also work in the library taking the cart around the cells. Both jobs are paying jobs and I make twenty five cents an hour Whoo hoo! Gets lonely in here sometimes. At night, I just read a newspaper or rest.

Do we have any new neighbors? Randy and Nancy tell me they come down to the house to keep an eye on you. God love them! Tell Randy to keep up with mowing the lawn. I don't want you to go outside and do it. If he can, he could also take the Pontiac out to get an oil change. Or Nancy can. Of wait, I forgot. Randy sold the Pontiac. I wish he would of sold the truck instead. He should of talked to me first. Oh well that's life I guess. I know he's doing what he thinks is right. He's looking out for you. I'm not mad at him anymore.

Well they are about to turn the lights out. I sleep good until the guards wake me up at six in the morning by banging on a trash can. You take care of yourself and I will see you soon.

Love,
Your son,
Rich

I'm still pissed that my dad has an uncaring attitude about the crimes he committed. He still believes that he did nothing wrong. But his letter isn't filled with hate and anger towards me or the rest of the word. Maybe doing hard time in a prison cell is finally teaching him a hard lesson when it comes to treating people with kindness and respect.

Daniel is traveling to Paris for a work related convention. He is allowed to take three people with him. Amelia and Rosa are a given. The last spot comes down to me, Gino, or Karen. Gino is unable to go as he still has military business to attend to-in Hawaii. Karen certainly could use the vacation. Karen is not crazy about flying. She has a fear of rising thousands of feet above the ground. She gets scared thinking about parachuting or a crash landing in the ocean.

I hurry to make adjustments to my work schedule. The Clarion is currently in a rare slow period. The kitchen staff is stocked with enough punctual, driven to succeed employees. When one of us requests time off, the others has his or her back. Rosa has been working too many late nights. Rosa's boss demanded that she take time off. Heck, it's only for one week.

"I'm sorry, but this is like, fucking awesome of your parents to invite us. I'll have to do something really special for them. For their anniversary."

"Randy! Your language. I can't wait to go either."

After a LONG five hour, maybe more and a two hour layover in New York, Rosa, her parents, and myself land at Charles de Gaulle airport. Daniel met with a dapper dressed, older man who was either a co-worker or his boss. Daniel motions for me, his wife, and daughter to come on over to the airport's shuttle service. The bus ride cruises along the winding streets right up to Courtyard Paris Arcueil.

The place reminds me of America's Courtyards. Only ten times fancier. I'm glad to have my leather jacket with me. The hotel could have turned down the AC. Besides, it's only like forty degrees outside. Before we left, I told Rosa that it wasn't right for Daniel to pay for both of us. Daniel received a discount courtesy of his work but that only covered some of the air and hotel cost. After all of us get settled in our rooms, I approach Daniel with a check in my hand.

"Here, you take this. I..Rosa and I want to contribute. Don't argue. It's not much but this will help with the cost of the trip."

The check was written for one thousand dollars.

"Wow, this is very considerate of you both. You are a selfless person. My family loves that about you. Thank you."

I was getting uncomfortable by his weepy behavior. I sure in the shit hoped he was going to hug me or kiss me on the cheek. A handshake would be enough. Of course, he did take the check. Daniel may be my polar opposite, with his no drinking, no smoking, no hidden sexual fantasies, I love my family blah blah blah, but he's generous and says thanks to those who give.

Daniel was unable to spend a lot of time with his family since he was giving company presentations.

"You guys go have fun and see all the sights. I've got my phone with me. I'll call you when I'm finished with my presentations. Then we can all do some sightseeing."

Daniel's meeting with his clients was at the Eiffel Tower. That is not the same as eating boxed Chinese at a cramped office. Rosa, Amelia, and I became tourists. Daniel would meet us later at the Champs Elysses.

The stores and events at Champs wasn't what got my attention. I did some research and discovered Champs Elysses is French for Elysian Fields. Elysian Fields is the name of a music group I enjoy listening to. The band plays a trip hop music style. Jennifer Charles, the lead singer, has a breathy and seductive voice. While walking around, I pick up information on the restaurants in Paris.

One of the restaurants nearby was the Citrus Etoile. Just from the small picture I'm looking at, this eatery makes the Clarion Restaurant look like a hot dog stand. Not that there's anything wrong with being a hot dog vendor.

Daniel meets up with us around noon time as promised.

"Are you ready go shopping and put my credit card in the intensive care unit!" Daniel says as puts his arms around his wife and daughter.

The area is a strip mall for the rich people. I see familiar clothing stores Banana Republic and Ambercrombie and Fitch. Another store is the famous perfume outlet Guerlain. Rosa bought a bottle of perfume from there for Karen. I went back to the Banana Republic and purchased three identical peach long sleeve generic shirts for mom, grandma, and Nancy. I also went inside a store showing a formula one race car on display. Paris is known for the Renault manufacturer. Renault builds formula one race cars. Some useless fact that I felt like sharing. I was unsuccessful finding a guy gift for dad, so I buy another tourist shirt. His is the color blue.

My idea of going to Citrus Etoile was okay with everyone else. Not like they were there before anyway. The fancy restaurant is known for its eclectic mix of California and French inspired dishes. I ordered the blue lobster oyster chicken. I'll give the chefs here credit on this one. The food was unique and delicious. Rosa and her family shared plates of seared red mullet and duck foie gras raviolis.

Foie Gras is expensive and for food, controversial. John told me its duck liver. Your food cost could take a shit if the dish doesn't sell. And you have sensitive animal lovers who are opposed to the harming of a duck. The same ones who cringe when someone orders veal.

Duck. That's a funny word. Even funnier is when you add Daffy or Donald in front of the word. The mood at the dinner table is too peaceful. I need to liven the atmosphere. I'm not an expert on ducks, but here's a joke about ducks that should bring any boring dinner table talk.

A farmer needs money bad because his crops are going bad. He has no choice but to sell his three prized ducks. He tells his three sons to take a duck then go out and sell the duck. About a half hour later, the first son comes running back to the barn. "Hey dad, I got twenty dollars for selling my duck!" "That's great son!" the dad replies back. About an hour later, the second son comes running back to the barn. "Hey pop! I got twenty five dollars for selling my duck!" "That's wonderful son!" the dad replies back. Then the dad gets curious. "I wonder how my other son is doing?"

Well, the third son was have difficulty selling his duck. He stops at a whorehouse then knocks on the door. A female prostitute opens the door. "Say, that's a lovely duck. I'll fuck you for it." She says. The son agrees. As the son was leaving, he felt bad because he had no money and no duck. So he goes back to the whorehouse. DING DONG. The same female prostitute opens the door. "Hi again, I was wondering, can I fuck you for my duck back?" the son says. The prostitute agrees. The son leaves but still feels bad because he only has his duck.

All of the sudden the duck gets loose and darts out in the street. Along comes an eighteen wheeler and runs over the duck. The driver gets out of the vehicle and runs towards the son. "Oh no, I'm so sorry. Here's fifty dollars to pay for your duck. The son walks home. The son's dad sees him and asks "Well, my first son got twenty, and my second son got twenty five. What did you get?" And the son replies back.

"I got a fuck for a duck, a duck for a fuck, and fifty bucks for a fucked up duck!"

After our drinks were poured, white wine for Daniel, red wine for Rosa and Amelia, and a strong Vodka cranberry for Randy, we all raise our glasses for a toast. Daniel's toast was nowhere near as funny as my duck joke.

"Here's to a wonderful time together with my lovely wife, daughter, and son-in law. Too many more dinners and wonderful times together."

Don't get me wrong. I love my new family. But what I crave is in front of my nose. A slice of baked cheesecake with warm ripe cherries smothered all over.

The only other sightseeing Rosa and I did was take in a visit to the Eiffel Tower. I snagged a photo of Rosa standing nearby. So now I can add saw the Eiffel Tower on my personal resume. Later on Daniel and Amelia found us.

"My friends found a golf course. I'm ready to play a round of eighteen."

"Afterwords we can go back to the hotel for dinner."

I didn't know how to play golf. To be honest I was a lousy shot.

"Randy and I were going to walk back to the hotel anyway. You know, be tourists."

"Be careful and have fun."

Once Rosa and I got back to our room, I was eager to have sex.

"Oh, I don't know about this. I know we are in Paris. And it is sooo romantic. But if my mom or dad come back…"

Rosa was nervous about having sex or even making love. She didn't want her parents to be a knockin' on the door while Rosa and I were a rockin' in the bed.

"Okay. We can just have what they call a French quickie."

I made that phrase up at the spur of the moment.

Rosa and I kissed each other's lips. I felt my tongue slide across her tongue. The taste of salt from her buds was intoxicating. She moans softly as I hand slide down her skirt and panties. She's become wet in her genital area.

"No No we have to stop. I'm sorry but my parents."

Fuck. I don't understand. We are married. We should be fucking our brains out until the both of us are unconscious. I don't care if her parents knock. I don't care if they open the door and catch us in the act. They can fuck each other in the other bed next to ours. Then after Rosa and Amelia comes, the ladies can switch off. Who am I kidding? Rosa leaves the room to find the ice machine. I had to go to the bathroom and hurry to jerk off just so I could be completely satisfied.

On the airplane ride back to the states, I read some magazines that has stories and pictures of the French countrysides. Paris is not all fancy hotels and grand scale landmarks. I could see Rosa and myself living in Provence. The farmland is beautiful and serene. I wouldn't mind working in a café. Every morning I would serve bagels, pastries, and coffee to the Paris working man and woman. I turn my head towards Rosa. She rests her head in my shoulder.

Back to reality. Nancy would make a great prison guard. She may not be as physical as the over macho male cyborgs, but she would hold her own. Tough and in your face. Nancy was bringing some of her clothes over. She also had a box filled with books. She's been talking with my dad more than anyone else in my family.

"So how's my dad doing?"

"He's holding up. Ready to come home."

"I guess he's still mad at me for selling the Pontiac?"

"I think he's over that. Ancient history as far as he's concerned."

"Last time I spoke with him, he was still working in the kitchen and library."

"He still is. He's made a friend in Leon. No wait, Cleo. He calls Cleo his main man."

"No kidding. Well I guess it's good to have an ally. I'm surprised though at how well he and this other guy who I'm sure is black are getting along."

"Right. Your dad is not a racist. He just doesn't like lazy people. Their skin color doesn't matter to him."

"So, not to be nosy but are you two going to move in together?"

"Oh, I don't know. He may not be out for several more years. I love my home. I'm not planning on moving any time soon. Your dad and I feel better that someone is here at night a few times to watch your grandma. He wants you to keep coming down too."

"I am very grateful to you for doing that. My grandma is too. I'll start coming down a little more too. How's his demeanor? Does he even bring up what happened?"

"Not to me. It's time for everyone to get past all of this. We all make mistakes. He's paying for his actions. No one is perfect. Anyway, like I said, he's being punished for his crimes."

13
TRAGEDY AND ADVERSITY

A list of situations that would cause me to have a rotten day.

A- If the Clarion cancels a large sit down banquet reservation for any reason. Bad weather. The date interferes with the twenty other appearances that the guests have. Our food delivery got all fucked up. Or even worse, if the hotel would ever file for bankruptcy. We spend so much money on new beds, a new mahogany bar, or a brand new indoor tanning salon. Simply put, the Clarion makes no money, I make no money.

B-Having to shell out a wad of money because our washer, dryer, dishwasher, A/C, fridge, toaster oven, spa, twenty inch color TV, my stereo system with dual cassette recorder and record player, her car, or my car konks out and needs to be replaced. Not fixed, nbut a whole new car. Or if the roof needs repair, or our basement floods, or our privacy fence needs mending, or the automatic garage door opener gets stuck each time I try to open it during a rainstorm.

All of the above shit is expensive and I don't have the cash flow anymore that everyone else thinks I do. Rosa's work place is not making much of a profit. Rosa continues to work not caring anymore if she makes less money. I tried to convince to leave there and work for a successful animal hospital. Rosa was adamant about staying at the cottage.

So now I'm having to pay for most of the utilities. And what the fuck are we paying cable for. We have five hundred channels and neither of us watch any of them. I am not going to keep paying a two hundred dollar cable bill. Rosa got all teary eyed at me when she started talking about the cottage losing money. The poor sheep and chickens and horses face being put down. Aw fuck, so what do I do, write a check for one thousand dollars to help pay for rent. Rosa might as well put an electromagnetic dog collar around my balls.

C-My penis stops working.

I'm proud of my penis. Born as a tiny stud then all grown into a grande mural. It's the perfect size and shape. Stocked full of cum ready to dispose at a moment's notice. I may not have a chiseled body, glistening white teeth, or golden tanned skin, but I'll put my eleven inch cock up against anyone else's. Just kidding of course about actually lining my jewel up against some other guys. Ew. When Rosa's lips are all over my penis, he's a happy one. The terrifying thought of it not working anymore gives me nightmares.

D-Rosa decides she longer wants to have sex. Ever. This scenario relates to my penis fiasco. Call this one D.1-Rosa up and quits her job because she has an epiphany and joins a convent. That means I would have to get rid of all my R rated movies because each one them includes at least one explicit sex scene.

E-Before arriving to work, I step in a large, heaping pile of fresh dogshit. The dogshit must have belonged to a great dane. A tiny dog couldn't possibly have released this much poop. I have no paper towels in my car. I resort to smearing my shoe up and down on our just mowed lawn. When I get to work I continue to scrape my shoe on the Hotel's back parking lot. The bad smell on my shoe stays with me all during work. People are going to think I shit my pants.

F-My record, cassette, and CD collection are ruined. I have several records and cassettes not even available on CD.

G-The Clarion's food and beverage director, along with the banquet planners and clients, change their mind about a particular food item at the LAST MINUTE.

This actually happened. Twice.

The first time was when I helped prepare Crème Brulee. I don't remember the exact number, maybe four hundred dishes worth. Anyway, a few of the guests that were attending the event were allergic to one or more of the ingredients. The chefs, including me, find out about this a half hour before we were going to serve them. Oh shit. Fred, John, Derrick, Paul, Dave, Tony, and me had to moves our asses fast to make and bake three large sheet cakes. Then ask if the sneezing dwarfs were okay with this dessert. The good news though is the entire Clarion staff got to sample our award winning Crème Brulee for a month.

The other time I recall is when the person who planned the menu for us to follow couldn't make it to the event. The person who took that person's place didn't like the Mexican theme. So we had cases of tortilla shells laying around for several months. The replacement person instead insisted on a surf and turf theme. Not only did that cost a lot more but several people who attended the banquet event didn't eat or care for the meal. This was the only time that I can recall where the Clarion failed to make a profit.

H-I wake up to read that ALL sales of booze, condoms, powdered doughnuts, Lollipops, Cheetos, Cheerios, Spree, Mike and Ikes, painkillers, chocolate milk, distribution of bottled breast milk, and canned whip cream are deemed illegal and therefore banned in the United States, Canada, Europe, Japan, Australia, and the island of Bora Bora. However, you can purchase knockoffs of the above products for a bargain price in the great land of Bangkok.

I-Rosa says hell no to letting me own a Jackhammer, sledgehammer, pet alligator, python, cougar, indoor swimming pool with a volleyball net and ten foot tall slide, machine gun, army tank, gentlemen's club, casino, thirty six sports channel package including the all new twenty four hour female tennis channel called FTP24, or a weenie cart-filled with smoked and grilled weiners.

All of the above situations would put a damper on my day. But I would deal with the situations and adapt. I can accept change. It is vital to keep a sense of humor because I'm about to learn the hard way that my family, mine and Rosa's, are about to deal with some serious shit.

The greedy old man who calls himself mom's landlord is nothing more than a lying, conniving, bullish thug. First, he jacks up mom's rent another one hundred dollars. He doesn't even have the balls to tell my mom face to face. Instead, she gets a letter from a company named Benton Properties. I checked with the better business bureau to see if this company was legitimate. They are. But that doesn't mean you can just shoot up people's rent whenever you feel like it.

I did some research on Benton Properties. Seems they have a history of taking ownership of low grade flats or apartments. Their plan is to promise prospective renters a safe and sound place to live in. The ads say low rent or peaceful area, shit like that. Then these vultures legally spike the rent cost just so the slumlords can spend the money received on blow. Now mom owes four hundred a month. She can barely scrape up the amount she owes now.

Before I went inside, I looked around the outside of mom's home. I don't see any improvements made on the building since she moved in. Tuckpointing needs to be done on her front steps. The second front step is crumbling apart. Her front screen door needs replacing. I can stick my middle finger inside the screen hole. Both of her bushes out front could use some trimming. The bush in front of her window obscures mom from seeing anything outside. I'll bring over my pair of bush trimmers the next time I visit her. I go back inside and lay into my mom as to what she knows about anyone fixing up her place and why she's in the hole.

"So what's with this asshole of a landlord of yours? He raised your rent but does nothing to fix up the place."

"I know I know. Jesse says he's getting on it. He needs the money to buy the supplies. He's struggling with money too."

"Who gives a fuck? I don't. You and Kate are shelling out twelve hundred a month. I've seen this guy before. He dresses like a pimp. He drives a Cadillac. The car has those retarded looking silver plated hubcaps. He plays that putrid hip hop. Believe me, he's loaded. You need to talk to him. Or I will."

"No No No please don't. Kate and Hank takes care of the lawn. And we don't pay for the trash, Jesse does."

"What about the guardrail and your one step? It's not safe. It's all busted up."

"That happened when a kid ran into it with his bike. Jesse knows all about it. He's working on having that fixed. I don't know what Jesse's going to do about the step. It's not that bad."

"Well he needs to hurry up. Is your air conditioner working? You need central air in this place."

"I've managed this long and I'm doing fine. Mine works. Besides I like using the fans. They're cheaper and blow plenty of cool air. I also have heaters in the winter time."

"Even so, I would be much more at ease if you packed up and moved into a better home and a better location."

"Randy, I'm not going anywhere. I've got Kate and Hank and Joan next door. We all get along and don't want to be spending money on movers."

"Okay, But I know you still have a pile of medical bills. I also see that you take several pills. I don't want you to have to stop or even cut down on your medication. I'm making great money. So like it or not, I'm helping you out financially. Here. Just do me a favor and don't tell anyone including your neighbors. I'm not there yet trusting everyone."

"Sigh. Kate and Hank don't get in any kind of trouble. They're good people. I won't say a word about what you are doing. I'm very thankful but it's not necessary."

"It's very necessary. Now you have a month's worth of breathing room."

My mom is being stubborn. She accepted the four hundred dollars that I gave to her but she refuses to move out. A few days later I read in our local newspaper about a fatal shooting that happened in her neighborhood. For the first time in my life, I was scared. I immediately call mom to find out what happened.

"Mom, I just read about a shooting that happened on your block! NOW will you think about moving out?"

"Randy, the shooting happened at the end of my block. I wasn't anywhere nearby. Kate told me that the police caught the person who fired the gun. Stop worrying okay."

"As long as there are gangs and drugs and thieves, and niggers living in your area. I worry. What if one of those bullets hit your window? I know Kate and her manly boyfriend are around, but not twenty four seven. Your area is becoming a crime riddled unsafe area."

"Oh stop it. You sound just like your dad. Not everyone who lives around here is a bad person. I make sure to be careful. I'm not moving anywhere."

"Fine. But I'm not giving up on this. Take care of yourself."

"You too."

Mom may be stubborn but at least she stands up for herself.

My grandma also chooses to live alone and stay put. She's not really alone. Nancy and I, even Rosa stop by to visit a few times each month. At least grandma is in a safer area. Many times when I drive down, I'll see her talking to her next door neighbor. Both of them are usually standing on her front porch. Her next door neighbor is another petite woman who needs to make sure she is protected.

The young girls I remember from the neighborhood are now mature ladies with kids of their own. Sometimes, I'll see one of them visit their mom and dad. At least the kids were smart enough to move away. The older couples who were living around here have either moved into nursing homes or passed away. Times have changed as a gay male couple has moved into the house three doors down from my grandma.

My grandma's mind is still sharp. She knows my name, birthday, wife's name, and consistently tells me to get my hair cut. Her eyesight is slowly getting worse and arthritis has kicked into high gear. She's accepted the fact that either Nancy or I now take her to the doctor or run errands for her. She wants to go go go but sadly her body says halt. She refuses though to sit around. She is always wiping down a piece of furniture of folding and refolding clothes and sheets.

"Since there's no way I can bring your washer and dryer up here and re- hook them, I'll make sure to help with your laundry. Don't you try walking down the stairs."

"Oh honey, it hurts my legs too much to do so. Nancy takes care of the laundry. I can still fold the clothes and bedsheets. None of you do a good job of folding them anyway.

"What about driving?"

"I think my driving days are about over. I will not drive at night anymore. I have a hard time seeing the lines. Claire still comes by and when she does we go the store together."

"Oh yeah, I remember her from down the block. How is she?"

"Good. She has her aches and pains too. Her son recently got married."

"Who, Darren? No kidding. I remember when he was a little snot."

"Not any more. He's a fine young man. He has a good job with the Post office."

"Good for him. Look, I know you can take care of yourself. I just want to make sure you're being careful."

"I am. Have you visited your father?"

"It's been a long time since I've seen him in person. We still write back and forth though. There's been no big changes or news to share. For a guy with little or no patience, he's hung in there."

"I'm glad. I miss him."

"Well pretty soon he will up for parole. I believe he will be released soon afterwards. No one has said anything differently to me. When he does come home the two of you will have all the time in the world to catch up."

What is it with these ladies who can't see that moving into a place with better amenities will make their lives less stressful? Not to mention mine?

My mom and grandma's health and well-being are on my mind all the time. I never saw this one coming though. A sudden, tragic, and heartbreaking loss. Rosa and Karen were huddled together on the couch.

"What's wrong?"

"Daniel passed away last night." Karen quietly tells me while consoling Rosa.

"Oh no. God. I.. I'm sorry." I give Rosa a meek hug.

"A heart attack took his life away." Karen pointed out.

Daniel didn't have any medical conditions that I knew of. He wasn't the workout freak but stayed active by travelling and keeping his brain intact by working on complex computer hardware problems. He was only fifty five years old. I wonder if his side of the family has heart related problems. I hope Rosa goes to her doctor for a checkup.

I should see a doctor myself. I haven't had a check -up since, well, never. Nah, I'm too busy creating innovative and delicious food at work. One of my latest creations is a puff pastry filled with sweet corn, bulgur, and a semi-sweet glaze. Besides, all the doctor is going to do is lecture me on why I should stop drinking (which I only do when Rosa and her family are not around) and being so hyperkinetic. It's not my fault painkillers and aspirin have become my favorite candies. My own blood and all their problems or goings-on is why I have way too much unwanted stress.

Where are my manners? Rosa's dad passed way. I spread the news to John, Fred, Albert and the rest of my kitchen workers.

"Hey guys, Rosa's father passed away. I'm going need a day or two for funeral leave."

"You take all the time you need." John says comforting me.

"Thanks Chef. Once I get the wake and funeral information. I'll call you."

Not only did John, Fred, Dave, Derrick, Paul, Tony, and Albert pay their respects at the wake, so did several of the banquet and restaurant servers. I walk over towards Albert.

"Thanks for showing up. Means a lot to me and to Rosa."

"My brother, we are all one big family. You just never know when the good Lord is going to reach down for you."

"Rosa honey, you remember Albert? My friend and co-worker from the hotel?"

"Yes. Randy has some great friends. Is that Derrick?"

"Yes Ma'am. He's the one who headed up our department's wreath."

"It's a beautiful display. Hi Derrick. Thank you so much."

"Your welcome. I wish we were all here under happier circumstances. I lost my parents at a young age too. I know they are all now in a better place."

Several of Daniel's relatives, near and distant, his co-workers, and friends all show up at the funeral parlor and funeral mass. I walk up to Amelia and embrace her.

"God, I'm so sorry. I wish I got to know him a lot better. He sure treated me well."

"Thank you. He really liked you Randy."

I also find and embrace Karen and Gino.

"Hi Karen. Hi Gino. I'm sorry for your loss."

"Thank you my friend. We all think of you as a member of our family. How are you holding up? Rosa's told me that your dad is in prison. I'm sorry to hear about that."

Gino showed me that he was not a selfish person. His dad just died and he's asking me about mine.

"I'm doing good. He's learning his lesson. To be honest, I don't think about it all that much. He's doing what he's told to do and seems like he's going to come out of this a better person. I stay focused on keeping an eye out on the family and still making time to be with Rosa."

"Stay in touch with your dad. The good times and the bad. Family is most important."

Rosa is kneeling on a small pew in front of the casket. I'm uneasy walking up to the casket. Plus I want to give Rosa alone time with her dad. Rosa looks up at me. I kneel beside her and start praying with her.

You would think Daniel was a former president of the United States or an A-list Hollywood actor. All of the church pews were filled in with men, women, and children who all knew Daniel at some point in his life. His co-workers, former co-workers, co-workers families, a local politician that Daniel was recently hobnobbing with. Amelia is the most selfless, caring person I know. Breaks my heart to see her and Rosa in tears.

Gino flew in from the Hawaiian Islands. His wreath of pink and red carnations had to be twice as large as the one my work sent. I think He made it a point to make sure that he and his military group sent the largest bunch of flower arrangements. Gino was also the one who insisted on having a full funeral mass. I think he went overboard with the proceedings. A ten piece choir was flown in from Daniel's hometown. Was it really necessary to sing Amazing Grace in Spanish? Which by the way is Sublime Garcia. That name sounds like a punky skateboarding rock band.

My choice of music would have been Elton John's song Daniel. I'm sure my song choice would have brought the house down. If I had the bucks to spend, I would have even fly in the piano wiz himself. I would request he dress the same way he did during his kinky 1970s pinball wizard days. If he's not up for vocalizing, I suppose I could lend my voice. I would make a bold attempt to get my voice up there real high during the part when I sing about Daniel being my older brother and scars not healing.

In addition to the live music, fourteen of Daniel's family members, not counting his now widow and daughter, spoke for about fifteen minutes each at the podium. I swear one of the guys talking needed a tranquilizer shot. Every five minutes she would shout out *Oh praise Daniel!* or *Our brother Daniel is now returning home!* When he blew his nose, he forgot to turn the microphone away. I thought a ship at sea was going to crash through the church windows.

Even my mom and Kate attended his funeral. I gave both of them the news but didn't expect either one to show up. They sat behind Gino. After the three hour (I kid you not) service was over, everyone gathered in the lobby for Coffee and Danishes. Those Danish setting out were made from scratch thanks to me, Dave, Paul, and Tony.

I meet up with Rosa and walk with her. We stroll into a hallway and stop at the back exit.

"I'm sorry. I guess I wasn't paying attention to where I ended up. So, whatever you need and wherever you need to be, you just name it or be where you need to be. And anything, you just name it, that you or Amelia and even Karen needs from me, just say it. I'm here for you. I love you."

"Hey it's okay. We'll get through this."

"Thank you. I love you too."

I was hoping to say goodbye to Amelia, Karen, and Gino. They were lost in the sea of mourning strangers. When Rosa and I get back home, I listen to the several phone messages. Most of them are from people who were unable to attend the wake or funeral and were sending us their condolences. One of the messages was from Wes Stanley. He's the head maintenance technician at the Clarion.

"Rosa. Rosa honey, you are not going to believe this but we had a power outage at the hotel. I'm being asked to come in and help restore our perishable food items. Seems that no one can get a hold of John or the other chefs."

"Will you be gone long?"

"I hope not. Man, I hate to see all the food go bad though."

"I understand."

"Trust me, I'll be back here soon".

I needed to get away for a short time. The Clarion's bar should still be open by the time I arrive. There better NOT be a power outage.

My dad has to be getting cabin fever. Or in his case, prison fever. When I do talk to him on the telephone, he sounds calm, almost content-like about being there. Prison is his home and life is being good to him. My dad and his new fast friend Cleo are now running the kitchen. I never would have imagined my dad learning baking skills from an older black man who happens to be serving two life sentences for murder.

From what my dad tells me, night time is a desolate time. My dad has lost weight. He's not fragile or pale, he's skinnier though. His eyes appear to be bloodshot and not from booze.

"Randy, you have no idea how tiresome it gets staying in here. Every day is the same day over and over. I get up, eat, sometimes shower, work in the kitchen, and go back to cell for a long time. Sometimes, there are days where I just want to end it all."

"I spoke with your new parole officer. He says when your parole comes up, you should have no problem with an early release. I'll even talk to the judge if you want. Remind him of the work you've been doing in here and that you stayed out any trouble."

"No, don't. Besides, I'm sure he knows. All I can do is wait."

"Trust me, these last few years will fly by. In the meantime Nancy has sort of moved in your place. She didn't move any of her large stuff but clothes and other smaller stuff. Sometimes I think she even spends the night. Between her and me, we are still coming down."

"How's mom?"

"Still gets around at home. She was talking about selling her car. She hasn't driven for a long time."

"I'd keep it for now. Is the insurance due soon?"

"Hmmm, I'll check. If it is coming up I can always take care of that. Maybe go year by year. I never thought about even driving her car."

"Does she even talk about me?"

"Oh sure. She figures you're doing everything you can to survive and get out. She's confident that you'll be released sooner than later. We all are."

"That's what keeps me going. Hey, does Rose and her family know about what I did or where I'm at?"

"I gave them the fast lane version. Told them that you got angry about getting laid off. I said you did some damage, got caught, and had a judge who went overboard in his decision. They are aware that you're in jail but I didn't tell for long. They were all shocked of course but Daniel understood where you were coming from. No one is treating me differently and I haven't said a word to anyone at my work. It's none of their business anyway. Oh, just so you know, Rosa's dad passed away. By the way, I haven't seen any more mail from any lawyers. It's been over a year."

"Good."

"Rosa and her family don't need to know everything that went down."

"Good man. Well, I can hear Jake or Butch all the way down the hall. One of them comes in to let us know visiting hours are up."

"All right. I'll keep in touch."

"Sounds good."

I slipped in the news about Daniel at the last minute. I don't think my dad was paying attention to what I said. I'm glad because I didn't want the subject of death to cause my dad to get any suicidal thoughts.

The Clarion's band of merry new management has enforced a brand new health and safety policy. Now all Clarion employees are required get annual physicals. What ticks me off is that the same management are a group of cheap asses who will not flip the bill. Our insurance is supposed to cover the exam at one hundred percent. That is, after you pay a two hundred dollar deductible owed to the insurance company.

My first rule when picking out a doctor is the doctor must be a female. There is no way any guy is putting his cold, clammy hands all over my body. And I sure in the heck am not showing my butt, balls, and cock to him. The scour the pages of my doctor manual searching for a general practitioner near my home.

Rebecca M. Stelvanik M.D. So…she's a Russian doctor? I call her office to schedule an appointment.

Before I meet the Bolshevik in person, her nurse gives me a once over. Sort of like having an oil, lube, and filter prior to replacing the engine. I can't begin to describe the pleasure of having a stick shoved down my throat, a piece of medical equipment pushed in my ear, the blood pressure arm thing squeezing left arm so hard that my arm loses all feeling for ten minutes, and best of all, her warm hand caressing my stomach. She good nurse leaves, and after waiting fifteen minutes in the exam room, my Russian caretaker comes in.

"Hello. Mr..Steven."

Dr. Stelvanik may have a Russian name but her accent is closer to Bosnian.

"Hi there, pleased to meet you."

"Tell me all about you. What is it that you do? What your family does?"

"Cut right to the chase. Okay. I'm a chef at the Clarion hotel. Been there for about fifteen years now. I've been married for about nine years. My wife is a doctor too. She treats animals."

"Wonderful. Are your parents still living?"

"Yes, my grandma too."

"How are they?"

"Fine I guess. I still see my mom often. She and a friend still visit my grandma. My grandma has trouble getting around. Old age I guess."

"What about your father?"

"He's busy with his own life. I don't see him too much."

"Sounds like your parents are divorced. Does that bother you?"

"Not at all. They split when I was graduating from grade school. I was too busy with grades and working to really think about what and why they split up. Like I said, I still see both of them now when I can."

"You work a lot of hours and still make the time to see your family."

"Yeah."

"Married or single?"

"Married to a wonderful woman named Rosa."

"Kids?"

"No, we both agree that our careers are just too important right now. Rosa's father recently passed. It was sudden too, so we're all still in a little bit of shock."

"I am so sorry to hear."

"So, how am I health wise?"

"You are in great health but your blood pressure is much higher than it should be. You are stressed. Are you always stressed?"

"I don't think so. Work can be fast paced. The hotel has gone through a complete change in bosses. It's too early to tell if the new bosses are going to make the hotel an even bigger success or drive the hotel six feet under."

"You seem tense. Do you not like these bosses you speak of?"

"They come from a different era than I do. But I'm confident that I can adapt."

"Good for you. Change can be scary but you have to search for the positive."

Right. I see a general health doctor and wind up with a shrink. She only needs to know what I tell her. Even if my mood was better, I still would not talk about prison or death to her.

"I know your work is important but I hope you and your wife make time to be together. You must also find time for yourself. You are a young man. Savor all your moments and find peace."

"Yeah, we do. We've been on a few trips already."

"Wonderful. I want to do some blood work. Just for test purposes."

"You mean a urine sample?"

"It's the only way."

"Okay. That shouldn't be a problem. I drank a half gallon of fruit juice before I came here. So other than relaxing more, I'm in great shape."

"During the day I want you to find a place where only you go to. Stay there and take deep breaths. Do this for twenty minutes a day."

Good idea. Maybe on my lunch break, I can make a quick stop at the nude girls bar.

The economy has had its up and downs. People would rather have parties at smaller, more cost efficient coffeehouses. One way the Clarion is saving money is by partnering with a temp agency. I would guess ninety percent of the temp workers are our banquet servers.

Many of the past hotel banquet servers have left to work elsewhere. After Joann left, Mike followed suit. He got a job as a purchasing representative working for a small country club. His position was never filled. Instead, John, Fred, or I call in the orders. Albert would be the guy who filled orders or stocked deliveries. But Albert is also leaving.

"Is it true that you found other work?"

"I have to go where the money is. I haven't had a decent raise here in five years."

"Yeah that's bullshit. You know how to cook right?"

"Yeah. My fiancé and I are think about moving to New Orleans. She works as a caterer. We may even start our own business."

"Awesome. Well Good luck. Thanks for showing me the way."

"Peace my brother."

Dave, Paul, Les, Tony, and Derrick have also expressed their displeasure of working in the kitchen. Inane scheduling, piss poor raises, and a lack of three hundred money making banquets have been contributing factors.

There were no teary goodbyes at the Clarion. Most of the time, you didn't even know the person had left.

Some weeks the banquet hall and kitchen is a ghost town. Once or twice in a month the hotel would host a banquet for one hundred people. We haven't had a party for over one hundred in almost a year. Lucky for me, my rounded experience as both a line chef and a banquet chef works in my favor. I can fill in the gaps when a cook goes on vacation or calls in sick.

Adding to my stress, I went into John's office to hand him some updated menus. A list of current banquet servers was hanging on his bulletin board. I see the name Kaylin Lawton. I forgot that Pete Lawton had two daughters. So Kaylin is all grown up. Kaylin would have been too young to really understand what happened to her family. She shouldn't recognize me. I don't know what her dad looks like, so I can't pick her out. Just play it smooth Randy. Kaylin doesn't know you.

I had to drive by the warehouse where my dad used to work. I made a few phone calls before, but never got an answer. Now I know why. The building is closed down. A for lease sign is out in front by the gate. The smell of burning ashes is still present. No one wanted to make any repairs. Several innocent people lost their jobs. I'm surprised that my dad didn't get sued by all his fellow workers. My dad will always be at fault. Remember what the doc said, I'm not about to let all of my dad's crimes stress me out. It's my dad's problem to deal with.

Charles and I are leaving the Rosemont Amphitheater. Hard rocker Eric Anderson still blows a new hole in my ass every time I hear him live. My fingers ache from hours of air guitar. My neck has a vicious kink from countless sudden jerks to the left and right. Charles and I had terrific seats. Row five. Dead center. The two twenty something girls in front of us couldn't stop shaking their tight, sweet little asses all night.

I had asked Rosa and Karen to come along. Karen already made plans with a girlfriend of hers. Karen and I will get together at a later date. Rosa is still mourning over the loss of her father. She's been staying with her mom. Not all the time though. I'm having a hard time getting Rosa to join me at my stress free place.

Back to the concert-sure the tickets were fucking expensive. Forty bucks a ticket. AND I had to pay seven more bucks to park. AND I got stuck buying Charles a five dollar bottle of beer. AND I had to put gas in my vehicle otherwise Charles and I were going nowhere. Charles' excuse was that he didn't get paid until NEXT week.

Charles and I had to get away to blow off steam. You already know why I do.

"So how's the new job coming?"

"It's work. That's all I can say. If it wasn't for that lying piece of shit Russell, I would still be at the Clarion."

"Yeah, I'm sorry to hear you got fired. I heard you and Russell got into a fight over you calling him the n word."

"Dude, he attacked me first with a knife. He was in cahoots with the new management. They were wanting to squeeze me out all along. And that stupid bitch Jane believed every lie told to her."

"Well for what it's worth, Russell is no longer at the Clarion either. He can join those other two retards at the unemployment line."

"You think I care. Russell can rot in hell. I hope the KKK finds him then lynches him by his fucking balls. Then they can set the bastard on fire."

I'm sure glad no black people are around us to hear any words that Charles are spitting out. I quickly inject positive vibes in the conversation.

"We have worked with your company before. Bolo Solutions? You may even get a call from me one day."

"Dude. Whatever. Just call."

"Anytime. I'll make you a busy and rich man."

Once I get home from drinking with Charles, I call Rosa to see how she is holding up. Once again, I end up talking to her mom.

"Oh, hi Amelia. How are you doing?"

"Better. Thank you for asking. I worry about my Rosa. She's still broken up."

Amelia tries to keep talking but starts to cry instead.

"Hey, I'm really glad I got to see Gino. I know I'll see him again this time under happier circumstances."

"He may be coming home for good. His time is coming to an end. He wants to come home and take all of us to Alaska."

"That's great. I already told Rosa this, but I want her to stay with you as long as she needs to be. And if you or Rosa or even Karen and Gino need anything at all from me, don't hesitate to ask."

"That's so sweet of you. We will get together soon. Oh, I forgot, thank you for the flowers."

"Your welcome. Take care."

There is a silver light shining in my personal universe with Rosa not circling around. I can watch bloody violence or softcore romance films any time and not get a lecture from Rosa. Rosa doesn't believe in white lies, or bending life's rules. I can spread myself out on the king size bed and not sleep vampire style. Damn. Our home is too quiet. Eerie. No wind blowing, only an uncomfortable still. I'm at my resting place.

14
CLUB CYN

The taverns, bars, and nightclubs are all becoming slim pickings. Let me share with you my history with the bars, taverns, saloons, and nightspots I have visited. You will see that once was a town flourishing with places to drink and be merry has become a ghostland where you drink one drink and never return.

I was visiting the Clarion's hotel bar even before I was deemed legal to mix vodka with my orange juice. The bartenders wouldn't risk serving me any alcoholic beverage even though I was more mature than most of the twenty year old yuppies who would frequent the place. On Sunday nights a stuffy old man would play a guitar. Sometimes he performed solo and other times a woman would accompany him. The lady had to be close to sixty but hid behind her old age with layers of make- up.

Maury's used to be the place where blue collar and white collar workers (besides me and Charles) went after work to vent against their inept colleagues. Now, all I see in there are college kids who talk about what's new in the digital world. Someone puts in five dollars' worth of music in the digital jukebox. After three songs by bland top forty artists I never even heard of, I throw a dollar bill on the counter and walk out.

Then I tried Ozman's. Ozman's isn't really a bar. It's a restaurant serving pub-style food such as loaded potato skins and greasy cheeseburgers. Just because you have a huge C or U shaped table in the center of the place, alcoholic beverages behind the c or u, stools surrounding the table, and an employee called the bartender doesn't make you an official bar.

Ozman's won't allow you to smoke inside either. Who in the hell came up with this ridiculous policy? What do you do when you go to a bar? You smoke, drink, and pick up chicks. The woman fixing my vodka cranberry didn't know to properly mix the ingredients. I've had orange juice that tasted stronger than the purple piss I was served.

Another unofficial new bar policy is too watch your language. Since these places have eating areas, kids are welcome in. So when I'm at the bar and the strange drunk next to me asks me *why do you like vodka cranberries so much* and I reply back with *because they taste like a teenage girls cum* I have to endure the wrath of an angry woman who roars out *Hey I have children here! Watch your mouth! Where's the manager!* The woman's all bent of shape probably because her own cum tastes like rusty hosewater.

The one tavern in South St. Louis that did allow, and still does, is the Melrose Club. There is no jukebox or piped in music. The Melrose Club is where you smoke, drink, and have meaningless conversations about life with the bartender and the stranger sitting next to you.

When I moved from the city to out west one of the first clubs I went to was America's Hub. This place was packed on the weekends as soon to be female newlyweds would come here with fifty of her uptight female friends to drink a lot of beer and dance with horny black breakdancers. The hub may have made dollars on Fridays and Saturdays but during the rest of the week, the Hub was dead. A few college kids would stop in for a beer or two. The hub's lack of business and money forced the owners to close down.

As long as I don't arrive home plastered off my ass, Rosa is okay with me frequenting the bars. She still would rather stay at home watching television or playing games on her computer. Sometimes she will take her mom out to visit a flea market. I'm hoping Rosa and I will have sex again soon. Cuddling is nice once in a while but let's get naked and fuck each other.

There's no other bar or club near our home that I care to visit. Many of them are hole in the walls that cater to biker dudes, roughnecks, or shady government officials who are using the bar as a front for their bribery and racketeering crimes.

The good nightclubs Mississippi Nights and Velvet have been replaced by lofts. Both located in the city, Mississippi Nights featured top Rock acts from all rock genres. Velvet was the place to be to hear pulsating dance music. And no top forty mixes thank God! The lofts were the brainchild of city officials, politicians, and business developers. They all misread the stats stating that club activity attracts crime. Oh, but the lofts were a better idea. Building these lofts attracted welfare collecting, piss poor minorities who take advantage of the cheap cost living. The dreck living in these units would show disrespect by trashing their place, scribbling graffiti on the walls, and throwing glass bottles out in the streets.

Club Cyn has only been open for eight months. It is nestled in West County where no homes are within a mile. A busy gas station and convenience store are across the street. The main highway access is to the right. I love the location. You don't have to worry about getting lost in any area that you are not familiar with.

I heard a rumor that Club Cyn has a wicked cover charge of twenty dollars. Might as well pillage the villagers if you can get away with it. Their hours of operation are Tuesday through Thursday nine PM to three AM and Friday and Saturday it's ten PM to four AM. The prime times for the late night breed of humans to release their energy.

During the week, Club Cyn is a cocktail lounge. Thirty and forty year olds who are desperate to hang on to their youth take a twirl on the dancefloor while listening to calypso and salsa music spun by a disc jockey. You can even take Calypso and salsa dance lessons very other Monday from seven to eight pm. The music will vary from euro disco to nineties dance artists like Culture Beat. Sometimes, Club Cyn will have a theme night. So far, there was polyester night, funk you night, and ya man night.

I'm waiting for Key Party night. A key party is a couples' only invitation. The men drop their house keys in a basket placed inside the front lobby. As the party winds down, your libido running wild, the ladies begin to randomly pick out keys from the basket. The guy who owns that set of keys is who the lady will be leaving the club with. The goal is for the two strangers to end up having meaningless sex with each other.

I have another stellar idea for Club Cyn promotions. Temptation Night. Here, a lucky man (or woman, I guess) has the chance to win a million dollars. All he (or she) has to do is resist sexual temptation with ten people. If he or she fails, they endure public embarrassment by the cub owners, staff, and patrons. If the willing participant succeeds, he or she will have their life changed forever. Not to mention the fact they have supreme willpower. Club Cyn already has a private room with bed included for the two (or more) to use. Rick and Barry will serve as the game show hosts. Angelina and I will be in charge of setting up the meets.

You think temptation is easy to play?

Guess again.

First contestant: the guy is a happily married man. He needs to get away from his wife for one night. His weakness is young girls. So, the game host (in this case the club owners) makes sure that any of the ladies who approach him start younger and keep going until the girls are under legal age. In addition to the cherrystainers, you could also find a contestant who is a frail man struggling whether or not he craves the men or the women. Toss a few queers his way and watch with evil satisfaction as the fragile minded guy caves in to his weakness.

Temptation is the kind of televised show our society needs. Enough with the bad karaoke shows, lame song, dance, and talk shows. Escaping the real world by delving into superheroes and crime solving is nice once in a while but sometimes you have to go to the place where your darkest secrets are exposed to the marshmallows of the world. Give them something they can really talk about in front of the water jugs.

Club Cyn doesn't advertise a dress code. On the weekdays, the dress is more casual. A person should never wear blue jeans to a nightclub but some do anyway. But on Friday and Saturday, the jeans stay at home. The sign on the window says *dress to impress.* That means, no sneakers, torn pants, camouflage pants, parachute pants, or T-shirts. Sweatshirts or sweatpants of any kind are verboten.

I get a kick out of watching the doormen turn away boys who violate this simple policy.

"I don't care how much money you have! The sign says dress to impress. I wouldn't let my own daddy in here if he was wearing goofy argyle pants and a drabby looking sweater. Go home and change! And you! You back there! This isn't a country western club! No cowboy boots are allowed!"

The women never have anything to worry about. Their weapons of choice for a night out are tight black mini-skirts with matching colored shoes. The owners give ladies leeway because the ladies show cleavage which attracts the men, who keep paying for the drinks.

John and I know the club's owners. Rick Monetti and Barry Carter.

Each of them hosted a small scale event at the Clarion. Rick, a pure New Yorker who migrated down south in the late 1980's was the key note speaker at his own seminar *Seize Time.* He handed me one of the brochures. He and his wife Angelina host motivation workshops emphasizing how to spot an opportunity and successfully take charge, be it education, work, or starting a business.

Barry, whose real first name is Barcino, was born in Italy. He used to work in the fashion industry. He still has powerful connections in the fashion world. He helped plan a designer show held at the Clarion. The event was even televised on a national cable channel. I'm surprised Barry left the glamourous world of fashion to become an owner of a nightclub.

Both Rick and Barry live by the code dress to impress. Their wardrobe consists of pressed, collared shirts, sport jackets with diamond cufflinks, navy blue or midnight black dress slacks with matching shoes and socks. The first time I saw Angelina, my dick got hard immediately. She is a smoking hot devil sporting a cotton white mini. God, her ass is so wrapped tight in that dress, it takes all my willpower and then some not to reach out with my hands and give those perfect ass cheeks of hers a full squeeze. Rick and Barry also both drive slick sports cars. Rick owns a silver Porsche. Barry cruises the night in his yellow Lamborgini. I can only imagine what each of their homes look like.

It should come as no surprise that the food served for both of their events at the hotel were high dollar. For Rick, he and his guests sampled on trays of pork tenderloin sliders and spring rolls. Barry's party went the seafood route. Small helpings of eel, shark, and octopus were sampled by all those in attendance for the show. There were no leftovers for the hotel staff. Rick and Barry's guests were vultures.

Rick and Angelina stayed a night at the Clarion. From what I heard, both were impressed by the courteous desk staff, the concierge's knowledge of where to go for night time entertainment, the food obviously, and how clean their hotel room was. Rick relayed all of his experiences back to Barry. Both of them made sure that their friends and acquaintances heard of the Clarion.

It was after Rick visited the hotel for a second time that he approached me with a gift.

"Randy, come here. This has been lovely, yes? Are you aware that I am also the co-owner of Club Cyn."

"No kidding. I know the place."

"Good. Are you a night owl, someone who craves the action?"

"I am a nightclubber."

"You and the staff here have treated me and my wife well. This is for you."

I was expecting an envelope stuffed with money. Instead I received a small business card.

"That's a Club Cyn VIP pass. Just come to the door any night and let one of the doormen know that you are with Barry, myself, or my wife Angelina. Have you two met?"

"Briefly. We said hello."

"That card will allow you to bypass the crowds. Bring your wife to my club. I'll see to it that you and your wife have an unforgettable evening."

"Wow, okay, I will. Or we will. Thank you."

Luck isn't always on my side, but today is a different day. Angelina runs into me right before I am exiting the hotel.

"Excuse me. Randy. I'm Angelina. We met earlier. Come, let's sit down. I'm buying this round. Pablo! A seven and seven please. What's your pleasure Randy?"

"Vodka cranberry."

"Make sure he tastes the Laroux."

"Thank you for the drink."

"Please, I had a wonderful time at the banquet earlier. You and the other chefs do a terrific job. The food was delicious."

"Glad to hear you enjoyed."

"You met my husband Rick too. Correct?"

"Sure did. He told me all about Club Cyn that he owns. Do you own or work there?"

"I help with advertising since I work for an ad agency. Here, let me give you this. It's a VIP pass. Let my husband or Barry know that you know me. Okay."

"I will. Wow, this is awesome. Thank you."

You fucking A better believe this. Most people scratch, crawl, cry, beg, and bribe to get inside Club Cyn. Fucking Randall P. Stevens has two free club passes.

Rosa was still in mourning over her dad's passing. I had to choose my words carefully so not to upset her.

"Rosa honey, I met some important people at the Clarion. Their names are Barry and Rick. They own the Club Cyn nightclub. Rick and Barry are helping our marketing department and kitchen staff with new advertisements. They want to meet with me and John to go over the plans and ideas. Both of them are at the club now and can't get away so they asked me to meet them there. If you need me to be here just say the word. I can reschedule."

"Oh no. I understand."

"I mentioned to Rick and Barry about you and your dad. They wanted me to tell you how sorry they were to hear."

"Tell them thank you."

"Are you going to be allright?"

"I'm better. I want to stay with my mom more. She always feels better when I am with her."

"Sure. As long as you need to be. I promise I will not be gone long."

I drive around the building searching for a place to park. All of the small lots were full of cars. The closest garage was two blocks away. I finally give up searching and pull up to the valet stand. I get out of my vehicle and approach the valet.

"Here's a five. I want you to be the one who gets my car when I leave."

"No problem sir."

Rick and Barry are standing near the club's front door. A tall, muscular man is standing next to Barry. Where in the heck did this giant find a suit to fit him? Rick whispers in Barry's ear, then walks inside. Barry sees me and waves me over. I hand over my pass to the formal giant. Barry unhooks the rope so I can go in.

"Enjoy your evening Randy."

"I will, count on it."

Count on it?! I wish Rosa was here with me. I stare out at the vast crowd. A sea of twenty and thirty year olds, male and female, frantically dancing to high energy dance music. The older couples stay in their chairs talking to one another. These are the high octane, high maintenance people. I love the female singer's voice. Seductive. I see Rick standing in front of the bar. I walk over towards him.

"Hi, I couldn't get Rosa, my wife, to come. Her dad passed way recently so she's still recuperating."

"I'm terribly sorry to hear. My condolences. I have work to do my office. You have a great time."

I looked around hoping to see Angelina. I guess she decided to stay at home.

An hour passes and now the club is packed with patrons. The boys are hoping to hook up with the girls for a fast one night stand. Only the desperate girls will give in. The bartenders hustle to serve the booze. I made plans to have lunch with Rosa and Amelia tomorrow. All I drink are fountain sodas. A soda or a bottle of water cost two dollars. Even with the sodas, I didn't want to come off as a cheapskate, so I tip the bartender a dollar per soda.

Dancing by myself is usually something I will not do. Certainly not in public. But here the swirling, spacey drug induced atmosphere pulls me on the dance floor. Women are dancing with women. Men are dancing with men. So close, their chests and butts make physical contact. Threesomes. Foursomes. Switch-offs. Club Cyn may have a strict dress code, but who you want to dance with is anything goes.

A younger than me lady wearing a snow white mini skirt shakes and gyrates alone on an elevated stage. She is not missing a beat. I walk out to the center of the floor. Sometimes, a smokecloud appears. Everyone's feet disappears. I feel like a fool not being able to keep up the hard techno beats. I smell perfume behind me. I turn to see who my female shadow is. She's not Angelina but still another oh my God diamond queen sexy. We start to dance together. She stays behind me, places her warm hands on my hips. Soon, a strange male straddles himself behind the female. I begin to wonder if the female is actually a man.

The heavy carbonation causes me to urinate more often. I have to wait in line to go. I keep waiting, discreetly holding my cock so I don't piss my pants. Come on, hurry up. I can't stand it when some guy stands at the urinal for twenty minutes and doesn't do a damn thing. What I should do is pull out my cock and then take a piss on the back of his pants. I'll bet he moves out of the way then.

After I leave the bathroom, I notice a hidden area located at the back end of the club. One couple together is kissing each other hard. His hand is up the woman's skirt. Another couple share in a bright blue drink from a tube. Rick and a cyborg are standing in front of a small wooden door. I walk back towards the bar and ask the bartender about the back area.

"So, what's behind the wooden door?"

"Our exclusive VIP section."

"What's different about it?"

"Let's say it's where you can let all of your desires go."

"Okay, so how do I get in?"

"If you have the money and Rick and Barry approve then you're in. But of either of them see something about you they don't like, you won't be coming back to the club anymore."

"I understand. How much to enter?"

"One hundred to start. That's all I know."

Holy shit. Rick and Barry are making a fortune running this place. I still have two hundred in my pocket. Club Cyn is ecstasy in the purest form. Here is where evil manifests itself upon you.

Just mentioning the name Club Cyn didn't help my case. Rosa wasn't angry with me for going there, she just wasn't comfortable being at a place where loud music would hurt her ears and sweaty bodies would gag her throat. Amelia was getting better. Time was the perfect cure for her and Rosa to mourn. Rosa's smile returned. She went back to work. Amelia went clothes shopping with her female friends. I convinced Rosa to be with me for one night only at Club Cyn.

Rosa and I meet Barry at the front door. I use my last VIP pass.

"Barry, my lovely wife Rosa. Rosa this is my friend Barry. He is one of the owners."

Barry takes Rosa's left hand, then bends down to kiss it.

"Wonderful to finally meet you. Come inside and enjoy yourselves."

I can't help but smile. Rosa and I are a well-known Saint Louis couple. My face is in various food magazines. Rosa's work was the subject of a recent television documentary. The horses, dogs, and baby calves are being trained to be company for people who have a mental illness. Strangers recognize us, point to us, and say hello.

"Since you're not comfortable being around crowds, there's an intimate area in the back we can sit at. Even dance a slow dance with few people watching."

"I'd like that."

"Good, come with me."

I give Rick a crisp one hundred dollar bill. His Thor like bodyguard unhooks the velvet chain.

"You must be the lovely Rosa that Randy speaks of. More beautiful than I imagined. Come. Let yourself go."

The door slams behind Rosa and I. Shit, I have goosebumps. We walk down a corridor, passing up a couple getting high and drunk. The area has makeshift dividers for each couple to have privacy. Well, it's not too private. One lady is topless. I see one couple making out in a corner. He must sense someone is watching. He turns around and smiles at Rosa and me. His van dyke is familiar. Oh, and the lady's large breasts are too familiar. No shit! It's Gary and Sonja!

"You remember our two friends who cruised with us?"

"Sure. Hi Sonja. Hey Gary. What are you two doing here?"

"My wife never stopping thing about you. Sonja even screamed out your name one time while we were fucking. I had to search for you, find you for my wife."

I knew from the moment when Sonja and Rosa were sunbathing together on the cruise ship that Sonja was sexually attracted to my wife. Aw hell, Rosa could have had a school girl fixation on Sonja. I just didn't know it. I pull the blue curtain across to give all four of us more privacy. The space is so compact that all four of us have to line up train style.

Gary faces Rosa. Sonja is right behind Rosa, already kissing her neck. I position my body behind Sonja's. I lean in to whisper in Rosa's ear.

"Don't be afraid. You're among friends. What we do to each other will be between us. Shhh. Sonja is a gentle, delicate woman."

Gary picks up where my haunting words leave off.

"You are so exotic my love." Those words are for Rosa.

"Escape with us to a place where nothing is taboo and no boundaries are made."

Gary and Rosa start kissing each other on the lips. I can hear Rosa whimper as Sonja puts her hand up Rosa's dress. My hand slides up Sonja, she also whimpers and moans. Gary is making similar noises. He must have his cock inside Rosa's pussy. I follow suit by pulling down my pants, then Sonja's soaking panties, and press my cock inside her pussy.

I wake up in a puddle of sticky cum and cold sweat. Jesus Fuck. I turn to my right side. I'm relieved not to have gotten any cum on the bed sheets. Rosa would be pissed. I carefully slide of the bed, watching closely if any cum runs down my belly. I walk fast to the bathroom and grab a bunch of toilet paper. It never occurs to me that Rosa, Amelia, or Karen could be in another room. I need to get my bearings. I'll drink some water. What in the hell did I drink last night? Did I try one of those blue drinks in a tube?

My hallucinations vary from night to night. Rosa is having sex with a different woman every night. Is she and Amelia and Karen having a sex kitten party without me? One of them brings a porn video over to watch. While watching the film, they have to masterbate in front of each other. When the film is over, they reenact the explicit sex scenes with each other.

I wish Rosa would spend more time at home with me. Instead, she's finding solace at her work. Her boss transformed an empty guest house behind the cottage into a makeshift place for Rosa to stay in. I've seen the place one time. Reminds me of a college dorm room. Rosa has a twin size bed, a small dresser, table lamp, and narrow closet. She uses the work area's bathroom and kitchen. The two of us can't fit in the room together, so I'm the odd man out.

Rosa and I are still in love with each other. I'm giving her space and time to heal from her loss. The minute I start on about not getting invited to her work-related parties or get-togethers with her family, then Rosa begins to tear up. She does a good job of making me feel guiltier than shit. Think about it this way Randy, when she's visiting someone, you got the green light to live the nightlife.

Rick and Barry want to throw a thank you party to show their appreciation to the people who have visited and supported their club. They even had plaques made to be given to certain patrons who have been VIPs since Club Cyn opened. I suggested two events.

"We could have a banquet for Club Cyn's owners, your wives, girlfriends and VIPs. Maybe even invite your closest friends and relatives. The Clarion could use the business. We've been steady but need more parties. We could also have a second party here at the club. This one would be open to the public. I'm sure my boss John could help out, I ask about a champagne toast. The kitchen can cook some appetizers to serve during the party. Here. This is a business card that has Sharon Taylor's name. She's the Clarion hotel banquet manager. We've had similar parties like this before. She's always willing to help out."

"Thank you. I love the idea of our club and your hotel working together. I'll give the card to Angelina."

I couldn't make it to either event. I promised my mom and grandma that the three of us would spend a day together. Then I promised Rosa and her mom that I would meet the two of them for dinner at Amelia's. I need to work on my scheduling. I met Barry a few days later at the Club.

"Our hotel party was wonderful. Great food and service as always. But, my friend, you missed a fucking great time. I, well Rick and I, hired ten strippers to entertain all of the guests. Man, there were nipples and tits everywhere. You want to know what else was great. The strippers had to give the club ten percent of all the money they got. Guys are fucking morons. They throw around dollar bills like pebbles tossed in the sand."

The Clarion may have made more money hosting other people's event, but Barry and his guests were the one you wanted to know. The actors, pro athletes, socialites, singers, investors and company CEOs. If any of them are staying at the hotel, you present them with free nights, all night booze, and a turn the other way when one of them snorts some coke. Barry puts is arm around my shoulder. Together, we walk into Barry's club office.

"The VIP pass is only the beginning. Here, a gift from me to you."

Barry hands me a sheet of paper. It's a typed list of eight female names. Their first names only. Theresa. Angie. Lea. Teri. Nicole. Teri. Samantha. Amber. Next to the names are seven numbers. Barry smiles and nods his head. He's going to give me the answer to the question he already knew I was going to ask.

"Those are the names of women who are seeking male companionship. I've met all of them. You have your blonde, brunette, big breasted, not so big but just as sweet, a bevy of gorgeous women who have more money than they know what to do with. Their husbands ignore them and treat them like shit. What these ladies want, they get. You call their number first. Tell the lady that you want to meet her. Usually the ladies will pay up to five hundred. Hell, I knew a lady who's not on the list anymore paid up to two fucking grand for one night. Anyway, they call me to help plan the evening. I find a discreet hotel where the two of you can meet. I can even provide a different car. Their dumbass husbands never find out. Ever."

"And nobody else knows?"

"The only other person who knows anything is Rick. If his wife knows, then she knows. Both of them assist me with the set ups. Trust me, this is all done in secret. Think about it. If Rosa isn't giving you pleasure in the bedroom anymore then these ladies are your problem solvers."

The extra money would come in handy. But how in the hell would I be able to pull this off without Rosa finding out? Rosa is finally coming home to stay. Her emotions are still fragile but she's starting to make peace with the death of her father.

"I missed you so much Randy. Want to hear some exciting news?"

"I sure do."

"I delivered a baby horse. Oh, it so wonderful to see the baby cradle up to her mom."

Oh shit, here come more tears. Wait, these are of joy.

"Well, they had a wonderful doctor caring for them. So maybe if you're up to it, we can go out. I'll take you to Club Cyn to do a little dancing."

"Oh, I don't know. I want to be with my animals. I also want to keep checking on my mom. How's your family doing."

"They're fine. My dad's parole hearing is coming out. He's getting anxious. Mom and grandma are still well. Nancy has been great"

"I know we haven't seen a lot of each other.."

"Stop that. Family is important. I'll only go out if I know you are staying at Amelia's or at work. That is if I even feel up to it. If you would rather I stay at home, just say the words."

"No, no. Just promise to be careful."

"I promise. Besides, I just got a change in my work schedule. Seems the day crew is short staffed. Guess I'll be turning in early in order to wake up early."

The blood in my veins is transforming into a sheet of ice. Rosa and I may be legally married, we still wear our wedding rings, but we are no longer husband and wife. We have become roommates. The woman I used to have sex with at least once a week has vanished. Where did Rosa disappear to? Where's the woman who would bake a lasagna in the kitchen wearing only a bra and panties? Whoever or whatever kidnapped her needs to know that I fill find Rosa and I will bring her back home.

The bright sun slowly vanishes from the sky. Ominous thick clouds have taken over. Then a bright crackle, one after another, lights up the night. The flashes appeared so fast that you lost count how many there were. Ten? Eleven! The thunderclaps are so loud one may think someone ignited a bomb. The final crack of lightening shut off the city's power. Light, however flickering it was, has disappeared. The heavy downpours could be heard but not seen. No one was prepared for the total darkness, not even the overpaid weathercasters predicted this kind of catastrophe. One of them announced moderate rains with some lightning. He made his money's worth. My gut tells me to call Rosa now. I breathe a sigh of relief knowing both of our phones are still working.

"Rosa, are you at work or with your mom?"

"I'm at my mom's place."

"Good. Stay there, and please don't think about driving home."

"I wasn't going to. It's horrible outside. The rain is hitting the glass so hard that I think the windows are going to bust out. My mom and I are staying away from them. Are you going to drive home? The streets may not be safe. Please wait at least until the rain lets up."

"I was already there earlier. I have one of the small living lamps turned on. The curtains are closed and the alarm is turned on."

"Thanks, I feel better. Where are you now?"

"Back at the club. I had to drop off some flyers. The blackout must have occurred right after I got here. Talk about good timing."

"Well at least you're safe inside."

"Do you have any light at all where you are at?"

"We have some candles burning. Oh, and I have a flashlight."

"Good. Make sure you guys have plenty of batteries. I don't want you or Amelia to open your doors for anyone. I don't care who you think it is. I would even put a chair up against the back door."

"That's okay. Neither one of us will be sleeping too much. Not with all this thunder and lighting. Thanks for caring though. You'll keep calling right?"

"Yeah, my damn phone battery is low. I'll ask if someone here has charger. I'll come home either when the lights return or in the morning."

Club Cyn was crowded tonight. The dark clouds hovering above didn't frighten anyone from coming here. I'm glad Rosa and I purchased a home security system. A sticker reading *mount securities* placed in the left corner of our front window isn't good enough. I paid over two grand for their elite package. Once our alarm is activated then triggered, a loud, piercing siren screams in your ear. 911 calls my phone and Rosa's seconds after the alarm goes off. The two sets of three floodlights, one set in front of the house and one set in the back, turn on.

Black people are not the only looters. You would be amazed at the crime a bored rich white boy would commit. If they aren't damaging your mailbox then they are keying the side of your car. Rick and Barry locked the club's back door. From time to time, one of the bouncers would step outside to make sure no vagrants were roaming around the back.

You wouldn't know there was a black hole outside from the inside of Club Cyn's doors. The strobe lights were spinning around creating flashes of white light. The disc jockey was playing a hard style of house music. Several males and females were dancing together, their eyes closed, unaware that our city was taken hostage by a power thief. Club Cyn has an established reputation for being the club to be at when you want to have a good time. You don't just walk into Club Cyn-you get an invitation. A typical innocent evening only slightly marred from the indulgence of alcohol and lust.

But tonight, innocence is gone. When darkness arrives, your sins, evils, and vices emerge. Lucifer and his prodigal son stand high above the podium. Or in this case, next to the disc jockey perched above the crowd. They look down upon the crowd with satisfaction knowing their malevolence is about to be spread among all the unsuspecting people.

"The cops have their hands full with all the looting. A serial killer will get away with killing for pleasure. Pity that police officers must waste their time and effort on these uneducated ingrates who must steal only to prove they can. I say let the looters destroy and kill one another. The less dreck we have infesting our society will be a victory for our kind."

"Our place here is a safe haven for the flock here with us tonight."

"We must take advantage of the chaos that has suffocated the pathetic outside world."

"What do you have in mind?"

"Allow the people to indulge in their fantasies, their addictions, and help them overcome their greatest fears."

"Excuse me father?"

"Yes?"

"For I am only a humble mixmaster but I want to earn my wings. I know how to start the night of our decadence."

"Tell me."

"I'll start by playing ethereal trance music. The music's hypnotic soundwaves will transport the night clubbers back to a time where taboos were shattered."

"You must not stop there."

"Of course not. Once the crowd is cast under, I'll switch gears and strip away their goodness. This is will be accomplished with brutal industrial dance.

"Perfect."

"But seductive dancing only? Surely you have greater evil planned?"

"Of course not. Soon, I will summon for a shower of white powder to fall. Let the people grab this powder to use among themselves."

"The music will force them to share not only the drugs but themselves among each other."

"Yes! The grandest orgy of them all!"

"It is not fair to the people that we stay up here as mere observers. They are begging us, all of us, to step down and join them."

The bursts of light burn and blind my eyes. Tonight's dress code went from formal to clothing optional. If you were not a part of the group of people fucking on the dancefloor, you were with those sitting at a table snorting coke. Addicts were lined up waiting to buy more coke or any pills they craved from Rick and Barry. Rick set out a large tray filled with amphetamines, barbiturates, speed, dope, reefer, rolled joints and angel dust. Barry put the money collected in a tan suitcase.

Barry brings out a large cart filled with bottles of rum, vodka, gin, scotch, elixirs, and cognac. A second line forms as people wait their turn to open their mouth so that Barry can pour a shot glass size of the alcohol they choose down their throats. Your first communion of unleavened bread and wine made you pure. Tonight's services will make you a transgressor.

With excess comes the challenge of willpower. I saw a man and woman lying on the floor. Their opened eyes were glazed upon the ceiling. I peered closer to their naked bodies. Powder was smeared all over their chests and faces. Blood was coming out of his right nostril. She didn't have a pulse. Poor amateurs. Tonight, your willpower will not stand a chance against our immoral acts placed upon you.

Strangers who never met rolled around naked with each other in a dark corner of the club. They would take turns at fucking the person directly in front of them. One guy with a large dick grabbed another guy's buttocks. The man with the large dick then butt fucks the other guy. Watching the one man sexually torture another weaker man was brutal. I had to turn away. A small tear ran down my cheek. For I knew this guy who was being fucked in the ass was going to die from AIDS before the year was over.

Barry put his hand on my shoulder.

"Son, I know you do not indulge in drugs. For your vice is indelicate sex. You share the same wicked temptation as my wife. She has long been a tainted woman. A whore among the innocent. But I still love her. I want her to succumb to her wiles. Go to her. This is be your final cast. Do not be gentle with her. For she must be punished!"

A woman wearing a black dress made out of a hard rubber was signaling for me to come hither. Her face was partially covered with a red and purple Mardi Gras mask. My heart pounded faster as I got closer to her. I kept jumping back every time I heard the whip she held crack to the floor. The crackling noise is even more frightening than lightning bolts striking concrete.

I do not revel or delight in S&M. I want my sexual experience to be without the toys and weapons. What good are your hands if they are tied up with rope or handcuffed to the bedpost? I use my hands and lips to give ultra-orgasms to every female I'm with. Getting a hard spanking across the bare ass is not my idea of pleasure. How would you like it if I returned the spanking to you only twice as hard? My capturer speaks first.

"Come with me darling. I have been instructed to satisfy all of your fantasies."

"Please no bondage. I want to engage in a 69, then switch from oral to anal, and for the climax, a three way with one of the female peasants here in attendance. I will lay down first, the lucky chosen one in the middle, and you on top of her."

"Ohhhh, you have learned well. Come! We will fuck each other with relentless passion! I will make you come then you will me come twice!"

The police were out all night patrolling the streets wearing their riot gear. The police failed at keeping the streets and neighborhoods safe. Homes were set on fire and destroyed. Convenient stores were looted. Cars remained parked up against the curbs. Many of the car windows were busted out. The result from a rock thrown by a heartless ingrate.

The homeless were robbed of their blankets, shopping carts filled with leftover foods, and their dignity. The blackout has extended into the next day. Enough time to paralyze the city.

Rosa made it home safely. Of course she waited to drive home until the sun rose. Our home was still safe and secure. No person would be foolish to try and break in our home. The first night of a citywide blackout terrorized many people. Except me. I gave Angelina the best fuck she ever had. The blackout had ruined many lives. But for me, all in all, not a bad night.

15
PUTTING ONE WALL UP, TEARING ONE DOWN

I was not going to make it home in time to kiss Rosa goodbye. The rain was so heavy that I couldn't see clearly out my front car window. All I could do was drive in a straight line and drive twenty miles an hour. If the cars behind me would honk, fuck them, they can go around. I decide not to take any chances. I call Rosa to let her know where I'm at.

"Hi Rosa, it's me. Are you home?"

"Yes. Thank goodness I made it home before the rain really came down. We lost our electric power. I'm nervous. It is pitch black outside and the rain keeps getting heavier."

"Well make sure the alarm is on. I would also keep in touch with our neighbors."

"Oh we are. Some of the guys are even doing a neighborhood watch."

"Great. Someone should check to see if the gate is operating."

"I think Kyle is. He's a brave man for going outside. Where are you at?"

"I'm in the police station parking lot. Last night, I stayed at a hotel near the club. I have to drop off some letters for my dad to sign. Then I want to talk to an officer about his upcoming parole."

"Are you going to drive home anytime soon?"

"Not sure. The streetlights aren't working but I should be able to get on the highway. I'll be home as soon as I can. There's a lot pf police cars in the lot across the street. I may pull in there for a while or find a diner where I can go in for a few hours. Anywhere where there is a lot of people."

"Be safe. I'll be thinking of you."

I've driven in hailstorms and ice pellets falling from the sky. I'm not going to let a blackout prevent me from getting home. I stare at the prison walls where they are keeping my dad hostage. The prison resembles a Scottish castle from the dark ages. The stone walls built to keep even the most deranged killer from escaping to the outside. All of the cells inside have become a personal stockade.

My dad has never mentioned to me the idea of escaping. Oh, like he would anyway. What if my dad received a denial letter from either a judge or the parole board? His mood changes from hopeful to discourage. My dad can't take one more year locked up. The only solution, out of desperation is to escape.

A riot breaks out in the prison shower facility. Several prisoners are pushing their way through the wall of armed guards. The guards shield themselves by firing back in the direction of the inmates. This causes several guards to drop and break their flashlights. The gunshots sound like firecrackers being released into the sky.

Cleo is a hardened lifer. He knows the prison walls better than the warden. Cleo developed a blueprint for escaping the first day he arrived. My dad and Cleo stop sweeping and mopping the kitchen floor. Tonight would be Cleo and my dad's best, and possibly only chance for a successful escape.

"Hey Rich, put your hand on my back and keep up with me!"

"We're getting out of here right?!"

"This is our only chance. We must escape now!"

"Do you know where you are going?"

"I know these walls better than the guards, come on!"

My dad and Cleo run down dark halls and corridors. Cleo's hand slaps up against the cold and wet concrete walls to make sure they are going the right way. The maze was tricky. One minute you run down a clear path only to be stopped by a solid wall made of concrete. My dad was so close behind Cleo you would think he was going to butt fuck him any minute.

"Come on, we're almost there."

They come to a black gate. Since the prison's power is shutdown, the gate does open. My dad and Cleo turn their heads for a second. No prison guards were chasing after Cleo or my dad. The guards were either restraining the other prisoners or they were killed by the prisoners. Cleo and my dad have made it to the outside.

"We're almost there! Hurry!"

Suddenly, a bright light shines in their faces!

"Freeze!" A guard yells out.

"Go! Go! Go!"

Cleo slips on the wet grass and falls to the ground. Rich turns his back to him."

"Go! Get out of here! I'm right behind you!"

Cleo pants heavily but manages to get up. Several shots are fired.

"Ahhhh!"

Cleo is shot in the back by a dead-on bullet. He falls face first to the ground.

"You..keep…running!"

My dad listens and runs into a wooded area. He stays low to the ground hoping that by keeping down so light will shine on him. He's praying that he finds more solid ground. My dad can hear the sounds of cars driving along the road. He runs until he sees a pick- up truck parked on the shoulder of the road. My dad climbs in the back and covers himself up using the wet tarp.

My dad is no longer a citizen. He is an escaped convict. My dad has no idea how far the truck is going. My dad would say that it would be his luck the pick -up truck is owned by a police officer. The truck drives for several miles. There is no going back to your family.

Who am I kidding? My dad may be a lot of things but a fugitive is not one of them. He wouldn't throw his life way. He wouldn't take the risk of getting shot. He's got Nancy and his mom waiting for him to return home. Before I drive off the prison lot, I say a prayer.

Dear Lord,

Please protect my dad. The prison is without any light. I do not want my dad to get hurt or worse. He's done some bad things to many people. But he's trying to be a better person. I'm scared that another prisoner may try to hurt him. Please keep him out of trouble and out of harm's way. I'm asking that you look over him tonight and for the rest of his time in here. Amen.

I call my dad the next day.

"Man, driving home was nerve racking. Only the car lights guided me home."

"I wouldn't have even driven home. Why didn't you just stay here or go to a hotel?"

"I did the previous night. I didn't want to leave Rosa home by herself. Didn't really matter. She spent the night at her mom's."

"How did you get around in your place?"

"I feel around. We did have one lamp turned on that provided some dim light."

"At least you had light. We had no lights except for the flashlights that the guards were carrying."

"So if they weren't around..."

"Then you better pray that you get to your destination without getting hurt or killed."

"Did you have to return to your cell? Or were you already in there?

"Oh definitely. A lot of us were outside since we just ate dinner. I was going to stay in the kitchen but Cleo wanted to go outdoors so I went with him. There were some guys who tried to escape. I guess they thought the guards wouldn't see them. You could hear the shots fired at them. I know none of the prisoners who tried to escape didn't make it to the outside. Their bodies may still be laying on the ground. There were some other guys who got stabbed by other prisoners Man, if you were on someone's shitlist then you weren't going to live. And all of this happened before we were ordered back to our cells."

"Jesus Christ."

"I didn't talk to anyone except Cleo or the guards. I hurried to get back inside my cell."

"I'm glad you didn't get hurt in any of this."

"I don't have any beef with anyone in here. Cleo and I stayed close by during the blackout. I watched his back and he watched mine."

"I guess it's good to have at least one ally."

"And no enemies."

"Do you share a cell?"

"No. The cells are too small. Sometimes it feels like living in a shoebox. All I have is a cot, a toilet, and a sink. I didn't sleep too much last night. You could hear the wind howling and the rain hitting the windows. That's how intense it was! This is the last place I ever want to be, but I'll tell you this, I was never happier to be in my cell than outside last night."

"I agree. I'm going to let you go. I want to make sure that my mom and grandma survived. I'll keep in touch."

My cell phone battery is running now. I need to make these next calls brief.

"Hello, Grandma? It's Randy."

"Say isn't this rain something. None of our street lights are working."

"Yeah I know. I'm on my way over. I should be there in five minutes."

"Is Rosa with you?"

"No. She's with Karen and her mom. I already called her and told her that I was seeing you."

When I got off the highway, I made a quick detour to avoid a certain area. I can see activity from my rear view window. A group of young adults, black and whites, were running into a clothing store. The store's front window had been shattered. The place didn't have any alarm. In fact, I didn't hear any alarms. Not coming from the stores or the cop cars. The adults were running in and out of the store with piles of clothes in their hands. Several of them were running down the block. Even in the pouring rain, desperate low class people will brave the weather in order to steal for their own personal gain. These criminals were taking advantage of a city paralyzed by the gloom.

I will never understand why the police are not relentless at stopping these thieves. This is a state of emergency! If the police feel outnumbered or overpowered then call in the National Guard. The plan is simple: Have an endless line of armed militants walk in union down the street. Every two minutes, every other militant turns around with their weapon pointed outward.

If our warriors are forced not to draw fire then tear gas becomes the weapon of choice. One toss into the crowd of unruly animals will make them scurry like runaway possums.

I sped through the streets but diligently kept an eye out on anyone near my car. My nerves calmed once I pulled in front of my grandma's. Several of her neighbors were standing on their front porches. I run up my grandma's front porch, bang on the screen door and wave franticly for her to let me in.

"Hello, is your back door locked?"

"Of course."

"Good, I'm going to go next door and make sure the back door is locked."

"I'm glad you're here. I feel safer."

"Is your television working? I want to watch the news and weather."

"I keep hearing police sirens then the cars go by."

"Yeah, a lot of stores are getting robbed or set on fire. These people have nothing to do with their lives except to destroy buildings, cars, and to injure someone. They all deserve to get shot by the police."

"I'm sure the police will make arrests."

"Not good enough. Once these buffoons are taken into custody they either post bail or can't be held because they are still a minor or the police don't have enough jail cells to hold them. That's why I say shoot the bastards. I know where there's an empty lot of land. It's near Rosa's work. You could have a bunch of the caught criminals be forced to dig gigantic holes. Then when of the thieves or looters gets shot, bam!, in the hole they go."

"Oh hush. Turn off the television."

After securing the back door with a chair up against it, I call my mom.

"Hi mom, it's Randy. How's everything in your area?"

"Black. All gloom and doom."

"Well don't be going out."

"Trust me, I'm not I'm going out anywhere."

"I hear a lot of noise in the background. Sounds like a party."

"I know. A bunch of us gathered in and around my place. Kate and some of her friends and some of Butch's friends too."

"Is Kate or her boyfriend at home?"

"Kate is. I don't know about him. Whoa!"

"Mom, what happened?"

"A loud noise happened somewhere around here. Sounded like an explosion. The noise is scaring the heck out of busterbut."

"Who?"

"Busterbut. Oh you never seen my little guy. He's a brown Australian terrier. I'm not sure if it's the thunder or the fire out back that's scaring him"

"What fire?"

"Oh, some people are starting a bonfire."

"In the rain!?"

"I think they put up a tent. I don't know. I need to check on Buster."

"How long has you had him?"

"About three or four months, I guess. Becky was moving. She asked if Kate and I could take care of him. Kate has bad allergies so she can't really be close to him. I'm surprised you and Rosa never got a dog or even a cat."

"Oh yeah that's all I need. I would be the one waking up at four in the morning so the dog can take his am shit. I'm not crazy about any cats either. I don't need that kind of pussy all over my bed."

"Get out of here Randy! Well I didn't wants old busterbutt to go back to the shelter. So he's here to stay."

"That's nice of you. The noises must be people taking advantage of the dark. Y'know, some oaf throwing a firecracker through a window. I already had to drive past a store that was getting robbed. Wouldn't surprise me if some of the stores in your area are set on fire. Do you have any lights at all?"

"Kate does. She keeps going in and out."

"You need to borrow a flashlight from her. And keep a lookout for anyone going into your backyard."

"Randy, you worry too much about me."

"Until all the drug dealers move out of your neighborhood, I will worry. I just want you to be careful."

"I will. Where are you at?"

"At my grandma's. I'll stay here overnight. I don't want her to be alone. Rosa is with her mom and Karen."

"I'll bet your father is going nuts."

"As long as he stays in his cell, he'll be fine. I'm sure the prison has plenty of back up and prepares for shit like this."

"I hope so."

"I'm going to go back over to grandma's. I'll talk to you soon."

"Okay bye bye."

I crashed on my grandma's couch during the blackout. I was awakened by the sounds of trucks and people yelling thank you. I couldn't sit still. I would sneak a peek from behind the curtain. The electric company worked around the clock to restore the power. The next morning felt calmer. Cars driving on the still damp roads and birds chirping were pleasant and welcoming sounds. The evil disappeared along with the profound immortality.

A week passed since the blackout. Then a woman named Jenny told me the sad and unexpected news over the phone.

"Hi, is this Richard Stevens?"

"No. I'm his son Randy. My dad isn't here right now. May I ask whose calling?"

"Oh, well I can call back at a better time."

"No you're fine. What I mean is my dad is away for a while. Who's this calling please?

"My name's Jennifer Steck. I'm Laura's sister."

"Oh wow. The last time I saw you was when I in grade school. How are you?"

"Good. Under the circumstances. Carl passed away last Wednesday."

"Grandpa Carl! Oh man. I'm sorry. How?"

"He died in his sleep. His health has been going downhill for a couple of years. He's been in and out of hospitals for a few years. He went peacefully so now he's in a better place."

"Damn. I'm so sorry. All this death is really getting to me."

"Excuse me?"

"My wife's dad passed away recently too."

"Oh, I'm sorry."

"Thank you. You're still living in Kentucky right?"

"Laura is. My husband and I are living in Houston."

"Um, okay. I'll give my dad and grandma the sad news. Can you give me your phone number? Hopefully my dad will call you and talk to both you and Laura. But he won't be able to attend the wake or the funeral."

"Why not?"

"Because he got into some trouble and is now in Jail."

"Oh no!"

"It's not as bad as it sounds. He just wasn't using his noggin."

"Jail?!"

"Yes. He's been there for several years. Really it's not for anything horrendous. He got caught messing around with his former employer but he's behaving himself."

"Well I certainly hope that everything turns out well for him. How is your grandma?"

"She's still kicking thank God."

"Wonderful to hear some good news."

"Do you have Laura's address? It's easier if I just write it down and put it in my wallet. And her number too? I want to at least call or write to her."

"Her address is 432 Pittman acres way in Lexington, Kentucky. Hold on. Her number is 859-410-2658."

"Great thanks, Oh your number too?"

"You can reach me at 713-569-3847."

"Thanks. I'll be seeing my dad sometime next week. I take it grandpa will be buried in Lexington?"

"Yes. His funeral is Friday."

"Okay, I'm going to try and see if I can get a few days off from work. Shouldn't be a problem. It will be nice to see everyone even though the occasion is a sad one."

"That would be lovely."

"Okay, well thanks for all the information. I'll let my dad know."

"Great. Thank you Randy."

"You take care of yourself."

"You too bye now."

My dad hasn't seen his dad since the last time my grandpa visited us. That was back in 1980 or 1981. My dad never did care for Laura. Grandpa Carl and Laura eloped in Las Vegas. After Carl divorced my grandma he wasted no time meeting then marrying another woman. I think this was back in 1978. My dad still has a postcard of those two standing outside by the welcome to Las Vegas sign. When Carl was married to my grandma, he was an auto mechanic for a semi-pro race car driving organization. His love of race cars carried over to my dad's love for the sport. It was Carl's dream to one day be race car driver.

After those two split up, they never really divorced, separated rather, Carl met Laura. Laura's dad worked for a bank. He was the stuffy businessman who frowned upon giving loans to poor people who needed extra cash. I was too little to understand why Laura's dad, what the heck was his name? Zack? Zeb? The passed away too at a young age. I wasn't even a teenager.

Laura persuaded Carl to give up his pipe dream of being a race car driver. She wanted him to work for her dad. Carl was not a well-off man. The idea of making three times as much money convinced Carl that he was in the wrong field. Only problem is that Carl was passionate about revving up race cars. My dad had mentioned to me a couple of times about how grandpa has an old race car in his garage that he was going to repair and rebuild. When I went to visit my grandpa one summer, I didn't see any race car in the garage. Instead, an ugly green station wagon was parked inside.

Carl stayed at his father's company for the rest of his working years. My dad thinks Laura manipulated grandma into giving up something he loved to do for a menial dead end job. After Carl and Laura retired, the two became homebodies. Content to living out the rest of their lives in a rural community.

I'm not sure how emotional my dad will get upon hearing the news. I should also tell my grandma and Rosa. I mean what's my dad going to do? I doubt the prison will give him funeral leave. First, I tell my grandma the news.

"So I got a call from Jennifer Steck. Do you remember her? She's Laura's sister. I don't know how or where she got my home number from? But anyway, she called to me that grandpa Carl died last week in his sleep."

"I haven't seen or spoken to them in a long time."

"I can give you the address where they were living or the address to the funeral parlor. I guess we should get a condolence card and some flowers."

"Just put them on the kitchen table."

"All right, I'll let dad know about this too."

"He may not want to hear about this. With him being away at all."

My grandma gave me the impression that she didn't care whether or not Carl was living or dead. I don't know all the details about her and grandpa separating. I'm sure my grandma had her feelings hurt and her heart broken. I never asked her what happened to them. She hardly spoke to the man anytime they did see each other again.

When I got to the prison, I had to first get with one of the guards. After telling him why I was there, he directed me to stay put in the lobby until someone came over to either get me or talk to me. About twenty minutes later, one of the prison guards approaches me.

"You Stevens?"

"Yes. Randy Stevens to see Rich Stevens. He's my dad."

"I told him you were here. He doesn't want to see anyone including you."

"Did you tell him why I was here?"

"Yes. He put both of is hands up in the air and told me to make sure that no visitors would stop by."

"Aside from hearing about his dad, which I would rather tell him face to face, how's he doing?"

"He behaves and stays out of trouble. Spends most of his time either in the kitchen or his cell. Makes my job a hell of a lot easier."

"I'm concerned that he's depressed."

"If he is, then he does a good job hiding it. He and Cleo are always cracking up in the kitchen. When he's outside, the two of them are usually on the steps talking to each other. His mood seems fine to me."

"I'm surprised. Happy but surprised. Thanks for the updates."

"Good luck sir."

I drive home and spill the news about my grandpa to Rosa. She is in the bedroom packing a suitcase.

"Are you spending the night at your mom's?"

"For a couple of days. I'm sorry I haven't had a chance to go to the grocery store."

"Don't worry. I can take care of myself. So listen my grandpa passed away last week. If I can go, I may drive to Kentucky to see some of his family. We should go together. I would love for my dad's side of the family to meet you."

"That's sad to hear. I don't know about going with you. I still want to make sure my mom is doing well. You should go with your mom and grandma."

Rosa finishes packing her clothes and races past me towards the bathroom.

"I'm running late, there's leftover pork and rice in the refrigerator."

Rosa dashes out the front door without even kissing me goodbye.

Is it just me or does no one give a fuck about Carl's passing away? Since my dad doesn't want to see me or anyone for that matter, I wrote him a short letter.

Dear dad,

How are you doing? I went to the prison last week to visit you. One of the guards told me that you didn't want to have any visitors. I thinks it's important that you know Grandpa Carl passed away. I got the news from Jennifer. She called your home phone. I just happened to be over there when she called. Talk about timing. Anyway, he's getting buried in Lexington, Kentucky. I'm going to drive down there to visit everyone. Unless someone brings it up, I will not say a word about where you are. The guard I spoke to says you have been staying out of mischief. That's good to know. Keep that up and you will be home sooner than later. I guess you are keeping busy in the kitchen. I know all about hard work from washing dishes.

Do you still work in the library? Grandma is going great. I still drive her to the hair salon or to the grocery store. Sometimes, Nancy will too. Oh, did I mention that Rosa's dad passed away too? Rosa's been having a hard time with this so I just support her as much as I can. On a happier note, I got a raise from my last job performance. Well that's about all I know here. Keep in touch.

Sincerely,
Randy

Weeks went by and I never received a letter or phone call in return. When I continue to talk to the guards, they give me the same news as before. My dad's going well, has not gone to the stockade, he and Leon are too busy scrubbing the kitchen floor to see me, and my dad still wants no visitors. He only exception he made was when Nancy stopped by.

I'm having a hard time believing that my dad and a black guy are getting along. Cleo has to be black. How many white guys do you know are named Cleo? I will keep writing to my dad even if he doesn't respond. He should be overjoyed that I'm keeping him in the loop about what's going on with me and our families.

John approved my funeral leave for three days. It's easy to repay him back. All I need to do is flex my schedule so that he, Fred, and any of the other chefs can take a day or night off without any hassles. I was unsuccessful at getting anyone from my family to go with me.

Once I arrived at Blue Grass airport, I searched for the Hertz rental car kiosk. I requested a mid-size car. What I got was a Volkswagen. Comfort Suites hotel was close to the airport. I pull in there to stay.

After changing clothes, I drive to the funeral parlor. Lexington is best known for their horse race tracks and home of the Kentucky Wildcats basketball teams. Rosa would love being here. The winding roads lead to several farms. Many of the people who live around here either own or breed horses.

When I arrive at the parlor, Jennifer and Laura are already inside.

"Hi. I'm Randy. Rich's son."

We embrace each other for a few seconds.

"Hi Randy. I'm Laura."

"It's been a long time."

"Too long. Let's step outside and talk for a minute."

Laura and I walk hand in hand and go into another room. A small table is set up with water, coffee, bread, and lunch meats.

"So…Jen tells me that your father is in jail. Is he okay?"

"Oh, yeah. He actually keeps busy in there from what I hear. I keep letting the guards know I'm here to visit. I think my dad is afraid of getting too emotional if he sees me. The whole situation with what he did was a big misunderstanding. Let's just say he got careless. His temper got the best of him. But he's learned his lesson."

"Good."

So how have you been, I mean, what have you all been up to you?"

"Well, to be honest, it has been quite stressful for the past five years."

"What happened?"

"Carl suffered a stroke. He actually had a few. His last one was a major one. He could hardly walk or use the left side of his body. I think he got released from the hospital too soon. He was stubborn and didn't do much therapy. Even when he was at home with me, he didn't want to do much therapy. I hired a nurse to help him out but he was mean towards her. Then I would try another one. Same thing. Pretty soon, no nursing agency was willing to help me. I had to rely on family. Carl meant well but you have no idea how trying these last few years have been."

"His stubbornness rubbed off on my dad."

"But not on you, I hope."

"No. I wish I would have kept in touch with you and him more. I feel bad. I could have made the time to come down here to give you a helping hand."

"That's okay. I'm touched that you came down."

"I'll keep in touch with everyone more. Not only with you but with Jennifer too."

Carl's funeral was brief. The only people who were there were related to him. None of his relatives told any stories. I get the feeling Carl wasn't the most pleasant person to be around. His state of mind from his stroke caused a lot of hurt and headache. I'm sure he went well though. The only person who recited any prayer was the funeral parlor clergyman. I drove with the rest of the motorcade to the gravesite. Carl already picked out his plot. His stone will be set underneath a large tree. No other stone would fit to the right of his. Another spot is reserved to the left of his.

When I arrived back home, I had planned on telling Rosa how my trip went. She firmly planted herself on the couch. The television was on but her eyes were gazed upon her cellphone.

"Hi there, I'm back."

Rosa doesn't even look up at me or say hello.

"So the trip went well. The funeral service was nice. Short and sweet."

Still no response of even a that's nice out of Rosa's mouth.

I go into the kitchen to pour myself a cold glass of chocolate milk. I look into the sink to see several dirty plates and glasses. I yell out to Rosa from the kitchen.

"So did Angela call in sick?"

Is Rosa even paying one ounce of fucking attention to anything I'm saying? I walk into the laundry room. The basket is still full of dirty shirts, pants, and towels. I walk back into the living room. Rosa's eyes are still locked into her cellphone screen.

"Rosa? Did something happen to Angela?"

"What? Oh, I fired her."

"Why? What happened?"

Rosa began to get agitated at me for bothering her.

"She wasn't doing what I asked her. The sheets aren't clean enough."

"Oh. Well I can do the dishes. Tomorrow I also…"

"No don't. I" LL take care of the laundry. You never do the laundry right anyway. I don't want all of my white and darks in the same load."

"Allright then."

I go back in the kitchen to begin washing the dishes. Rosa is yelling at me but I can't hear her with the water running. I turn off the water as Rosa steps into the kitchen.

"Just leave all of it! I'm not going in to work tomorrow. I'm going to wash everything. Just leave the dishes alone."

"Okay. I was just wanting to help."

Rosa didn't respond back to my remark. I started talking again about my grandpa's funeral.

"It was nice to see Laura again. She's related to my dad. I also saw her sister and a few people I haven't see in a long time."

Rosa wasn't paying any attention. I could have said that I went to Kentucky to gamble, drink kegs of beer, fucked all my female cousins one after the other locomotive style, blew three fourths of our joint account on the finest pot and shine and had to take the ride home by bus. Rosa was only interested in what was happening in her world.

I decide to change the subject.

"So how is work going?"

"Fine. I want to watch and hear this."

I figured one night of her rude behavior was the result of her not getting enough sleep at night. But this kind behavior from her was growing to once a week. Then twice a week. Any time I would bring up wanting to hire someone new, Rosa would say no.

I didn't understand, Rosa doesn't want a professional cleaner to take care of our home but Rosa doesn't do any mopping, dusting, or even dish washing. I had to buy a package of paper plates. Or I would eat something out of my microwave bowl. And any time I did wash a dish, Rosa would point out the spots I missed. This coming from someone who didn't grow up around hard labor.

"I made sure the dishes are clean."

"Don't put any of them away! Just leave them! There not clean!"

"Are we still going over to your mom's?"

"No. She's coming over here. I told you this. You never listen. I said she may be spending the night."

"Oh, well we can all go out."

"I'm not going out anywhere!" Why would I take my mom out?" It's in the middle of the week."

I don't care what Rosa said. I know for a fact that Rosa never mentioned anything about her mom coming over. Rosa has gotten into a bad habit of telling me one thing then changing her mind at the last minute. Then she blames me for not paying attention to her. She needs to see a doctor about her mood swings.

"I was talking to Rick yesterday from work. He wants to meet up with me at the club."

I didn't care if Rosa believed me or not. I wasn't going to stick around here if Rosa was going to have her PMS moments.

"Fine. Leave."

"Call me if you or Amelia need anything."

Club Cyn isn't too busy tonight. I watch the men and women gyrate to the thumping techno music. I wish someone who I know other than Rick or Barry would come inside. I feel alone. Where's my companion for the evening? I certainly wasn't going to invite Rosa. Her pissy mood would have been a buzzkill. There's a man and woman are sitting next to each at the end of the bar. The man is trying to get the woman to leave the club with him. Everyone in the club is with someone, either talking, kissing, or dancing together.

"Ready for another one?" The bartender asks me, eager for a tip.

"Sure."

"Have you seen Angelina tonight?"

"You mean the owner's wife?"

"Yes."

"No not tonight. You know her?"

"I know all three of them. I've been helping with any parties that the hotel I work at hosts for them."

"Right on."

The bartender would ask me the same question relating to my having a drink four more times. I would stare down at my empty glass before responding with a yes. One vodka cranberry would be too weak. The next one would be too strong. This guy needs to take bartending 101 all over again.

"Can I get a cup of water?"

Drinking water helps dilute any alcohol in my body. I pull up my sleeve to look at my watch. It's only eleven thirty. My money is going away fast. Rick and Barry have become pals of mine but charging me the same five dollar price for a small glass of booze is nuts. I slide off the stool and head towards the bathroom. When I reach the closed in toilet, my forehead leans up against the wall as I urinate.

Oh shit, I need to stop drinking. There's no female coming in the club to meet you. You are all alone tonight. You are too drunk to call an escort.

I can walk through the club and out the door without stumbling over my own feet. I even remember where I parked my car. Once I get in, I can't help but take a piss again. So much for going to one of those twenty four hours diners. Now I'll have to find a twenty four hour fast food drive thru. The cold wet piss stain is causing my left leg to itch.

The bright lights blind me in the eyes. I stay on the correct side of the road. I know when to stop and go. No flashing lights or sirens are behind me. I keep my speed to the limit or a few miles underneath. I pull into the driveway and stop inches from the garage. I can't find the garage door opener anywhere. I walk fast up to the front door. The house is dark. That's good, Rosa doesn't need to see what my pants look like.

I throw the pants into the washing machine. As I'm putting on a fresh pair blue jeans, I fall on the bed. I struggle to get myself up and go to the bathroom. I grab a bottle of painkillers and pop three of them in my mouth. Then I take out the two tacos I ordered. After eating, I put my pants into the dryer. Instead of going back into the bedroom, I fall back first on the couch. I have perfected the remedy for avoiding a throbbing headache caused by a hangover.

Rosa and Amelia were sound asleep on the bed together. Our sofa is one of those where there's a hideaway bed tucked inside. It never occurred to me that either one of them could have been awakened by the noise coming from the machine. Later in the week, when Rosa finally did some laundry she questioned why the washer was used earlier.

"Did you do a load of clothes?"

"Yeah, I had to do a pair of my jeans. I spilled some sauce on them."

You made a mess with the soap. If you don't know to properly use the machine then don't wash anything. Now I have clean this up first."

"I'm sorry."

"Don't be sorry. Please just don't use the machine again."

Living with Rosa has become my own personal prison. Maybe I'll search for one of those cheap studio apartments. Or one of those extended business suites. Make up some kind of story like our department is going to be a part of a convention. I'll be gone for two days. If that doesn't work out, maybe I'll visit the prison my dad's at. Ask the warden if he has any empty cells.

I wonder if my dad even reads my letters that I wrote to him. He plays the tough, unemotional alpha male while he's in prison. I'm going over in my mind what kind of conversation my dad and this Cleo or Leon or whatever his name is are having when they work together.

"Time to make our money again huh?"

"That's all we have in here boy is time."

"Whose turn is it to wash?"

"Shit, I don't know. Tonight was fish with cheese. The plates and pots are going to be a motherfucker to scrub. You wash this time and I'll dry and put away."

"Thanks a lot. So I got a letter from my son. The letter says my dad passed away. He thinks I can just leave here and go to the funeral. My boy doesn't always use his head. But at least my son and his wife are still together."

"I feel you. Many times I wanted to put my kid's heads through the Goddamn wall. They think with their dicks instead of their brains."

"You have any grandkids Rich?"

"Not yet. At least none that I know of."

"You got a girlfriend waiting for you?"

"Sure do. Ready and waiting."

"That's what it's all about. Having someone wait for you on the other side."

"What about you."

"Shit, I alienated my family years ago. That's okay. I don't need a woman wrapped around my neck, never did. I keep waiting for one of my daughters to visit me but they never do."

"How many daughters do you have?"

"Four"

"Wow, all grown up huh?"

"Oh yeah. My oldest daughter is thirty five. Or thirty six. Shit, I forget. But it's probably all for the best. They all moved away and went on with their own lives. Hell, I don't know if I'm a grandpa or not. I'm sure I have a bunch of grandkids. When I was around, none of my kids never wanted me in their business anyhows. All of my daughters had different boyfriends who just wanted to stick their dicks in them. I hated all of their boyfriends. None of them could hold down a job, one of them got arrested for grand theft auto, most of them would be cheaters. If I threatened any of them with a knife then I was the villain. They never talk to me about anyone anymore. That's probably a good thing. I'd end up killing one of them."

"Shit if I had a daughter who got pregnant by a loser I'd hammer the punk to the wall Jesus style."

"Amen brother. But you know? Sometimes you got to be on your own two feet. They are adults. If she wants to learn the hard way about life, then she will learn what happens when you get pregnant before you even turn sixteen. Not like any of them are going to give a fuck what I have to say."

"That's what your kids do. You have their best interests but they defy you anyway. My son doesn't smoke and knows better not to drink and drive. He's not street smart but stays out of trouble."

"Sounds like a good kid."

"He tries. You know between the two of us, we run this kitchen. Now if they would only let us use knives to cook with."

"Ha! Boy they won't let me near a pearing knife!"

"Or even a dull one! Hahahaha!"

"Man, shit! Hahaha!"

Maybe my dad enjoys being in prison more than he does at home. At least in there, he doesn't have to deal with the stupidity that most people possess. He's no longer angry at his boss or the way life has treated him. My dad is thinking what he did happened in the past and all is forgotten about. I say my dad got lucky. If Jeff would have died soon after he went into the hospital, my dad would have gotten life or even the death penalty. His new friend of sorts, has taught him a hard lesson in humility.

16
AMENDS

Change is inevitable. The only way I'll accept change is if the change benefits me. When you start changing polices and procedure that end up hurting someone or make another person's day miserable then what good does that change do? It's the same old phrase-don't fix what was never broken. No one listens. Too many of these hasty and awful changes are happening in my life all at once.

The Clarion hotel now has new owners. The old owners were close to retiring and instead of closing the place down or promoting anyone from the inside, these rarely seen in pubic dinosaurs have dollar signs bored in their eyes. The hotel is now run by a group of three men who have rhyming first names-Ron, Don, and Juan. Real quick, I need to back up. The empty parking lot across the street from the hotel was converted into a sand volleyball court. A national sports station even televised one summer event. The swimming pool had a cash bar built right in the center of the pool. Those two amenities were the main reason why the hotel raked in the money during the past few years.

Ron stared into the future. Of course his vison resulted in mass failure. He managed to build more rooms with internet access. He called the rooms' chateaus. Are we back in Paris? He also eliminated our popular continental breakfast and replaced it with a café serving organic breads, pears and kiwis, and a mocha flavored coffee that tasted like melted bm. The smell of the fake coffee seemed pleasant, but believe me, the first time I swallowed, I was throwing up all day.

The public wasn't buying into Ron's new vision of what the Clarion needed. The regular guests are now staying at the Renaissance. The owners of the Renaissance stole the Clarion's ideas of having a weekly open lobby bar for the guests, surf and turf menu items on Fridays and building a brand new indoor pool and spa center.

Don is a complete imbecile. He refused to order new vacuums, floor buffers, and side door that leads into the banquet kitchen. The ones we currently use need repairing or replaced altogether. The rooms now were looking dingy and pee stains were visible on the bathroom tile. Our side door sticks when you want to open it or close it. The hotel had the money to spend on the new equipment. Instead, Don got Phil fired for mismanaging money and decides to spend any hotel profit money on a very expensive new menu overhaul. Don also installed a security camera that hovers over the front lobby. He is the newly self- created Clarion hotel spy.

Juan is my new boss. I have a hard time understanding most of the words that come out of his mouth. He may excel in baking a cake but his English skills could use some polishing. Juan hated working with Fred. They were always arguing over food preparation. Fred got wise and put in his two week notice. I have no idea where he's working at now. Wouldn't surprise me if he went to any one of our competitors. John had enough of the three bozos lack of business knowledge that he leaves the hotel with NO advanced warning to become a silent partner at the Renaissance Hotel. And the train kept moving out-then Robert left, followed by Paul, Albert, Tony, David, Derrick, and Les. Hell, I lost all my boys!

The only employee who stayed on that I cared about was Jerry. I hope Jerry forms a backbone and takes no shit from these dillholes. Ron didn't care if anyone left, he already had someone lined up ready to replace each one of them. All of his replacements were former line cooks who couldn't properly marinate a chicken even if the chicken marinate manual fell in their laps.

I was debating whether or not to stay or go. Juan made the decision easy. Instead of serving surf and turf with starch, the kitchen was going to serve all organic and gluten free dishes. OH PEEE UK! David had called me earlier to talk more about the shit -all disaster that was becoming the Clarion hotel.

"Hi Randy. Good to hear your voice again. Are you still at the Clarion?"

"Not for long. The new menu sucks and my new boss is a dildo. My hours vary from afternoon to evenings without much notice. Everyone from our crew is long gone. All the chefs here are rookies out of college. They all got fed up or just didn't like how the hotel was changing everything. One after another they all put in their notices. The chefs no longer dish out the surf and turf. Instead it's all seaweed and kale. The guests, especially our long time regulars don't like the new menu."

"Haha. So tell me how you really feel about the place. Have you applied anywhere else?"

"I have my feelers out, that's about it. It helps to have an establish hotel listed on my resume. How's it going with you at the Coranado Club.?"

"Yes it does. It's Friday night every night and double on Saturdays. Hey listen, if you are interested, there is an opening here for a night shift line cook. You would work Monday through Friday nights only, we have plenty of weekend help. I know it would be a step down, but at least you would be preparing similar dishes like we were at the Clarion. It would be just like the old days. And believe me, we get busy on the weekends. Let me know soon though, I think the position will be filled soon."

"I will. Thanks for the inside scoop. Good talking to you."

I was on my way home when I forgot I had to pick up some aspirin for Rosa. After I pick up her drugs, I go to the hardware store. I need to get car emergency supplies. I buy a first aid kit, a can of fix it flat, a giant flashlight, four D size batteries to put in the flashlight, and a twenty inch metal chain. The chain will be used if I need any extra traction, a substitution sand or gravel.

Charles has moved all the way down to Staunton, Missouri. He got a job working part time at a local copy and print shop. He and I agree to meet halfway at a Tully's bar. Like heck it was halfway, I was only five miles from Staunton. The few homes I did pass were spaced out by at least a mile. When you live out here you will get your privacy. Charles is living in a condo unit about a half mile from the bar. Tully's is a popular, crowded place but that's probably because there is no other bar around here for the locals to go to.

I had given Charles the short version of what happened to my dad. He couldn't remember much of what I said so he makes it a point to bring the subject up.

"So dude, what's up with your father? The last I heard from you is that we was arrested."

"He got fifteen years for all of his crimes. His parole coming up though. He should be getting an early release."

"Damn dude, that's fucked up. There are people who do far worse than destroying property and making threats. Man, there are people who I want to just kill you know. That judge was just making an example out of him. I'm sorry."

"Don't be. He learned his lesson."

"Yeah, well don't you do anything stupid. He can handle himself in prison. You on the other hand would get raped, beaten, and tortured all in the first day."

"Fuck off. I can take care of myself. Besides, I'm not about to do anything foolish and jeopardize my career. So, how's the new job?"

"The job is a job. I only make twelve an hour. I deserve more."

"I hear you. I'm tired of all these people wining about their wage. They're not like you or me. We work hard for our money. These fast food workers have the simple task of hearing an order, getting it right, and handing the shit over. I mean you cannot fuck up an order of chicken nuggets. Well apparently you can if you are a dumbfuck who presses cheeseburger on the register instead of nuggets. And I lost count how many times they consistently fuck up my burger by putting ketchup on it after I clearly say NO KETCHUP! I speak English. It's not my fault you had to learn English before you were hired. They all should be thankful that we even allow them to work. They want fifteen dollars an hour?! Be happy you make eight."

"Damn dude. You're worse than me. Shit, I created a monster."

"Oh I'm not done yet. Be glad you don't work at the Clarion anymore anyway. The print stuff is now handled by a low grade outside company. I saw some of their samples. The designs were on the same level as a fourth grader learning how to color for the first time."

"Haha. I believe you dude, I believe you!"

"Let's have a toast. To our new beginnings and continued success!"

"To our friendship."

After that visit, Charles became a ghost. His phone number is disconnected. I never met any of his friends, so I don't have any way to reach out to him. I didn't feel like driving all the way down to Staunton. I figured Charles would call me if he wanted to talk. After four months of no phone calls from him, I deleted him from my contacts.

Charles wasn't the only person I knew that vanished from my life.

"Hey dad, just calling to say hi and that grandma and Nancy are going good."

"Great. How's work and Rose?"

"Surviving on all fronts."

"So now big news to share?"

"Oh, here's some news for you. You remember your friend Trent?"

"Oh yeah. I haven't seen him in ages. He never visited me once."

"Well, that's because he passed about two years after you left."

"Awww. That's sad. Do you know what happened?"

"Well, this is just what I heard around the car show campfire. Trent was dating a guy and…"

"What! A guy?!"

"Yes. Several of the guys I talked to also knew Trent said that he was dating a man. Anyway, from what I heard, Trent and whoever he was dating had a bad breakup."

"Oh sheeit."

"This is where I think people blow the cause out of proportion. People say he committed suicide over them breaking up."

"Oh shit. Who would of thought?"

In addition to humans, the letters also stopped coming. No more lawsuits and no more monies to be paid. Pete Lawton passed away. Let's see- Daniel, grandpa, Trent, and now Pete. My first thought is that Pete died from the injuries suffered at the hands of my dad. Not so, Pete's family had a cancer history. Jeff rehabbed quickly from his car related injuries but not from his colon cancer. All of this I know because Pete's daughter Kayla spread the news to several employees. I never had or have the courage to tell Kayla how sorry I am not only to hear about her dad dying but for my own fathers' actions towards her family. My fear is that she will hate me and start crying in public after she finds out who I am.

I've lost count how many letters I have written to my dad. He's only responded to four. All of his letters to me were repetitious. How is work? How are you and Rosa? Are you making a million dollars? How does my house look? How's mom? He is not aware of Trent and Pete's passing. I'm not going to tell him either. He can find out on his own. I'll play dumb if he asks me about it later. My dad is calm and I don't want the news to upset him or get him to gloat. I made an appointment with my dad's parole officer. I want to hear from him what my dad can and cannot do once released.

"Mr. Stevens. Guy Tisdale."

"Thanks for meeting with me. I just want to know what's going to happen with my dad once he's out."

"Depends on whether or not he stays clean and doesn't violate his parole."

"Like what?"

"I know he will be placed under house arrest for six months. He will have to wear an ankle bracelet. We'll know if he takes it off. After that, he will be allowed to go out, even travel out of the country if he wants. But if he is caught going out before then or if he is caught making any threats to Pete Lawton or his family then he will be arrested."

"Well Pete is dead, his family has moved, and the company is no longer in business. I doubt he will cause any trouble. I'm glad he has wear a bracelet. Keeps him on a leash for a while. So, you will let him know all of this, right?"

"Yes. He will know what he can and can't do."

"Thanks a lot for the info."

My dad survived eleven years in prison. He's about at the age of retirement. His finances are not great, but since I took out a few grand and put them in an account under my name, he has money. I got clarification about my dad's solitary confinement. He can go outside. On the porch. To the garage. He can't go anywhere over ten miles.

A week before my dad's return home, I drive over to his place. I mow and trim the lawn. I bring in bags of non- perishable food items to place in the pantry. There are ten two liter soda bottles, five packages of chocolate chip cookies, five cans of beef stew, two cans of beer nuts, four large bags of regular potato chips, and one family size bag of plain M&M's. I also stock the fridge and freezer with a gallon of white milk, gallon of chocolate milk, bread, butter, chocolate ice cream, and Salisbury steak TV dinners.

I go next door to say hello to grandma. She's asleep on her couch. I walk past her and stop at her bedroom. There are some envelopes and letters on her night stand. One is a letter for my mom, another for Nancy, and one for Jeff Lawton. Jeff's envelope has a yellow sticker glued on top. I rip open that letter.

"Dear Pete Lawton and Family,

You may not remember me. My name is Rich. I used to work at PowerSTL manufacturing. About ten years ago I was let go from there. I was angry, furious, and pissed off. I took all my anger out on you and your family and the company. I even drove my car on your front lawn and plowed into your front porch. I fired shots at you and even ran you over with my car! What in the heck was I thinking! I wasn't thinking! My mind was all messed up. I got caught and was arrested. The judge showed me no mercy. He made an example out of me. I was sentenced to fifteen years in prison. My girlfriend says the company is no longer around. I won't ask where you relocated to. That is history. During my time in prison I was lonely. I missed my family. My mom, son, girlfriend, and even my ex wife! I was mad. Mad people do crazy things without thinking. Humans make mistakes. Boy did I make a huge one and ended up paying for them. I'm going to retire. I have way too much catching up to do. Life is short. I should of went to the president. Maybe I would of received some kind of compensation pay. I ended up with no pay. If I hurt you bad, I hope you are healed. I hope you got your porch fixed. I am asking that you forgive me and let's put the past away for good. Thank you for not going after my son and my mom. Neither of them deserves to be punished over my selfish actions.

Sincerely,
Rich Stevens.

The postmark date on the envelope is dated something 2006. Even of the letter did reach Jeff, he was already dead. I know my dad wrote this letter to help him with getting an early release. My dad swallowed his pride and kissed plenty of legal asses. My grandma is still sleeping. I read the letter written to his mom.

Dear mom,

Greetings from the big house!

My parole is finally here! You have no idea how lonely and depressing it has been in here. There have been many days where I just said fuck it and wanted to end my life. Talking to Randy and Nancy and writing to you has been what's kept me going. It will feel sooooooooooo good to sleep in my own bed again. In here you sleep on a mattress that is as hard as a brick. And it would be my luck that my mattress has a spring that has popped out.

I have been keeping myself busy by working in the kitchen and library. Cleo is my main man. He and I make a good team. He will do most of the cooking. I help him and I also wash the pots and pans. Cleo works fast and keeps me on my feet. For a black guy, he doesn't act like one. Cleo works hard and takes pride in his work. He is in here because the judge ruled against him in an armed robbery.

Cleo says he was the victim of mistaken identity. I believe him. Cleo isn't the kind of person who would rob someone. He got twenty years in the bighouse for his crime. If I'm not working in the kitchen, I wheel a cart around that has books and magazines in it. Twice a month a minister will come to the prison. When he arrives then the lunch room becomes a church. Cleo and I both attend.

I have been praying at night and God has answered. I'm so happy that you and Nancy have become friends. She tells me all about taking you to the doctor and to the grocery store. Make sure you keep taking whatever medication you need to take. Does Randy help you with keeping track? God love both of them!

You have remained healthy and happy because of them and because of Regina. We are all family. We made it through the good and bad times together and came out of it together! I'm super proud of Randy's success as a chef. I hope that he is willing to share all the money he has been making with us. He told me that he has two welcome home gifts waiting for me when I get home. UH-OH! I can't wait to see what they are. Knowing him he's probably baked a giant cake with a moveable top. I'll bet a stripper pops out of the cake.

Not sure if I'm going to go back to work. I'm too old to go on job interviews. I'm ready to retire. You and I, and Nancy should take a long vacation. How does that sound?

Sometimes, I tell the guard that I'm feeling sick. I only do this to do to the infirmary. When I'm at sickbay I can take a nice long nap. The beds there are more comfortable than the ones in the cells. There are too may rough people in here. People who have murdered someone and gave it no thought. I stay away from them and mind my own business. I don't want to do anything that will mess up my parole. I am ready to COME HOME! I even wrote a letter to my former boss and told him how sorry I was for doing what I did. The lights are about to go out so I will stop writing. Take care and I will see you soon!

Love, your son
Rich

Hmm, my dad sounds sincere. Next, I read the letter he wrote to Nancy.

> *Hi sugar lips!*
>
> *It's the love bandit.*
>
> *I'm walking tall and looking good. I'm on my best behavior doing everything the guards tell me to do. My parole officer knows all about my good behavior. I am making amends with my former company. I want to put all of this behind me and start over. I miss you so much! I know that you have been taking care of my mom. THANK YOU THANK YOU THANK YOU! There is no way that I can ever pay you back. No amount of money or gifts. I will never stop saying thank you. I learned my lesson not to destroy property or hurt people.*
>
> *There are several people in here including my friend Cleo who are here for life. I don't know how any of them make through the days and nights. I would go nuts. You, mom, Randy, and Gina writing and calling me is what kept me going and gave me hope that I would survive.*
>
> *I'm ready to go home and then take some long naps and trips. There are some people who would of left their old man if he went to jail for a long time. Thank you for staying with me. I'm going to repay you back for the rest of my life. When we retire we can rent one of those big campers with a built in kitchen. We can cruise up and down the highways all across the united states.*
>
> *Love always*
> *Rich AKA The love bandit*

My dad even wrote a short letter to my mom.

Greetings from Alcatraz!

It may not be Alcatraz but it is close. Dark, cold and quiet. Are you still living in the same place as before? I have one suggestion. Save up your money and buy a burglar alarm. You will feel safer and so will I. Randy tells me that you don't want to move out. I understand, my mom won't move out either. My mom has lived here for seventy years! I know she's not going anywhere. Besides, she's too young to go into a retirement home!

I will never be able to repay you for all the help and times you drove down to visit my mom. I will have to borrow money from Randy. He's probably running the hotel by now. I hope he is willing to share his good fortunes with you and me. Hey, are you going out on any dates? You deserve to have fun and be happy. Uh-oh, the lights are flickering and means lights out around here. Take care and I will see you soon.

Sincerely,
Rich

I hear movement in the living room. I put the last letter down and walk out of my grandma's bedroom.

I didn't go with Nancy to the prison pick up my dad. I figured the two of them would want some alone kissing time with each other. My heart is racing. How does grandma remain calm? Nancy opens my grandma's front door. Behind her, emerges a man who I do not recognize. He's older in the face. The brown hair is gone, replaced by gray. My dad bends over to give his mom a long hug.

"Holy Jesus, the place is still in one piece."

My dad's eyes begin to tear up. I wasn't about to run into his arms. The two of us were never loving or emotional towards each other. I didn't see any reason why we should start now.

"Welcome home."

Those were the only two words I could say to him.

My dad walks into the kitchen. He stands still, staring at the walls. Then he walks into the hallway and then to the back bedroom. He is silent as he walks. My dad could break down emotionally at any moment. He is desperately trying hard not to cry. He walks back into the living room then plops down on the couch. The small black ankle bracelet wrapped around his ankle becomes visible.

"Oh this feels so good! I am going to sleep for an entire week!"

"Yeah, I'll bet the mattress here will feel a lot more comfortable."

"You better believe it. Sometime in the future I'll want to make an appointment with the doctor. Have him or her give me a through checkup."

"I can always make an appointment with my doctor. She's a six foot Russian witch doctor who takes pleasure putting objects in your eyes, ears, throat, and behind."

"Oh great! I think I'll pass on her."

"I did a few things for you to help keep you occupied since you will be at home most of the time."

I choose my words carefully as not to anger or upset my dad.

"Rosa and I made plans this weekend but either next weekend or when I get a few days off I'll come down to see you. In the meantime I called the cable company. You are set up with the extended basic channels plus you get one premium channel for one year. Here's the list of all the channels you have. There are two remotes to use. This one turns the TV on and off, changes the channels, and controls the volume. The other remote is used to control the VCR. Nancy or I can show you how to work this one. It's not as difficult as it sounds. I also subscribed to a hot rod and classic car magazine. The first issue already came. It's over on the table. You'll be getting eleven more issues. Call them both a birthday and Christmas present. And all your tools and car cleaning supplies are still in the garage."

"I can't drive anytime soon. Is the truck still running?"

"Oh yeah. I've had the truck at the mechanic. When the time comes that you can drive, the truck will be ready to go."

My dad kept shaking his head and forth as I was telling him what I did.

"Randy Oh Jesus. You went way above and beyond."

"You're welcome. All I ask is you do what your parole officer tells you. No arguments and no breaking any rules."

"Trust me I will. This bracelet isn't coming off."

"One day, after you can get out, then you and I can go to the bank. We can get your own account started up again. You do have money here, I have the dollars in a white envelope. But I still have some of your money in an account with my name on it only. I will start transferring that money back to you. There hasn't been any letters from any attorneys for a long time. Nancy and I also want my mom to keep coming over. My mom can help grandma get dressed and cleaned up."

My dad nods his head in agreement. His actions surprised me.

"Regina can stop by anytime she wants to. I will even give her gas money so she can be here. I will never forget what she or any of you did for my mom while I was gone."

Nancy gets up to put her coat on.

"It's getting late and I have to get up early. I'll call you tomorrow. I'm so happy and thankful you're home and safe."

My dad and Nancy kiss each other on the lips for a long time. After Nancy leaves, my dad walks over on my side of the duplex.

"Nothing's really changed over here. The place is dustier. The one chair that was there is now at moms. I still have your old playboys in a box. There in the basement."

"Hahahahahaha. You can take them with you if you want."

"I don't have any reason to."

"I know you need to be getting back home so go ahead and leave. We'll talk more."

I look at my watch to see what time it is. A few minutes before seven. Rosa has been with Karen and Amelia all day.

"I need to call Rosa. She knows I'm over here."

Her phone keeps ringing, so I'll leave a message.

"Hi there, I'm still over at my dad's. I'll be home in a couple of hours."

"I guess she is at her mom's."

"So do you want to watch a movie? Do we still have Stripes?"

"Yeah. All of your films are still in the closet. You might be only person on the block who still has a VCR. Are you hungry?"

"Nancy brought over a plate of food, a boneless pork rib and some carrots. Plus, we got all that food in the icebox thanks to you."

"Right. I know you though. You'll just eat ice cream and cookies"

"Yeah, and then I'm going to have beer nuts and M&M's for dessert. Hahaha!"

Laughter is what both my dad and I could use after some stressful times.

So far, my dad has not violated his parole. He has not taken off his ankle bracelet. He even wears the bracelet when he goes to bed. My dad has mastered the skill in the fine art of channel surfing. With over two hundred channels, you would think he would find something to interest him. He watches a lot of drag racing or old black and white action films.

"Here's some flyers of upcoming shows I copied for you."

"Oh thanks. I'll look at these later. The truck is looking good. I've got her all cleaned up."

"Are you planning on driving once your house arrest is done?"

"Oh sure. Nancy got me a copy of the driver's manual. I have to take all the tests over again before I can get my license. I don't know if we will go to any shows. The truck isn't really ready. I'd rather sell the truck and buy one of those campers. Then Nancy and I can go on long trips when the weather is nice. I guess you need to study for driving those too."

"I'm sure you'll pass."

"Oh I will. But it doesn't hurt to study."

Any thoughts I had of my dad still holding a grudge are slipping away. My dad has yet to bring up his work, Pete, or even Trent. There were two stuffed bags leaning up against the back door.

"Before you leave can you take out those bags? I threw out all my old papers relating to my work. I also threw out clothes that don't fit me anymore. You can take my Playpens. I would hide them from Rose. Heehee."

"Rosa. And no I'll pass on the playpens. Want me to help you clean up the house?"

"No, I'll do all the cleaning myself during the day. Keeps me busy."

"Okay then I taking off."

"All righty, so I guess I'll see you soon."

Not only does my dad look different, he sounds different. His composure is calm and relaxing. He doesn't use a cuss word in any of his sentences. He's grateful to everyone who watched over his mom while he was away. The time away in prison may have reformed my dad but the cynic in me still doesn't trust his motives. Is his behavior all a ruse? Time will tell if and when he returns to being the angry, hateful human being I grew up being around.

17
A DIFFERENT KIND OF HATE

The first few years being married to Rosa were the happiest times of my life. Yeah, those words are sappy and redundant, but it is the truth. On our weekends off from work together, the two of us would do what we called half and halfs. That is, for one day the two of us would do something I enjoyed. Maybe a night out at a nightclub or a bar. Then the next day, we would visit quaint antique shops or watch a romantic comedy together. If I had to play board games with her and her family, she would have to attend a hockey game with me. The point of this was to embrace and appreciate each other's activities and experience them together.

Lately, being together has come to a screeching halt. Rosa slept all Saturday morning and into the early afternoon. Instead of arguing about trivial shit like crumbs left on a plate, Rosa just treats me like I don't exist. Rosa still makes the effort to go into work. But after work or on her day off, she hibernates and shuts herself off from the outside world.

"Rosa honey, would you like some lunch? I can go to The Fish and Chips deck and pick up some crab cakes and fish tacos?"

"I'm not really hungry, I'll have a bowl of cereal."

"Okay, I can always find something here to eat. Does seven sound good? That way you'll have plenty of time to take a shower?"

"What's at seven?"

"The film. Starts at eight. Then we going to have a drink at Club Cyn."

"Oh…I'm not up to it today. My stomach has been hurting. If you want to still go.."

"Not by myself. Maybe I'll go to the bar though."

Yeah, one Rosa huddles herself back into the fetal position on the bed, I know she won't want to get up until the late afternoon. Rosa only communicates with friends and co-workers by texting on her phone. Texting is basically typing a message to someone then pressing the send button. All done on your own phone. It's the most impersonal way to have a conversation with someone. My preferred way of communicating with someone is face to face. No wait, nose hair to nose hair.

When I make lasagna or made from scratch tacos and biscuits, I make enough so that Rosa will have some. She tells me that she will eat some but doesn't. So I end up eating all the food or in some cases end up throwing the shit out. At first, she was signaling me out, now she doesn't even go out with her friends from work. No more clubs, casinos, or bars.

She even refuses to go to any flea markets with Karen or her mom. Rosa would rather sleep all day or sleep late, drink hot tea, and firmly plant her rear end on the couch. All she does is watch Spanish speaking soap operas or reality style shows that deal with relationships.

One afternoon, Rosa was sitting kumbiya style on the couch. She was watching a program, about what I have no idea, wiping tears from her eyes with several tissues.

"Rosa honey, what's wrong?"

"Oh, it's just this program. A young man has feelings for another man. He finally has the courage to tell everyone but has to face ridicule from his family and the town people. It's so sad."

"Yeah, what's the world coming to? People need to be more sensitive and stay out of it all if it doesn't even concern them. Need some more kleenax?"

"No, I'm okay thank you though."

I sure in the shit hope this is not what all my weekends are going to be like. Rosa has expressed in a roundabout way that she wants me to be at home more when I'm not at work. Fine, but let's do something that I would like to do. Or let's go back to the trendy restaurants and flashy nightclubs. I am not going watch fucking boo hoo stories all day.

Rosa had stopped going to church. Amelia persuaded her to start going again. I even told both of them that I would go. Amelia has made peace with Daniel's passing. Amelia still cries when she comes across a picture of the two of them. But, she is moving on with her life. She has returned to the salon. She goes out more with her friends. Karen and Amelia have invited Rosa to go with them to local wineries. I pass. Rosa feigns illness or cancels at the last minute.

Rosa has maintained her focus at work. The only difference is now she doesn't want me to see her at work. That is, on her lunch break or for any surprise visit. Her reason was a lame excuse:

"Oh listen, I'm not allowed to have any visitors at work anymore. We have a new policy regarding non employees. It's for the safety and sanitary of the animals. I'm not excluding you alone. It's everyone. If my mom or aunt come by that might be different. It's not you okay. It's the work policy."

At what point on our lives did I go from being your husband to a low life visitor? I shrugged off everything she said. Anyway, each time I offer to bring her food to work, she shuts me down. I'm too busy. We have an emergency at the cottage. I'm not hungry. Pasta noodles give me bad gas all day. My mom is stopping by and we are having lunch. Don't forget to pick up a box of ultra- fresh tampons. The roads are flooded this way. One of the horses' piss is green. The dog is terrorizing the chickens. Yawn, I'm too tired to eat. One pathetic excuse after another.

A week later, Rosa informs me that her brother Gino will be stopping by for a quick visit. His tour in the military is ending. Rosa didn't seem to want me to see the guy.

"When Gino visits it will only be for a few days. He has a new job lined in North Carolina. He's just stopping by to say hi to me, my mom, and Karen. The four of us are getting together at Cardel's Restaurant. You'll be a work right?"

"Yeah, but maybe I can work out a trade. I would love to see Gino. It's been a while since we talked. I'm sure he could go for a drink."

"Gino doesn't drink. And you shouldn't either. Don't get mad, it's just that my mom wants to spend time with him before he leaves again."

"Hey I understand. I'm not upset. And your right, my schedule is all over the place. It's cool. Just let him know I said hello and hope everything goes great for him."

"I will, thanks."

Well fuck you too bitch. I mean what's the big deal about me not seeing your brother. Just because he's a computer expert and some American war hero doesn't mean he's better than me. I thought I was a part of your family. I care about you, Amelia, and Karen. Although right now my caring for you is becoming less and less. You rarely ask how my mom, dad, and grandma are doing. Quite frankly, I don't give a fuck if you don't give a shit anyway. Aw fuck it, I'm not about to ball over this. I have enough shit to deal with at work and still making sure my dad doesn't get a hair up his ass and starts misbehaving.

Here's another situation that was a big surprise to me. Nancy sold her house and has moved in with my dad. She hired professional movers to pick up her large queen size bed, couch, dresser and twenty inch TV. Some of her friends and I helped bring over boxes of clothes and other personal items of hers. There is a lot of furniture in my dad's house. For now, Nancy's furniture is in the basement or I my old room. My dad and I are in my old room reminiscing and planning for the future.

"You never got rid of the old bed? I remember you spending a lot of time down here by yourself. Makes me wonder what you were doing."

"Funny. I had everything I needed, except for a fridge. And no, the mattress sags and I think a spring has even popped out. I couldn't sell the damn thing. See that over there? That's the old stereo system. The eight track still works, I just don't have any working eight track cassettes."

"We should throw the bed away."

"I think I'll be turning this room into my own man cave. Nancy will use the spare bedroom as her own getaway place. Hey! Listen, after I get the truck all cleaned up and looking good, Nancy and I are going start going to more out of state car shows and cruises. There's a real good one in Piggott Arkansas. We'll let you know when we are going and you and Rose can go with us."

"Maybe, I'll have to check my schedule. So, Nancy decided to move in with you. Are you okay with that?"

"She got a real good price for her home. I know she will closer to her work and my mom loves her. She also won't be paying high taxes anymore."

My dad and I walk upstairs. Nancy is sitting on the couch watching a TV program. My dad sits right beside her then pulls her in closer to him. When in the hell did my dad start cuddling?

"Hey Randy, did you take any pictures when you went on trips to the Bahamas or to Europe. Get a load of Mr. Moneybags and all his travels. Heehee. I never got to see any pictures. I hope you took some! If it were me I would go through at least five rolls of film. Wow, did you see the Eiffel tower while you were in Paris? I want to hear all about your cruise. Where will you go next? To the moon?"

"Not any time soon. Your bracelet comes off in a few days. You'll be the one leaving."

"Boy will that feel good. I've done everything I was supposed to do. I have one final visit with the parole officer. Nancy and I would like to go to Las Vegas but will probably go to Branson instead. Branson is just like Vegas only you see Mickey Meadows instead of Willie Taylor. You and Rose are always welcome to come too. Ohhh. I also want to go to Kentucky to see my dad's grave. We'll do that before we go to Branson."

"No, that's cool. The two of you could use the alone time anyway. Rosa would rather stay at home or work long hours. Or spend time with her mom and aunt. Sometimes we'll make weekend plans or plan to do something on my day off but then Rosa changes her mind at the last fucking second. Puts the rest of my day in the shithole. I wouldn't mind if Rosa changed her mind one time but she's been making a habit of doing this. She also calls me at the last minute to say that she's spending the night at her mom's. So I end up eating at ten at night. And if I do eat before she gets home then she has a tissy fit because she hasn't eaten yet. I can't win but I grin and bear it."

"Geez Randy. I know. And you women. They change their minds. You just have to go with the flow. You have to remember that she is still hurting from her dad passing away. Remember when you finally told me about this. It takes time. You need to be patient with her. She feels more comfortable being with her mom. And her mom needs her now. Don't get worked up. I know she still cares about you."

Either my dad read books about how to be sensitive and not a belligerent asshole while in prison or he is saying all of this sweet talk to make himself look good in front of Nancy. Either way, all of his all gee whiz that's life attitude is giving a bad case of the heebie jeebies.

I continue to pour on my bile of contempt.

"I hear you loud and clear. I'm not being pushy at all. But you know women, no offense Nancy, if I call and tell her that I'm at the Clarion's bar having a drink with friends and I'll be home later then Rosa get into one of her moods and pretty much demands that I hurry up and come home. I don't know why. We aren't going anywhere. And then Rosa hired someone to clean the house. Then she fires her later on! Rosa seems to think that I can't do a simple task like throw sheets in the wash or take a mop to the floors. Want to take a wild guess as to who paid for this service all by themselves? And I'm not even done yet. If I want to watch any TV, I have to watch the program in another room because Rosa gets all offended when she hears someone say fuck, shit, or pussy. Oh well, I know I'm married for better or worse."

My dad and Nancy couldn't stop laughing while I was venting. The two really started laughing loud when I said fuck, shit, and pussy.

"He really is your son!" Nancy bellows."

"Oh Randy. You are a married man Randall Stevens. Rosa's just being Rosa. She's going through a rough patch. You need to support her. Be nice and don't do or say anything that would upset her. She'll get better. Just hang in there. Hey, if you ever need or want to get way, you are always welcome to stay here. This is still your home. I'll make room in the garage. Hahahaha!"

I smile and give my dad the middle finger. This causes my dad and Nancy to resume laughing at me.

"You are too much. You want to stay here and have dinner with us? Nancy has T-bone steaks on the grill."

"Nah, I'll pass. I need to get home."

"Okay then, so I guess I'll see you and Rosa soon. We all need to get together. Be sure to say hello to grandma before you leave. She misses you."

"I will. Bye Nancy."

"See ya."

Rosa has been calling to let me know if she is working late or staying at her mom's.

"Hi there. Listen, I'm not coming home tonight. My mom isn't feeling well and I want to stay with her."

"Sure. I'll be fine. Tell your mom I hope she feels better."

"I will. Bye."

I thought about going to the Clarion's bar. There is a new female bartender working there. From what I hear, she's single and loaded up with a pair of huge tits. It's not a payday week so my cash flow is low. Shit, I don't want to stay at home. By myself. I pull out my wallet and find Karen's number. After three rings, she answers.

"Hello?"

"Hi Karen, its Randy. Rosa is spending the night at her mom's place. It's nice outside. Would you..want to get together?"

"Well, I'm not wanting to go out anywhere. If you want, you can come over here. We can play some Wii bowling or golf."

Karen's new adult toy is a Wii console. You hook the box up to your TV set. Then you buy games such as Jeopardy, Monopoly, or Slot Poker. The toy comes with two remotes that you use to control the games with. The entire device is like playing an arcade game or board game using your TV set as the monitor.

"Sure, sounds great. When should I come over?"

"Anytime. Leave now and I'll see you in about an hour."

Before I arrive at Karen's, I stop at the grocery store to pick up a vegetable and ranch dip tray for the two of us to share. The official time it takes to get from my place to hers is fifty six minutes. I arrived in forty three. That includes the stop at the store.

"Hi Karen, good to see you."

"Hey there, come on in."

Karen has no desire to go out. She's wearing her pajamas. For a woman about to turn sixty, she still takes care of her body. She has put on weight, but she has an exercise bike in the corner of her living room. Her additional weight doesn't bother me. Besides, I'm more turned on by women who don't resemble undernourished boys.

"Want a beer?"

"No Thanks."

"I made a tuna casserole. There's some left in the fridge if you want any."

"Okay thanks."

Now if I were married to Karen instead of Rosa, I would bet that Karen and I would be at Club Cyn. Our bodies would be thrusting together in sync with the music. All of the sweat and penetration would force us to go in the back area of the club.

Karen whipped my ass in the bowling game 205 to 105. She's obviously been playing against the computer. I fared better in the golf game. In each round, I was able to get my ball in the hole by the fourth try. Of course, Karen got a hole in one in the sixth round. Karen wasn't bashful about winning. Her big breasts went bouncing up and down every time she jumped up and down in excitement. Then I would jump up and down in excitement.

"I've had enough beatings in one night. Can I have some casserole?"

"Sure, I'll have a plate too."

"Thanks for inviting me over. I guess I was just bored. Didn't feel like going to the bars."

"Don't worry about it. I have the film Cast a Deadly Spell. Have you seen it?"

"No. The film has Tom Harrington in it right?"

"Yeah."

"Cool. I like his films."

After we eat, Karen and I go into her living room. Karen grabs the DVD and puts it in the machine. I take the high road by sitting in the rocking chair next to Karen's couch. Karen lays down on her couch.

Karen is a heavy sleeper. The film is on, the volume is a tad loud for my liking, cars speed and honk at one another, but Karen doesn't wake up. She is also is faint snorer. The only way I know Karen hasn't died is by watching her chest go up and down. I'm not paying any attention to the film. This film is going on and on. Another half hour goes by and Karen is still asleep. I keep staring at her body. Her face, arms, breasts, and legs. Most of the time, I stare at her chest and middle region. Karen's left arm is hanging down off the couch. Her right one must be wedged in between her side and the couch.

I pull off my grey T-shirt. Then, I slowly unbutton my blue jeans, then unzip them. I pull out my cock and start stroking it. I stop stroking when my cock becomes hard. I already had my shoes off. I keep my eyes on Karen while I slowly pull my pants and shorts down, then off. Man, my heart is beating so fast! Both of my hands are shaking. I slide off the chair and kneel up against the couch. I'm thinking Karen will open her eyes any second. No, she's still sleeping. I reach over and begin to unbutton her shirt. Once I finish, I spread her shirt open. Oh my God! Her breasts are so beautiful! I bend my face down and begin sucking her left nipple. Then I start sucking her other one. While I'm sucking her right nipple, I slide my hand down her pants. Karen is not wearing panties. I am stroking her cunt and at the same time sucking her nipples.

I feel my cock becoming limp, so I start stroking it again. I want to fuck Karen so bad and so hard! I stand up and begin to pull down her pants.

"Ahhaoohh!"

Karen suddenly wakes up. I immediately put my hand over her mouth. I'm not pressing down hard, but use enough force so she can't scream.

"Shhhhh! I'm not going to hurt you."

Karen's eyes become wide. I glance at her, her look back at me is one of shock and disbelief. But she never screams. I keep one hand over her mouth and use my other hand to yank down her pants. She could help me by just pulling them down herself. I can see her pubic hair. I finally get her pants down to her ankles, and pull them completely off.

I don't say one word. I spread her legs out. I reach over to kiss her on the lips. Her lips are too tight for me to stick my tongue inside her mouth. I press my cock up against her pussy and push it inward. Dammit. Karen is tight down there. I bend down sand start sucking her pussy. This time, my hand is pressed down harder on her mouth. Sucking did no good as her pussy is still too tight for my cock to go in. I clench my teeth in frustration. I begin stroking my cock very fast. I keep stroking until I cum all over Karen's chest.

I finally take my hand off of Karen's mouth. I use my own shorts to wipe my cum off her chest. I hand Karen her pajama bottoms. Karen and I don't say one word to each other as we get dressed. My hands are shaking so bad. Karen's face is hard to read. Is she angry? Still in shock? She never screamed NO! She didn't fight or pull away? It was like she was allowing me to have my way. She probably thought I was being too rough. Shit! What I should have done is caress her neck. Give her kisses on the lips. Why did I have to be so rough? I had to say something to her.

"I never meant to hurt you. I love you and I wanted to have sex with you."

Karen doesn't respond to anything I say to her. She can't even look me in the eyes. Shit, so much for her feeling the same way about me. I finish getting dressed and decide to leave.

"I never meant to hurt you Karen." I close Karen's front door not even turning around to look at her.

I look at my watch. Fucking one in the morning. I go into the basement and grab two gym bags. I start packing up my shirts, pants, shorts, and work clothes. I grab my toothbrush, toothpaste, comb, and hairspray. I toss the bags in the back trunk of my car. Shit! I forgot my safebox. The safebox has my tax papers and other important personal documents, mostly work related in it. I grab the box from the closet then go back outside to my car so I won't forget it when I leave. I need to get some sleep. I crash on the couch. My eyes keep opening up because I'm waiting to hear the sound of a police siren.

Another morning waking up by myself without Rosa next to me. Today is my day off. My mind is not on work, rather it's waiting to hear from Karen, her family, their attorney, or get a visit from the fuzz. Two hours later, no calls and no fuzz. I couldn't fret about what I did last night all morning. My plan today is to give the Clarion my official one week notice. Even though Juan can kiss my ass, I want Jane to give me a letter of recommendation. In addition to applying at the renaissance, I also applied at Mac's Grill and The Exo Spot. I have an interview with all three places during the week.

My boss isn't around for me to say buh-bye so I head to Jane's office. The employees are allowed to go to personnel and give notices there. Before I hand over my paper to Jane, she motions for me to sit down. She is talking to someone on the phone. I'm getting restless waiting around for her to finish. I glance at my watch. Thirty minutes later, Jane finally hangs the phone up.

"Sorry about that. Randy as you know this hotel has undergone many changes in the past few years."

My employment must not be important to her because when her phone rings again, she picks up the phone and begins talking to whoever is on the other line.

"Can we hurry up with this? I interrupt. "I have to be somewhere."

Jane gives me a frown, then tells the caller that she will call back.

"I apologize. As I was saying… the Clarion has gone through changes in both the kitchen and guest experience. Chef Juan and Mr. Gladden believe that your skills no longer fit into the new dining experience. They want to work with…"

I interrupt for a second time and take charge of the conversation.

"Listen, I'm well aware of Juan's obsession with changing the whole menu to be all organic and gluten free and this other herby shit. He's not even going to bother training me, much less have the balls to say I'm gone to my face and that's fine. I don't want to cook any food that I'm not even going to eat. These idiots are driving away the few customers we have left. You need to fire all of them and rehire the guys back who are the reason this hotel made a fuckload of money."

"Excuse me, there is no reason for you to use that language. I'm going to ask you not to or I will call security."

"Can I just have my last fucking paycheck? Thank you."

"I'm sorry you feel this way. I'm calling security to escort you out of the hotel."

"You mean Art? That guy wouldn't know how to shoot a water gun properly. Besides, the guy is pushing seventy. Like he's going to outrun me."

Art may move slower than a turtle but his hearing is still intact. Hell, here he comes now.

"Come with me sir right now!" Art barks out!

"Hi you doing Art! You taking me out to my car? Well let's get the fuck out of here! The new chef is a coward who doesn't have the sack package to even talk to me face to face. Jackass. Everyone in this dump can bend down and suck my ass!"

"You need to shut up right now!"

As Art escorts me through the hotel hallways, I decide this is a good time for me to let him and the hotel guests and employees know how I feel about be pushed out.

"Fuck you and yo mama! If fact, I'll fuck her while you are forced to watch. Let her see what a real man can do. What are you going to do? Shoot me in the back if I run? Put your hand over my mouth? I'll kick you in the balls so hard you won't feel them for a month! This new menu is nothing but faggot garbage! I hope this place goes fucking bankrupt! I'm going to tell everyone who bad this place sucks! The bed sheets smell…"

Art grabs my arm and shoulder hard then pushes me out the front door. A police officer is waiting outside. My first thought is that Karen told the cop about her being raped. Instead of going home, I'm riding with him to the police station.

Officer Nobrainz barks out a demand.

"Come with me sir! Where are you parked?"

I point to my car, parked a few feet down the lot. As I'm pointing to my car with my right hand and finger, I use my left arm and finger to give the hotel's front door the middle finger. I take my keys out and squirm my arm away from the cop.

"If you come back here sir, you will be arrested for trespassing. Please leave now."

The policeman watches me get in my car, start the car, and drive way. I look in my rearview mirror. The friendly fuzz is still standing the parking lot. Art is standing next to him. If those two are the face of the Clarion's security I feel for the guest's safety.

I drive on the highway disgusted at everyone who had a hand in my getting canned. I wish I knew how to make a homemade bomb. Send the hotel a nice little care package. And I can kiss goodbye any letter of recommendation huh?

What I should do is call up my outlaw comrades. Fred, Albert, Derrick, Les, Tony, Paul, Dave, and Mike. I tell all of them that we must unite and teach the current hotel staff a lesson. We would meet in a vacant garage and plot our revenge. Everyone I called was more than willing to join me. They too were angry for getting tossed out.

Everyone brings their own weapon of choice. Fred is clutching a wooden baseball bat. Albert, Paul, and Dave bring their own handguns. I don't know the specific kinds. I only know when they are fired, bullets fly out. Les twirls a long 2x4 with both of his hands. Derrick and Tony go the old west route and have shotguns at their side. Those two could have left their cowboy hats at home. I wasn't trying to recreate the OK corral shootout. The only weapon I own that would cause any damage is my twenty inch metal chain.

The Clarion gets an F when it comes to their security. I've walked into the hotel's front door several times with my gym bag slung over my shoulder. I could have a gun or a knife inside my bag. The only time I have ever seen a security employee is when one of them is behind the front desk flirting with the agent on duty. The security department is located in the basement. The basement! These cop academy rejects get winded just walking up a ramp to enter the back door that leads into the banquet kitchen. The hotel has no guard on duty patrolling the outside parameter. Any employee could be running a backdoor drug trade or brothel and get away with it.

All of us ride together in an unmarked white Chevy van. Derrick's cousin works for a salvage yard. His cousin was the one who lent us the van.

"This van may look like shit but it has a souped up engine. If we need to make a fast getaway, this baby will fly."

As we pull up to the adjoining lot, I park the van in the spot reserved for the hotel manager. Everyone is anxious to leave the van.

"Wait." I tell everyone before exiting the van.

"Someone else will be joining us. I made a call to someone who can lead us into our quest of carnage."

None of us really had any taste of satisfaction from destruction. We were all rookies who never fired weapons out of distain before. But I knew someone who did. A man who didn't care about the feelings any human being. A man who only knew retaliation and retribution as the solution. A man who would lead his followers, his sheep, his students into the depths of unadulterated carnage.

A gigantic black four wheel drive pick-up truck races past the van. The truck comes to a screeching halt near the hotel front doors.

"Before we go any further, is there anyone who is having second thoughts?"

"Fuck no!"

"Let's kick some ass!"

"It's time for payback!"

"Let's teach these pricks a lesson in respect!"

"I'm ready!"

"We are united my brothers, we began here together and we end this together."

"No turning back now. You all read the bible? Revelations 6:8. A pale horse comes. The rider's name is death. And all hell follows! Our leader is here. Let's move out."

Emerging from the truck is a man I have known all of my life. A scowl on his face and red eyes burning behind his chrome sunglasses. Not one for hellos or tearful reunions, he motions for all us to start walking towards the hotel's front door. No words are necessary as action will be taken. He leads, we follow. Fred was about to take his bat and bust out front door glass pane. Our leader holds him back with his right arm. Then he reaches down to his pants and pulls out the most frightening weapon-a loaded colt diamondback.

BLAM BLAM BLAM!

There goes the glass! Several shattered pieces fly inside the hotel's lobby. Albert kicks in the busted door parts. The rest of us walk in with our weapons engaged. I glare over at Art. His normally squinty eyes grow wide in disbelief.

"Hey! Hold it right there!"

Art fidgets as he attempts to pull out his starter pistol. The damn thing isn't even loaded. Paul fires off one shot that hits Art in the chest. Art crumbles to the ground. Art never even had the time to use his radio. I watch over him and begin to shake when I see a pool of blood form under his frozen body. My shaking calms down and a smile forms on my face. I need to kill more.

Les, Fred, and I begin using our chains, bats, and two by fours to destroy the counter, tables, chairs, desks, and walls. The scared employees are screaming in fear. We showed no remorse. If a pitiful guest got cut with glass or hit with wooden splinters, we didn't care.

The man clutching the diamondback still had bullets of his own to use.

"Where are the people who wronged you? Point them out."

We continue to walk pass the bloody carnage towards the restaurant.

"Over there!" I yell then point out.

BLAM!

Via con dios Don!

The back of Don's head hits hard against the wall. A perfect red and black circle forms on his pale forehead. His eyes remain open while he slides down the wall.

"Hey! He's another one!"

BLAM! BLAM!

Sayanora Ron!

Two fast gunshots from Derrick's gun made deadly contact with Ron's chest. The little fucker is still breathing. His cries of *oh God please don't I have children* were useless. He was losing blood and consciousness. Ron fell forward so hard on the carpet that stumbled back a bit myself. Oooh, the sound of his face cracking and his bones breaking, my God! I feel a hand push me forward.

"Keep moving."

BLAM BLAM BLAM!

The two other hotel security guards never stood a chance. Both of them were unarmed. Neither of them even were able to call for help. Derrick made all of his shots count. Derrick took out any poor sap around us who thought he or she could be the hero of the day.

We reach the restaurant area. All of the customers are either running towards the kitchen or hiding under tables. Derrick and Tony begin firing shots. Some of the customers ran for cover by locking themselves in a storage closet. Paul and Dave kicked down the door. No survivors and witnesses. The four frightened people hiding out all met their maker.

Tony was not a good shot. Bullets were flying everywhere. The water glasses shattered, the plush chairs torn apart, and the dining room walls were riddled with bullet holes. A sad case of being at the wrong place at the wrong time. The young chefs working in the kitchen met their maker on this day.

My former fuckface of an incompetent boss comes out into the lobby. David and Paul are pushing him towards me.

"Not too close. I don't want his blood splattered all over my good causal shirt."

Juan is trembling so much that I can see a visible wet stream down the front of his pants.

"You're a pathetic piece of shit."

The cops weren't coming to help him. All of the hotel phone lines were disconnected. I might have heard him babble *no please stop I'm begging you.* No one could understand what he was saying. He could have been saying *ubabababo.*

Without saying one word, the man who became the follower's prophet hands me the Colt Diamondback. I caress the large shiny gun. I stare into the terrified eyes of a man who doesn't realize that in a few seconds his wife will be a widow and his children will be orphans. A shiver comes over my body when I hear the gospel according to vengeance.

"Shoot the motherfucker dead."

The shot rang so loud I couldn't help but let out a frightening *AAAH!*

The recoil from shooting the gun was so strong I began to fall backwards. Instead of dropping to the floor on my head like I thought I would, I'm leaning at an angle. My head is resting up against something hard. I pull myself up then turn around. Throughout my life, in grade school, then high school, up to my marriage and to the present age I now know he meant well. He had my best interests. And most important to me, the man who was a racist, a bigot, and a selfish, greedy, mean, spiteful man has my back.

Jerry's life was sparred. He may have been off that night. Tonight will be the night I absolutely get a good night's sleep.

18

ONE FINAL RIDE (AND THE AFTERMATH THAT FOLLOWS)

Rosa filed for a divorce. I saw this coming a mile away. If she wants to throw our marriage away in the dumpster, then fine by me. I have no intention of trying to make our marriage work. I'm not about to beg for any kind of reconciliation. I bask in the glory of being a single man once again. A different woman every night in my bed.

Karen couldn't hold back her guilt any longer. She blabbed to Rosa and Amelia that I sexually assaulted her. Karen is a liar. A part of me wants to ignore all of her accusations. I have a bad feeling though that Karen is going to press charges. I need to call Barry and find out if he knows a good lawyer.

"Hi Barry, its Randy. I'm in some serious trouble. In addition to the divorce, I may have a rape charge coming."

"Rape charge?!"

"The accusation is all bullshit. Karen is the one who instigated the entire thing."

"What happened? Please tell me you didn't get rough with her."

"Of course not. Karen was already naked on her couch. She was giving all kinds of signals. I succumbed to her wills. When we were having sex she never said no. I think I got me enough proof to prove that I never raped her. But even so, can you help me out?"

"Let me give you the name of someone who may be able to help. His name is Ben Tate. His number is 567-9898."

"Who is he?"

"A divorce lawyer. He's one of the best, never lost a case. He handles messy splits involving infidelity. He's not cheap though."

"Okay thanks, I'll call him. Can you do me one more favor? I am giving you my bank account number. You have my permission to withdraw all the money out. I have two accounts, one I'm sure will be depleted from the divorce. I need you put my money from my other account somewhere safe until I can get a hold of it."

"What's the account information?"

"Central States Bank. Randall Stevens is the primary name. Account number is 24681012. There's three thousand in the account. I owe you big for this."

"Keep me informed as to what's going on. Come see me after your hearing."

"I will, thanks bye."

I make the call to Barry's lawyer.

"Hi, Mr. Tate? I'm Randy Stevens, Barry Carter gave me your number. I need your help with a divorce and a rape charge."

"A man who cuts right to the chase. Let's meet and talk about what is going on first. Let's see, how does tomorrow at four work for you?"

"Fine. I'll see you then, thanks."

The next day, I drove to Ben's office. His office is located inside one of those large buildings that rent out several small businesses. Ben reminds me of a retired military sergeant. His hair is short and neatly trimmed. His face appears wrinkled and serious. I don't see any ring on his finger. I'll bet he's gone through a few messy divorces himself. Ben's secretary buzzes me in his office.

"Hi. I'm Randy Stevens. I'm here to see Mr.Tate."

"He's expecting you. His office door the second one on the right."

"Excuse me. Mr. Tate?"

"Come in."

"We spoke on the phone. I'm Randy Stevens."

"Ah yes. A friend of Barry's. Please sit down and tell me what happened?"

"Here's the story in a nutshell. A woman I know named Karen has feelings for me. Sexual feelings. She's paraded around nude in front of me. Her bathroom door was opened one time. She knew I was watching her stand naked in front of the mirror. She's touched my body in a sexual matter at a recent party. She wanted me to come over to her place. She never said no or stop. She didn't even push me away. When the sex was over, she got dressed without saying a word. All of her signals were telling me that is was okay to have sex with her. I didn't hurt her physically. She has no bruises of any kind. I never forced myself on her."

"Are you related to Karen?"

"No. She's my ex- wife's aunt."

"Have you and your ex-wife ever have any arguments that escalated into a violent fight?"

"Not at all. Seems kind of strange. We never argued. Hell, we barely disagreed on anything. I never hit Rosa either. Or any of her family members. We just grew apart. Her career became her top priority and not our marriage. I was focused on my career too. That's the main reason we never had kids."

"Were you faithful to her?"

"Always. I admit I looked. I did before we were married and that vice carried over while we were married. But I never, never, had sex with another woman during our marriage."

"Have the two of you discussed any arrangements regarding property and money?"

She can whatever she wants insofar as the house or the furniture inside. She's a greedy bitch. Pardon my language. She made it so that I can't get in the house anyway."

"Okay then, I have your statement. What I can do is present this to her or to your ex- wife's attorney. The rape charge is rather weak. Sounds like a case of he said she said. I'll be focusing on the divorce hearing not any rape charges against you. If you're willing to give up or relinquish your tangible items then hopefully, they will settle."

"But can you help me if Karen does press charges."

"Unless she has solid evidence that you did indeed rape her, I doubt she will want to take that to trial. What you told me a minute ago is what I'm presenting to the other attorney."

"Okay then. Thank you for all your help."

"Your welcome. I'll see you soon."

When my lawyer and I met Rosa and her mom at the divorce hearing, Karen or Gino was not present. Rosa hired two lawyers, both females, one black and one white, who sat so close together that one of them could have had a hand up the other's dress.

"Okay everyone, let's begin. Have the two parties come to an agreement on the tangible items?"

"My client has been under a tremendous amount of physical and emotional duress. We ask that you keep in mind Ms. Carvella is still in mourning over the passing of her father. She is asking for sole ownership of the house and sole owner of any monies in the bank accounts. She is convinced that Mr. Stevens has committed adultery and show no compassion over his actions."

Rosa's second lawyer, the black one, then puts her two cents in.

"In addition to our reasonable requests, I'm asking for a permanent restraining order against Ms. Carvella and her mother Amelia Carvella. The order also names Gino Carvella and Karen Moreno."

"Mr.Tate?"

I whisper in his ear before he starts talking.

"Yes Ma'am. My client is willing to give Ms. Carvella the home. He has already removed his name from all joint bank accounts. I have a bank document for Ms. Carvella. She will need to sign this so that her bank can complete the transaction. We are also prepared to bring forth documents showing that my client did not rape or sexually molest said name Karen Moreno at any time during his marriage."

"Ms. Moreno is not pressing charges. She only requests, along with Ms. Carvella a restraining order against Mr. Stevens."

"What about the stuff inside the home? Some of the items belonged to me and me only."

Now it's Mr. Tate's turn to blow in my ear.

"Take it easy. Remember, you already told me that Ms. Carvella could have all tangible property."

What Rosa received: The house, her car, all of the furniture including MY stereo system, a painting of a house setting in the snow that easily was worth ten grand, and a lump sum of twenty five thousand dollars. I only had around twenty four thousand in one of my bank accounts. As a bonus to Rosa courtesy of the judge, I also have a restraining order against Rosa, Amelia, and Karen. In other words, I can no longer come within five miles of any of them.

What Randy got: The only good news for me was that no mention of any rape came about. Even so, I did get the dirty shit end of the *you are fucked* stick. I'll be more specific: Two medium size boxes crammed with my clothes. All of the clothes were stuffed inside without any care. My good dress pants got all wrinkled. And as a second bonus to Rosa, the boxes were left outside overnight while the cold rain poured down. The only items that didn't get wet or ruined were my toothbrush, toothpaste, and deodorant. I was allowed to pick up the boxes that were sitting on MY lawn. I wasn't sure if Rosa was even home. I didn't see any police car around. I walk over to pick up the boxes. I throw them both in the backseat of my car. After slamming the door so hard that dogs began barking, I lean up against the driver's side of my car. I can see two young kids, both boys maybe age six to ten, playing catch in their front lawn. I unlock my car door then release my venom before getting in.

"THANKS A LOT FOR RUINING ALL OF MY FUCKING CLOTHES! AND MY FUCKING LIFE! I HATE YOU! YOU WORTHLESS FUCKING CUNT!"

I feel vindicated. Those two kids learned fast how men react when their ex fucks them royally. Both of them run into the house behind the lawn they were playing on. I get out of the area fast. The last thing I need is for some mom to stop me and scold me for saying fucking and cunt in front of their kids. I would make a great teacher of in the class of how to prevent your ex-wife from stripping you bare.

Lesson 1-sign a prenup.

Lesson 2-keep a separate bank account with YOUR NAME ONLY

Lesson 3-Don't quit your job, keep money flowing

Lesson 4-Have enough friends to help get you out of any jam

Lesson 5-Keep a good enough relationship with a least one parent. That way if you need to use one of them as a last resort, your mom or dad will be there (if they both have passed then be sure to have a great relationship with one of your relatives).

I'm driving over to my mom's. It has been a long time since I've visited her. First, I want to let know about dad's release and the fact that he is okay with her coming down to visit. Here's a crazy thought-My dad tells my mom to move in with my grandma. I also want to let her know from me what has happened with Rosa and me. I'll leave the part about trying to fuck Karen out of the conversation. I'm sure if she goes to the same salon as the other woodpeckers, she will hear all about the false accusations.

I pull up to the red stoplight. The roads are vacant. The pitch black sky is starless. C'mon light change so I get going. All of the sudden my driver side window shatters.

"Oh shit!" Oh God!"

The man was wearing a grayish hoodie so I couldn't make out most of his face. He was leaning in my car pushing me to the side. My heart is beating faster than it has ever been. Where the hell are the cops! I maintain control of my car but swerve from side to side on the road.

"Please don't hurt me!"

My attacker pays no attention as he continues to fight for control of my car. I am able to press down on the gas. I have no idea if I'm going to hit someone or run into something. My foot comes off the brake as the car makes hard contact with something. I can't see what. I remember having a can of hair spray under the front seat. I am able to grab the can, then pop off the lid. The man trying to steal my car slipped and fell to the ground. I am able to open the driver side door to get out. I then start spraying the liquid in his face.

"Ahhhhh!"

He screams out loud so I must have made contact in his eyes. I didn't care if I blinded him or not. This is not a dream or a fantasy. I am getting carjacked! I hurry up to find my chain. I move quickly in case this guy is a fast runner. He does start running but I am able to grab his right leg and heave it in the air.

"Ahow!"

The thief falls to the cold ground face first. Maybe I should have sped off after I sprayed him in the face. But I am outraged. Rosa wiped me out financially. Karen snitched on me. I was fired over not fitting in to the hotel's new shitstorm of awful ideas. I hated driving through this stinkhole of a neighborhood. And worse of all some miserable puke has the audacity to steal my car. I wrap the chain around my right arm and hand.

POW POW POW POW!!

He lets out scream after scream!

"Take that you stupid bastard! Who do you think you are?! This is my car! It's all I got! I'm sick and tired of being shit on!" From now on nobody takes advantage of me."

My arm finally gets tired of swinging. Any welts should be forming on the vagrant soon. I hope he bleeds to death.

I quickly stop hitting the guy once I hear police sirens. Oh now, the police arrive! Police officers never did excel at timing. They are either having a two hour coffee break at the local burger joint or they want to hide out in parking lots waiting to catch someone going fifteen miles in a ten mile an hour zone. I throw the bloody chain a few inches from where I was ruthless beating the pile of shit. I fall to the cold ground feigning to be injured.

"Officer! Officer! Please help me! I was carjacked by this man! Help me!"

"Take it easy sir, are you okay?"

"I think so, I had to use force against this guy. He grabbed my chain from my trunk and began using it on me. I had no choice but to retaliate and hit him back. Oh shit!"

"Okay just calm down. Do you need an ambulance?"

"I don't think so. I'm just scared. I'm shaking."

As the one officer pulls me up and helps me to the squad car, I look over at my attacker. Another cop helping him up has to restrain him as the poor schmuck tries to run away.

"Hold it right there! We're going to sort all of this out."

"Just relax and tell me what happened."

"Okay." I have to catch my breath.

"I was stopped at the light. All of the sudden my driver's side window shattered. This guy forces his way in. I press on the gas and drive and end up crashing into the bus stop thing. The wait area. I reach for my spray and was able to spray him in the face. Somehow my trunk pops open. From the force from hitting the wall. I still had had my spray but I got a hold of the chain that was in my trunk. I just keep spraying. I did hit him with the chain. But I had to. I was afraid he might have a gun or knife on him."

"So he forced his way in through your driver side window?"

"Yes busted it out with something. It just shattered."

"But only you sprayed him and struck him with your chain?"

"Yes. I got scared and used a chain to defend myself. I thought he was going to attack me."

"Okay, wait right here."

I couldn't hear a word what the two cops were saying. They were also speaking to the little varmint. They would talk and write on their notepads. Soon, one of the officers comes towards me.

"Okay sir, we're going to take the man who you say attacked you down to the police station. I'm also having a separate squad car bring you down."

"Am I being arrested?"

"Right now we want statements. Do you want to press charges against that man?"

"Yes."

"Okay. Here comes the squad car. You go with him. We'll get an official statement from you."

"What about my car?"

"Either my partner, the other officer or I will call a tow company. You can get the information at the station."

"Shit. Okay."

Once I get to the station, I'm led into a small room. This station is in another location than the one I was at when my dad was arrested. So at least I shouldn't recognize any cop or detective.

About a half hour later a young man enters the room. The man is built like a bodybuilder. He must have graduated recently from detective school. He's a young and fresh faced adult with acne. After he flips a page of his own pad, he sits down across from me.

"Mr. Stevens. I'm working with the officers on what happened. So I want to be clear. You were at a stoplight, then had one of your windows shattered caused by someone attempting to break in?"

"Yes."

"Then a struggle occurs for control of the vehicle. You press down on the gas pedal which causes the car to crash. Then you spray with other person with what was a can of hair spray. You also used a chain that was already in your possession. The chain was used by you in defense, according to you. Am I correct?"

"Yes. I never wanted to hurt the guy only defend myself."

"Okay, I'm still talking to the other guy about the incident. So you'll stay in here."

"Can I make a phone call to my dad?"

"Not yet. You haven't been charged. I need to make sure that I have all statements made. I'll let you know so be patient and wait here."

I wasn't wearing my watch so I had no idea what time it was. For all I know it's the next day in the very early morning. My only concern was that my attacker will say he was attacked by me. He could deny carjacking me at all. But why would I drive with a busted out window. Especially in a nigger infested part of town. Did this guy lose the weapon he had to have had on him? I am going to need the public defender to help me out. Damn. I already had Barry help me with my divorce. I don't want to keep bothering them will all my troubles.

The door to the room I'm in opens and in comes in Mr. Academy and someone who is probably the public defender.

"Mister Stevens, you are not being charged at this time. You will need to appear in court. He'll give you all the information. Once the two of you are finished then you are free to go."

"Okay. Thank you."

"Hi Mr. Stevens, I'm Bill. I have copies of statements from you, the other man involved, and the police officers on the scene. I'll present these statements in front of the judge. You will need to be present. Is there anything you want to tell me or ask me?"

"What about the other guy? Is he being arrested for attacking me?"

"He has been charged."

"So what happens now? I mean will he be at the courthouse with me?"

"I can't divulge too much information as he is being escorted elsewhere. I doubt you will see him there."

"I did what I did in self -defense. Will I be able to tell the judge this?"

"It's a part of the statement you gave. The judge will have a copy of everything you told me and the detective."

"Okay. Well thank you."

"Listen, just tell the truth. You said you used force to defend yourself. I believe no crimes were committed here. You did use aggression which may be used against you. I'll do everything I can to push for no jail time."

"Okay. Thank you. I'll see you on the 7th."

I call a cab in order to get back to West County. I decide to stay the night and one day at a motel. For a second, I just thought about getting on a plane to a far way destination. The next morning I call my dad to let him know what's going on."

"Hi, dad. The reason I'm calling is that I need to let you know what happened to me last night and what I did so just listen for now. I was driving over to mom's place and while I was at a stoplight I got carjacked."

"WHAT!"

"Don't worry. I'm not hurt. Unfortunately as I was driving off, the guy was still hanging on to the car. I ended up crashing into a bus stop."

"So the car's totaled?"

"Yes the fucking car is totaled! But I'm okay!"

"Okay calm down."

"Anyway, in order to defend myself I had no choice but to spray him in the eyes with some hairspray that I had in my car. This guy also went after my chain. I was able to get the chain away from him"

"A chain? Why did you have a chain in your car?"

"I keep one in the trunk. Hell, I don't know. I'm glad I did have one though."

"All right. I'm just glad you are not hurt."

"It's not necessary for you to be in the courtroom. I can call you from there after it's all done. The public defender says my case is solid. The judge may question my use of spray and a chain but overall I wasn't intending to commit a crime."

"Will you be here in the city?"

"Yes. Since the incident happened there."

"What's the date?"

"The 7th"

"What time?"

"Says nine am."

"All right."

"I'm not going to fret too much. I was told the other person is being escorted elsewhere. Hopefully, my self-defense will save me."

"It will. Don't worry. You may have to serve a month tops. Man oh man. What does Rosa think about all of this? Or does she even know?"

I pause for a minute then answer him.

"No, I haven't told her and I'm not going to either. Rosa and I are getting divorced."

"WHAT!"

"Relax. This is for the best. Rosa and I are way apart. We don't love each other anymore. Neither of us have any desire to see any therapist either. I'm not about to have some quack shrink tell me how to salvage a marriage that is beyond repairing. Fuck it. I mean I still care for her and her mom too. I want her to go on with the rest of her life. So don't be calling anyone. I'm moving on with my life. I meant what I said about calling her."

"I don't even have her number. Can't the two of you work it out? Maybe you need to see a marriage counselor."

"The divorce is pretty much final."

"Okay. We can talk more about it at a later time."

"When I can, I'll come down to visit you and grandma. I'll have another car soon. I've already looked at two cars for sale. They are both from a dealer. I'll make sure to have the car I buy go through a diagnostic test before I actually buy it. I let you know how everything turns out."

"Good. You call me right away. Do you hear me?"

"Yeah. I'll talk to you soon."

I get a phone call from some guy who was probably Rosa's lawyer.

"Mr. Stevens. My name is Bernadette Massa. I represent Ms. Carvella. You and your attorney are required to meet us for a follow up regarding the divorce hearing. Can you make it in next Wednesday at 9am?"

"Yeah, I'll call my attorney. If that day or time doesn't work for him then he can call you himself. Will this be the last time I see you and Rosa?"

"Yes, as long as all you and Ms. Carvella are in agreement over all said items."

"Great. Maybe after the housecleaning of my ass, you, me and my lawyer can all go to the strip bar to have are our faces pushed inside the pairs of some big boobies. How does that sound, you fucking dyke?"

"Goodbye Mr. Stevens."

Rosa sold our home and thanks to her lesbian lawyers, got all the money from the sale. Rosa stole all the monies from our accounts. Thank God I had Barry take my money from my own account and put that money in a safe place. I treated Rosa as a queen. I gave her love, support, and grieved with her when her dad died. I showed respect to her mom, dad, and brother. I adapted to her flexible and demanding work schedule.

What thanks do I get? Besides a costly divorce? A restraining order from a vindictive bitch named Rosa, an ungrateful whore named Karen, and a mentally challenged failure named Gino who isn't worth the piss I sprayed on side the commode in the courtroom's bathroom.

My dad had to show up at the courthouse. He even had to bring Nancy with him. Not once, did he shout something out or cause a scene. Instead, he would look at me with sad puppy dog eyes. Nancy's face was hard to read. Who knew how she felt about what happened to me or the guy who attacked me. I would think she would be the kind of person who would also use lethal force to fend off someone coming after her.

My dad is to blame for my newfound attitude and behavior. He convinced me to be pushy, aggressive, and to treat women as useless sex objects. Now, I don't even recognize the man anymore. He's change is appearance. From stubble all over his face to a clean shaven baby face. His hair is cut short with neatly trimmed sideburns. All of his hair is mix of light and dark gray. His blue jeans have been washed and pressed.

As I leave exit the courtroom, I am allowed one phone call. I give my dad the satisfaction by letting him know what's going to happen to me.

"You were right. I have to spend twenty days at a correction facility. The place a detention center for adults. It's not really jail so no bail was set. From what I understand though, there are police and guards here.

I don't understand why I have to. I told them I was afraid for my life. My lawyer said something like I did use force."

"I know Randy. It'll be okay. Just watch yourself, do what you are told to do, and you'll be out of there in no time. If you need a place to stay, we'll make up a bed and room for you. Remember, you always have a home here. Nancy and I are going to Florida next month. We are having Regina and a caregiver come over here while we're gone. You can stay here while we're gone and be a really big help."

"Okay, I'll see what's going on."

"All right, hey does your work know about everything?"

"I was let go from the Clarion a while ago."

"Oh no! Why?"

"Trust me I'm happy. None of my friends and co-workers are there anymore. The menu has changed for the worse and I wasn't happy with the food choices. I've been talking to my friends and former workers, the one's I like, and I'm going to have interviews with other places. With my experience and commitment to showing up, I'll be hired soon at any of the places I go to."

"I know you will. God, first the carjacking then the divorce and now your work gives you the heave ho. I don't think anymore can happen to you."

"Look at this way. I'm getting a new car. Well at least a good used car. My friends Barry and Rick have bent over backwards to help me get back on my feet. I'm not hurt or in prison. Rosa and I have gone our own ways. I did hock my wedding ring though. Got two hundred for the damn thing. And I have plenty of good leads for a new job. I'm going to use some of the money to buy a new shirt and pants and the rest for food."

"Listen to me. You helped me out more than you know while I was away. I'm putting some money in an envelope. The next time you come over here take it. I know you are going to need some."

"Thanks but.."

"Don't but me or argue."

"Fine. I'll get it."

"So you learned your lesson?"

"No. And if I ever get attacked again, a chain will not be the weapon I use to defend myself. I'm going to the shooting range to learn and apply for a gun. I will never marry another woman again. Instead, I plan on having several one night stands. All I'm going to do is fuck them and then tell them to get the fuck out of my life. Once I have enough money saved up I'm moving far away from this shithole of a town. Jamaica sounds really nice."

"Hold on Randy, you need to relax. I know you're all uptight and scared over what happened. Just have a good night sleep. Listen to me very carefully. Take it from me, getting crazy is not the answer. You don't want to end up where I was."

"I know. You're right. Okay, so I got to go. Phone's dying. I'll keep you informed."

"You do that."

I'm too broke to call an escort. Even a trashy one who does pro bono blowjobs. I need some alcohol to take the edge off. I have enough money to go to a corner hick bar and order two draft beers.

Aftermath

I can breathe a sigh of relief. My time spent in A.D. was boot camp for the dregs on society. I do not belong in the same cramped quarters as the drug users, drug sellers, thieves, vandals, male hookers, drunks, vagrants, misfits, queers, derelicts, and every other kind of dreck on society. I have wined and dined in Paris. I have soaked in the sun rays on a luxury cruise liner. I have eaten in five star, award winning restaurants. I've prepared food for company CEO's and CFO's. I slept on a king size bed. My friends and I sipped white wine and ate samples of crabmeat and lobster tails. I have been the playboy swinger and wife exchanger. I pulled in forty five thousand a year; that is after the government snagged their share.

No more. I lost all my privileges and luxuries.

The silver lining in all of this is I haven't received any more phone calls from any lawyers or from Rosa's family. None of them can write to me anyway since I no longer have a valid address. I have yet to get any kind of lawsuit relating to the night I attempted to have sex with Karen. I erase Rosa, Amelia, and Karen's phone numbers from my list of contacts. All of them no longer exist in my new life.

I meet up with Rick at Club Cyn. He wants to talk to me about my future plans.

"Did Rosa throw you out for good?"

"I never gave her the satisfaction. Walked out on my own. Her lawyers were going to give me orders. I told all of them to kiss my ass. Then I packed up and moved out."

"Where are you staying?"

"For now, a motel."

"I know someone who has an apartment for rent. The place is in Overland. Rent's cheap, I think around three hundred a month. Here, the owner's name is Josh."

"Have you seen the apartments?"

"Once. Josh does a good job taking care of the tenants."

"Thanks. I'll give him a call."

To be honest, I didn't want to live in the Overland area. Comparing Overland to Chesterfield is like comparing a brand new, just-from-the-factory Mercedes to a beaten down, rust everywhere Rat Rod. Overland is the rat rod.

"How's your job hunting going? Any good news?"

"Not yet. But I still have more leads to follow up on."

"Angelina, Barry and I talked about this. You can come work for me and Barry."

"You serious?"

"Yes. I could use a doorman. I lost Dylan last week. He was shot during a stick up. Poor bastard was just buying smokes. And this new guy I hired is a useless fuck. He was letting all of his underage friends into my club. He couldn't even take out the garbage without busting the bag and letting the shit run all over the back alley. I'm firing his black ass and want you instead. Besides, Barry and I want to start serving food to our customers. Nothing fancy. Pizzas, pastas, and a good hamburger. I know you can cook. So what do you say?"

"I..I don't know what to say. Thank you. I owe you for this big."

"So that's a yes huh?"

"Yes!"

"All right. Hey just don't let minors in here or anyone who can't read the sign that says dress code enforced."

I'm not ready to see my dad or Nancy. I will never tell my grandma about my divorce or my time in the faux prison. Besides, I'm sure my dad will give her his version of what happened to me. I still had some money to tie me over until I get paid. Three thousand dollars. I'm considering moving out of the states and going to Paris. Oh wait, I committed to Rick that I would begin working at Club Cyn. He's never steered me wrong so I owe it to him to stay true to my word.

Staying at the motel gets lonely. I pull out my wallet and take out the folded yellow piece of paper. I flatten the paper out and begin reading the names and numbers. I close my eyes, breathe heavy, and dial the first set of numbers. Shit, Theresa doesn't answer. I dial the next number. Shit, that number is disconnected. I keep dialing all the numbers. Either the number is no longer in service or the phone just keeps ringing.

I'll have to call Rick for some new leads. They may have put an end to the entire side business.

"Hi Rick, Its Randy. I was just wondering if you or Barry had any new or different names and numbers of women. The ones I'm calling are not in service. Thanks Bye."

Then I give my mom a call. I want to know how she is.

"Hi mom, it's Randy."

"What's up?"

"Just calling to see how you are doing."

"Fine. This new medicine my doctor has me on makes me drowsy. But I don't go out that much anyway. You know there was another shooting in the area. This is the third one in a month."

"We have been over this time and time again. You need to move out. The area is no longer a safe place for you to be. Maybe you can talk to dad about living with grandma on a permanent basis. You could help take care of her and that would offset any rent."

"What, no I'm fine. I always make sure my front and back doors are locked when I'm at home. Don't go out at night anymore. I can't see the lines in the road! Besides, Kate and her boyfriend are here too. We all look out for one another."

"Even so, you should think about it. So thanks for driving down to help take care of grandma."

"Randy, she's my grandma too. I thinks all those years in prison has changed your father. He is much calmer and nicer to be around. I think Nancy is good for him too. Maybe they'll get married. Ha!"

"Right. The jury is still out for me. You know what I mean? He's being a good boy now. He'll always put grandma first. I'm not concerned about that. You just be cautious and call me the minute he does or says anything that's out of line. Okay, well I'm glad you're doing well. Be safe and take care of yourself. Shoot, I have another call so I'll call you later and talk more."

"Okay. Remember, I love you."

"Love you too."

I return the phone call from Angelina.

"Hi there, sorry I did not return your call earlier. I was on another line."

"It's okay. I've been out of town. Rick told me all of what's happened to you. I'm so happy you were not injured. I hope the person who attacked you spends a lot of time in jail."

"I wasn't hurt much. Just a few scrapes here and there. The guy who carjacked me might have spent some time in the hospital. I fought back out of protecting myself. The cops told me that he's going to jail in another state after he's released from the hospital. Maybe he'll have a relapse while still the hospital. I don't care if he lives or dies."

"Good for you. We don't need people like them anyway. Rick told me you were interested in some female companionship? Let me make a few calls. I'll bet you're ready for some female loving."

"I am. You, Rick and Barry have really helped me out. Did either of them tell you about my working at the club? I'm looking forward to it. I'll repay all of you back somehow."

"Yes, and no you won't. You were very helpful with promoting our Club. We owe you a debt of gratitude. Without you, our club wouldn't be nearly as successful. We're your friends. We take care of each other. Have dinner with us next week and we will talk about what it is you were asking for."

I am no longer afraid. I can walk down the block, pass up two thugs cementing a drug deal, and not worry if I am going to get robbed, beat up, or even shot. I continue to walk down the street, staring at the dim street lights from above. I cross the street, pass up the used car lot and stop at Benny's Tavern. I sit on a hard stool pressed up against the bar. A beefy black man limps over towards me.

"What can I get you?"

"Bud Light."

I turn my head to right then to the left to see who else is in the bar. At the end of the bar, close to the front door is an older black skinned man. He's got three bottles of beer in front of him. On my other side is a black woman close to my early forties age. Is she alone or with someone. I finish my drink and walk down towards her.

"Hi, May I join you?"

"If you want."

I motion for the bartender to come towards me. His noticeable gimpy leg makes him walk slowly.

"I'll have another beer and whatever she's drinking it's on me."

The young lady turns her head towards me and points to her empty glass.

"It's a rum and coke. Thanks."

I finish my first and second beer in silence. I have to squint my eyes to avoid any upcoming forehead pain. The lady sitting next to me wasn't much for talking. I wonder if she's here because she and her boyfriend had an argument. I would be the perfect man for her to have jealous sex. I come to the realization that I'm not going to make it with her so I get up and walk out.

"Have a good night."

"Take care my friend."

The next bar that I can see through my half closed, dilapidated eyesight is located on the next block. The cold blowing wind is making me cough. Tucking my chin underneath my coat, I move along keeping in step with the cold breezes. I pass a homeless person lying on a bench. I suddenly shiver as I realize that I could be that person who now lives outside.

Acknowledgements

I raise my glass of ice cold beer and say thanks to God, Mom, Dad, Dave, Paul, Tony, Stephanie, Nick, Brianna, Ethan, all of my relatives, Jackie, Charles, the inventors of vodka, cranberry juice, pens, pencils, notebooks, flashdrives, and painkillers.

I also want to say thank you to all of the musicians, actors, actresses, and everyone else who had a hand in the movies and songs I have listed in this book. Watching a terrific show or listening to killer music is what inspires me to push myself and believe that I can succeed.

About the Author

ADORES (OR IS FOND OF):

Booze, smoking in bars, women, intelligence (those two would have to go together), free speech, the south, money, success, excess, good music, sex, indulgence of any kind, shocking the hell out of people, risking everything for the glory, and candy corn.

DETESTS (OR CANT STAND)

Sour milk, lofts, most men, stupid people, people who are too damn close behind my car while I'm driving, people who make left turns that prevent me from going past the yellow light, people who bitch about how bad their lives are but do nothing to fix it, professional (and I use that word loosely) athletes who make millions of dollars but have no true talent (I mean how hard is it to catch a baseball, throw a football or toss a ball into a net), horrible music (I'm talking to you top 40 genre), not getting any, boredom, and melted chocolate on my fingers.

Printed in the United States
By Bookmasters